EXILE

BY

ELLE BRICE

Moonshine Publishing:

www.mshinepub.com
or ellebrice95@gmail.com

Follow on social media at:

www.facebook.come/daywalkersaga
Instagram: @ellebriceauthor

Printed in the United States of America

OTHER BOOKS IN THE SERIES

ACKNOWLEDGEMENTS

TO MIGUEL—THE LUCAS TO MY NICOLA

PROLOGUE

EULESS, TEXAS OCTOBER 17

Ryan Aspen dug through his boxes, trying to find his tube of blue oil paint. It had been a hassle moving into his new place and even more of a hassle trying to unpack. Two weeks and he'd barely touched two of his boxes. He'd been so busy with his art classes and preparing for the grand opening of his studio that everything else was low on his priority list.

It hadn't been his idea to move to Texas, let alone tiny old Euless. He hated it there. It was too hot, too small, and it stifled his creativity. He'd been given no choice. Where the coven went, he would go also. He'd been answering to them for the past thirty years. While the coven gave him a family when he had none, they sometimes smothered him.

Frustrated, he raked his hands through his dark hair and sat on his stool. The art piece he was working on required blue to mix with the orange to create the shade he was going for. He wished he could be more organized and hadn't thrown everything together so quickly. He would have to settle for water paints instead.

His whole life he'd settled. Like he'd settled for a place as a council member instead of an elder. Like he'd settled for coven duties instead of pursuing his dream of painting for a living. Like he'd settled for Simeon's plan instead of being with the woman he was falling for.

Someone knocked on his door and he set down his brush. He hoped it wasn't Simeon, speak of the devil. He'd already been grilled with special instructions for what he needed to do, and he didn't need another lecture. He wanted a little bit of time to enjoy his painting before he would have to set it aside, again, for the coven agenda.

He opened the door and smiled. This was just the person he'd been wanting to see. She was beautiful and only became more beautiful each time they saw each other. Her auburn hair hung long around her shoulders and her golden eyes danced with mischief. She stood leaning against the door with her arms crossed.

"What are you doing here?" he asked.

"Seeing you, of course. Is this a good time?"

"It's always a good time."

Taking her by the waist, he pulled her inside and shut the door. He crushed his lips to hers, and she returned it with earnest. She was the only upside to this move across the country. He would get to see her and that made everything worth it. He led her over to the couch and he lay down with her on top of him. Her kisses were intoxicating, and he couldn't get enough of them.

"Does he know you're here?" he asked, still lightly kissing her lips.

"No. He's so busy these days that he barely pays attention to me."

Ryan sighed and stroked her arm. It killed him that they had to sneak around. He wanted to be able to walk down the street with her — be able to have her over at the house during the day and not worry about anyone seeing her arrive. That couldn't happen until her ties were cut.

"You should tell him," he said. "He's going to find out eventually, right?"

"In time. I'm waiting for the right moment. Everything is just so hectic right now and he's got a lot on his plate."

"Well the moment it's unhectic, you should speak up." He kissed her neck, just where he knew she liked it. "I want you all to myself."

"And I feel the same way. We'll be together, I promise."

She got up and wandered over to his canvas. She was the only one he let see his work before it was finished. In the past, he would show his father, but after he died, Ryan was left with no one he cared about. Not until this woman came into his life.

"I have an idea," she said. "I want you to paint something and put it for sale in your gallery. If someone buys it, I'll tell him about us. If not . . . you're going to have to tell him yourself."

Ryan chuckled. "All right. What painting are you suggesting?"

Giving him a seductive smile, she kicked off her shoes. She started undressing herself, and his heart pounded. In all his years, he'd never done a nude painting because he couldn't find the perfect model. Now the perfect one stood right in front of him.

"You're a masterpiece in the making," he said. "You're comfortable with this?"

"It's not like you haven't seen me before.

"I know but everyone who goes through my gallery will."

She looked at him from beneath her lashes. "I don't mind. It's a small price to pay if it means we'll be together."

2

It was a small price. He had to admit that her idea tempted him immensely. It would work, without a doubt. She had a gorgeous body, and someone was bound to buy a portrait of her. Plus, he wanted to have an excuse to stare at her curves for hours and then make crazy love to her. It would all be worth it.

"Let's go outside," he said. "I know the perfect place to do this."

1

EULESS NOVEMBER 10TH

Hawes, we have a ten-fifty on West Boulevard. Do you copy?"
Someone said over the scanner.

Cadet Beau looked over at me. "Do you know what that is?"

I tried to run the codes through my head. There were so many to remember but having been an officer for three months, I was starting to get better and picking up on the codes quicker. Mona's flashcard technique probably saved me.

"Someone under the influence of drugs?" I asked.

"Perfect. And it's about four blocks from here. You up for it?'

I chuckled. "Is anyone?"

"Good answer."

Flipping on the lights, I headed in the direction of the reported sighting. At first, I thought being a police officer would be just like working with the MITF, but I was pleasantly surprised to find that it was way better. The guys weren't shady and every officer I worked with had great integrity. Not everyone was like that, but unlike the MITF I wasn't afraid of any conspiracy to commit murder or conduct illegal experiments.

We'd moved to Euless, Texas at the end of August. After Gallard got us settled, he left with David and Solomon to try and gather more people to support our cause. I didn't want to just sit around and wait for Gallard to come back, so I decided to get a job. With Solomon's help, I was able to get a hold of the documents stating that I'd completed the required police academy training. All he had to do was change my last name and the date I finished. I'd applied at the Euless police department and was now in my second month.

Granted I still had to ride with someone more experienced for the required training process. I enjoyed my job. Police officers I trusted. Immortal Task Force officers I did not.

Slowing to a crawl, I turned on my side floodlight and shone it throughout the neighborhood. I really hoped that this was just a case of someone strung out and wandering the streets. I wasn't in the mood for any danger.

"There!" Beau said.

Right after, I saw a strange hooded man walking in circles. He was mumbling to himself and twitching like crazy. This was going to be a long night.

I parked the car then Beau and I got out. Whoever this guy was, he was either on something or mentally unstable. We approached him slowly until he noticed our presence and turned around. He was skinny and balding.

"Hey, man," I said. "You doing all right?"

"No," he said. "No, no! I'm clean! I promise!"

Oh boy.

"Are you sure about that?"

"Go to hell! I'm not going back there! I'm not!"

I put my hands up. "Okay. We're not here to corner you. We just want to ask a few questions."

Beau shot me a side glance and I figured he was okay with how this was going. I had dealt with several similar circumstances before, but I was still new to this.

The man started crying and wiped his eyes with his jacket. Whatever he was on was making him erratic — angry one second and emotional the next. Mixed with alcohol and a deadly weapon and he could be highly dangerous.

"I tried," he said. "I tried to be clean. It's so hard. So, so hard!"

"I know," Beau said. "My brother was addicted to cocaine. He relapsed several times, but he got through it. He's married with kids now. It may seem bad now but when you look back, you'll realize you were stronger than you feel in the moment." He held his hand out. "Just come with us and we can get you help."

The man took his hands out of his jacket pockets, revealing that he had a gun. Beau reached for his and I quickly pulled mine out as well. I really hoped that this guy wouldn't shoot because I probably wouldn't be able to shoot him.

"Put the gun down, man," Beau said. "This isn't worth your life."

"I'm not going back there!"

My enhanced vision picked up on every movement he made. I saw his finger beginning to curl around the trigger. The gun was pointed at Beau and it was aimed high. If this guy was lucky, he would get a throat shot. Worst case scenario, right in the cheek. I wanted to at least shoot the guy in the leg, but by then the gun already went off.

Against my better judgement, I tackled Beau to the ground at a speed no human could move. I then drew my own gun and put a bullet in the stoner's thigh. The man yelled, dropping his weapon and fell to the ground.

"You okay, man?" I asked Beau.

"Yeah. Thanks to you."

We both got up and he went over and kicked the man's gun away then cuffed him. I called for a bus and backup over my radio. I realized after that my hands were shaking. This was the first time I'd been shot at on the job and though I was immortal, it still rattled me. Ever since what happened with Henry, I was slightly on edge.

Once the guy was in custody, Beau and I gave our statements then drove back to the precinct. I would have to go through the routine of meeting with a Post-Incident manager. I finished all necessary procedures then turned in my weapon. Everything took about five hours.

Shutting my car door, I began to unbutton my uniform shirt as I walked into the house. Working night shift wasn't as easy as I thought it would be, but I was getting into a routine. It was around four o'clock, which meant I had about three hours before I had to get up again.

We had been in Texas for three months and for now, things were normal. All my family lived next door to each other for convenience and it was just Lucian, Kevin, Abe, and me looking out for the women. Not that they needed looking after. Cherish was basically good enough for four men. We had a peaceful life in Euless, and I loved not having to worry about danger or conspiracy for a change.

I went into my room and smiled when I found someone in my bed. Colton spent most of his nights in my room as of late, and I enjoyed coming home to him. He made my time away from Micah more bearable.

I showered and changed before crawling in next to him. All the stress on the job was worth it because I had him to come home to.

Around seven, he stirred a little then twisted around until he was looking into my eyes. This had become a routine since he hardly ever slept in his own bed. He'd been excited because it was bigger than the one he had back home, but soon his homesickness took over and he preferred my room over his.

"Good morning, bud. You sleep okay?"

"Uh, huh." He yawned. "Did you 'rest anyone last night?"

I nodded. "Just one guy. He was sick and he tried to hurt someone. I stopped him before he could."

"He didn't try to hurt you, did he? I don't like it when people hurt you."

He hugged me and I held him tightly. I hated that he'd witnessed Henry trying to kill me, and he would probably never forget that. More than anything, I wanted him to have a normal life where he wasn't around danger or violence.

"Why don't you go get dressed," I said. "I'll make you breakfast."

We both got up and Colton bounded down the hall into his room while I went into the kitchen. We had parent-teacher conferences, and I had taken the day off so Nicola and I could go.

On Colton's first day, being the over-prepared dad that I was, I opened his school supplies and organized them in his pencil box. Probably a little overkill, but I used my OCD to avoid the real issue. It was the first time I left Colton somewhere other than in the care of a family member. I was very protective of him and worried he would be found. Lela kept assuring me he would be fine, and I couldn't let him miss out on school. So, I put aside my concerns and enrolled him in one of the preschools closest to the house.

The front door opened, and I smiled when Nicola came in. She looked great these days. Healthier than she had in a long time and more beautiful than ever. We were slowly but surely getting comfortable as a couple again.

We had agreed that in the two months we were together before we separated for some time, we had moved pretty fast. We were both going through quite a bit and since most of our issues were behind us, we were focusing on becoming less dependent on each other emotionally and having our relationship based on the right things.

Of course, this was all advice we'd taken from Lela. If it were up to me, I would have had her move in with me so I could spend every night with her.

"Good morning, Nic," I said. "Excited for conferences?"

"Totally. It's so weird that five years ago my parents were going to mine and now I'm the one going for my child." Nicola came into the kitchen and stood next to me. "J.D. wants to know if you and I want to go to town later. She's getting bored at home."

"She's not driving you nuts yet?"

"No! J.D. and I are tight. We're like *The Three Musketeers*, with her being Porthos and Robin being Aramis. I guess that makes me Athos. It's Abe that drives us crazy. He's like d'Artanian—the annoying tag-a-long."

I smiled at the thought of the three women being roommates. What I wouldn't give to be a fly on the wall at their place for a day. J.D. was so busy that she could make me dizzy while Robin was sweet, yet talkative. Nicola wasn't as blunt with them as she was with everyone else and I could tell she was getting close to them.

"Colton, breakfast is ready!" I called.

The sound of thudding around in the living room told me that Kevin and he were still wrestling, so he wouldn't even care about his food until either Kevin wore him out or he got hungry. Colton and Kevin had been attached at the hip since the moment they, met and I wasn't about to interrupt their roughhousing.

I slipped the spatula under the browning pancake and flipped it to the other side with ease. I had gotten into a routine over the past few months. If I didn't have structure to my days, I would go crazy thinking about Micah and what he might be going through. The nightmares were bad enough without my imagination running during the day.

When I finished making the pancakes, I set the stack on the dining table next to the bacon and eggs. Usually, I would settle for fixing him a bowl of cereal and orange juice, but Colton expressed that he missed his mom and I thought having pancakes might cheer him up. It cheered me up as well. I couldn't imagine Colton getting through this if it weren't for Kevin. He was my savior.

As I put down a fork for Colton, Kevin came in with the bubbling child riding on his shoulders. Since his release, Kevin had gotten into better health. He drank blood regularly and he looked less like a hobo. He never told us what he endured while in MITF custody, but I never pushed him to say anything. He was dealing with it in his own way.

"Pancakes?" Colton shouted excitedly.

"Yeah bud! Indulge yourself."

He sat down and started eating, shoveling the food into his mouth. I ruffled his hair then sat down next to him. Nicola sat to my right and occasionally stole bites of my food. Kevin got some blood from the fridge, filling a glass for each of us. I only took a little, though. Blood in large quantities still made me antsy, but not as wild. In four weeks' time, I had managed to get to a place where blood didn't set me off in a violent frenzy. It also helped that no one in my family appealed to me.

"That boy gets stronger every day," Kevin said. "At this rate, he'll be stronger than any day-walker by the time he's a teenager."

"I'm glad you're working with him," Nicola said. "It's better that he learns to control his strength now than when he's stronger. I don't think I'd have it in me to run him down with my car."

The three of us laughed and Colton looked extremely appalled that she would suggest such a thing. I was relieved that Colton was away from Scott and any person who might use him for evil. His strength would be handy when he got older, but I didn't want him to be a weapon. Not on my watch.

"How are the pancakes?" I asked Colton. He couldn't answer because his mouth was too full, but he smiled. "I know they're not . . . mom's pancakes, but I tried."

"I miss mom." He chewed a bit. "Can I see her?"

Nicola and I exchanged glances. I didn't know how to answer that. I'd promised myself in the past that I would take Colton to visit Regina once every couple of weeks, but that was before Scott banished me from Miami and we moved to Texas. Every time he would ask to see her, I would have to come up with a way to stall.

"Maybe sometime in the future, bud. I know you miss her, but it's not a good time right now."

"Okay."

I blinked. He was so easy to please, and I'd always known this, but I was afraid as he got older, he would start asking more questions and stop taking no for an answer. Kevin gave me a sympathetic smile and I knew he understood. He'd gone through the same thing when Robin was little and having difficulty accepting her parents' death.

"So, what are we going to do tonight since it's your day off?" Kevin asked. "Can we please go somewhere?"

I chuckled. "It must suck only being able to go out at night. If you want, I could ask Lela to babysit Colton and we could —"

"Party? I couldn't have thought of a better idea myself. While I'm not dying of boredom, I'm researching the best night clubs in town. And apparently, this place has all of two. If you don't mind driving into Arlington, we might have more options."

It had been a while since I'd done anything fun. Taking on parenthood was more of a challenge than I'd thought. Colton had to come first before everything, and I loved him like crazy. However, being a parent and a working man required more work than I thought it would. I had a lot more respect for parents now.

"I'll talk to Lela after I drop Colton off," I said. I finished off the last bit of blood in my glass and stood up. "Okay, bud. It's time for school."

He finished his eggs then took off to his room to put on his jacket. I changed into some nice jeans and a polo. I would probably be the youngest dad there, but I wouldn't let that bother me.

Colton skipped out the door then I closed it behind me. Nicola strapped him in, and we were going to leave when a loud screeching of tires turned our attention to the street. A car came speeding around the corner and came to an abrupt stop merely centimeters from my car. It shut off and then the driver got out. Abe couldn't have gotten up as early as we had, so I assumed he'd gotten back from spending the night somewhere. He put his sunglasses on as he walked towards us.

"'Morning," he said. "Why are you lovebirds standing out here?"

"Why, we were waiting for you!" Nicola said.

He laughed. "Sure. Well, I hate to jet, but I'm very hung-over, and I need a shower. See you."

Abe stalked off towards the house Nicola shared with Robin and J.D. then went inside. After all this time, he'd kept his promise to watch out for Robin. He technically lived with Kevin, Lucian, and me but he spent most of his nights in the extra room at their house. I had been right to predict he would be Robin's new favorite. They were almost inseparable, and we hardly ever saw one without the other. Abe still had his hook-ups, but then he would dutifully go back to Robin's side.

The school was barely five minutes away from the house, so we got there quickly. We each held one of Colton's hands, and his backpack was strapped onto him and secure. As always, we had to pretend it wasn't obvious we were the youngest parents there.

When we got to his classroom, we let go of his hands and he ran off to play with the other kids who were waiting for their parents. There was a whole line of them waiting their turn to have a meeting. His class consisted of twenty kids, but some came in the morning while others came in the afternoon.

One mom next to me kept sifting through her purse. She appeared to be in her mid-thirties and had brown hair. She wore khaki slacks and a nice blouse.

"I can't believe my daughter is in school," the mom said. "In my mind she's still a baby."

"I know the feeling. Which one is she?"

She pointed to the little girl in a pink jumper with brown braids on the swings. "That's my girl— Delaney. She cried all night before her first day, and now she's excited about school. Which one's yours?"

I pointed at Colton. "That little guy."

She smiled. "He's adorable. I can tell he's yours." She held out her hand. "I'm Michelle Covington. Single mom."

I shook her hand. "Lucas d'Aubigne. Married dad."

Michelle laughed. "I'm trying to figure out if I should be worried. Isn't it usually the kids who are doing poorly that need conferences?"

"Not necessarily. My son is actually doing very well. I think it could mean a number of things."

The door opened and a couple came out, signifying that it was our turn.

"Well, I guess it's us. It was nice to meet you, Michelle."

"The pleasure was mine, Lucas."

The conference went well. His teacher had a lot of good things to say and her only concern was that Colton liked to keep to himself a lot. He would join in the recess games if invited but he would never ask. I wasn't too worried. Micah had been same way at that age, and he turned out just fine. Colton was only adjusting to being in a different state and away from home.

"*The pleasure was mine, Lucas,*" Nicola mocked while we were in the car. "She totally wants to do you."

"Nic!"

"You know I'm right, though. Why else would she point out that she was single? Plus, she has homewrecker written all over her. Didn't she see you come in with me?"

I did get the sense that she was hitting on me, but I would never respond to it. She was friendly in a lonely housewife sort of way.

"Even if you are right, I'm not interested. I have you and I'll only ever want you."

"Unless you get tired of waiting for me after five hundred years."

Before she'd turned into a vampire, the thought that I would lose her one day was always in the back of my mind. I kept telling myself that I would be prepared for that moment and then it was right before me as she was in my arms bleeding to death. I realized then that I couldn't live without her.

"I will never get tired of waiting for you. Can I ask you an honest question?"

"You always can. Be warned, I may be brutally honest in my answer."

"It's what I love about you." I came to a stop at the red light. "Were you mad at me when you realized what I was doing? When I gave you my blood, I mean."

Nicola didn't answer right away, and it made me nervous. I said that I loved her honesty, but this might not be an answer I wanted to hear. I would hate it if she resented me for the rest of her life because she specifically said that she didn't want to be an immortal. I'd gone against her wishes in turning her.

"When I thought I was dying, the only thing going through my head was what I would miss," she said. "When you gave me your blood . . . I don't know. I didn't fight it because I knew I would have a second chance to be a mother to Colton. Do I like being a vampire? No. But it's a sacrifice I'm willing to endure for him."

My stomach knotted. She'd said she allowed it to happen so she could be with her son. She never said she'd done it to be with me. I wasn't sure how to take that. If Colton weren't in the picture, would she have chosen to die? I didn't want to think that.

I looked down the road and noticed the traffic had slowed down. There were a dozen police cars and their lights were flashing. It reminded me of the day I found out about the three gang members who were disemboweled. Euless was a small town, though and hardly any crimes occurred there. It was why we'd chosen the city for a place to hide.

It was technically my day off, but I still felt like I should stop. I saw someone I knew was on the scene. We got closer to the lights, and I rolled my window down. He recognized me and came over to the car.

"Hey, Lucas," Beau said.

"Why are you still on the job?"

"Someone was killed two hours after the druggie incident. A young man about fifteen years old. Vampire attack. His throat was torn, and he

11

was missing most of his blood. The cause of death appears to be a broken neck. They think whoever did it was remorseful and decided to kill him before feeding on him."

Normally, such a crime wouldn't be a big deal, but I had to remember this wasn't Miami. Euless and the surrounding cities were known to have the least amount of vampire activity in the state of Texas. They didn't even have a task force but only trained a handful of the local police officers on how to handle vampires.

"Any leads?"

"Not yet. Don't worry about it, Lucas. Go enjoy your day off and I'll fill you in tomorrow."

I nodded then drove off, a million thoughts going through my head. How was I going to enjoy my day off with this going on?

"It might just be a drifter," I told Nicola.

"I hope so. Then again, it could be a mortal trying to frame someone. We both know that some people do that."

We remained silent during the drive home and I kept obsessing over this attack that occurred. We'd been living such a peaceful and violent free life for the past month that the crime rattled me. The last thing we needed was some immortal exposing us. Whoever killed that boy, I hoped they were long gone.

2

Robin fiddled nervously while she waited for the man to finish typing on his tablet. She'd spent hours preparing for this test, and it would crush her if she failed. This was her chance to prove herself— to prove that she wasn't a child and that she could function in the adult world.

Finally, the man put his iPad down and smiled. "Well congratulations, Miss Shepherd. You passed the driver's test."

A long exhale escaped her lips. At least she could do one thing right. It would have crushed her if she wasn't able to pass the test.

"Thank you for your time," she said.

"My pleasure. Now let's go inside and get your picture taken."

She unbuckled her seatbelt and got out, nearly sprinted to the door. When she went inside, Abe stood up from his seat and smiled.

"Well?"

"I passed!" she said. She gave him a light hug then pulled back.

"Of course you did, babe! I taught you well."

"I couldn't have done it without your help. Thank you for teaching me how to drive."

He nodded then she went over to the instructor who told her to stand on the red line against the wall. She gave the camera her best smile, the light flashed, and then she stepped away. The machine made a whooshing sound then spat out the plastic license. They gave it to her then she went with Abe out the door. She felt like a new person. She was a licensed driver and her next mission was registering to vote.

EXILE

"Can I drive us home?" she asked.

"I don't know. The Scion is Lucian's baby. And we still have to stop at the grocery store, if you recall."

Robin gave him the most pathetic look she could muster. She really wanted to drive up to the house so Lela would be surprised. Robin hadn't told her because she was afraid she would say no. Abe wasn't busy and he successfully sneaked her away.

"Oh, no. Robin don't give me those eyes."

"Please! It won't be as much of a surprise if I just tell her. She has to see me behind the wheel too."

He sighed then gave her a half smile. "All right. I suppose since the house is five minutes away, letting you drive wouldn't hurt."

She then took the keys and got into the passenger seat. Once they were both buckled, she pulled out of the parking lot and got into the road. Abe looked tense while she drove, but he didn't say a word. She drove even more carefully than she had during the test and made sure to leave extra space between her and the other cars just to give him peace of mind.

"What are you getting at the store?" she asked.

"Just a few things for myself. J.D. offers to pick up what I need, but she always buys a different brand than I request. I think it's her way of saying she's still mad at me."

"You mind if I borrow some money. I need a few things as well."

"Sure, babe." He handed her a credit card. "Use this. It's my back-up."

They arrived at the store and they both got out. He promised he wouldn't be long, but she wanted to look around. She rarely ever got out since she had to rely on transportation, so she welcomed any chance to go into town.

Checking over her shoulder, she made sure Abe wasn't around then hurried to the feminine care section. She had to learn quickly that life wasn't as simple as it used to be. Ever since her parents were killed, her eyes were opened to how cruel the world was.

And then the two men assaulted her, and she was never the same after that. She grew up overnight and lost her innocence. Oh, she would smile, and laugh at J.D.'s jokes, and pretend nothing was wrong. But she was dying inside. Lucas healed her physical wounds, but she would always be scarred.

Now, her life might get even more complicated. Over the past few months, she hadn't felt quite like herself. She would get sick in the morning, and strong smells made her nauseous. Robin assumed she just had the flu, and after three months the vomiting stopped.

Then she'd started feeling the butterflies. About a month ago, she'd become convinced something was inside of her. Instead of asking J.D., she went online to try and figure out what could be wrong. That's how she'd found herself in the grocery store buying a pregnancy test.

She tried to pass the time by pretending to look at everything on the shelves. She stood next to a woman holding a baby in a carrier. Robin stared at the tiny human for a little while and it smiled at her. She tried to smile back but then the baby's face scrunched, and it started crying. The baby's wails unnerved Robin and she wanted to get away from there. She grabbed the first test she saw and hurried to the pharmacy counter.

Once she'd paid, she took the white sack and headed for the tobacco machine. These days, it was a lot easier to get cigarettes. They'd developed a system that could read a person's info from their driver's license to determine their age then the person would choose the brand from a selection on the screen and the box would come out through a chute. She'd figured this out a while back when she'd stolen Lela's and used it to buy cigarettes.

After going through the procedures, she reached down to grab the pack but then she felt someone's hand on her butt. Instantly, fear spiked through her and her heart raced. On instinct, she turned around and kneed the guy in the groin. He yelled in pain and hunched over. The kid couldn't have been more than fifteen.

"What the hell?" the kid shouted. "Are you crazy?"

"Am *I* crazy? You're the one touching me inappropriately!"

"Look, I accidentally brushed you. You're blowing this out of proportion!"

Her anger building, she shoved him backwards. He started to lunge for her when she grabbed the first thing she could find. There was a broom display on the end of the aisle. She hit him in the gut and when he fell.

It's my body!" she said. "You have no right to touch me!"

Someone came up behind her and in a panic, she jabbed him too, causing him to double over. When she realized he was wearing a police uniform, she gasped and dropped the broom.

"I'm sorry officer!" she said. "I was frightened. That boy assaulted me and —"

"That's all right, beautiful," he said in a pained voice. "You can club me any day."

The officer recovered and straightened his posture, smiling down at her. He was only a few inches taller than her and had eggshell-brown eyes. His chestnut brown hair was shorter on the sides and slicked back on top. With one sweep of her eyes she saw that he had a lean physique, like Lucas.

Another officer joined him and hauled the kid up from the ground, cuffing him. Robin felt bad that she'd hit the officer, but she didn't feel bad for hitting the kid. He'd crossed a line and she was never letting another man do that to her again.

"Hey, McPherson, you coming?" the officer asked.

"I'll be out in a minute, James. I need to get her statement." He turned to her and smiled again. "That was some impressive work there. The Euless police department owes you their thanks."

"I don't know what came over me. Is he going to jail?"

"That's a definite possibility. He's been groping women in several stores for a week now. We wouldn't have caught him without you. You're a hero."

She wasn't expecting him to be friendly. His voice was kind and warm — not like the officers that had hurt her. But she'd learned from that situation not to trust a man just because his job was to protect people. Henry and Ash had been nice until she saw them for what they really were. She was now paying the price for being so trusting.

"Are you going to arrest me?" she asked.

He laughed and the sound of it made her stomach do flips. His good mood was infectious, and she was smiling before she realized it.

"For what?"

"Assault and battery? I hit that kid several times. Plus, I don't feel bad about it, so that probably means I won't get a good deal in court."

"Not to mention you assaulted a police officer. Your rap sheet isn't looking so good is it?" He gave her a teasing smile. "What's your name?"

"Robin Shepherd."

"Robin. I like it. I'm Officer McPherson, but you can call me Erik."

She couldn't look into his eyes anymore without feeling flutters, so she cast her gaze down and fiddled with her hands. She'd never felt this way before. Men made her nervous except for those close to her. But this man made her feel excited. She needed to push these feelings away. There was no way she would trust a police officer ever again.

"You're not from around here, are you?" he asked.

"No, sir."

"Sir? Does my uniform make you nervous?"

Robin nodded timidly and forced herself to look at him again. His kind smile sent a shock of thrill through her body and she hadn't been prepared for it. She didn't know why, but she wanted him to keep talking. She shouldn't have wanted that, yet she was torn between wanting him to continue talking to her and wanting him to go away.

"You're really beautiful," he said. "I'm usually not this straightforward, so believe me when I say this."

"People say I look like my mother."

"Then I'm sure your mother is stunning."

Her nervousness skyrocketed. His compliments made her uncomfortable, but not in a bad way. She couldn't decide what she should think of him. His uniform was intimidating, but if she looked at his face, she felt otherwise.

"I should go." She picked up her paper sack from the floor. "Abe is probably looking for me."

His smile disappeared. "Abe? Not your boyfriend, I hope."

She chuckled. "No. He's my friend."

Erik let out a sigh of relief then turned his mouth up in a grin. "Thank goodness for that. It would ruin my day to find out you're already taken."

"Robin!" Abe called to her. She turned to see him coming towards her and heat rushed to her cheeks. Why was she embarrassed that she was talking to this Erik McPherson? They were just having friendly conversation.

"I was looking for —" Abe looked at Erik. "What's wrong? Is she in trouble?"

"Not at all, man. I was only talking to your lovely friend here. I was going to ask for her number, but we hadn't gotten to that yet."

"I don't think that's a good idea."

Robin shot him a look to try and get him to stop talking. It was embarrassing enough that he'd showed up without him getting all protective of her. It had been comforting at first to have someone strong and capable at her side but now it was suffocating her. She really cared about Abe, but she needed him to back off a little.

"All right. I guess I can get a hold of her some other way. I'll probably catch her attempting citizen arrest or something. It was nice meeting you Robin, and I hope I see you around. Hopefully next time, I'll be out of uniform."

He winked at her before going on his way, and Robin watched him until he walked out of the door. She let out a long sigh and looked back at Abe.

"When he says out of uniform, did he mean he would be naked?" Robin asked, genuinely confused.

Abe started laughing so hard that tears were streaming from his eyes. Robin blushed, embarrassed that she'd yet again made a mistake. She'd learned educational things from Danielle Shepherd, but her friends had taught her the ways of the world. She'd also had the unwelcomed privilege of hearing everything that went on in Abe's room whenever he brought someone home. All the while, there was still a lot she didn't know about.

"Come on, babe. I should get you home."

They got back to the house and thankfully, no one had noticed they were gone. She was no longer thinking about her maybe-pregnancy but had something else on her mind. Erik McPherson. He was extremely attractive and their chance encounter had gotten her curious. Did Lela feel this way about Gallard? If so, Robin could see why they married so quickly. Not that she wanted to marry the guy. Besides, he was a police officer and policemen were off limits. That didn't mean she couldn't think about how good he smelled or how his laugh gave her butterflies. The real kind, this time. Thinking was innocent.

"Why was that police officer speaking with you?" Abe asked.

17

"They were trying to arrest someone, and I apprehended the suspect."

He stopped walking. "Did you just say *apprehended*?"

"I'm expanding my vocabulary. Melody says I've gotten to the seventh-grade level of my studies. And I watch a lot of TV. I'm more advanced than you know. You should have seen me, Abe! I kicked him and then I beat him with a broom. He deserved it though. He was a pervert."

"I need to start training more with you. It's impossible to stay at your side twenty-four seven, and I want to have peace of mind knowing that you can defend yourself."

Abe knocked on Lela's door and Robin grew anxious. Would Lela be mad that she did this behind her back? Robin hadn't meant to keep her in the dark. She wanted to surprise her. Then again, she was hiding the fact that she was buying cigarettes using her sister's I.D. and smoking them at one in the morning when everyone was asleep. There worse things Lela could be upset about.

Lela opened the door and smiled at Robin. "Hey, you two. What brings you here?"

Robin took her new I.D. from her pocket and handed it to Lela. "I got my license!"

"That's great!" Lela pulled Robin into a hug. "I'm so proud of you, hon."

Lela invited them inside, but Abe said he had something to do. Nobody questioned him and Robin went in alone. Melody was on the couch reading a romance novel and Cherish was apparently at Robin's house spending time with J.D. Robin always wondered what they spent their time doing. Lela had her salon job in Arlington, but the other women were still unemployed.

Robin sat next to Melody and Lela bragged about Robin's achievement. Melody was even more excited and hugged Robin as well. Robin knew that this was something people normally did when they were sixteen, but she was proud of herself anyway.

The excitement finally died down, and Robin set her bag on the floor then picked up a newspaper from the table. There was a story on the front cover about a new art gallery that was opening in town. Nicola had been raving about it from the moment it was announced. She had been taking art classes from the guy who owned it.

"I can't believe Abe took you to get your license," Melody said.

"I asked him to teach me about a month ago, and we practiced in that abandoned parking lot by the library. He even let me drive home. My next challenge is learning how to drive stick."

The newspaper got boring, so she traded it for one of the romance novels on the table Melody had in a pile. She was the biggest romantic Robin had ever met and she loved that Melody was dating David. She hoped they would get married one day.

"Melody, when did you meet David?" Robin asked.

"Oh, wow." Melody closed her book. "It was nineteen ninety-four. He wanted to know how to become mortal again. I was surprised since most vampires don't wish to reverse their immortality. I thought he was so handsome, but then he told me he was doing it for a woman— your mother. I understood what it was like to want to be with someone I loved, so I told him."

"Was it love at first sight, or something corny like that?"

Melody laughed. "No, hon, it wasn't. I wouldn't lie and say that I wasn't intrigued. But it took seeing him a second time to get me interested. We came back to life close to the same time and he was such a gentleman. He made me want to rethink my life as a permanent widow, and I'm so glad I did. I love him very much."

Robin pondered on this for a while. She wondered if it would be the same for her if she saw Erik again. Would he still be interested? Why didn't she just give him her number? What would Abe do about it?

Who was she kidding? Erik McPherson was not someone she should be thinking about. She had faith that he wasn't the only attractive guy out there. But she did worry that Erik would be the only one to give her butterflies.

"I want that someday," Robin said. "I want to be happy like you are."

"I'm sure it will happen, hon. Your guy is out there somewhere and when the time is right, he'll show up."

3

J.D. took a swing at Cherish and groaned when she missed. This was probably the tenth time she'd failed at making a hit. They'd been sparring for nearly an hour and she hadn't made any progress. She'd thought she would be a natural. She'd never been more wrong. The fact that Lucian was watching embarrassed her further.

After Cherish found out that J.D. had a pension for getting caught during attempts at spying, she concluded J.D. would not make it as an undercover agent so she decided to teach her self-defense instead. J.D. had been up for it in the beginning but hadn't anticipated the humiliation.

"Again," Cherish said.

"This is rubbish! You're too fast for me — I can't hit you."

"Come on! You're a d'Aubigne, you can't give up. Forget that I'm strong because if you fight someone else that's just as strong as me, they aren't going to go easy on you."

Cherish put her arms up in a defensive stance with her feet as wide apart as her shoulders, and J.D. did the same. She wasn't ready to give up just yet, but she felt like her progress went backwards instead of forwards. Cherish had spent years in Asia learning every form of martial art ever invented and J.D. was no match for her prowess.

J.D. managed to dodge a few of Cherish's blows, but they had been mediocre ones. J.D. attempted to kick her but Cherish blocked those as well with her foot. J.D. aimed for her face and made the mistake of ducking. Cherish's boxing glove clipped her right in the nose. The blow sent J.D. onto her back. Her nose throbbed but wasn't bleeding.

"Oops! Hope I didn't knock out any teeth," Cherish jabbed.

"Careful, darling!" Lucian said.

"She's fine, dad. J.D.'s tough, aren't you?"

J.D. covered her face with her hands while she waited for the throbbing to stop. That was when she got an idea. She would never be able to overtake Cherish with fighting tactics, so the only other way was to fake her out. J.D. then started moaning and pretended to cry.

"Oh, come on," Cherish said. "I didn't hit you *that* hard!"

"Tell that to my nose!" J.D. said, her voice muffled through her gloves.

She continued to whimper as she heard Cherish come closer. She kept up with the façade, waiting for just the right moment. When she was sure she had Cherish completely distracted, J.D. did a quick sweep of her leg, knocking her off her feet and Cherish crashed to the ground, causing her to laugh.

"Bloody hell, I'm good!" she said. "I can't believe you fell for that!"

Cherish laughed too. "Touché. You may not be a skilled fighter, but you excel at acting."

J.D. was about to speak when she heard someone clapping. She turned her head to see her brother.

"I'm impressed," he said. "I haven't seen anyone best Aunt Cherish in a fight since . . ."

"A very long time," Cherish agreed.

Lucian held out both of his hands, taking each of theirs and hoisted them off the ground. J.D. didn't let go of his hand right away but when she did, her skin was still hot from his touch. It had been too long since he'd touched her and she missed him like crazy.

"What brings you here, Abe?" Cherish asked after removing her gloves. "I know it wasn't to see me get knocked on my ass."

He glanced at J.D. for moment then looked away. "I came to see my sister. We haven't spoken much these days."

"There's a reason for that," J.D. said, purposefully avoiding looking at his face.

"Why don't we give them some time to catch up," Lucian said.

He and Cherish linked arms, and J.D.'s heart sank as they walked away. She wished they wouldn't leave her alone with Abe. She couldn't stand him, and the sight of him made her want to hit something.

J.D. wandered over to the tree and hit the punching bag over and over, channeling all of her frustrations into the bag. As soon as she was old enough Cherish had taught her of this method to release the pent-up energy she had. As a child, she'd found it hard to sit still and beating on a bag full of Styrofoam proved to help.

"Are you really going to ignore me?" he asked.

"Yeah, that's the plan."

You're hiding your thoughts from me, sweetheart, a familiar voice said. *What's wrong?*

21

She stopped punching the bag for a moment and held onto it, pressing her forehead against the cool material. Just hearing her father's voice lessened her anxiety. What would help even more would be if he could physically be there to hold her and comfort her.

Ever since she was five years old, she could hear the voice of her father, Jordan. It frightened her at first because she thought he was a ghost, but then she heard stories of Lela and how she'd experienced the same thing with Lucian. She swore never to tell anyone her secret because she was afraid of what people would think. Her mother and Gallard already worried about her enough.

Being a potential immortal was more stressful than anyone could imagine. As children, her family would keep a close eye on her and her brother. She lived a life of constant fear and safety. She understood why they treated her this way. If she were to die, whether by an accident or murder, she would become immortal and sustain herself on the blood of vampires. The only one who she could talk to was her father.

Nothing you want to know, dad.

Come on! If I don't talk to you, I have nothing to do. Tell me what's on your mind.

She chuckled to herself. Her father's comic relief was one of the many things that helped her get through each day. When she'd started having feelings for Lucian, she had to learn quickly how to block some of her thoughts from him to avoid any lectures. She knew her father didn't approve of him, but she was determined to show him that Lucian was a changed man — not the one he'd used to know.

It's my brother. I have a feeling he's going to make a speech about suddenly giving a damn about me.

You should talk to him. I don't like that my children aren't getting along.

That's not helpful.

"Why are you here, Abe?" she finally said.

"I've put this off long enough. We have issues and we need to work them out. We can't continue to live like this."

"And what inspired this sudden need for reconciliation?"

She punched the bag but the he grabbed onto it to keep it from swinging.

"Robin and Lela, actually. I see how close they are, and it bothers me that we're not like that. I couldn't visit sooner because I was in the middle of several contracts with this new men's cologne and had to do commercials and photo shoots —"

"I don't want to hear about your glamorous life. You obviously care more about your career or you would have come sooner."

"I do care. Why do you think I'm still here?"

"I think Gallard guilt tripped you."

He flinched and she knew she'd hit the mark. If anyone could talk sense into her brother, it was their uncle. He hadn't been able to convince Abe to stick around, but he had gotten him to come to the states for a few holidays. After he turned eighteen, Abe returned to London and never looked back. In return, she ignored him as well.

"As far as you're concerned, I'm here for the duration. I quit modeling to prove it, and I'm going to help our family fight this vampire eradication thing. I owe it to you, and I owe it to dad. Just let me prove that I mean it this time."

He walked away, his words ringing in her mind. He quit modeling? She knew he'd taken time off when he came to Miami and never would have guessed he would give up that life. He'd been doing it since he could walk. Maybe he was really going to stick around. No. She couldn't let herself be fooled again. He hadn't been there when she really needed him, and she wasn't getting her hopes up now.

She started punching the bag again but was interrupted once more.

"Punching bags again, I see," someone said behind her.

J.D. turned to see Lucian coming across the yard. She hadn't expected him to come back. He looked as handsome as ever in his dark jeans and navy button-up. He'd cut his hair a little shorter, which made him even more desirable.

Speak of the Devil, Jordan said. *Has he finally come to his senses?*

Let me get back to you on that, dad. We'll talk later, okay?

"Are we speaking again?" she asked with a taunting smile.

"I did not know we weren't."

"Oh, really? Then why haven't we had a real conversation in five weeks?"

He hung his head. "I thought you were angry with me. After the situation with Lucas' mistaken death, I wanted to give you space. I also did not know how to react to your advances."

Lucian walked up to her until he was close enough for her to smell his cologne. She was only dressed in a sports bra and volleyball shorts, but she didn't mind that he was staring at her body. She welcomed his gaze now that she no longer blamed herself for Lucas' near death.

"I was just over at Lela's," he said. "It appears Abe took Robin to obtain her driver's license, and she passed. That girl does everything she puts her mind to."

"Is Robin your new favorite now?"

"You're sexy when you're jealous." He reached up and slid his thumb over her cheek. "It has been too long since you last kissed me."

"Then what's stopping you?"

He lowered his hand and put both into his pockets. She couldn't understand why he was holding back. She loved him and he knew it. She was waiting for the moment when he would say it back to her and until then, she would be content with the stolen kisses and longing stares.

She stepped closer to him and slipped her arms around his waist. He didn't react at first then held her as she looked up at his face. His eyes were intense as ever and she could sense that he was holding back everything he wanted to say.

"I spoke with Gallard last night. He believes he's close to finding Arnaud."

"That's wonderful news! How long do you think it will be before they come back?"

"Time will tell. For now, I am going to make the most of the time we have without his eyes on us."

He leaned down until his lips met hers, and she surrendered to his kiss. The weather was already warm, but she could feel her body growing hotter as it reacted to his touch. He ran his hands over her, and she allowed it, not wanting him to stop. She wanted all of him, and if it weren't for her roommates, she would suggest that they go straight to her room and do what she knew he wanted.

Lucian finally stopped kissing her, and she was out of breath. She hated that they had to keep their relationship a secret. Only Lucas knew of them and it was killing her every day that she was forced to pretend that she only saw Lucian as an uncle or family friend.

"I want you," she whispered in his ear.

"And I *you*. But we can't. Not yet."

She pouted. "If it's because of Nicola and Robin, I'm sure they won't be here for a few hours. Nicola is next door with Lucas."

"It wouldn't do because I would want more than just a few hours with you."

He kissed her again, causing her to relax in his arms and allow him to support her with his strong arms. She started moving forward to hint that they should go inside, but he didn't budge. A low chuckle rumbled in this throat as she continued to attempt to push him. She wanted to protest, but doing so would force them to stop kissing, and she didn't want that at all.

He was finally the one to end it and she nestled her face into his chest. She hated this— having to hide that they were together and settling for stolen kisses in the backyard behind the tree. Sometimes it was hard for her to look Cherish in the eye, knowing that she was fooling around with her dad behind her back.

"How long?" she asked. "How long do we have to sneak around?"

"I do not know, darling. I know that Gallard suspects that you have feelings for me, but he does not know that they are reciprocated. I am not so much concerned about the others as I am for him. He's your surrogate father and he's the one I will have to convince it is a good idea for us to be involved."

"Is that why you won't touch me?" she looked up at his face. "You don't want to go against his approval?"

He nodded then wrapped her in a firm hug. "When he returns, I will say something. I promise you. Until then, we must try to resist temptation."

4

I finished hammering the last nail and wiggled the wood to make sure it was sturdy. After I'd dropped Colton off at school, I'd gone to a local toy store and purchased a swing set. I was in such a good mood that it had inspired me to relax and do a project. Colton said that he liked the one at the Taylors' house, so I went out and bought him one. It was made of wood and came with simple instructions on how to put it together.

It was finished, and I was eager to show it to Nicola. She was inside keeping Kevin company. He didn't get to go out much because of his inability to be in the sun. I felt bad that he was often left alone. Sometimes, I would transfer him over to Lela's in a box but other than that, his place was inside the house on the couch. He was really looking forward to our night out.

Nicola came out of the house and smiled when she saw the finished project. The wood had a smooth finish and was a mahogany color. I'd spent a pretty penny on it and trusted that it was sturdy. Colton was tough, but I didn't want him to fall off. Nicola was even able to sit on it without causing distress to the screws.

"Colton will love this, Lucas." She stood up, hooking her thumb through the belt loops of her jeans. "You're a great dad, you know that?"

"Thanks, Nic. And I know you'll be a great mom once you have the chance to be one to him."

She cast her eyes down then brought them back up to me. She looked like she had something to say but was holding back. Our conversation from earlier came to mind and I grew worried. I was always wondering in the back of my mind if she resented me for turning her. We weren't as close as we used to be. Then again, her losing her sister probably played a major part in that. We were both still a little wrecked.

"Hey." I pulled her into my arms and hugged her. "What are you thinking about?"

"Seeing you out here putting up this swing set for our son makes me happier than you can know. Four years ago, when he was taken from me, I never imagined I would be able to do this. To take him to school or raise him with a man who I would be proud to call his father. I love you so much."

Nicola met my lips with a kiss, and I welcomed it wholeheartedly. I pulled her against me, basking in this moment, and her tongue found mine. She slid her fingers through my hair, kissing me more deeply by the moment. She hadn't kissed me this way in a very long time. I didn't know what had inspired her to let loose, but I didn't care.

"Tonight," she said. "I want you tonight. If you'll still have me."

I stared into her eyes to see if she was serious. Her pupils were dilated, but her eyes were honey brown, which meant she was relaxed and completely serious.

"I'll always have you," I said. "Are you sure? I thought you wanted to wait until we were engaged."

"No. No more waiting, no more putting it off."

"Okay, um . . . are we prepared? I love Colton, but I don't think having another child would be smart right now. I've heard enough jokes from Kevin about how d'Aubignes are fertile that I want to be extra careful."

Her expression darkened a moment then she said, "I've been on the pill. I started it a month ago. We'll be fine. I already talked to Kevin, and he said he would be happy to crash at Lela's. I don't think it will be hard to convince Lucian to crash on my couch." She gave me a soft kiss then smiled. "So, tonight?"

"Tonight."

I heard someone loudly clearing their throat and we turned to see Kevin standing on the porch in a spot void of sun exposure. He was probably getting tired of being the only one without a significant other, besides Robin and getting envious of all the PDA he was exposed to.

"What's up, Kev?" I asked.

"I called J.D., and she said that she and Robin are in for tonight. I figured it would be boring if just the three of us went out."

"I agree. Should we invite Lucian? I doubt he'll want to spend the night talking with his daughters."

"Yeah, I'll ask him. And we should ask Abe too."

"Eh," Nicola and I said in unison.

"What? Yeah, he's a little vain, but he's a great guy. As my late best friend's spawn, I've made it my task to look out for him."

"Think we could *not* invite him and say we did?" I asked. "All he'll do is pick up some other woman and keep everyone up all night. I swear all the guy does is bang and lift."

Kevin gave us a scolding look. I would forget often that he was really supposed to be in his forties and his inner elder would come out sometimes, though he'd stopped aging at twenty-two.

"Speaking of, guess who I saw getting all handsy in the backyard?" Kevin said, his young side returning.

"Was it us?" Nicola asked. She purred in my ear sending a wave of pleasure through my body. I had to quickly recover so I could continue with the conversation.

"No, J.D. and Lucian. I thought the neighbors were going to get a live show. When did that happen?"

I laughed. Though we often made dirty jokes about J.D. and Lucian behind their backs, I knew she genuinely loved Lucian. Because of what happened to me the night she'd confessed that to him, she revealed to me that she'd cooled the jets between them so she could get her priorities in order. I was glad they were together again. I wanted her to be as happy as I was.

We still had plenty of time to kill before we had to pick Colton up, so Nicola and I went over to Lela's. Robin told us about her achievement, and we decided to go to the new art gallery in town. There was an open house event going on from nine to six and since we had nothing else to do, we decided to go. Even J.D. tagged along and only gave a little fuss about Abe coming, though we couldn't convince Lucian. He had no interest in art.

I immediately recognized the building as the one that had been available for lease. I'd driven by it a few times and was curious about what it would turn into. An art gallery was the last of my guesses, but it made Nicola excited. She'd been waiting for weeks for this place to open.

When we walked in, I was amazed at how crowded it was. I didn't take Euless as a city full of art geeks. Baseball, maybe, but not art. Most of the people were dressed nicely too and I felt out of place. Even more so than I did at the school. J.D. was wearing one of Lucian's shirts and had it tied in front with a tank top underneath. Robin was probably the most dressed up in her soft pink sundress.

We split off into two groups with Nicola and Abe in mine, and we started at the far left. Nicola recognized some of the artists, and I listened intently as she told me about each painting and gave her opinion or made a comment about the brush strokes. She used to be very quiet when we first started dating, only speaking to make a snide remark, and now she was becoming herself again. I fell more in love with her each day.

We came across one painting in particular that was so astonishing that even Nicola was speechless. She'd had something to say about all of them except for this one. I furrowed my brow and cocked my head to the side, trying to see if my mind was playing tricks on me. She had to be thinking what I was thinking.

"Is it just me, or does that look like—"

"Like you?" Abe said, coming up behind us.

Nicola nodded in agreement. So, she was thinking the same thing, and so was he. The painting was of a woman, or rather a nymph. She was nude and lying in a bed of flowers. Her red hair fanned out around her, and her golden eyes were the most captivating thing. She was undeniably the spitting image of Nicola.

"I don't know if I should feel awkward or be impressed," Nicola said.

"You don't have to feel awkward," Abe said. "You're hot."

I shot him a warning glance, and he laughed.

"While your comment was kind, I'm not half as gorgeous as she is," Nicola said.

"I like the way you look." I studied the painting some more. "You have that woman's eyes."

"Yeah sure."

"No, I'm serious." I stood behind her and rested my hands on her waist, sliding them down. "And you have her shape."

She moved away from me. "Lucas! We're in public. Control yourself."

We laughed so hard that we didn't even notice that someone was standing next to us. Nicola recognized him and greeted him enthusiastically.

"Ryan, hey!"

"It's great to see you here, Nikita. I knew I could count on your appearance."

Nikita? I knew they had become friends through the art class, but I didn't know he had a nickname for her. Part of me was suspicious but I could see why he was drawn to her. She'd blossomed into an amazing person and one couldn't help but fall in love with her confident and lively personality.

"This is a favorite of mine as well," Ryan continued. "It's called 'La Donna Dai Capelli Rossi.' The Red-Haired Woman. No one knows the artist or the woman in this picture. The time it was painted is a mystery as well."

"We were just pointing out that it looks like Nic," I said.

"I realized that after I bought it." He held his hand out to me. "Ryan Aspen. Owner of the gallery."

I shook his hand. He was a friendly guy and stood about an inch shorter than me. He had brown hair and grey-blue eyes with a tan that hinted that he was from a different country. Unlike his visitors, he was dressed as casually as we were. He even had a little paint on his forearm, probably from something he was working on.

"Lucas d'Aubigne."

"Nikita was right that you look like an angel."

"It's true," she said, hugging me close to her. "He's my angel."

"Are any of these paintings yours?" Abe asked with a patronizing tone.

"Yes, three actually." He walked away and we followed him over to an oil painting of another woman, only this one wasn't facing forward and she was completely dressed. "I did this just recently. I think it's my best one so far, so I put it up anonymously in hopes that someone will buy it."

"It's very well done," Nicola said. "I love the way it's dark around her head, as if her thoughts are being shadowed and hidden. The background is incredible too. Did you get that color by mixing blue and orange?"

He raised his eyebrows. "Impressive. Not many have been able to catch that right away. That reminds me. I wasn't going to advertise it just yet. I wanted to see how well the opening went first. I'm thinking that I could move the art classes here and do them more than just twice a week."

Nicola's eyes widened with excitement. "I would totally sign up! Two days was never enough for me to get lost in my painting."

"Actually, Nikita, I was thinking you could teach some of those classes."

She did a small snort. "Yeah, sure."

"I am serious. You are more advanced than any of my students. They could learn a little something from you. Besides, with the gallery, I may not always have the time to teach. I could use an assistant. I would pay you, of course."

"Okay, well . . . I guess I could give it a try."

He gave her a flier with the class details then went off to talk to more visitors. Nicola's mood had brightened, and I could see in her eyes that she was more excited about this class than she was letting on. I was glad that she might have something to do. She was very talented, and if teaching made her happy, I would be happy.

5

Robin held her breath as the timer went off. She'd wanted to wait to take the test but couldn't handle the suspense. She needed to know if she was going to be a mom or not. The sooner the better.

Letting out a sigh, she went over and picked up the test. The instructions had been easy enough, so she didn't worry about doing it wrong. The box said two pink lines meant yes one line meant no. And right now, she was staring at two pink lines.

She set the test down then put a hand over her belly. The results only confirmed what she'd known in her heart. While not huge, her stomach had become significantly rounder. Somehow, she'd managed to hide it with looser-fitting clothes.

For now, she would try to have a good time and worry about the baby later. She still had at least a few more months before she would deliver. She learned from her research that babies typically took nine months to grow. If her calculations were correct, she was five months along.

Still, she wanted a smoke. It would take the edge off and relax her some before going out. She'd successfully hidden the pack in her purse, so she nonchalantly went out the back door then went to the side of the house through the gate. Sticking the cigarette between her lips, she hit the button on her lighter.

Taking in a drag, she closed her eyes then let it out. Already, the burn was distracting her. She would never admit it, but large crowds had begun to stress her out. She hated being surrounded by people she didn't know and the thought of getting separated from her friends and family gave her anxiety. It had even been hard doing the drive test without Abe. Being alone with the instructor made her nervous and it was a miracle she didn't fail.

Her nights were often plagued by memories of the assault. So much so that she sometimes gave up sleeping altogether and watched TV with the Bluetooth headphones on the couch. She would often have a smoke to wake her up and then rely on adrenaline the rest of the time. She still slept, but only after making herself exhausted. No one had caught on to any of her habits yet and she wanted to keep it that way.

When she finished, she found a rock to smash it with then wet it a bit with the tip of the hose before tossing it into the neighbor's trash. She didn't want to be careless and risk someone finding it in their bin. Not that her family regularly dug in the garbage. She went inside to gargle mouth wash and spray on more perfume.

A moment later, J.D. poked her head into the bathroom and gave Robin an approving thumb up. J.D. looked amazing as well. She had on a shimmering backless sea green dress that matched her eyes and flattered her body very well. Her lips were crimson, and she had on dark brown eye shadow.

As for her own outfit, she couldn't believe that J.D. had convinced her to wear this tonight. It was white with three-quarter sleeves and hung in a deep V, almost to her waist. At least the shirt tucked into the shorts and didn't reveal her baby belly. She did like her makeup, though. Nicola had done it for her, and her eyes were covered in a sparkly, gold eye shadow and her lips were a soft pink with shine. She'd even straightened her hair for the first time, and she resembled Lela more so with this style. For once, she actually felt beautiful.

"You're very pretty, J.D.," Robin said. "That dress makes you look like a mermaid."

J.D. laughed. "Well coming from you, I'll take that as a compliment. You're stunning, R. Nic, on the other hand . . ."

"Hey!" Nicola yelled from her bedroom. She then stood in the doorway. Of the three of them, Nicola was the most casual in her black pants and layered green tank top. Her makeup was subtle as well with a nude lip shade and her hair was pinned up. "I'm not the one with a million-dollar inheritance. I can't afford nice clothes."

"I have two words for you — Sugar Daddy. Just swipe Lucas' card. I'm sure he wouldn't mind."

The two women walked away, and Robin took one last look at herself in the mirror and decided to smile. She was going to do her best to enjoy herself and pretend that everything was all right. That she hadn't been attacked. That she hadn't been forced to grow up in a short amount of time. That she wasn't going to be a mother in four months. She'd gotten through the day without sinking into a deep depression. She was determined to keep it that way.

When she went into the living room, she walked into the middle of a conversation between J.D. and Nicola.

"No way! You and Lucas are going to seal the deal?" J.D. asked.

"Yeah. It's long overdue, and I think I'm finally ready."

"And, are you sure you're safe? I know you said you went to the women's clinic a month ago."

Nicola rolled her eyes. "Okay, *Dr. Jordin*. Thanks for the advice."

"What? I'm looking out for you. We don't want you getting knocked up, now do we?"

Robin began to sweat a little. "Uh . . . Speaking of knocked up, I did that to someone today," she said, suddenly remembering her heroism at the drug store.

J.D. cracked up laughing. "What? Robin, what are you talking about?"

"I hit a guy with a broom. I knocked that guy to the ground! You should have seen it! Even the police said I was a hero."

She couldn't believe how eager she was to talk about Erik, even if she hadn't mentioned his name. Thankfully, Abe hadn't told anyone about the encounter, and she wanted to keep it that way. No one needed to know about something that wasn't really anything.

"I wish I was there," Nicola said. "I would have demanded that they pay you and put you on the front page of the news."

Robin followed J.D. and Nicola outside where they met up with Kevin, Abe, Lucas, and Lucian. They were going to take one car to save on gas, but as soon as the three men saw Robin, they stared at her in shock.

"J.D., was this your doing?" Kevin asked.

"Yeah, and?"

"She's not going out like that! Find her something else to wear."

"Why?" Abe asked. "I think she looks great."

Robin felt uncomfortable as she listened to them argue. Again, her brother was fussing over her like she was some innocent little girl who needed protection. Abe was always there to stick up for her, but this was getting out of hand. She wanted to stick up for herself. If she wanted to be treated like the woman she was, she was going to have to demand for such treatment.

"She's too young to be dressing like that," Kevin said.

"Last I checked, she was older than me. Am I too young to dress like that?"

"Stop!" Robin shouted, startling everyone. Her brother and Abe grew quiet. "Kevin, you're not the boss of me. I'm a grown woman who can drive, and you can't tell me what I can and can't wear!"

Without another word, she got into the car, sliding over to the far left and let out a long exhale. Nicola climbed in next to her and gave her hand a squeeze. It felt good to finally speak her mind. Everyone else got in as well and began having conversation as if nothing had happened. Kevin looked back at her at one point and smiled, which meant to Robin that he was sorry, and she smiled back.

Her confidence washed away the moment she stepped into the night club. The music was so loud that she could barely hear herself think. Everywhere, there were people swinging their hips and dancing incredibly close to each other. She'd seen this kind of dancing in the music videos J.D. liked to watch on TV.

Immediately, J.D. dragged Lucian towards the center of the crowd and forced him to dance. Robin wasn't quite ready to dance yet, so she skirted towards the bar and found a stool to sit on. Lucas followed her with Nicola at his side.

"How's my Robin Bird?" he asked.

"Fine."

"Hey." Lucas lifted her chin with his finger. "What's wrong? Not still upset about Kevin, are you?"

"No. Kevin was just looking out for me. It's so crazy in here. I might get lost."

Abe lifted her off the stool by her waist. "Dance with me. I know it will make you feel better."

She was going to protest when he took her hand and twirled her in a circle then placed his hand on her back, swaying her from side to side. She laughed and gave in to his pleas. She got used to the rhythm and soon was dancing comfortably with him. When they'd first met, she was interested to know what Jordan's son was like. He was a d'Aubigne, which meant he could either be extremely reserved or a party animal. Her first impression seemed to hint that he was a little of both and it was proved after they spent a lot of time together. She'd grown to know and love both sides.

"You're a good dancer," she said.

"So are you. I think you get it from David. I hear he puts Patrick Swayze to shame."

Robin frowned. "Who's Patrick Swayze?"

"You've got to ask J.D. to watch *Dirty Dancing* with you sometime. The original of course, not the remake. You won't regret it."

A faster song began playing and J.D. began dancing with Nicola in the same way they would at their house. Robin didn't do anything at first but then started swaying to the music and soon she was getting just as much into it as they were. She laughed, surprised at herself for letting loose. She noticed Kevin was staring at her in shock but that didn't stop her.

Lucian, who hadn't been dancing as enthusiastically as the others, sneaked up behind J.D. and rested his hands on her waist so that their bodies were moving in sync. Nicola started dancing equally as suggestive with Lucas and Robin realized that this was quickly turning into a battle of the couples. She, Abe and Kevin watched with jaws dropped as they executed risqué moves.

Somewhere during that time, a woman had roped Kevin into being her partner, leaving Robin alone and she went over to the bar to take a break and get a glass of water. She then remembered she had her I.D. with her and showed it to the bar tender before ordering a mimosa. She sipped it slowly while watching to see who would win. To her, it appeared that J.D. and Lucian were ahead of the game.

Abe found his way over to her a few moments later and took a seat on the bench to her left. She gave him a sideway glance to look at his muscles. He was always doing pushups in the living room to keep them up. She hadn't seen arms that big since Jordan and she liked the way he smelled too. He was wearing a different scent tonight.

"Why aren't you dancing with some pretty woman in here?" she asked.

"Because I'm yours tonight. I need to make sure no more guys hit on you."

Robin frowned. "Why? Is it really such a bad idea for me to experience being hit on like everyone else?"

"Yes, it's a terrible idea. I know what kind of a guy I am and I would rather not have someone like me come after you. Or any guy for that matter."

"Why not? Shouldn't I be able to have fun too?"

"No. I'm the only man in your life, babe. You're going to have to live with that."

She punched his arm, and he laughed as he went back to join everyone on the dance floor. She couldn't have him as her bodyguard forever. Eventually, someone would come along and take over and she hoped that she could fall in love with a good man just like her sister had. That would never happen with Abe always lurking around.

"Need a refill?" The bartender asked.

She blew air out of her mouth then turned around. Alcohol sounded like a great idea. She, J.D., and Nicola drank sometimes when no one was around and she figured a few drinks wouldn't hurt.

"How about a Gin and tonic," she said. "Make it a double."

He poured the drinks then she downed them one right after the other. She loved to feel buzzed and the effects of the cigarette had worn off. The alcohol burned down her throat and she took a deep breath. May the games begin.

As she turned around, she happened to catch a glimpse of a familiar face. There was no way she could have missed him because he was standing there looking attractive and friendly as usual with that white smile and adorable cheekbones. It was Erik McPherson. Instantly, she began to panic. Why was he here? Had he followed her? No, that was ridiculous. He probably came here because there weren't many other places to hang out for adults.

When she caught his gaze, his eyes lit up and he pushed his way through the crowd towards her. He wasn't wearing his uniform anymore, but had on a white t-shirt with a black jacket and blue jeans. He looked significantly less intimidating in these clothes and she had to admit that she liked what she saw. It wasn't helping her attempt to elude him.

"Of all places, I never would have guessed I would run into you here, Robin," he said. He looked her up and down causing her to blush. "Wow. You are . . . breathtaking."

"I hope so. If I wasn't taking breaths, I would probably die."

Erik laughed, but it wasn't a condescending laugh. She liked the way it sounded and the way it made her stomach flip. Why did he have to be so darn attractive? She was supposed to be avoiding him.

"Who did you come here with? Not another guy I hope."

Robin nodded. "Four guys, actually." She felt eyes on her and spotted all four of the men staring in her direction with stern gazes. The same gaze Kevin gave her when he'd tried to order her to change. She prayed that they wouldn't come over and shoe Erik away.

She pointed in their direction. "The blonde one is Lucas. The brunette is Kevin, my brother, the other brunette you met earlier is Abe, my best friend, and the redhead is Lucian."

"Hey, I know Lucas. He's in my department."

"Really?"

"Yeah. We work on different shifts, but I still see him from time to time. Aren't you lucky having all these men to look after you?" He gave them a wary glance. "I don't think they like it very much that we're talking."

"They think I'm still five years old, but I'm not."

"How old are you, if you don't mind my asking."

"Twenty-eight," she stated proudly.

He raised his eyebrows and whistled. "Well, I'll be. I'm smitten with an older woman. I just turned twenty-four this June."

She smiled to herself, suddenly feeling more mature. He was younger than her and that boosted her confidence.

When it was obvious that Kevin was coming their way, she had to act fast. She grabbed Erik's hand and pulled him away so they could get lost in the crowd. Once she couldn't see Kevin anymore, she put her arms around Erik's neck and coaxed him into dancing with her.

"Wow. What happened to the timid woman I met at the store today?"

"She grew a pair," she replied. She'd heard J.D. say that about someone before and was appalled when she'd learned what it meant.

Erik laughed again, bringing a smile to her lips, and she found herself moving closer to him as they swayed. She spotted Kevin again just as the music changed to something fast paced. They locked eyes and he looked livid, just how her Mark used to look whenever Aaron did something that made him mad.

Feeling defiant, Robin changed the dance to how she was moving before. She moved her hips from side to side and then shook her head around, making her hair flip. Erik stared at her for a moment then started getting equally as enthusiastic. Copying a move she'd seen J.D. do with Lucian, she put her arms around his neck, drawing him so close to her that their bodies were touching.

"Robin!" she heard her brother shout. "What the hell are you doing?"

Erik quickly backed away from her and she glared at Kevin, folding her arms. She'd thought their talk earlier had put a stop to his babying, but she'd been wrong.

"Easy there, man," Erik said. "We were just dancing."

"I'm so sure. I saw you with your hands all over her."

"I would never overstep my boundaries with a woman, especially not one as amazing as your sister. Believe me, I have my own sisters."

Kevin shifted his gaze to Robin. "Who is this guy?"

"Erik McPherson. He's a police officer and we met earlier today. He's not a stranger, he works with Lucas and he's nice."

"Sure. Remember the last time we met a *nice* police officer?"

His words cut through her like glass. He was right — she'd trusted the last man she'd met with a badge — two of them even and because of them she was forever damaged by what they'd done. Kevin nearly died because he'd killed to protect her.

"I don't know what some other officer has done to wrong you, but I assure you that I have no ill intentions," Erik said.

"You probably don't, but just the same I would rather you not set your sights on Robin. Kevin put an arm around her. "Come on, little sister. We're done dancing and the others want to grab dinner before we head home."

She nodded and began following her brother when she looked back at Erik. He winked at her, sending the butterflies aflutter. How could he still be flirting with her after Kevin had all but told him to get lost? His confidence was intriguing and though it had ended abruptly, she would carry the memory of their brief dance for a long time.

The group went outside, and J.D. took her hand, making her do a twirl and was in an extremely good mood. Robin was feeling happy as well. Even Nicola was giddier than usual, and the three women danced all the way to the car.

They were about to get in when Robin heard shouting along with laughing. It sounded like a group of men, but she wasn't sure. The others heard it too because they got quiet and listened. A woman screamed, sending the three men running in that direction. J.D. and Nicola followed behind and Robin did as well. Whatever was going on had to be serious if there was so much yelling.

When they finally arrived, she saw that there was a group of twenty-somethings. Two of the men were holding a woman back by her arms while four others were beating on another man with a crowbar.

"What the hell are you doing?" Lucas shouted.

"Get out of here! This isn't your concern!" one of the men shouted back. Robin looked at the crying woman and momentarily saw herself in her. Robin had felt equally as helpless when the two officers hurt Kevin and made her watch.

"You made it my concern the moment we showed up. Why are you hurting this man?"

"*Man*? He's not a man, he's a parasite. And this whore is a parasite lover. We caught them kissing in the club and we decided to show them what happens when you mate with a monster."

Robin quickly grabbed Kevin's hand and he hugged her to his side in understanding. Was everyone here this intolerant to immortals? If so, what would they do if they found out about her family?

"Get out of here," Lucas said. "Leave him be or you will have to deal with me."

"Oh, yeah?" The guy with the crowbar dropped it to the ground and approached Lucas in an intimidating manor. "What if I beat you first, pretty boy? Are you an immortal lover too? Do I need to teach you the same lesson?"

"Go ahead. I'd like to see you try."

The man acted like he was going to walk away then swung his fist toward Lucas' face. Lucas grabbed the man's fist before it made contact and shoved him to the ground. Robin was afraid there was going to be a fight, but she wasn't afraid that Lucas would lose. She was afraid the police would show up and they would get in trouble. Then again, Lucas was the police.

"Get up, you intolerant scum bag," Lucas said. The man didn't move so he grabbed him by the shirt and forced him to his feet. "If I ever hear that you or any of your friends are participating in hate crimes against immortals, I will make you regret it. Now get out of here."

"Are you stupid? You're outnumbered."

Lucian and Kevin stepped forward and so did Nicola. Robin wasn't sure why Nicola was getting involved. She wouldn't stand any more of a chance than Robin or J.D.

Lucas nodded towards Lucian. "See this guy here? He chopped a guy in half once. I wouldn't mess with him. And my uncle here, well . . . he's been messed with one too many times. I wouldn't take a stab at his hornet nest either."

He shoved the guy away and the group of men shot him annoyed glances before walking back into the bar. The vampire on the ground finally got up and Robin could see that his injuries were healing. His girlfriend rushed over to him and threw her arms around him.

"Why did you do that?" the man asked. "You shouldn't have helped me."

"Why not? If I don't help you, no one will. Take care of yourself, okay."

Without another word, Lucas walked towards the car and the rest of them followed in silence. Robin's admiration for Lucas had doubled in those few moments. He did what he thought was right and if everyone did that, maybe the vampires wouldn't be persecuted anymore. It was all she could think about while they drove home and for the first time in a while, she had a glimmer of hope that someday, things could be different.

6

Nicola tried to go inside the house, but I grabbed her hand, pulling her close to me once more. I'd loved dancing with her at the club and couldn't wait to spend the night with her. *Really* spend the night, and not just having her next to me. I'd probably annoyed her when I'd asked several times at the club if she was sure if she was ready, and she kept replying yes. I didn't sense any nervousness in her voice, so each yes would make me more excited.

"Is there a reason you have me out here and not in there?" she asked as she fiddled with my belt.

"You'll see. Let's stay out here for a moment. Anything you want to talk about? Life, love, death?"

She laughed. "Well, how about I ask your opinion on Robin's new suitor?"

My stomach turned thinking about it. The idea of Robin being romantically involved with a man bothered me for reasons I knew everyone else felt. Not eight months before, I'd found her dirty and crying in the Sharmentino house. She was only about eleven then and now she was a woman. While the rational thing to do would be to forbid her from seeing this guy, the softy in me was just glad that she was finding some joy in life. She'd been too sad these days.

"I can understand why Kevin sent him away. I felt a little bad, though. He's a nice guy from what I've seen of him at work. We can't blame her for doing exactly what we were doing. She probably wanted to see what it was like."

The front door opened, and J.D. came out with Lucian and Abe. I nodded in thanks then J.D and Lucian went off down the street to go for a walk. I would have to add that to my list of activities to do with Nicola.

"Hey," Abe said. He waved me over then whispered in my ear. "I left you something on the counter."

"Thanks?"

"Thank me later." He patted me on the shoulder then continued next door.

As we walked into the house, I covered Nicola's eyes and she didn't ask any questions. I guided her through the living room, down the hall. I'd invested in Cherish's help with some of what I planned because she was the only one who was okay with it. After asking if Nicola could live with me in the house and having Kevin live with his sister and J.D., I was bombarded with lectures from Lela about premarital sex. I didn't want to go through that again, so Cherish promised to keep these plans a secret.

I stopped in front of the bathroom door and removed my hands from her eyes. This was sort of a surprise for me as well since I hadn't seen the end-results. The large bathroom was transformed into a romantic setting. The tub was filled with delicious smelling bubble bath and there were rose petals sprinkled on top of the suds. Candle's lined the edge of the tub against the wall and there was a piano playing lightly on the iPod doc in the corner.

"I thought we could start here," I said. "That way, we can get comfortable with each other."

"It's perfect." She turned around and kissed my cheek. "Why don't you get in? I'll join you in a minute."

She went down the hall while I took her advice and got undressed. I then remembered Abe said he'd left something, and I found said item on the counter. It was a new box of condoms. Honestly, I hadn't even thought of getting my own, so it was probably a good thing he had my back.

Thankfully, the bath had its own heaters, so I wasn't worried about the water being cold. I got in and slowly lowered myself until I was sitting. The scent was wonderful — not too manly and not too feminine. The heat relieved tension in my back that I hadn't realized was there.

I heard movement and opened my eyes to see Nicola standing in front of me. She'd taken her hair down and was wearing Lucian's azure, silk robe. I would have laughed if she hadn't looked so stunning. I was going to speak when she dropped the robe and no words seemed to justify her.

In the past few months, Melody had put her on a strict high protein diet so she could get her up to a healthy weight, and she already showed results. Her ribs weren't as prominent and her hips had filled out, giving her an amazing figure.

"I was wrong," I said. "You are way more beautiful than the woman in that painting."

"Oh sure," she said, casting her gaze down. She exhaled then walked over to me and got into the tub opposite me so that we were facing each other. She sank down until the water came to her collarbone then rested her arms on the sides.

"I can't believe you planned all this," she said. "This is the most romantic thing you've done for me."

"I've never done anything romantic for you."

"That night at your apartment was pretty romantic. Though it's hard to think of that day without feeling sad."

I'd almost forgotten about that. It was the night Mona died and we were separated for a month. That was a very low time in my life, and I never wanted to get that low again. I couldn't imagine being depressed with the most beautiful woman in the world taking a bath with me.

"Nice work helping that vampire tonight. I always knew you had this hero complex but seeing you in action makes you extra sexy."

I laughed. "I wish I could have done more. I may have threatened them, but I have a feeling they aren't going to stop."

"Typical Lucas. You go above and beyond and you feel like it's not enough. What you need to do is relax."

She drifted over to me and put a hand on my back to push me forward then sat behind me with her legs circling mine. She began to massage my shoulders and I closed my eyes. Usually I was the one to give the massages, but it was nice to receive one. I gently caressed her legs, running my fingers up and down the top of her thighs. She responded by kissing my neck and her hands moved across my chest.

"Come here," I said in a low voice. I shifted so that she could come back around and lay so that her legs were slightly tangled with mine and I gently kissed her. I slid my hands over her back, pulling her against me and slowly kissed her more passionately.

"Should we move this party elsewhere?" I asked.

"Yeah. That sounds like a good idea."

After we dried off, she put on the robe, and I carried her into my room, staring into her eyes the entire time. They were green and her hair was changing shades like crazy. She was stunning no matter what her hair color was.

I closed the door behind me then set her down so I could pull the covers back. She took off the robe and lay down first and I slid in next to her and kissed the side of her neck, making a trail down to her collarbone.

I stopped kissing her to make the most of this moment. I could have waited longer, but I was so happy that we were finally here. She smiled at me as if to tell me that she was still fine — that she wanted this just as much as I did.

"When did you first have feelings for me?" she asked.

"Really?"

"Yeah. You never told me, you just surprised me by asking me to the beach."

I thought back to sophomore year of high school and tried to pinpoint the specific time. That was when I'd developed a crush on her, but after Henry asked her out, I tried to get over it because he always won, and I didn't think I would ever have a chance.

"It was six years ago," I said. "You signed us up to do the Christmas festival for disabled children. The festival was over, and we were closing the carousel and this one girl with severe cerebral palsy hadn't gotten a chance to ride. You begged the carnie to leave it a few minutes. You sat with her on the sleigh."

"Any decent human being would have done that."

"Possibly. But to me it was the kindest thing I'd ever seen. And I knew then that I would want you forever. As long as my forever would last anyway." I rested my head against hers. "Your turn. When did you first have feelings for me?"

She grew quiet for a moment, and I waited expectantly for her answer. Had it been the day I'd healed Mona at the beach? Or maybe it was when I'd gotten sick and she stayed with me in the hospital waiting for me to wake up.

"It was in third grade," she finally admitted. "We'd been playing hide and seek in my parents' backyard, and we hid together under that bush. Then I kissed you. I knew you saw me as your friend, but from then on, I knew that no matter who I ended up with, I wanted you to be the last guy I ever kissed."

This was amazing. She'd had feelings for me long before I'd ever considered letting myself feel that way about her. If only one of us had spoken up, we would have already been together. At the same time, I didn't mind how we'd ended up a couple. She was mine now, and I planned to keep it that way.

"I remember you threatened to punch me in the throat if I told."

Nicola chuckled. "I threatened you several times throughout our childhood. It was my way of saying I liked you."

"I wish I'd known. I would have come up with my own phrase for you."

My lips found hers once more, and we picked up where we left off. Each kiss became more urgent and she tangled her legs around me. I started kissing her neck and exploring her body with my hands. Her body responded to every touch and it ignited my own desire.

I heard a low moan in her throat and before I knew what was happening, she flipped me onto my back and pinned me down. I was still getting used to her strength and she'd surprised me. She then kissed me once more, only this time was different. Instead of being loving, it was more primal.

As she kissed the space between my neck and shoulders, I felt a sharp pain and realized she'd just bit me.

"Whoa, hey!"

Nicola instantly stopped and stared at me in shock

"Oh no," she said, her face forming a grimace. "Lucas, I'm so sorry!"

"It's okay . . . I'm just surprised." I studied her face. "What's wrong? Are you okay?"

She shook her head then sat up. I noticed that her fangs were still emerged. Her eyes were black as well.

"Is there a blood bag in here?" she asked.

"Um . . ." I looked around my room and finally spotted what I was searching for. "There's an old one in my trash can."

Nicola clenched her jaw. "I thought I smelled it. Damn, now I'm thirsty. This is the worst time to get cravings."

"I see. Do you want me to get you some blood?"

"No. I mean, I don't know." She sat with her legs over the side of the bed and wrapped her arms around her middle. "I hate this."

I warily reached over and touched her shoulder. "It's no problem for me. I could bring you some."

"No. I hate blood. I can't stand it. The one thing I hate more than anything is the one thing keeping me alive and it pisses me off."

My heart lurched. She sounded incredibly angry. I had a feeling there was more to it than just her not wanting to drink blood. This had to be building and building for months.

"Talk to me," I said. "What are you thinking?"

She sniffed then sat up a little. "I hate being a vampire. I hate that I can't sleep at night because I can hear every little sound in the neighborhood and beyond. I hate that I can't go to the meat department at the grocery store without my stupid fangs coming out. I hate that Henry shot me and forced me to choose between this and dying. I never wanted this life and it's taken away everything."

I kissed her shoulder. "I'm sorry you feel that way. You must hate me too for doing this to you."

Nicola turned around. "No, Lucas. I could never hate you. But I can't lie and say that I'm happy. I love you, and I love that I can be with my son, but I'm miserable. I'm sorry, but I can't do this tonight."

Getting up, she wrapped the robe around herself before leaving the room. I threw on some boxers and sweats from my drawer then lay back down. I tried to wish away the feelings of disappointment. Her words would haunt me for the rest of the night, and I didn't think we could just pick up where we'd left off like I'd hoped. Especially not with the worried thoughts in the back of my mind. She was miserable and it was my fault.

7

J.D. yawned as she poured herself a cup of coffee. She'd stayed up late talking with Lucian on the porch, and he had to be the one to force her to go to bed before she passed out. He said he was going to sleep on the couch since Lucas had requested no one be at his house that night, but he'd left in the middle of the night after making a phone call. J.D. was jealous that Lucas was able to have romantic alone time with Nicola. She wanted that with Lucian, but he'd made it clear that he wanted Gallard to know about their relationship and be okay with it. That may never happen.

Lucian came out of the bathroom and into the kitchen then put his arms around her while she poured creamer into her coffee. She chuckled and leaned against him, longing for the time when every morning could be like this. He slid his hand up her shirt and she giggled.

"Lucian Francis, we are not alone in this house!"

"Yes we are. I transported Kevin to Lela's and Robin is there as well. We're safe."

She set her cup down and swiveled around in the circle of his arms to face him. He smelled incredible with his expensive cologne and freshly clean scent. His hair was still damp from the shower and his eyes stared down at her with a desire that made her dizzy.

"Where did you go last night?" she asked. "I got up to get a glass of water and you weren't on the couch."

"I was speaking with Gallard. He wanted to give me an update about what they were doing."

"You call him every night. Even Lela doesn't call that often. Are you in love with him?"

"Deeply. In fact, I may leave you for him unless you kiss me."

It was all a joke, but she kissed him anyway. She happened to be wearing another one of his shirts and he started to unbutton it. She was shocked at this gesture but didn't question him. He stopped at the third button and dropped his hand.

"We shouldn't do this. I have not discussed us with him yet."

"You're kidding me. What did you two talk about then?"

"Nothing much."

He turned his eyes from hers and her chest tightened. Something wasn't right. He always had difficulty making eye contact when he was bending the truth and it hit her. He was lying. He'd flat out lied to her face about talking to Gallard.

And you want to marry this guy? Jordan asked. *Come on, J.D., you can do better than him.*

Like you haven't lied, daddy. To Cherish — Gallard — oh, the list goes on and on.

Okay, I get your point. But don't forget, he did the same thing to Lela. He deceived her into his bed, and he'll do the same thing to you if you're not careful.

"What did he say?" she asked Lucian. "Where are they right now?"

"He said they were heading for Nebraska, I believe."

"Uh, huh. And where in Nevada are they going?"

"I do not know. Maybe Vegas? Gallard has old acquaintances there as well."

J.D. shot him a disgusted look and pushed her way out of his arms. She went to her room to get dressed and angrily tugged on some jeans to compliment her red halter top. She heard Lucian come in but didn't acknowledge him.

"I am confused, darling. Why are you angry with me?"

"Why am I angry?" She shoved her foot into her left flat and wiggled it until her heal went in. "How about the fact that you are a liar?" She put on her other shoe before turning around to face him. "You told me that he was in Nebraska and then you said he was in Nevada. I'm not an idiot."

His eyes dropped in shame and she walked past him and out of her room. She wanted to go over to Lela's and share company with people she knew would be honest. She passed by Lucas' place and stopped when she saw him come out onto the lawn.

"Hey! I have a question," he said.

"If it's dating advice that you want, then I'll tell you this — don't trust anyone. Relationships are pointless, especially when your boyfriend is a big, fat liar."

He chuckled. "Wow. I don't think I'm going to ask about that, but you might be able to help me. Have you seen Nicola?"

46

J.D. frowned. "No, I assumed she was with you. Did she do the classic screw and ditch?"

"She did the ditch part, but we never got to the other. She got upset about something and left. I thought maybe she went back to your place."

J.D. let out an angry shriek, startling Lucas. "That liar! I'm going to kill him!"

"Whoa, calm down! Who's a liar? Who do you want to kill?"

"Lucian! He left in the middle of the night and he told me he was talking to Gallard on the phone. But there's no way a phone call lasted eight hours." She took a deep breath to keep from losing her temper. "It appears that while your girlfriend was supposed to be seducing you and my . . . Lucian was supposed to be on the couch, they were off somewhere all night doing who knows what."

They both grew quiet for a while, letting the truth sink in. What J.D. wanted to know was why Lucian spent the whole night with Nicola and lied about it. Better yet, why did Nicola give up her chance to sleep with Lucas to run off with Lucian?

The paper boy rode by on his bike and tossed a paper, sending it flying towards them and it landed a few inches from J.D.'s feet. Her temper boiled once more and she picked it up and prepared to throw it at the back of the paper boy's head when Lucas grabbed her arm.

"Hold on, I want to read this."

"Since when are you interested in local news?"

"I'm cop now, remember?"

He removed the rubber band and unfolded the paper, holding it so that they could both see it. There was a report about a young man who was killed by a vampire two nights ago. Only this time, it was a double headline. A girl was killed the night before with the same M.O. The neck was broken, and she was drained of blood.

"The report says she was killed sometime around one a.m.," Lucas said.

"Oh, no." J.D. started to tremble. "Lucian and Nicola were out around that time."

A million theories were going through her head. During one of their late-night talks at his apartment, Lucian had told her his entire story, starting with his life at the convent as a child. He'd never hidden any part of him from her and she'd always admired him for his quest of redemption. It was why she'd fallen in love with him in the first place.

One part of his past came to mind. He'd said that when Cherish was born, he'd seen himself in her—a potential killing partner and protégé. He wanted her to be the best vampire ever created and together establish dominance in the immortal world. He'd raised her to be a fighter long before he planned to turn her. Years later, he'd wanted to do the same thing with Lela, only he'd ended up falling in love with her and he'd changed his heart because of her.

"Lucas, you know Lucian's story, right?" she asked.

"Yeah. Lela wrote about it in the journal she gave me. Why?"

"What if after twenty years, he'd decided he didn't want to change? What if he's attached himself to Nicola because he wanted her to be his new protégé?"

Lucas failed at stifling a laugh. "Are you serious? That's the worst-case scenario you came up with?"

"Well, the worst-case scenario would be that they're cheating on us with each other, but if you think that's the worst, more power to ya."

"No, they're not cheating. And he's not turning her into his killing protégé. You're getting worked up over nothing."

She sighed. "You're right. I'm just getting carried away because he's never lied to me before."

J.D. linked arms with him and they made their way towards Lela's house. They both needed to get their minds on other things or else their paranoia was going to get the best of them. They walked in since the door was unlocked and were greeted by a sudden burst of laughter.

They went into the living room and found Lela, Cherish, Melody, and Nicola sitting on the couch while Kevin sat across from them next to Robin. The women stopped laughing as Lucas and Nicola exchanged an awkward glance.

"Hey, you two!" Lela said. "Come in, we were just talking about bad dating experiences."

"What a coincidence, so were we," J.D. said with blatant sarcasm. Things instantly grew even tenser between Lucas and Nicola. J.D. was experiencing her own suspicions towards her friend. She and Nicola had grown incredibly close after moving in together and she'd never once questioned her credibility. Both Nicola and Lucian had some explaining to do.

J.D. and Lucas found a place to sit and the conversation resumed.

"Did Colton get to school all right?" Lucas asked Lela.

"Yes. He barely even said goodbye. He must really love his class."

In a stealthy way of trying to catch Lucian in his lie, J.D. decided to bring up the topic of his so called phone conversation with Gallard. Chances were that if Gallard had talked to Lucian about where he was, he must have spoken with Lela as well.

"Has anyone talked to Gallard lately?" J.D. asked.

"I have," Lela said. "He said they were in Nebraska."

J.D. instantly felt terrible. She often forgot that Lucian wasn't completely in the know of all the states and easily could have mixed them up. She would have to apologize to him. But he was keeping something from her, or else he wouldn't have had such a questionable look in his eyes while they were talking. He might have talked to Gallard, but that didn't explain where he he'd been all night.

"Did you hear about those murders that occurred over the past few days?" Lucas asked. J.D. was glad he'd brought this up. She wanted to know their opinion on the matter.

"What murders?" Cherish asked. The astonish in her voice piqued J.D.'s interest.

"Two people were killed, both by vampires. One girl and one guy. Nicola and I drove past one of the crime scenes."

"Well, it wasn't any of us." Lela looked at Kevin. "Right?"

"Why are you looking at me? I'm on a strict blood bag diet. Besides, I've never fed on women."

"That leaves Lucas and Lucian."

"Nope," Lucas said. "I haven't fed from the vein since . . ."

He didn't have to finish that sentence. Even if his brother had done despicable acts, it was hard for Lucas to talk about Henry. Lucian wouldn't talk about it either and J.D. wondered if that had anything to do with his recent odd behavior.

"Well, my father didn't do it," Cherish said. "We were out last night."

Melody raised an eyebrow. "Out doing what? I don't remember hearing you leave."

"Catching up. We've hardly seen each other with Solomon and me living in England and him living in Miami."

"And you didn't hear anything about a murder?"

"Fine, I'm guilty. I did it in the library with a candlestick."

Everyone but Melody started laughing. They all knew that Cherish wasn't responsible because she fed on vampire blood. She would neither let Lucian kill someone nor feed on anyone. It was pointless trying to find the culprit when he or she was obviously not someone related to them.

"Whoever it is, they better pass through," Lela said. "The police are going to start searching and the last thing we need is for a repeat of the post Orlando massacre paranoia."

The group nodded in agreement. However, something still wasn't sitting right with J.D. If Lucian had been out with Cherish all night, why didn't he just tell her? Better yet, where was Nicola? The three of them weren't together, were they? And if so, what were they doing?

8

Robin gasped as the Vanquish lurched yet again. With the new freedom of her license, she wanted to learn how to drive stick shift and J.D. gladly offered to teach her. As usual, Abe decided to tag along. So far, it wasn't going so well, and she was having difficulty remembering which gears did what.

"Sorry," she said.

"That's okay," J.D. said. "We're in a parking lot, so we're not in danger of hurting anyone. Give it another try."

Robin took a deep breath then managed to get the car going again. J.D. had given her markers for where she was supposed to stop and where she needed to shift gears in order to accelerate. The stopping part wasn't hard, but the gears were so confusing. All her confidence from getting her license was fading with each lurch of the car.

She approached the marker and did the smoothest stop she'd done all day. She still didn't quite shift as quickly as she needed, but she began to make progress. Two hours later and she could shift spot on. J.D. cheered for her and hugged her in excitement.

"Great job, hon! I think I've made a pro of you, yet."

"Because no one drives stick like you, right sis?" Abe asked from the back seat.

J.D. quickly unbuckled and reached back, slapping the side of his head. Robin laughed. He deserved it for that disgusting comment.

"We should celebrate by stuffing our faces with something greasy," J.D. said.

"Can I drive us?" Robin asked.

J.D. looked hesitant and Robin understood why. She may have succeeded in mastering J.D.'s parking lot course, but it was another thing to actually be on the road where she couldn't afford to stop too late and ram into someone. On the other hand, she would never learn unless she practiced the real thing. She was a quick learner.

"I guess you can try. We'll go someplace close just to be safe."

Robin squealed with delight then put the car in gear so she could leave the parking lot. There was a taco shop about a quarter of a mile away so she decided to go there. To be extra safe, she waited until there were absolutely no cars coming before she pulled onto the road. She loved that Euless was small and she really liked living there. Miami was too big with too much crime and violence. Here, it was easy going and she wasn't afraid to be out at night.

At least until the murders. She wanted to believe Lela's theory that the vampire was probably someone passing through. She'd had enough of dangerous people, vampires and mortals alike. But danger seemed to find her family no matter where they lived.

When they got to a light, the vibration from someone's bass rattled the car. An orange sports car that looked like it came out of a sci-fi movie pulled up next to them. Two guys were in it and the guy in the passenger seat gave her the eye then nudged the driver who looked at her too. The way they were looking at her reminded her of Ash and Kai.

The driver revved the engine once then again for a longer period of time. He kept doing it and Robin was confused about why they were wasting gas.

"They want to race," J.D. said, rolling her eyes. "It's the car. People automatically assume you're a street racer."

Curious, Robin put her foot on the peddle and revved her own engine. The sound was exciting and gave her an adrenaline rush. She looked over at the guy one more time then back at the light. She was going to do this.

"Robin . . ." Abe said. "I know that look. That's not a good look."

The light turned green and she shifted gears before speeding up then shifted one last time. The car next to her began to pass by but then she sped up, getting ahead. It seemed like the other guy was going to win for a moment there, but then she gained on him and passed by.

"Yes!" she shouted.

"Robin the light!" J.D. said.

Her eyes widened as the light went from green to yellow. She was going a good fifty-five miles an hour in a thirty zone. Right when the light changed to red, she blew through it and the camera flashed. The rush of racing was quickly replaced by fear and she pulled over.

"Oh no!" she said. "J.D., I'm so sorry!"

"Don't be. That was the most excitement I've had since they made triple stuffed Oreos. Plus, I run red lights all the time. I probably have like six tickets, but my motto is—"

"They can't fine me if they can't find me," Abe said. "I taught her that one."

"It's not like they can arrest me. I have diplomatic immunity."

Robin raised an eyebrow. "How?"

"My grandfather was a Duke and when he died, it made my father the new Duke and since he's no longer alive—"

"*I'm* the Duke of Idlewood," Abe said. "And that makes my sister officially, The Lady Jordin Christophe."

"Wait! What about Gallard and Lucas?"

"Gallard is a Marquess and that makes Lela a Lady as well. Lucas is an Earl. If the MITF knew that he was a peer, they wouldn't be able to touch him. Speaking of, did you know that Kevin is a Marquess too? Solomon is a Duke as well and since Kevin is his only living male relative, well. You get the point."

Robin started to ask more questions but then she saw red lights flashing behind her. She was more scared than ever. What if they took away her license? She'd only just gotten it the day before and she'd already made a traffic infraction. She never would have done this in with automatic transmission. She shouldn't have insisted on driving.

"J.D. I'm not a Lady or a Duchess. I can't get away with this!"

"Don't panic. Just do as I say." J.D. reached over and undid the first two buttons of Robin's shirt then tugged down her camisole, making her previously modest outfit into a risqué one. "There. Ten bucks says you get out of a ticket."

"What if the police officer is a woman?"

J.D. blinked. "Then you better hope she's gay or else you're screwed."

"So, *that's* how you've skipped out on tickets," Abe said. "Genius."

Someone knocked on the window and Robin reluctantly rolled it down. When she turned to look at the police officer, her eyes widened, and her heart palpitated. It was Erik.

"Well, well. It appears that fate has brought us together again," he said.

Robin nonchalantly pulled her camisole a little higher. It was one thing to try and flatter a stranger, but another to appear trashy in front of a guy she was attracted to. Of all people, it had to be Erik McPherson who saw her run the red light.

"I'm really sorry," she said. "I'm learning how to drive stick shift, and I panicked when the light changed." This was a huge lie, and she kind of felt bad for it. She held out her wrists to him. "Let's get this over with."

He chuckled then knelt down so that he was eye level with her. "Why do you always think I'm going to arrest you? Are you secretly a criminal? Should I be checking the database for beautiful blondes at large?"

She didn't fight the smile forming on her face. He had an amazing ability of washing away her fear with each compliment.

"Holy hell!" J.D. said. "Erik McPherson?"

Erik smiled at J.D. "I thought this was your car! Only one girl in Texas drives a classic like this."

J.D. got out of the car and so did Robin and Abe. J.D. ran around the side and hugged Erik for a really long time. Robin's stomach tightened, and she was surprised at herself. She was actually jealous of her friend hugging a guy she was attracted to.

"How have you been?" J.D. asked. "I haven't seen you since I graduated."

"I'm great! Got a good job. James is on the force too."

"How do you know each other?" Robin asked.

Erik slung an arm around J.D.'s shoulder. "We go way back to high school. J.D., my friend James, and I spent a lot of time together. She took James to homecoming and then went with me to my senior prom. Every guy at school was jealous of me."

J.D. laughed. "It's because I'm British, right?"

"And because you're gorgeous."

"Robin, this is Erik McPherson. We went to the same high school when I lived with Lela. Erik, this is my cousin Robin and my brother Abe."

Erik shook Abe's hand then smiled at Robin and she forgot her jealousy instantly.

"We've met," Erik said. "She helped me catch a pervert at the convenience store and then I had the privilege of dancing with her at the bar last night. I think it's fate that we've met again."

"Well, kind sir," J.D. said, "since this is her first offense, I think we should cut a deal. If you let her off with a warning, Robin will go on a date with you."

Robin's eyes widened and she looked at J.D. with appall. How could she get her in this situation? She would rather have the ticket than suffer the embarrassment of going on a date with him. She'd never been on a date. Heck, she never talked to anyone who wasn't in their circle of people. She could have slapped J.D.

"If anyone else had offered, I would have been appalled that one would think I take bribes. But for a beautiful and funny woman like her, you don't have to ask me twice."

He winked at Robin, and she felt her cheeks grow hot. Why did he have keep to calling her beautiful? He was making it harder for her to resist his flirting, though she did admire his perseverance. Any other man would probably run for the hills after receiving Kevin's overprotective Sharmentino glare. Erik was immune to it.

"We live on 3903 Hawthorne Avenue," J.D. said. She wrote down something on a piece of paper then handed it to him. "Here's her number.

She never goes anywhere so call her any time. We should get a drink sometime too! She can't have Sexy McPherson all to herself."

He laughed. "Will do."

Erik pocketed the number then took Robin's license as well as J.D.'s insurance and registration for protocol purposes. When he returned, he gave the papers back and smiled at Robin.

"I will be calling you, Miss Shepherd. Until then, I wish you luck on your learning experience. I'm sure you'll be driving stick with your eyes closed in no time."

When he walked back to his car, Robin admired him from behind by looking in her side mirror. She raised an eyebrow, impressed that he looked just as good from the back as he did the front.

"Did you just look at his ass?" Abe asked.

"No!" Robin blushed, embarrassed that she'd been caught.

"You totally did, you little vixen!" J.D. threw in. "I think you're smitten with Sexy McPherson. You should be thanking me for giving him your number."

"I'm not smitten," she insisted. "And I wasn't looking at his butt either."

She and J.D. switched seats and continued on their way to the taco shop. After the fact, she was terrified of the idea of going out with Erik. What made her feel a little less wary was that J.D. knew him personally. If she thought he was safe, then he probably was.

While they were waiting in line, J.D. left to use the bathroom, leaving Robin and Abe alone. She started counting the seconds before he would say something intrusive or over-protective. He lasted all of twenty.

"Are you really going out with that guy?" he asked.

"I guess. Why do you care?"

"Because I do. I want to make sure he doesn't have bad intentions."

"Like *you*, you mean?"

He chuckled and draped his arm around her. "Robin, I would never have bad intentions concerning you."

That comment bothered her for some reason. She and Abe were friends, but he'd never flirted with her. He hit on Nicola and Cherish all the time but never her. She was just as close to him as they were. Closer even.

"Why not? Am I too innocent for you? Are you afraid you're going to corrupt me?"

"You're not innocent in the sense that you're naïve. I know better than to think that after everything you've been through. But I do think you're too good for me. That's why we're friends and not bed buddies."

Too good for him? He obviously had no idea that she was slowly becoming a chain smoker or suffering from insomnia, and drinking J.D.'s wine when she wasn't around. She was far from good.

Feeling even bolder, she asked. "If I wanted to hook up with you like those other women, would you say yes?"

He turned to her with shock in his eyes. It had been an honest question and she wanted an honest answer. She wanted to know if he saw her as someone desirable or if he just saw her as a child.

"Yes," he said. His expression bore a seriousness she'd never seen from him before. "In a heartbeat."

Robin's phone rang and it broke her trance. Her hands shook as she took it out of her pocket. It was a number she didn't recognize, but she had a feeling she knew who it was. She answered it on the third ring.

"Hello?"

"I believe that a particular blonde who tends to beat up strangers and run red lights owes me a date. Is said felon free on Friday at noon?"

That was it. She could no longer fight her attraction to him, and she didn't want to either. After only three encounters, he had her hooked and boy did she not mind being hooked. Abe could shoe him away all he wanted but Erik had snagged her heart. She wasn't completely sure about how she felt in terms of his status as a police officer, but for now she would try to see past his occupation because the man behind it was irresistible.

"Friday at noon is perfect," she said. J.D., who had come back, discerned what the call was about and did a happy dance around her.

"Great. I will see you then. Until we meet again, I will be thinking of you."

Long after he hung up, Robin couldn't stop smiling. She gazed out the window while she ate, certain that nothing, not even a rainy day, could dampen the good mood she was in. She was going to experience her first date and she knew the three-day wait felt like an eternity.

9

When I saw Colton walk out of his classroom, I waved so that he would know I was there. Nicola was with me, but we'd barely spoken on the ride over. Ever since she'd walked out on our romantic night, things were awkward between us. We weren't exactly fighting, but not talking about it was worse, in my opinion.

Colton saw us, and he smiled big as he ran towards us. His running always made me nervous because sometimes he tended to run a little too fast. His strength came in random spurts as well, but Kevin was working with him to make sure there were no accidents at school.

As Colton grew closer, I noticed there was a bruise to the left of his right eye.

"Hey bud," I said. I knelt to his level and inspected the mark. "What happened to your eye?"

He shrugged.

"No, a shrug is not an answer," Nicola said. "What happened?"

"Some kids were being mean to this other kid and when I told them to stop, they hit me."

"They hit you? Did you tell someone?"

"Excuse me!" someone called.

I stood up to see a middle-aged woman coming towards us and I recognized her as Mrs. Archibald—Colton's teacher. I'd met her during Colton's orientation in late August and she seemed like a sweet lady. But her expression told me that I was about to see a different side.

"It's a pleasure to see you again," Mrs. Archibald said. "I wish it were under better circumstances. Would you two mind stepping into the classroom?"

We followed her into the classroom. It looked like a very fun place to be. There was a corner devoted to toys, with a dollhouse and Hot Wheel cars and another for reading with beanbag chairs. It was only the second day of school, but the walls were decorated in the student's drawings.

Nicola and I sat in front of the desk while Mrs. Archibald sat in her office chair. She took off her glasses, setting them on her desk then folded her hands. Whatever she was going to say, I had a bad feeling. Had they figured out that Colton was taken? Had he gotten into a fight and accidently hurt someone?

"Mr. and Mrs. . . ." She looked at her paper.

"D'Aubigne," Nicola and I said at the same time.

To elude suspicion, Solomon had helped us with the necessary papers that made the public think we were married. Nicola was more than happy to take on the d'Aubigne name, but we weren't ready for a real marriage at the time. Four months later, that had changed for me. I was definitely ready.

"Right, sorry. I'm so used to people with names like Thompson or Smith. Anyway, the reason I've called you in here today is that I'm concerned for your son. He's been saying things to his classmates that have me worried."

Nicola and I exchanged glances, and I took her hand in mine. I forgot that I was upset with her or that I had any suspicions surrounding her disappearance. Our son might be in trouble and we needed to put our differences aside to deal with it.

"What kind of things?" I asked.

"We were doing a project where the kids drew a picture of what they want to be when they grow up." She opened her drawer and pulled out a paper then handed it to me. "He drew this."

Nicola and I looked at it and did our best not to laugh. There were two men in the picture, and one had shoulder length black hair, jeans, and a green t-shirt while the other was dressed in a grey uniform. There were arrows pointing to each and the one over the man in jeans said *Gallard* while the other said *Bad Guy*. It was a picture of Gallard punching an MITF officer in the face. I had no idea where he came up with it, but thought it was endearing that Colton looked up to his grandfather.

"He said he wants to be a vampire that saves people," Mrs. Archibald said. "I know children have their imaginations, but I can't imagine where he got that idea."

"Probably all those *Angel* re-runs," Nicola said as-a-matter-of-factly. "I mean, have you seen David Boreanaz? What guy doesn't want to be him?"

Mrs. Archibald looked extremely appalled. I squeezed Nicola's hand to let her know that I found her joke funny, even if the audience wasn't appropriate for such a remark. Who could blame us? We were twenty-two and twenty-three-year olds who'd been thrown into parenthood so suddenly. We were still learning all the do's and don'ts.

"I'm afraid there's more," she said. "When I asked him about the drawing, he said that he knows some vampires and that they're nice people." She put her glasses back on. "Now I know you're new in town, but I must inform you that such claims are grounds for investigation."

I sucked in my breath, quickly exhaling so she wouldn't notice I was nervous. An investigation? This was the last thing we needed right now. Sure, Kevin was the only one who would be deemed suspicious, but we could always hide him. I was afraid that with more digging, they would figure out that Lela was an escaped convict and that Colton had been theoretically kidnapped.

"When will this investigation happen?" I asked.

"As soon as possible. I'm sure it will be fine, but I wanted you to know that I was only upholding the law by reporting this."

"Pardon me for saying this, but I hardly think a little drawing is as harmful as my son getting beaten on the playground."

"Excuse me?"

"He has a bruise on his face. He said he was hit by some kid. Do you know anything about this?"

"No, he never said a word. I assumed he'd had an accident on the playground."

"And you didn't think to ask? Look, Mrs. Archibald, I don't want to cause trouble. Personally, I think it's a waste of time because I've already undergone a background check for my job, and I came up clean. However, I will cooperate with this whole investigation thing, but I ask in return that my son be watched a little more carefully. Agreed?"

She nodded. "Agreed. Once it's all cleared up, everything will be back to normal. Colton will continue with his class, and we can forget it happened."

If only it were that simple. I didn't say these words out loud but said goodbye to her and we joined Colton outside. He was playing with a yoyo that Gallard bought him before he left. I studied the bruise again and was amazed when I saw that it had faded to the point of barely being noticeable.

"Come on, bud, let's go home," I said.

He tried to run ahead, but Nicola lifted him off the ground and swung him around, causing him to giggle. It made me happy seeing him getting along with his mother. I was worried that this investigation might go sour and split them apart again. It nearly killed Nicola when he'd been taken away from her as a baby, and I didn't want that to happen again.

We got back to the house and Colton couldn't get out of the car fast enough. He was eager to get inside and play with Kevin, like he did every day. It would be nice if he could make some friends at school so he wouldn't be around us bloodsuckers all the time and maybe he would have a new dream for his future.

"We should go talk to my mom," I said. "She should know about the investigation."

Nicola looked up from her phone. I hadn't even noticed she was texting until then.

"Uh . . . yeah. Definitely. Could we go after dinner? Or better yet, you should go alone. Spend some time with your mom."

I frowned. "Why can't you come with?"

She put her phone in her back pocket. "I have to do something."

I scoffed and folded my arms. She was hiding something from me. We knew each other's darkest secrets, we'd shared intimate moments, and though we hadn't consummated our love, I still felt closer to her than anyone.

"What's the real reason you're not coming?"

"It's kind of an obligation. I'll call you later, okay."

"Does it have anything to do with why you left last night? I know you were upset, but I really think we should have a serious discussion. If you want to wait longer, I have no problem with that. I only want you to be honest."

She wrapped her arms around my neck and hugged me tightly and I held her with the same force. I didn't have to worry about breaking her anymore, so I held on as if she could disappear at any second. I could feel her slipping away. I had her in my arms, but she wasn't fully there.

"I love you," she said softly. She pulled back and looked into my eyes. This time, they were honey brown. "We'll talk when you get home from work, okay?"

I leaned down and kissed her, hoping that somehow it would convince her to open-up to me, but she pulled away, ending the kiss abruptly.

"I have to go. I'll text you later."

I dropped my arms, allowing her to walk away and my heart broke. Something was putting a rift between us and I didn't know why. We'd been fine up until the past few days and now we were drifting apart. This was more than just the honeymoon season being over because it never really started. There was so much I wanted to share with her, but instead we were becoming strangers again.

"Are the lovebirds having problems?" I heard someone say. Cherish came walking over from next door.

"I'm not so sure," I replied. "Can I ask you a personal question?"

"You can ask me anything you want."

I thought about how I would word this.

"Let's say someone had to change. It's a big change, and the person is having a hard time adjusting. This person is very unhappy but there's no way to take back the change. What would you do to try and help them?"

"If it were me, I would let that person figure it out for themselves. We can't always fix everything and that includes the people we love most. If you're there for that person as someone they can vent to or as a shoulder to cry on, they will be grateful. Just give it time."

I gave a half smile. "All right. I guess I'm just a little disappointed that our night was cut short."

"Wait, she left you? After the bath and the candles? I was pretty sure you would keep her around for the next two days."

"Not exactly. She left before anything happened, and I didn't see her until the next day. I thought she was out with Lucian, but you cleared that up."

Cherish frowned. "Why would you think she was with my father?"

"J.D. came up with that theory."

"Oh, Lord, that girl. I love her, but her mind churns up things out of nowhere. She's just like her mom. But she hides her deepest feelings, like her dad." She rubbed my arm. "I wouldn't worry about Nic. She adores you. But if you're suspicious, follow her. It's what I would do."

I went into the house and dialed J.D.'s number then waited for her to answer. Kevin had given Colton a snack and they were watching *The X Files*, just like they did every Thursday afternoon. They wouldn't be paying attention to me, so I stayed in the room.

"Hey, Luke, what's up?" J.D. said once she'd answered.

"I think you're right about Nicola and Lucian hiding something. She's acting funny and keeping secrets from me."

"What do you suggest we do, Sherlock?"

I looked out the window and saw that Lucian had pulled up in the Scion. Nicola walked over to him and they talked before she got into the passenger seat and they drove away together. This fueled my frustration even more.

"How about a little reconnaissance? The d'Aubigne Duo has some spying to do."

10

Nicola walked around the room, observing her students as they practiced their shading. This was her first class, and so far, she loved every minute of it. Agreeing to teach had been a great idea. While she loved painting, she loved sharing her skills even more and watching others progress in their technique.

The only downside was that the rift between her and Lucas kept interfering with her work. She'd caught herself daydreaming several times during the class but managed to save face. Ryan noticed and acted professional about it. She didn't want to discuss her relationship problems with anyone, especially him.

"Nicola?" one student in the back said. "I can't quite get my shading right."

She smiled and went over to the woman. Most of her student were middle-aged people who probably needed a hobby with their kids away at college. Marionette was a sweet old lady who always wore pink.

"Hmm," Nicola said as she studied the drawing of the teacup. "Try pressing a little harder. Your blending stick is tougher than it looks, so it can take it."

Marionette smiled and began shading once more. When it looked like it was working, Nicola walked away and observed from the front once more.

Ryan came in at that moment and smiled when he saw her. She appreciated that he trusted her to teach alone and didn't hover. He let her have her own curriculum and offered to be of help if she needed any advice.

"You're doing well," he said softly.

"Let's just hope we can get more students in here. It's too quiet with just three people in the room."

"I already have a few who want to transfer from mine. They're curious to know about my beautiful new assistant."

The smile left her face. "Ryan . . ."

"I know. These past few months have been torture. I hate seeing you every day and not be allowed to kiss you or touch you."

Nicola quickly looked away from him. She wished he wouldn't say such things. It was hard enough that she felt vulnerable without having to deal with Ryan's flirting. She'd sensed Lucas' concern when Ryan had called her by her nickname. She'd asked him not to use it in front of people, but he wouldn't quit.

She excused herself from the room for a moment and gestured that they go into the hall to talk. She didn't want to have this discussion with an audience.

"You know why we can't. Lucas—"

"Doesn't deserve you."

Nicola grimaced and turned her attention back to the two students. Thank God they had music playing so they wouldn't hear this conversation. Why couldn't she just teach in peace? It was all she wanted.

Someone walked into the gallery, and the two of them looked over. It was a man— maybe thirty-five, average in height with dark hair and eyes eerily similar to hers. He had glasses and dressed like an old man in his knit sweater tucked into his corduroy pants.

"What are you doing here?" Ryan asked him.

"I came to see the, uh, gallery." The man crossed his arms behind his back. "You've done well with the place."

"I see." Ryan put a hand on her back. "Nicola, I'd like you to meet Ezekiel— Zeke, this is my new assistant."

Nicola smiled, offering her hand and Ezekiel took it.

"Pleasure to meet you," she said.

"Zeke is my brother of sorts," Ryan explained. "His father took me in when my parents died."

"That was kind of him. Not to be weird or anything, but Zeke it appears we have the same eyes."

Ezekiel raised his eyebrows.

"Ah, yes. Very astonishing, considering the trait is the rarest of eye colors. Most commonly found in Asian territory, or even the Americas. Statistics prove that one is more likely to have red hair than amber eyes, which is fascinating considering red hair is the rarest hair color."

Ryan rolled his eyes. "Ignore my brother. He's somewhat of a geneticist."

62

"I think it's interesting," Nicola said. "My sister wanted to be a forensic scientist. I'm sure she would have studied topics of that sort."

Ryan pressed his lips together. "Uh . . . Nikita, my brother and I are going to lunch. I'll be back before your second class, so no need to worry about leaving the place unattended."

"Okay." She smiled at Ezekiel. "It was nice meeting you."

He gave her a polite bow then walked out of the gallery with Ryan. He was the most interesting person she'd ever met. No one in this century bowed anymore. Not in America anyway. And his style — she couldn't get over how old fashioned he dressed. But she liked him. Something about him was very likeable.

Nicola started to go back into the classroom when she saw a familiar car in the parking lot through the window. It was J.D.'s Vanquish. She looked closer and saw both J.D. and Lucas were in the car.

"Oh, hell no," she said, seething with anger.

She knew exactly what those two were doing here. Lucas kept asking her to talk to him, and she'd needed some space, which was why she hadn't elaborated on where she was going. Besides, she thought he would remember she'd agreed to teach the art class.

Throwing open the door, she marched over to their car. The two of them got out and she glared at Lucas. She didn't care that J.D. was there since she'd probably wanted to follow Lucian. That was her business.

"What are you doing here?" she asked. "Are you following me?"

"Yes," Lucas said. "I saw you leave with Lucian and you wouldn't tell me where you were going."

"Are you my keeper now?"

"No, I'm your boyfriend, and I don't appreciate being lied to. I've been lied to my entire life and I'm not going to put up with it anymore."

"Okay, here's the truth. I wanted a ride to my art class and Lucian offered because he needed to go to town anyway."

Lucas let out a sigh and closed his eyes. "The art class. I completely forgot about that. Nic, I'm so sorry. I forgot, and when you left without an explanation, it completely slipped my mind."

"Well I'm glad that was cleared up for you."

"Can you blame me? You disappeared the other night and then you leave without saying anything. I wanted to know what was so important that you put our son's problems on hold."

Anger surged through her, and she felt her eyes change to black.

"How dare you? You know I love Colton as much as you do! I will discuss this with you tonight like I said I would. I just needed a few hours."

"Nicola, this is serious. If they find out about us, they could take Colton away. Do you understand that?"

Tears stung in her eyes. How could he think she didn't realize that? He should have known by now that she dealt with stress by painting, which was exactly why she'd wanted to go and teach. It soothed her, and she knew that afterward she would adequately be able to have this discussion. It terrified her that Colton might be taken, and his words hurt her.

"I don't want to talk to you right now," she said. "We'll talk later when you're calm and not making irrational comments."

Without looking back, she went back into the gallery. She leaned against the door, taking a few deep breaths. She couldn't have her students see her this upset. She wanted to cry but fought back the tears.

When she was composed, she took held her head high and returned to the art room. The two students were talking to each other and comparing drawings. She smiled when she saw their work.

"Great job, you two! You caught on very quickly. Now, let's try to get some color in these pictures."

The hot water from the shower poured over my head, soothing the tension in my body. I had been completely distracted at work and was glad nothing really life threatening happened. It wasn't good for someone in my profession to be distracted. It was a slow night with two tickets and one arrest for drunk driving. The rest of the time, I sat in my squad car and chastised myself for my accusations against Nicola.

I finished rinsing off then got out. I was about to go to the sink and shave when I was startled by movement. Nicola was sitting on the edge of the bathtub, staring down at the floor. I'd been so deep in thought that I hadn't heard her come into the house, let alone the bathroom. She'd said we would talk when I wasn't being irrational, and I felt calmer than I had been that afternoon.

She didn't say a word, so I continued with what I was going to do. I finished shaving half of my face before she finally stood up and came over to me. Still, neither of us spoke, even as I rinsed my razor and dried my face with a towel. I set it on the counter then looked at her for the first time.

"I already talked to my mom. She said that we're going to hide the blood bags and make Kevin mortal for a few days. Problem solved."

She took my hand, slipping her fingers in between mine, and I gave her hand a squeeze.

"I would be just as devastated as you if they took him away," she said. "It hurt when you implied that I didn't care."

"I know. I'm sorry I made you feel that way. And I'm sorry that I forgot about your class and accused you of keeping secrets. I'm a clueless ass face."

She laughed. "J.D.'s favorite insult. You may be an ass face, but I still love you. All is forgiven?"

I kissed her cheek. "Definitely. Stay with me tonight, okay? We don't have to do anything. I only want your company and I want to listen if you have anything you want to talk about. Besides, I always sleep better when you're next to me."

Someone knocked on the front door, and I got dressed quickly so we could go answer it. I was curious to know who it was since everyone we knew was comfortable with walking in the house without a knock. I opened the door and stared at the unexpected guest, or rather guests. It was two men and one woman.

One man had a russet complexion with distinct African clothing and a matching hat. He had eyeliner, but it looked more cultural than a style choice. The other had leather pants that were so tight they could have been mistaken as his skin. He was pale and had hair grown past his ears, like Micah, only his curled up at the ends. He had a goatee and a toothpick hanging out of his mouth. The woman, however, was very striking. She had medium length brown hair and light green eyes. She was rather endowed and wore clothes that accentuated her figure.

"So, yer Gallard's boy?" the goatee guy said. He had a Scottish accent.

"Who's asking?"

He stuck out his hand and I shook it out of common courtesy. I wasn't about to let them in until I knew who they were. Nicola, and I were very capable of fighting him off, but I had Colton to think about.

"I'm Terrence Hawte. Pronounced *howt*, not *hot*. I don't appreciate jokes, so please call me Terrence."

"Oh, right!" I said. "You're the guy whose name my dad used when he was arrested. You were the bouncer at his bar."

He nodded then looked at Nicola. "Do I know you?"

She smirked. "No. I don't hang out with Scottish people on a regular basis."

"I do know you! Yer that woman Kevin brought to the bar. Yer brother was Curtis, right?"

The smirk faded from her lips. "You must be talking about my mom. I'm Nicola."

"Ah. I see the resemblance now. I'm sorry about your uncle. He was one of the few mortals I could tolerate."

She shrugged. "Thanks. To be honest, I don't really remember him. I was only nine months old."

I realized we'd completely ignored the other man, so I took initiative and held my hand out to him and he took it.

"My name is Ramses. My brother and I are the last of the first generation of night-walkers."

"It's good to meet you Ramses, I'm Lucas."

"And I am Celeste. Arnaud's sister," the woman said. She took my hand in hers and gave me a seductive smile. "I see that you are your father's son."

"It is nice to meet you as well, Celeste. Please come in."

Nicola and I stood so they could sit on the couch. Kevin was over at Lela's so it was just the four of us. We didn't say anything at first and Terrence kept looking around and sniffing. He wouldn't smell anything but vampire blood, including Colton's.

"I hope you didn't come to see my dad because he's not here," I said. "He's been gone for about a month now."

"We know," Terrence said. "Who do you think sent us here?"

I raised an eyebrow. I knew that Gallard called Lela on a regular basis, but he'd never mentioned sending anyone our way. This was a good thing— it meant he was successful in finding people to stand on our side. Things were starting to look a little less hopeless.

"I have come in honor of your father's ancestor, Jordan," Ramses said. "If it weren't for your uncle's heroism, none of us would be alive right now. Your father wants to finish what he started, and I am willing to as well."

A door opened down the hall and I heard little footsteps. Colton must have woken up from a nightmare. I knew he hadn't heard the company because he could sleep through a hurricane. Sure enough, he entered the living room, rubbing his eyes and yawning. "Who are these guys?" he asked.

I went over and lifted him into my arms. "These are Gallard's friends, bud. They came to see us."

"This must be your . . ." Terrence began to say but I gave him a cautioned look. We still hadn't told Colton I was his father and hadn't decided when to break that news. "Little brother," he finished. "Gallard told us about him and Jordan's kids too. You d'Aubignes are a fertile group of people."

Nicola laughed, and I didn't fight a smile. It was true. My mom got pregnant with me when Gallard was mortal, and Colton had been conceived in one try of artificial insemination. Not to mention J.D. and Abe who were the product of one night shared between their mom and Jordan.

"Are more coming?" I asked. Colton had long since fallen asleep on my shoulder.

"He's traveling with Arnaud," Ramses said. "They've convinced Jordan's friend Ivelisse to come here as well. She wants vengeance for her brother's death."

I remembered that name from Lela's journal. The brother, Estebon, had saved Lela's life, as well as mine, by pushing her out of the way of burning debris. He'd died in the fire, along with Bodoway.

"Wait, did you say Arnaud? He's on our side now?"

"Did he ruin your life somehow as well?" Terrence asked. "Never cared for the man."

"He threatened to kidnap Colton if I didn't help him bring Celeste back." I didn't want to get into that, so I changed the subject. "That makes four of you? If you add Solomon, my dad, David, and everyone here, that makes fifteen of us." Nicola nudged me and I realized my error. "Fourteen, excuse me."

"Make that thirteen," Terrence said. "Celeste doesn't count for anything. Unless it entails being on her back."

"Cretan," Celeste hissed. "And whose fault is that?"

"You know each other?" I asked.

"*Know* her? We were engaged when she slept with Gallard. I threatened to expose Arnaud's shady brothel, and to keep me quiet, Arnaud had me nearly beaten death. Gallard had Bodoway turn me to save my life. It was why I forgave him of his indiscretion with Celeste."

"Wait . . . you and Gallard hooked up?" Nicola asked Celeste. "Does Lela know?"

"I'm sure she knows," I said. "My dad doesn't keep secrets."

"Speaking of, is your mother around here?" Terrence asked. I was thankful that he'd changed the subject.

"She's next door, why?"

"We don't exactly like each other."

The door opened, and I almost laughed when Lela walked in with Cherish, Kevin, and Melody. How she knew we had company was a mystery since none of them came by vehicle. She took one look at Terrence and they groaned in disgust. He wasn't kidding when he'd said they didn't like each other.

"Hello, Tight Pants," she said with zero enthusiasm. "Gallard said you were coming, but I hoped it wouldn't be that soon."

"Pleasure to see you as well, Lela. Still Gallard's ball and chain I see."

Lela elbowed him in the ribs, and I tried not to laugh. Terrence, however, could barely sit down he was in so much pain. I almost felt bad for him.

Ramses stood up and she gave him a friendly hug. They exchanged a few words before he returned to his seat and Ramses filled her in on what he'd told Nicola and me. Nicola texted Lucian to let him know we were having a meeting and while everyone did introductions and catching up, he arrived with J.D., Abe, and Robin not five minutes later.

"Where is Gallard now, do you know?" Lela asked Terrence. He nodded to Ramses, who answered instead.

"He found me in Egypt a few days ago. When we last spoke, he told me they were heading for Sinai. He was different than when we last met."

That caught my attention. "Different how?"

Ramses looked hesitant to answer. The way Lela was acting, she must have known what he was talking about. They needed to speak up because I wasn't in the mood for anymore secrets. I already had my fair share of them.

"He has your gift, Lucas," he continued. "Arnaud gave it to him so he could return it to you. The power made him human. He has a heartbeat and his touch is warm. But he hasn't used the power at all. He feels it isn't his to wield. He plans to send David and Arnaud to gather more men while he and Solomon go to Mount Sinai."

"Mount Sinai? As in the mountain where the Ten Commandments were made? Why would he go there?"

Lela came over to me and took my hand. "He wants to learn more about why we exist. He believes that the power Maximus passed on to Jordan that was then passed to you is the key to saving our kind. Since Maximus is dead, all he has to go on is myth. Maximus used to be a man of God and Solomon thinks the only way to get the whole story is from the source."

"He wants to talk to God?" I asked. "Why does he have to go to Sinai to do that?"

"Maximus believed that vampires don't have souls," Ramses explained. "That is what Jordan told me. Without a soul, we are permanently separated from him."

"It explains why I was trapped in darkness when we died," Melody said.

"So how would Gallard speak with God if he is a vampire as well?" Lucian asked.

"I don't know, Mr. Christophe," Ramses said. "I don't know."

11

Robin paced back and forth in Kevin's living room. It was eleven-fifty and Erik would be there in ten minutes. She'd changed five times and borrowed clothes from Lela — a black and white tank top with denim capris. J.D. put some nude eye shadow and mascara on her. She wasn't as dolled up as when she went to the club, but not too casual either.

A door down the hall opened and Abe came into the room. He was shirtless, again and strutting around like he was on some sort of catwalk. Maybe he wasn't doing it on purpose but that's how it looked to her. He used this strut whenever he was looking for a date. He didn't used to walk that way around her.

"Off to your date?" he asked with a hint of spite in his tone.

"If you must know, yes. He's picking me up."

"What a gentleman. You know, I can always go with you. I could stay at least a block away, so he won't notice."

"No, you can't!"

He moved even closer. "What about my promise? I'm never supposed to leave your side."

Her annoyed gaze softened, and she gave him a hug. She loved his hugs almost as much as Gallard's. She also hated that Abe still felt guilty for not being there to help her. He shouldn't. He couldn't have known someone would try to hurt her and Kevin. Abe wasn't a vampire and therefore not expected to be the big strong man.

"You have to stop blaming yourself," she said. "It wasn't your fault."

A car door shut, and she widened the distance between her and Abe. She pulled back the curtain to see who had arrived. It was Erik and he'd come in a silver four-door Dodge Ford. She loved trucks. She liked the loud sound they made when the engine started and the feeling of being high up— like no one could touch her.

"You have to go," she said.

"What for?"

"You're half naked, and I don't want Erik to get the wrong idea."

He nodded. "You know, you're a lot more capable of taking care of yourself than I give you credit for. I promise I won't ruin your chances with Erik but . . . he may have competition."

Her thoughts left her impending date and she stared at him as he walked away. Things had been awkward between them ever since their conversation at the taco place. He'd admitted he wouldn't turn her away if she approached him, and that had her confused and curious at the same time. She wouldn't do it. Abe was her friend, nothing more.

Erik knocked, and she took a deep breath before answering it. She had to shake off Abe's comment about competition so she could focus on this date. Not that there was anything to focus on, besides not making a fool of herself and accidently blurting out that she was practically a zombie. She just had to stick to normal conversation topics, and everything would go well.

He greeted her with a smile and held up a bouquet of yellow roses. He was dressed how he was at the club, only he had a different shirt and no jacket.

"For me?" she asked, hardly able to contain her joy.

"Unless there's another beautiful felon here named Robin, these are most certainly yours."

She took the roses from him and smelled them. The petals tickled her nose and she had to hold back a sneeze, but they smelled wonderful. "Thank you so much! I'll keep them until they die."

Lucas came into the room at that moment and she showed off her roses to him with pride.

"Hey. What's going on?" he asked.

"I'm here to pick Robin up for a date," Erik said.

Lucas raised an eyebrow. "You're a brave guy risking the wrath of Kevin." He took the flowers from her. "Robin, I'll take these to J.D. and she'll put them in a vase."

"You working today?" Erik asked.

"Yeah, the night shift. My schedule is kind of weird this week, but they said it would go back to normal. It was good to see you."

"Likewise. Don't work too hard."

Lucas left and Robin grabbed her purse. While she and Erik walked to the truck, she thought about holding his hand. Lucas always let her hold his hand, but they were family and it was different.

Erik opened the door for her, and she was about to climb in when she felt him put his hands on her waist and lift her onto the seat. Her body tensed under his touch and she hoped he didn't notice. While he had proved many times to have good intentions, she was still trying to get comfortable with him.

"I know you're a tall girl, but I couldn't help myself," he said.

"Thank you. Next time, I'll lift *you* into the truck to make it fair."

"I'm holding you to that."

He winked before shutting the door and she fought the effervescent butterflies. Usually they would go away after a few moments, but this time they continued for quite a while. The smile left her face, and she rested a hand on her stomach. It wasn't butterflies she was feeling. It was the baby.

Erik got in on the other side, and she quickly dropped her hand. He could never know of her condition. He wouldn't want to be with her if he knew. Before long, she would be huge and no longer able to hide it. She hoped that she could hold out on revealing the news for a while longer. She just got him and didn't want to lose him just yet.

"Where to, beautiful?" he asked.

"I don't know. I don't really go places very much. Where do you like to go?"

She let him think while she tried to will the butterflies to stop. They were making her nauseous and the last thing she wanted was to get sick while on this date.

"Want to see a movie?" he asked. "I think there's a new one out. A sci-fi I believe."

"We should go! I love space and aliens. Science was my favorite subject in school and I used to want to study biology, but I was never able to go to college and I do want to try and go someday but—"

"Damn! It seems I've found the golden mine. Is science your weakness?"

"Oh, I was talking too much, wasn't I?"

"That's okay. I like the sound of your voice."

He leaned over and she froze. Was he going to kiss her? The last time someone kissed her, it hadn't been her choice and it was awful. She'd sworn that she would never kiss anyone ever again. But as his face grew closer to hers, she wondered if kissing Erik would be so bad.

When he took her seatbelt and buckled it for her, she relaxed. It was silly to think he would kiss her. They didn't know each other well enough. She was on this date mostly because she knew he would keep asking if she declined and because she was curious about him.

He pulled up to the movie theater and he insisted that she let him open the door for her. As before, he lifted her out of the truck then surprised her by taking her hand. She looked down at their joined hands in wonder but didn't pull away. It felt nice— his grip wasn't too tight but made her feel protected. His palm was a bit rough like he'd done a lot of hard work and it was endearing. They walked inside and he bought a bag of popcorn for them to share and a Dr. Pepper for her.

They gave the usher their tickets then he held her hand again as they went to their seats. He told her of all the new editions that had been added over the years and how he'd first gone with his parents when he was eight. Hearing him talk about his childhood made her curious about what it would have been like if they were friends when they were children. Granted, she would have been older, but she had a feeling she would have adored him then.

"Tell me about yourself," she said. "I want to know everything about you."

"Everything? Well, let's see. I was born in Arlington, I have two younger sisters, one that is almost ten years younger than me, and both are currently in high school. I became a police officer when I was twenty-one and haven't looked back since." He smiled at her. "Now that I've told you my life story, why don't you tell me yours?"

"I don't think you want to know. My life is kind of sad."

The smile left his face. "Sad? How so?"

Where would she start? Should she tell him that her mother and father were murdered in front of her then she was held hostage for two months? Or about her aunt and uncle being killed in a car accident? Or that someone dropped her on her head to get back at Lela? Furthermore, that she couldn't remember anything after that and the last thing she remembered was waking up in a cemetery?

She chose to give him a censored version. If he knew her family was tangled up with vampires, or worse, that they *were* vampires, he would be more likely to run.

"I grew up in Miami with my mom and two brothers. My dad . . . my mom's husband, Mark, left us when I was a baby, but he spent time with me on the weekends. My mom died, and we don't know where he is. I have two brothers and one sister, but my oldest brother died a few years after my mom." This part of the story she had to omit a few details. "I had an accident recently and I was in a coma. I woke up about seven months ago."

Erik's eyes widened. "You were in a coma?"

"Yeah. For about twenty-two days. Anyway, I'm better now." She thought a bit. "My family is of regal background. Lucas is an Earl."

She let him take a moment to react to this information. She'd dumped a lot on him compared to his stories of reckless pranks and scabby knees.

"Lucas is an *Earl*? Of what?"

"I'm not sure."

"Does this mean I'm on a date with a princess?"

She laughed. "No, I'm not a princess. I don't have a title, but I'm related by marriage to people who do. My sister is a Lady."

"Well, I am honored that a noble lady like yourself is willing to spend time with a lowly commoner like me."

He winked, and she smiled. The lights dimmed, making her sad and excited all at once. She didn't like not being able to see his face, but she was looking forward to the show. The entire room lit up as images came to life. The new technology took 3D to a new level. They didn't even need glasses. There were even smells incorporated into the movie experience to make everything more realistic.

During the middle of the show, a bright light flashed and for a second, she saw that Erik wasn't watching the show — he had his eyes on her. She stopped paying attention to the alien attack and looked at him. It had grown dark again, but just knowing that he was there was thrilling enough.

When the lights turned on, the magic disappeared. The show was over, and it was time to leave. He took her hand again, to her delight and led her through the crowd. When they got outside, the Texas sun seemed too bright. She longed to be back under the artificial stars in the dim light.

"What do you think of this low-class entertainment?" he asked with sarcasm.

"It was almost as good as Christmas."

"Wow. That good, huh? What about it was so great?"

"You. I like spending time with you, and I hope that we can do this again."

He lifted their joined hands and kissed the top of hers. "I think I can arrange that. Next Monday is the Thanksgiving Festival and Euless does it every year. I have to work for part of it, but if you hang with my family and wait for me, I'll join you close to sundown."

Her heart palpitated. "Your family? Like your dad?"

He chuckled. "Yes. And my mom and two sisters. I know it's early to meet the parents, but when I'm sure about something, I'm very sure. I'm not letting you get away, beautiful. You're stuck with me until you get sick of me."

As they walked back to the car, she forgot her worries. If he was serious, then he would be around for a while. The people in her life were always leaving and she didn't think she could take it if she lost someone else. And he said he would only leave if she got sick him. One thing was certain — she was falling for him and there was no way she could get sick of Erik McPherson.

12

I lay outstretched on the couch while Nicola sat at her canvas and painted. I invited her over since she hadn't stayed at my place the night before and I loved watching her work. She always had this concentrated expression on her face, with one eyebrow slightly raised and her mouth set in a firm line. She was beautiful.

The show on TV no longer interested me so I got up and sat on the coffee table, admiring her creation. It was a portrait of Robin and Erik from the night at the bar. They were dancing and looking into each other's eyes. I could feel the affection as if the two were in the room.

"You see everything, don't you?" I asked.

"I do have an eye for noticing things that other people don't." She set her charcoal down. "I wish we could be like them. Not a care in the world — not on the run from the law, no vampires."

I didn't take that comment personally. I was sure that everyone in my family wished that they could be normal again. Kevin was the only one in our group who had turned by choice other than Solomon and even he expressed his regret over a decision he'd made when he was only seventeen. I was born a vampire due to the chance of DNA. Gallard was right about Micah getting the better deal. He had no blood lust.

"I think I know how we can spice up our relationship," I said. "We may not be getting intimate, but there are other things we can do."

"Lucas, I'm sorry that—"

"Don't be sorry. I told you, I will wait until the end of the world for you. Until then . . ."

I took off my shirt. She stared at me with confusion and I continued to undress.

"What are you doing?" she asked.

"Isn't it obvious?" I took off my shoes and started with my belt. "I want you to draw me like Jack drew Rose."

She burst out laughing at my *Titanic* reference and I smiled. I hadn't heard her laugh in a while, and it was music to my ears. She was right about Robin's relationship being simpler than ours. We weren't allowing ourselves to have fun because of how serious things had been lately, and I wanted to change that.

"Lucas, put your clothes back on."

"No. Not until you draw me first."

I shucked my pants off and she rushed over to me. "I'm not going to draw you!"

"Why not? I want to be famous like you."

I finally removed my boxers and her cheeks turned red. She'd seen me before, but it was flattering that I still made her nervous. She didn't say a word, and I went over to the couch and lay down, striking the same pose that Kate Winslet did in the movie.

"Draw me."

"You're crazy, Lucas Taylor." She sat on her stool and tore the first drawing off then started taking her paints out of her art bag. "If I'm going to do this, I want it to be serious. You're going to have to lay there for a long time."

Once she got out her necessary supplies, she wrote, *Do not disturb. Art in progress* on a piece of paper and quickly opened the door and taped it to the front, making sure to lock it as well. When she returned, she walked over to me and studied my body. Her gaze was starting to make me blush now, but I didn't say anything. She took the throw blanket on the couch and draped it over my shoulder.

"There. I know the blanket is brown, but I'm going to make it red in the painting. Could you flex your muscles too? The arms turn out better when I depict them that way."

As she started painting, she eyed me seductively from behind the slate and it took everything in me to not break my stance and take her into my arms. I wanted her so badly and lying there in nothing but a draped blanket wasn't helping. Her eyes flashed to an alluring green and it caused my heart to pound. She must have heard it because she chuckled.

I probably lay there for about two hours before she finally stood up and showed it to me. I managed to take a small nap after she'd finished with my face. She'd gotten down the important details and planned to touch it up later.

This portrayal of me was even more realistic than the one she'd done for Mona. She said that she planned to depict me laying on a stone altar instead of a couch. I was impressed and convinced that she'd gotten way better, if that were even possible.

"I love it," I said. "You didn't have to really paint me. I was kidding."

"Too late. I'm pretty sure this is my best work yet. I can't wait to show Ryan."

"What!"

"Kidding! Sort of. He asked me to show him some of my previous work. I don't have any of it here in Texas, but he doesn't have to know I did this today."

I wrapped the blanket around me as I studied the drawing. "Hmm. You kind of made the goods a little small."

"Whatever! Did you want me to make it so big that it's the only thing people see?" She wrapped her arms around my waist. "I put the most effort in your face because I love it so much. I love seeing your face every day and I think it's your face and not your body that's worth a million dollars. In my heart, anyway."

"You only like me for my face?"

She laughed. "I love all of you, Lucas d'Aubigne. Mona was right, though. It's very cute."

"I can't believe she told you about that!"

"You remember how she was. No secrets. And it's no secret that I adore you."

Her lips met mine and I forgot all about that stupid incident. She slid her hands down my back and then tugged off the blanket. I lifted her up from the floor and carried her over to the couch and lay her on her back then continued kissing her. I was right about this activity spicing up our relationship.

She slowly pushed me so I was sitting up then moved to the floor. I sat up, about to question her when she put her mouth on me. My entire body reacted to it, and my limbs grew limp as I surrendered to her.

As she pleasured me, my hips involuntarily moved. I'd never experienced anything like this in my life, and my brain felt like it had turned into mush. I couldn't speak or think. All I could processes was how amazing this felt.

Nicola didn't stop until I had my release, and she handled it like a pro. I finally opened my eyes, looking down at her and she smiled.

"I didn't expect you to taste like champagne," she said. "I could get used to this."

I picked her up once more, laying her on her back. She smiled and leaned forward, giving me a hard kiss. I tugged her closer to me and wrapped my arms around her as the kiss deepened. I felt light, as if my body no longer weighed anything and the electric bolts shot through every limb and even my fingers.

"Lucas," Nicola whispered. "Look around."

I glanced around the room and nearly had a heart attack. Everything, including the coffee table, TV, end tables, canvas, and lamps were floating at least two feet off the ground. Through further examination, I saw that the couch we were on was suspended in the air as well.

"You amazing. Lucas d'Aubigne," she said.

Nicola turned her attention back to me and as soon as her lips met mine, everything came crashing to the floor. The impact made us roll off the couch and I stood up. Unsure of what else to do, I grabbed my clothes and started getting dressed.

"I've never been able to do that before. I could make the objects shake but never get them to levitate. It was you who helped me."

She blushed then stood up as well. I was completely dressed and I wasn't really sure what to do with myself.

"You should tell your dad," she said. "He would want to know you're harnessing your abilities."

"Yeah, and what am I supposed to tell him? Hey dad, guess what! I was going to sleep with my girlfriend when we noticed everything was levitating."

Nicola laughed. "Oh wow, you're right. Better not tell him that you can access your power in the throws of passion."

Someone knocked on the door and I wondered who it was. Then I remembered the note. I opened the door and smiled when I saw Lela.

"Hey mom! What brings you here?"

"Cherish and I are going for a run. I thought you'd like to join."

I looked at Nicola and she smiled innocently. She knew as well as I did that if Lela knew what we were up to, we would get a major lecture. She was such a mom in that way.

"You go ahead and spend time with your mom. I want to finish the painting."

"Ooh! What are you working on?" Lela asked.

Nicola quickly blocked the way to her canvas and Lela looked suspicious.

"It's a surprise. I like to wait until I'm finished before I show people. Lucas can see because he's my muse."

I laughed and kissed her forehead. "I'll go change and meet you outside, mom."

Ten minutes later, we were in athletic gear and stretching on the sidewalk. I was kind of in awe when I saw Lela's calves. They were muscular from possibly years of running and even through her tank top, I could see that she had the workings of a six pack. She was serious about her exercise and I was glad I'd had some blood or else this was going to be a difficult workout.

Cherish, however, packed her muscle in other places. She had toned arms and gluts any woman would be jealous of. She wasn't the average woman you would see at the gym. She could inflict real pain.

"How far are we going?" I asked.

"Does Duncanville sound good?" Cherish asked.

"That's twenty minutes away in driving standards. It would take eight hours to walk there."

"Not if we're at our top speed," Lela said. "We could get there in fifteen minutes if we run as fast as we're capable. I've done it so many times I could do it blindfolded."

I believed her. I'd never really pushed my running ability because I never had the time. I was looking forward to this run. I wanted to spend time with my mom as well as find a way to let the levitation incident sink in.

Lela took off first and then we ran after her. She started out at a normal speed then gradually went faster until she would only appear as a blur to anyone who saw. I trusted that they'd preplanned a route that was discreet. I sped up until I'd caught up with her and she smiled at me. Gallard once told me that he only lost a race to her one time, but I was beginning to think he was exaggerating. It was taking everything in me to keep up.

We were out of Euless in less than five minutes and crossed Interstate thirty. It was a mind-blowing experience outrunning cars that were going seventy. I was going so fast that I could barely feel my feet touching the ground with each stride.

While I ran, I thought back to the moment I'd shared with Nicola, though I was supposed to be de-stressing. The memory of her kiss and her touch still made my heart race. I felt like I was floating instead of running. My whole body started to hum, just like when I healed Robin and Mona, and I closed my eyes.

I came out of my trance when I felt someone grab my leg and pull me down. My stomach did a flip from the fast movement and I crashed the ground. The two of us rolled for a while and then down into a ditch. Once the disorientation wore off, I looked over at Lela and Cherish.

"What just happened?" I asked.

"What happened?" Cherish said. "You were flying up in the air is what happened! I had to yank you out of the sky before anyone saw you!"

I was flying? I couldn't have been flying. I could when I was in animal form, but not while I was human. It must have been because I was thinking about Nicola. She'd been the one who helped me successfully use my levitation gifts. Could I also make myself fly?

"Mom, what's happening to me?"

She reached over and took my hand so she could help me stand. We didn't go anywhere for a while but remained silent. No wonder I couldn't even feel the ground before. It's because I wasn't even on it. My uncle gave me a lot more than just the ability to heal.

Though it was getting dark, we decided to walk home so we could talk. I confided in them about Colton's increasing strength and asked for parenting advice concerning his request to see Regina. Talking with Lela was like talking with a friend more than a mom, which made it so easy. It was like I'd known her my entire life. In a way, she reminded me of Mona.

"I think I can explain the flying thing," Lela said. "Lucian did the same thing after Maximus gave him his power. We were dancing and the next thing I knew we were up in the air."

"I wish I could have seen that," Cherish said. "But he'd used his power to block out everything to keep you hidden."

"That's right," I said. "I remember you wrote about it. I thought Maximus' power was destroyed when you gave him your blood."

Lela sighed. "So did I. None of it makes sense and I'm hoping your father can get some answers." She stopped walking and turned to me. "Do you resent your gifts? Do you ever wish that you hadn't been born with them?"

"No. And I regret ever giving my healing gift away. There were other ways I could have handled Arnaud's attack. I could have said something to Gallard sooner or . . . anything but what I did. I was protecting Colton. When he took that gift, I felt like he'd taken an arm or a leg. It feels like something's missing."

She smiled and took my hand in hers, walking closer to me. The gesture said it all— that she felt the same way when she was separated from me. I was miserable during those months they were gone and though I blocked out the years in between, I could recall the depression I'd felt all those years ago.

Lela stopped walking for a second and I stopped with her. We weren't in a hurry, but I was curious about why were stopped in the middle of Arlington. She squeezed my hand and smiled as she faced the house on the block.

"What is it?" I asked.

"I wanted to show you something." She pointed towards the house. "This is where your dad, David, and I lived back when I was fifteen. I may have lived in Miami during my childhood, but this is where I really grew up. Where I got to know your dad and where I fell in love with him."

I admired the house that had so much history. It wasn't too big, maybe two stories and had four steps leading to the door. The yard was small, but well kept. The driveway was slightly cracked and it was obvious no one had lived there in years.

"It's kind of creepy that you married your fake dad," I said. "You know that Robin dating your ex's son is bound to make you cross paths with Tyler sometime."

"Excuse me?" she and Cherish said simultaneously.

I knew I was busted. After Erik introduced himself to me, it clicked why his last name was so familiar. Back when Lela was in high school, she'd dated a guy named Tyler McPherson. She wrote about it in her journal and when she'd told him about what she was, he broke up with her and cut her out of his life. Fast-forward twenty-four years and the same guy's son had somehow made his way into our lives. I didn't want to say anything because I figured it would come up eventually.

"What do you mean Robin is *dating*?" Lela asked.

"She's not dating. She went on *a* date. They met earlier this week and now he's in love."

"Wow. That girl has a lot of explaining to do." Her annoyed expression softened. "Erik McPherson. I've always wondered what happened to him. J.D. was close with him in high school. I was worried about it at first, but no issues ever came up. He's a lot like his dad. Kind and considerate."

Our comfortable silence was interrupted when we heard a car approach. I thought maybe it was the owners who had come home, but they parked on the other side of the street. Three men got out of the car and I didn't recognize them. From their features, I could see they were night-walkers. The third man, I wasn't so sure about.

"Long time no see," the man first man said. He was tall, only a few inches shorter than me, and he had dark hair. The other two men were standing behind him as if he were their leader. I noticed he was looking past me, and I turned to see that his gaze on was on Cherish.

"What are you doing here, Simeon?" Cherish asked.

"Is that any way to greet your son?"

My eyes widened. "Son? You have a kid?"

"What the hell do you want?" Lela asked. "I thought we'd seen the last of you in Orlando."

"No, no, my pet. I have merely been biding my time before I pop in." He looked at me. "You must be Lela's son. Did they ever figure out who your father is?"

"State your business and get out of here!" Lela said. "You've done enough damage already."

"I need to speak with my mother. Alone."

Cherish rubbed her face with her hands then crossed her arms. I was still reeling from the fact that she was a mother. Lela never mentioned that bit in the journal. I did, however, remember something about a Simeon who tried to take advantage of her. If this was the same guy, I wouldn't want him anywhere near our family. Not after everything we'd been through with Nicola and Robin.

"Why can't we talk here?" Cherish asked. "Whatever you want to say to me can be said in front of my sister-in-law and nephew."

"Believe me, you will want to speak privately. Look, I'll take you to dinner and have you home by ten. What do you say, *mom*?"

I didn't feel comfortable letting her leave with this guy, son or not. He gave off a bad vibe and I was usually good about sensing when someone had bad intentions.

"Fine, I'll go," Cherish said.

"Cherish!" Lela protested. "You can't be serious!"

"Don't worry about me. I can handle myself."

She gave Lela's hand a reassuring squeeze then touched my shoulder before getting into the car. Simon nodded to Lela in goodbye then shot me a condescending glance as he got into the driver's seat. I kept my eyes on Cherish until I could no longer see them down the road.

"Should we be worried?" I asked Lela.

"Not sure yet. Come on, hon. If she's not home by ten, then we'll worry."

13

Nicola was doing something with J.D. and Robin so I used this opportunity to spend more time with my mom. Everyone else had gone out to dinner and we chose to stay in. I helped her make breakfast for dinner, which I learned was also a favorite of hers. We also shared a love of grape juice and Italian food. The more I got to know her, the more I could see we were definitely mother and child.

Once the food was cooked, we piled our plates then sat on the floor in the living room. We figured it was a good night for a *Jaws* marathon and she popped in the first one. Since we'd both seen it many times, we kept making commentary and talking throughout the film. Still, the uneasy feeling hadn't left since we got back. My mind kept going back to Cherish and I found myself checking the clock.

"You're worried about Cherish, aren't you?" Lela finally said.

"That obvious?" I set my plate on the coffee table then leaned back against the couch. "It was clear that her reunion with her son wasn't all rainbows and sunshine like it was when we reunited. What's the story there?"

"Where do I even start?"

She hugged her knees to her chest and grew quiet for a few moments. It must have been pretty bad if she was hesitant to talk about it. I had a bad feeling that this tale was going to be ugly, like when Robin told me what happened to her. While I waited for her to speak, I studied her face. In the dark, Lela appeared even younger than ever. I couldn't believe she was supposed to be forty years old. She looked like a young girl.

"Simeon Atherton went to college with my parents," she said. "They were really good friends and even stayed in touch for years after. I never met Simeon until I was thirteen. From the get-go I could tell something was off." She paused. "And then when I was fourteen, he tried to rape me."

It took everything in me not to lose it. I wanted to get up and go find Cherish and demand that she come home and get away from that monster. Why did the women in my family have to deal with all these perverts? It sickened me and I wanted to ring the neck of any man who dared harm those I loved.

"How did you get away?" I asked.

She smiled at looked at me. "Your father saved me. We hadn't known each other long, but he protected me like I mattered to him. I knew in that moment he would always hold a place in my heart. So anyway, after that happened I didn't see him again for five years. By then, he'd teamed up with Mark Sharmentino to try and expose vampires to the world. They did it for different reasons. Mark wanted to exterminate them because of what they did to my mother. Simeon wanted to stop hiding and try to take over the world or some stupid thing like that. In a way, they both failed and they both won. Vampires are now a target and the world knows we exist."

We sat in silence for a bit. It was amazing that this Simeon guy had played such a big part in the treatment of immortals. Because of him, they were being incarcerated all over the country and had little to no rights. We were now trying to clean up his mess and that somewhat pissed me off. If he hadn't been such an egomaniac, we could be living peacefully right now. I wouldn't have been taken away from my family and we wouldn't be on the run.

"What did he mean by that comment he made?" I asked. "About you finding out who my father is."

Lela laughed. "Oh, that. Well, back when I first found out I was pregnant, no one believed that you were conceived when your father was mortal. Everyone thought you were Lucian's. Lucian was the only one who knew Gallard was your father."

I frowned. "Why did they think it was Lucian?"

"They believed something happened between us that didn't. At the time, your father and I were having problems. Of course that was before I figured out it was really Lucian possessing his body. I got to a really low place then. But that was then and this is now." She smiled at me. "Now I have you, your father, and a wonderful extended family."

"Yeah, our family is pretty awesome."

She linked her arm through mine and rested her head on my shoulder. We finished the rest of the marathon in silence but it was a comfortable silence. Our time together was wonderful but also bittersweet. We had so much to make up for — twenty years to be exact. I would hate to miss that

83

much of Colton's life. No matter what it took, I wanted to make sure I was there for every big moment in his life.

14

It was finally Monday and Robin could barely contain her excitement. She hadn't seen Erik since their date, and she wanted to see his face again— to hold his hand and to hear his laugh. He was so kind and good to her. She even slept more soundly than she had in a while and it had been two days since she smoked. This was a good sign. Today, she was going to meet his family and she wanted to make a good first impression.

As she sat on the porch, she was surprised when her sister came out of her house along with her aunts. They were dressed for the weather and had bags as if they were planning to go somewhere. No one ever mentioned to her that they'd planned an outing.

"Are you ready to go?" Lela asked.

"Go where?"

"To the festival. Remember, we talked about going yesterday?"

Robin had forgotten and she'd also forgotten that she never told Lela that she planned to go with a date. Heck, Lela didn't even know she'd been on a previous date.

"I actually already have plans."

"Oh?" Lela's tone became suspicious. "With whom?"

She swallowed before answering. She knew Lela would find out eventually and now was as good of a time as ever to reveal her possible new relationship.

"He's really nice, Lela. He's funny and polite. He always holds the door for me, and he takes me for walks. He's twenty-four and he's a police officer."

The other women let out an impressed *ooh.*

"What's this dashing officer's name?" Melody asked.

"Erik McPherson."

Lela set her mouth in a straight line. "So I've heard."

"Uh oh . . ." Cherish said. "This is about to get awkward."

"Why?" Robin asked. "What's wrong?"

"It's not him so much as it is his father," Lela said. "Robin, I used to be engaged to *Tyler* McPherson when I was eighteen. When he found out I was a vampire, he broke it off and asked me to stay away from his family."

This wasn't what Robin was expecting. She was falling for the son of the same man who broke Lela's heart. Why hadn't she recognized the name? She'd heard the story before. Lela never bashed the guy, but her relationship with him had changed her life.

"When is he coming?" Lela asked to break the silence.

"He'll be here any minute."

"You can still call it off. I'll say you aren't feeling good and then when we keep turning him away, maybe he'll get the hint."

"What?" Robin said. "No! Don't make him go away. He's a nice man."

"I would hate to ask you to compromise a friendship because of something that has nothing to do with you, but I don't think it would be a good idea to be around him. He could easily trace you back to me."

"J.D. can be his friend, but I can't? That's a double standard and you know it. Besides, he's not a friend, Lela. I . . . I want to be with him like you are with Gallard." She held her head high with a confidence she'd never felt before. "I want to be his girlfriend. And if anyone has a problem with that, then I say too bad."

"Robin, are you sure you're ready for that kind of relationship?" Melody asked. "Being romantically involved is very messy. You don't need messy right now."

"Oh, come on guys!" J.D. said. "Let the girl go on her date. Erik's a great guy!"

Lela shook her head. "I'm sorry, Robin, but I'm sticking with my answer."

Robin's heart broke, and she tried not to cry as she went inside. She should have known this was going to happen. It didn't matter what Erik's last name was. She was sure her sister would find some way to keep her from seeing him. Because in her sister's eyes, Robin was still a child and she hated that people saw her that way.

When she heard Erik's truck rumbling, she peaked out the window between the curtains and watched him get out. Lela and Melody walked over to him and Robin could tell what her sister was saying by the disappointed expression on Erik's face. He gave Lela a polite smile and shook her hand before getting back in the truck. Tears stung her eyes as she wondered if that was the last time she would ever see him. She didn't even get to say goodbye.

Not feeling like doing much, she sat on the couch and drank tequila while she listened to sad music. After the others had left for the festival, she let herself cry for about a half hour before pulling herself together. She tried to watch TV but anything that even hinted at love or romance made her burst into tears. She was never going to experience that. Not if her family had anything to do with it.

Around ten o'clock someone knocked on the door then Abe came in. He had a bag of food in his hands, and he sat next to her on the couch. She was glad he came because she felt so lonely and she needed someone to vent to.

"J.D. told me what happened. She asked if I could check up on you. I brought McDonalds."

She smiled for the first time all morning. For being extremely cocky, Abe could be very sweet. Robin thanked him then took the food and ate it in small bites.

"She didn't even give him a chance," she said. "Lela is so convinced that Erik is just like Tyler, she judged him based on his last name. Besides, she thinks I'm five, just like Kevin does. I'm always going to be the five-year-old Robin that needs to be babysat."

"You know she is only trying to look out for you, babe. A gorgeous woman like you needs protection."

Robin blushed. "Yeah, but I wish she would worry less. She of all people should know what it's like to want someone to love her."

He nodded. "I wish I could say I understand, but I don't. I've been photographed and chased by companies my entire life. Several women have offered themselves to me, and I've never been turned down. Well, except by you."

Robin smiled. "Have I ever told you that you're kind of arrogant?"

"No. You're too nice."

"You should work on that. Maybe you could have a real girlfriend if you actually put as much effort into being a good person as you do making yourself look nice."

"Smart girl. Too bad Erik has to be without you this afternoon. I guess you're stuck with me. Not that it's much of a sacrifice. People used to pay money to be this close to me. And they don't even know I'm a Duke. I'm practically royalty."

She rolled her eyes, ignoring him. Talking with Abe distracted her from her disappointment, but it didn't change the fact that she wasn't at the festival where she wanted to be. If only she could be like J.D. and sneak around like she did with Lucian.

Her own thoughts formed a fanatical idea in her head. Lela had told her that she couldn't see Erik, but there wasn't really anything stopping her. What if she snuck into the festival to meet him without Lela's knowing? It would be so easy.

"What are you thinking?" Abe asked.

"I'm thinking I should follow my heart. My heart is saying Erik is a great guy and I shouldn't pass up the opportunity to be with him." She stood up from the couch. "I'm going to the festival."

"No offence, but defiance doesn't really become you."

"Well, it's going to have to. I respect Lela's opinion, but I am also entitled to my own."

"How do you plan to get here?"

Robin gave him her best puppy dog eyes. She was certain he wouldn't let her drive the Scion by herself, so the only other option was to have him drop her off. She had Erik's number and she could text him and figure out where he was. It was pure genius.

"No, not the sad eyes!" Abe said. He pinched the bridge of his nose for a moment then looked up at her. "All right. I will take you. But if anyone asks, you forced me at gun point."

Robin quickly put on her shoes and they were on the road five minutes later. She was so grateful to Abe for understanding her situation. Plus, sneaking around was fun. She'd never done anything bad or rebellious and she felt she was entitled to a little defiance since she'd missed the teenage years. It wasn't like she was out doing drugs or breaking the law. She was going to spend time with Erik and his family having good and innocent fun.

"Are you sure you don't want me to help you find him?" Abe asked after he parked.

"No, I'll be fine. Its daylight out, so I won't be in danger of getting snatched."

"Street racing, sneaking around, smoking. I think I like this side of you. It's kind of sexy."

Her heart lurched. How had he known about the smoking? She kept her packs in places no one could ever find them. Had he seen her?

"You thought I didn't know?" he asked. "I checked my credit card information to keep on my bill. It said the last purchase was at a Nicotine slot and you are the only person I let use that card."

"Why haven't you stopped me?"

He shrugged. "We all have our secrets.

Robin looked away for a moment. She still hadn't told anyone about the baby, and for some reason she really wanted to tell Abe. He was her best friend, after all. She didn't have to worry about him spreading her secrets around.

"Abe," she said.

"Yeah, babe?"

She dropped her gaze, looking down at her stomach. Today, she'd felt a little extra round so she'd made sure to wear something flowy.

"I . . . I, um. I mean. I'm —"

"Hey." He reached over, taking her hand. "It's okay. You can tell me anything."

Robin did her best to hold back her tears. "I'm . . . pregnant."

Abe went completely white, but he didn't stop holding her hand. At least a minute passed before he finally spoke again. She was afraid of hurting him, which was why she hadn't told him sooner. She knew how guilty he felt about what happened, and she didn't want this news to make him feel worse. She didn't blame him one bit. He couldn't have known what was going to happen that night.

"Robin . . . how long have you known?"

"A week." She swallowed, "I bought a pregnancy test at the store."

"But you . . . I mean it's been five months since . . . And you didn't know?"

"No one told me how I was supposed to know! I never knew anything about sex or how to get pregnant, it just happened!" She calmed down a bit. "I wasn't feeling well. I thought I had the flu, but then I started growing. So, I looked on the internet."

Abe groaned. "You had to find out on the internet? Why didn't you ask me?"

Her cheeks flushed. "I . . . I was embarrassed. I felt stupid for not knowing."

He squeezed her hand. "You listen to me. You aren't stupid. I will never, ever make you feel stupid. If you want to know something, just ask and I will tell you with no judgment. Okay?"

She nodded. "Okay."

Abe winked. "That being said, are you sure you want to keep it? If Erik finds out, he might not be as cool about it as I am. It's a lot to throw on a dude you've barely dated."

"I hadn't thought of that." She sighed. "What if . . . he thought it was his? Would it be different?"

He shrugged. "I don't know, babe. You're pretty far along. He's not going to buy it when you give birth three months from now."

"Then let me tell him when I'm ready. Please? I want to handle this at my pace. For now, I want to enjoy what little time I have left with Erik."

"Just don't wait too long, babe. If you need anything don't hesitate to call. I will be around here, probably annoying my sister."

"Thanks, Abe."

She paid the entrance fee and began searching for Erik. He would probably be working right now so she would have to look in places where a police officer might be. It helped that the uniforms were dark so she could spot them easily.

Twenty minutes passed and she still hadn't found him. She'd circled the entire area, passing by every booth and every ride. The food area was crowded and had a few officers at each corner but none of them were Erik. She was worried that it would be night fall before she found him, and she didn't feel comfortable being there alone in the dark.

Her last option was to ask one of the other officers. They would probably know where he was. Other police still made her nervous, but there wasn't much else she could do. She spotted one standing next to a booth selling homemade beer. He appeared friendly so she built up the courage to approach him.

"Excuse me, officer, can I ask you something?"

"Sure. What can I do you for?"

She unintentionally assessed him. He was more muscular than Erik and had light brown hair and violet eyes. He reminded her of Aaron. When Lela told Robin how Aaron had been the one to turn her and that he'd later tried to kill Lela and Lucas, she didn't know how she should feel. She'd always loved Aaron and hearing that he'd turned against the family broke her heart.

"I'm looking for Officer Erik McPherson. Do you know where he is?"

"I happen to know exactly where he is. Follow me and I'll take you to him."

He left his post and she followed him. Why hadn't she asked someone before? It would have saved her a lot of walking and she already would have been with him. But the anticipation of seeing him was almost as great as actually going to meet him.

Erik stood next to the security headquarters with a bottle of water in his hand. She spotted him before he spotted her. He was talking to some brunette woman who had a baby in arms. He looked slightly morose and she wondered if it was because of the canceled plans. Well, they weren't canceled anymore.

Robin practically sprinted towards him. He locked eyes with her then flashed his handsome smile. He was wearing his police uniform, but it didn't bother her anymore because all she saw was the man behind it — the man who would never hurt her or humiliate her like the other officers had.

"Hi, beautiful!" he said.

She blushed and gave him a hug. This was the first time she'd ever hugged him and when he put his arms around her, nothing ever felt better.

"I thought you weren't feeling well."

"I had a slight case of Overprotective Sister. Nothing a small dose of Defiance couldn't cure. Abe helped me get here."

"You sneaky little thing. I'm glad you decided to come because my family was just as disappointed when I said you had to cancel. So, are you excited to meet the McPherson brood?"

She gave him a nervous look and he laughed. He took her hand in his and kissed it.

"It'll be fine. They're going to love you. I've never introduced a woman to my parents before, but I know I'm making the right choice. They said they are by the bull-riding arena. I work until five, and then I'll come rescue you." He stopped and turned to face her. "Are you sure you're okay with this?"

"Of course. I want to meet your family. And I can't wait until I can spend time with you too."

He smiled and rested his hands on her waist, pulling her closer to him. By the spark in his eyes, she could tell he wanted to kiss her, and this time she was ready for it. He leaned down until his lips were an inch away from hers and she closed her eyes. She could feel his breath on her face, but he never touched her because a loud man disrupted them.

"Hey Rick! What are you dilly dallying for?"

"I still have a half an hour, James. Go bother someone else," Erik said.

"Like who?"

The officer that had helped her find Erik kissed the woman with the baby and then kissed the infant's bald head. She never would have guessed the two were connected.

"Why didn't you tell me you were dating Broom Girl?" the man asked.

"*Broom Girl?*" Robin asked.

"You're kind of famous at our department," Erik said. "James, Emily – this is Robin. Robin, this is James, my partner, his wife Emily, and their son Miles. He's my best friend, but don't tell anyone."

Robin shook both of their hands and smiled at the baby. She loved babies but no one in her family had any. She was the youngest for so long and now the smallest person in her circle was Colton and he was four. Little Miles giggled and took his feet in his hands, holding them up in the air.

"Well, I left my post, so I'll catch you later," James said. "See ya, Rick. Em, I'll meet you and your parents at the parade later."

Once James had walked away, Erik held her hand again and they continued walking.

"Why don't you want anyone to know he's your friend?" Robin asked.

"He's a good guy, but his family doesn't like me. His dad hates my dad because . . . you know what, that's not important. Let's get you safely to my family, okay?"

When she spotted his family, she instantly knew he belonged to them. Happiness radiated from them like a beacon of light. The mother was short and had chestnut blonde hair and green eyes. The two daughters had the same color of hair but had blue eyes. One was short and the other was the same height as the mother.

"Ma, hey!" Erik said. He gave her a hug then motioned a hand towards Robin. "Look who showed up after all."

"Oh my gosh, Erik! She's adorable! I'm Amanda McPherson. You must be Robin."

"I am. It's so nice to meet you, Mrs. McPherson."

She laughed. "Please, call me Amanda. Or better yet, call me Mandy. Girls. Girls!" she waved over the two young women by the fence. They cheerfully came over and smiled at Robin. "These are Erik's sisters." She rested her hand on the shoulder of the shorter one. "This is Nadia, my middle child. She's seventeen and the other is Imogen, she's fourteen and my baby. Girls, this is Robin Shepherd, your brother's girlfriend."

"Mom, we've only been on one date," Erik said.

"It doesn't matter, we know she's a keeper already," Imogen said. "After what happened with J.D., you need to act fast. If you don't marry her, I will just so she can stick around."

"Immy!" Amanda said.

"It's okay," Robin said. "J.D.'s my good friend. Her uncle is married to my sister."

That was downplaying it. J.D. never mentioned anything happening between her and Erik. Either she'd failed to bring it up or she hid it from Robin on purpose to eliminate awkwardness. It didn't matter anymore. The cat was out of the bag.

"Oh?" Amanda looked at Erik. "You never mentioned that."

"It's how we met. She introduced us."

"Go do your job," Nadia said. "We'll take *real* good care of Broom Girl."

He rolled his eyes. "Don't call her that. I should never have started that." He looked around. "Where's dad?"

"Avoiding Mayor Chase Newbury," Amanda said. "I saw his daughter-in-law earlier."

"Yeah so did we," Erik said. "Well, I should go. I'll see you later, beautiful."

He winked at Robin before disappearing into the crowd and his sisters surrounded her, giggling and laughing. Robin wanted to do the same thing, but she was still working on breaking out of her bubble. She didn't used to be a shy person. She was the kind of girl who would happy strike up a conversation with a random stranger on the street. Not anymore.

"Come on," Imogen said. "I'm starving, and I bet you are too. Our dad is by the chili dog stand."

Robin allowed the two girls to link arms with her and they walked in the direction of the food trolleys with their mom not too far behind. There were so many food options that Robin felt overwhelmed. There was a truck that sold chicken and waffles, there was a van that had Chinese food, and there was another truck that had clam chowder.

"You're so quiet," Nadia said. "Do you not like to talk?"

"I do. I'm just nervous."

"Was it Immy's comment about your friend? It's not as serious as it sounds. Erik had a thing for her, but she only saw him as a friend. He moved on and now he has you. It all worked out perfectly."

"Exactly," Imogen said. "You should meet our dad. He'll ease your nerves in a heartbeat. His teddy bear-like personality is what won him the sheriff election."

Robin stopped in her tracks. "Wait. Your dad is *sheriff*? As in the boss of the police department?"

The sisters laughed. "Yeah," Imogen said. "Didn't Erik tell you?"

If Robin was nervous before, she was terrified now. Not only would she have to try and expel any suspicion that she was connected to Lela, or rather Diane Fontaine, but now she had to hide the suspicion from the sheriff. If he ever found out who she was, he could investigate into her family and find out that they were all vampires. They could be run out of town, or worse—arrested.

"Robin, don't worry!" Nadia said. "I told you — daddy's a teddy bear. If Erik loves you, he'll love you too."

They approached the hot dog stand and Robin held her breath. and Robin held her breath. The smell wasn't doing anything for her upset stomach, and it was taking all her willpower not to vomit. She was also completely nervous about meeting Erik's dad, even if he had the reputation of being a teddy bear.

Nadia let go of her arm and tapped on the shoulder of a man who was talking with someone else in line. He said goodbye to the acquaintance then looked at Robin. She saw a lot of Erik in him. They had the same kind eyes and friendly demeanor. Robin was impressed that he still had all his hair since most men his age showed signs of a receding hair line.

But when he looked into her eyes, his smile left. She began to panic and figured she'd been made. She looked a lot like Lela, only she resembled their mother more while Lela resembled David. Could he really notice the resemblance?

"Daddy, this is Robin," Imogen said. "Robin, this is my dad and the Sheriff of Euless, Tyler McPherson."

"It's a pleasure to meet Broom Girl," Tyler said. She held out her hand and when he took it, he looked at their joined hands for the longest time then brought his eyes up to hers. "Have we met before?"

"Daddy!" Nadia said. "Of course you haven't. She just moved here a few months ago, remember?"

"Right." He continued to stare into her eyes and oddly enough, it wasn't making her uncomfortable. To her, his eyes looked like they had a deep sadness that someone could only see if they'd experienced something heartbreaking.

"Okay, now that we're all acquainted, why don't you join us at the rodeo?" he said, his mood changing.

"I would love to, Mr. McPherson. I mean *Sheriff* McPherson."

"Erik was right, you're so polite. You may call me Tyler. I'm only sheriff to criminals."

Nadia and Imogen pulled her away, chatting away about anything and everything. Tyler didn't act strangely around her anymore, so Robin wrote it off as her own paranoia. He wasn't someone she couldn't trust. Lela said that he was a good guy and that the only reason he'd broken up with her was because he couldn't handle the truth of what she was. Robin wasn't a vampire anymore, but that wasn't really something that needed to be told.

Robin sat between the sisters during the rodeo and did her best to pay attention. The bull riders were impressive, and the equestrians were beautiful in their sparkly boots and sequined hats. By their skill, Robin guessed that they'd been practicing for years.

It made her wish that she hadn't had twenty-two years of her life robbed from her. She was too old to try to get good at something. She'd been tutored by Danielle and now by Melody, but what she really wanted was to get her GED and go to college. No one would let her, though. They wanted to keep her in a little box and never let her really experience life. It was even a wonder that they didn't snatch her license away.

When the rodeo ended, the family moved on to play games. Robin didn't participate, but rather enjoyed watching the two sisters as they competed against each other. Tyler stood next to her in silence, and she found herself feeling less nervous around him than before. There was no way he could link her to her sister.

"Erik tells me that you're from Miami," he said. "Must have been a tough place to live."

"At times. There was a lot of crime and it's not safe to go out after dark. It's different here. I'm not as afraid and it's peaceful."

He nodded in agreement. "I had the option of going to college, but my heart was in law enforcement. I wanted to save people. So, I finished with my associates degree then applied to be in the academy. I was an officer for fifteen years before I ran for Sheriff." He turned to her. "What about you? Ever think of a career in law enforcement, *Broom Girl?*"

Robin never really thought about a possible career. She was just trying to get through her high school studies. Would she really be good at the job? She may have stopped one criminal, but she was still afraid. Her assault had made her extremely timid and she would probably freeze in the line of danger.

"I don't think so. I'm not very strong."

"Then you should consider a desk job. You don't have to leave the comfort of your office and you don't have to be out in the field where it's dangerous."

"Tyler, are you trying to recruit her?" Amanda said.

Tyler pulled her to his side. "You know it. I'm still trying to put together that task force. After the recent crimes, Chase finally agrees that we can't get by with just a few trained officers. SAITF is going to start breathing down our necks. Besides, we could use more women in the force. There's too much testosterone around the office."

"But we need big strong men to take care of this place. It's your guys that keep this town safe from vampires."

A lump formed in Robin's throat. These were the words that she'd been dreading the entire night. He was for the eradication of vampires. That probably meant that Erik was too. She could feel their relationship crumbling before her. If he found out about her family, nothing would stop him and his dad from taking them away from her.

"Not completely. That parasite that killed those kids is still out there. I really shouldn't have taken the day off."

"Yes, you should have," Amanda said. "You've been working long hours the past few weeks and you owe it to yourself to relax. You can't solve the case if you're exhausted."

The girls cheered as they finished the game and the three of them turned their attention to the giant stuffed animal that Nadia received. She could barely carry it, so Tyler offered. The conversation switched to something more pleasant, but Robin still had her mind on what he'd said. The hard part was that she had a feeling that she knew why he felt this way about vampires. Maybe Lela wasn't the only one who'd suffered a broken heart from their breakup.

15

A chunk of ice cream plopped onto Colton's shirt and Nicola laughed as she tried to wipe it off. I'd worked at the festival all morning and was just now joining my two, favorite people. Nicola informed me that Colton was having so much fun on the rides that he didn't even want to stop for a food break. He needed something in his system, so we convinced him to have ice cream, which led to tricking him into having a hot dog as well. He'd begged us to let him get a big cone and it was melting faster than he could eat it.

"I'm sorry, Nicola," he said. "I didn't mean to ruin my new shirt."

"That's okay, bud. It's nothing a little Tide won't cure." She scooped off the blob in one swipe. "There. It's a good thing you ordered vanilla."

"I did because I knew I would spill."

I smiled as I watched them interact. Nicola had been right about us really needing family time. I hadn't been this happy in a very long time and spending the day with the woman I loved and our son was just what I needed. I was getting closer to Nicola as well since she'd been staying over every night. I was beginning to feel like we were a married couple, which was a good thing.

Colton finished the last bit of his ice cream then stood up from the bench. I could see in his eyes that he was ready to get back to the rides, but I wanted him to let his food settle so he wouldn't vomit.

"Hey, bud, why don't you go on that horse ride first?" I suggested.

"Okay!"

Nicola and I each took one of his hands and we headed in the direction of the ring. We still hadn't run into anyone else in my family, but I hoped

I would catch Robin. Not that I didn't trust Erik to take care of her, but I was still concerned.

We found the arena and arrived just in time for the previous ride to end. I let Nicola walk Colton over to the ride and the carnie helped him onto the pony. Colton looked so happy up there in his riding helmet. I took a picture with my phone then sent it to Lela. I felt like such a dad in that moment, but it was a good feeling. I was starting to get comfortable in that role and I could see that Nicola loved being a mom.

She came back over to me and we watched as the carnie commanded the ponies to start walking in a circle. I slipped my hand into hers and rubbed my thumb against her knuckles. I hadn't told her yet, but I'd made plans for Colton to spend the night with Lela. It wasn't hard to convince him since Kevin was over there too. He wasn't due to move back until the investigation was over and I was a little confused about why no one had stopped by to respond to the supposed vampire activity.

Tonight, I wanted to forget about those worries and try a redo of my romantic night with Nicola, and this time I would propose. Before he left, David had given me his mother's wedding ring. In case I would need it, he'd said. It had been sitting in my drawer since then and I felt like this was the perfect time to use it.

"You're good with him," I said. "You're making everything easier. I think you fill that hole that Mona left."

The smile left her face and she squeezed my hand. We didn't talk about her much, but when we did, either one of us or both of us would start crying. Colton had taken it hard when he learned Mona was gone and couldn't come back. Regina and Scott had tried to sugar coat it since they'd believed that he was too young to understand death and when I'd come back, he thought that it meant Mona could as well. When I'd explained it to him, he fell apart and cried for hours.

"I miss her so much," Nicola said. "And poor Micah is dealing with this alone. When they told me you took your life, my mom kept me from falling apart. She was there for me and I am so lucky that I had her."

"And I'm lucky that I have you, Nic. I wouldn't get through losing Mona or leaving Micah behind without you. You and Colton both are keeping me together. I love you for that."

She wrapped her arms around me and gave me a soft, tender kiss. We kept it subtle so we wouldn't be *that* couple that made out in front of everyone. I felt more love in this kind of kiss than any other we shared.

"I need a hit," she said. "Could you cover while I drag one of the carnies behind the ring toss tent?" My eyes widened and she laughed. "I'm kidding, Luke! I have a little bottle in my bag. I'm going to drink it in the bathroom. Hold my jacket for me?"

I took her jacket from her and kissed her cheek as she walked off. Her joking about her vampirism was a good sign. We'd talked about it a lot over the past few days and she assured me she would make a better effort at making the best of her situation. I wanted to support her but I didn't want her to pretend to be happy either. We would have to take it one day at a time but J.D.'s theories were always popping up in my head when I least wanted them

Her jacket vibrated, and I discerned someone was texting her. I took her phone out of her pocket and looked at who it was. It was a message from Ryan saying, *A little bird told me you would be at the festival. If we don't bump into each other, you should check out the local artist's booth. It's quite impressive.*

Out of curiosity, I opened the message and started scrolling up to read what they'd been talking about previous to that. I felt kind of guilty invading on her privacy, but I was concerned.

One conversation stood out to me. He said, *Since there are more students, I was thinking I would add an extra day so it's not so crowded*, to which she replied, *I'm available for whenever you need me.* He replied with, *You're a great teacher and probably my favorite part of the class too. I should have hired you weeks ago.* She never responded to that and the next message from him was the one he'd just sent.

I heard Nicola come up behind me, so I put the phone back just before she took her jacket back.

"You know, you look really hot in your uniform," she said.

"Thanks." I hugged her to my side. "I'm thinking of changing before the parade so people don't think I'm on duty."

"Is he still on the pony?" she asked. I nodded. "Wow, that's a long ride."

"I think he might have gone back for a second one. So, these art classes. You never talk about them. How are they so far?"

"They're great! I like teaching with Ryan. He took art classes in Italy. He's very talented."

"I see. How many people are in your class?"

"Two. But there were more people on Thursday, so there were three of us all together."

"Ever do one-on-one sessions?"

"It was just Ryan and me on Tuesday, but it wasn't weird or anything. We listened to the radio and practiced mixing colors."

"Uh huh." I decided to just be completely honest. "He texted you by the way. Said something about how you're the best part of his day." I looked her in the eye. "Am I going to have to pay him a visit?"

A flash of horror flooded her gaze. "Lucas, please don't. He flirts with me, but I don't respond to it. It's innocent, I swear."

"Really? It looks like he texts you quite a bit. More than I do."

She fought a smile. "Lucas, are you jealous?"

"No, I'm not jealous. I'm annoyed. I don't feel comfortable with you spending time with a man who makes advances on you."

"But it's okay for single mothers to flirt with you at school?"

"That's different and you know it. I don't get constant text messages about how wonderful they think I am, and I don't spend hours alone with them."

I could see she was getting irritated as well. Her eyes flashed to the grey for a moment.

"I told you we had one session with the two of us. One. The rest of the time I've taught a class on my own, and we switch off every other day." Her gaze softened a bit and she took my hands. "Don't worry about him, Lucas. I love *you* and nothing is going to change that."

While we were walking, I got a text from Lela. She asked if we wanted to meet up for the parade and Nicola said she would like that. We'd had our family day and I didn't mind joining everyone else. They were family too.

Out of the corner of my eye, I noticed that Nicola was looking incredibly sad. She probably didn't know I was paying attention. Though she was next to me, her eyes showed that she was far away.

"Hey. What's wrong?"

"I'm not feeling that great, to be honest. I think it was something I ate."

I frowned in confusion. If she was drinking blood regularly, her body should have been insusceptible to sickness, like mine was. I hadn't had so much as a sneeze after I changed my diet and she was a first-generation day-walker. She would be even more immune than either Lela or Gallard.

"Talk to me, what's really going on?"

"I just feel sick. I'm going to head home." She glanced over at the pony ride. "Tell him I'm sorry I had to go. You have fun at the parade."

She gave me a lingering kiss. It wasn't loving or passionate. It felt forced, and I didn't like the dread forming in my mind.

Since it was dark, she was able to disappear at lightning speed without anyone being able to see. With her absence, came the same depression I'd experienced when we'd broken up over a stupid fight. Only this time, it was her secrets that were breaking *my* heart. Whatever had caused her mood change, it wasn't a bad reaction to carnie food.

I took a deep breath before hurrying over to the ride. It had just ended, and the kids were getting off. I kept my eye out for his shirt, but I didn't see him anywhere. All the children returned to their parents, and I watched a new set of kids get onto the ponies. He was nowhere to be seen.

"Colton?" I scanned the crowd for his yellow shirt. "Colton, where are you?"

I jogged ahead and checked the lines of every ride I came across. I checked the ring toss and then resorted to looking in the bathrooms. He was nowhere to be found I was starting to panic. I'd never lost him before and this wasn't the first time I'd taken him into a big crowd. I'd been so distracted with worrying about Nicola that I wasn't paying attention.

I tore out of the bathroom and continued looking everywhere. "Colton!"

"Excuse me," someone said.

I turned around to see a man holding Colton's hand. I recognized him as Simeon, Cherish's son. Colton looked terrified so I quickly picked him up and hugged him close to me.

"Do you know how scared I was!" I said, trying not to shout. "I thought I'd lost you for good!"

"I'm sorry. Nicola looked sad, and I wanted to win a prize to make her feel better."

I turned my attention back to Simeon "Thank you. I appreciate your helping my son." My heart lurched. "Brother. I mean my brother."

By Simeon's expression, I knew he'd caught on to my Freudian slip. It didn't matter, though. Colton was back with me, and I never intended on letting him wander off again. I should have been more careful. I hadn't been that careless when I was just his brother. The last time I had been this panicked was when he'd fallen out of the boat during a fishing trip we'd taken back when he was three, and I never wanted to feel that again.

"No problem, Lucas. I understand what it's like to worry about a child. My son went missing twenty-three years ago. To this day, I wonder what happened to him."

My heart sank at that thought, and I tightened my grip on Colton's hand. I couldn't imagine having Colton taken away for twenty minutes let alone twenty years.

"You are Cherish's nephew," Simeon continued. "She spoke highly of you when we conversed the other night. Are you close?"

I nodded. I wasn't about to go into my relationship with her with this man. I didn't know if he had ill intentions or if he was a friend or foe. Cherish never spoke of that night with any of us. He was creepy, and even Colton felt uneasy around him.

"Then we're practically family." He smiled. "Shall I call you cousin?"

I raised an eyebrow. "No."

"No?"

I covered Colton's ears before I spoke. He didn't need to hear what I would say to Simeon.

"You think you can show up here and pretend you want to be family? I know what you did, you bastard. I know what you did to my mom, and you're lucky my dad didn't finish you off that day. I don't care that you're Cherish's son. Scum like you have no place in my world. So do us all a favor and leave town."

Simeon's eyes flared with wrath, but he didn't show it in his body language. He remained calm. I almost expected him to make a move.

"Glad we could chat. I will leave you to the festival," he said. He turned to leave then stopped. "Oh, and tell Nicola that I adore her painting. She should model more often."

Chills went up my spine as he walked away. And how did he know about Nicola? How had he known about that painting? Sure, it resembled her a lot but how would he connect it to her?

I texted Lela to find her location then headed in that direction. I wanted to tell Cherish about my run in with her son and warn her to keep an eye out. I had a feeling Simeon wasn't going to listen to my warning.

I set Colton down but held onto his hand tightly. I wasn't about to let him get lost again, and I was angry at myself for that. We were almost to Lela and the others when I was surprised to see Terrence, Abe, and Kevin coming my way. It was well after sundown, so they could be out. I didn't think a southern festival was Terrence's scene.

"Hey, guys," I said. "What are you doing here?"

"There is literally nothing to do in Euless, so I we popped in here," Terrence said. "Where's the mamma?"

"You mean mine or . . ." I signaled at Colton with a subtle nod.

"Yours. I'm trying to keep my distance. Don't want her to body slam me or damage my ego."

"What's an ego?" Colton asked. "Are you talking about the waffles?"

The four of us laughed. It helped having Colton with me. He was soothing my anxiety over Nicola's sudden departure. Eventually, I would have a serious talk with her, but I wasn't about to hash it out in the middle of a festival.

They decided to follow me to find the other women, despite Terrence's apparent feud with Lela. We found them next to a bar tent, each with a beer in hand and some cowboys in tight shirts were flirting with them. From far away, I could hear that Melody and J.D. were trying to imitate their southern accents and were failing miserably. They sounded like they were from a different country and not one that was in the U.K.

"Lucas!" Lela said. "Glad you're here. Where's Nicola?"

"She went home with a headache and Colton wasn't ready to leave. We found some strays along the way."

"Some very, very hot strays." Terrence waggled his eyebrows at Melody who flipped him off, and I had to cover Colton's eyes. I was pretty sure he'd seen and heard worse from being around Henry, but I was trying to maintain as much of his innocence as possible.

"The only thing hot here is your pants," J.D. said. "How are you not dying? I couldn't even wear jeans in this weather."

"Vampire, sweetheart. No heartbeat, no sweat glands. We're lucky that we can even cry."

"Hey, have any of you by chance seen Cherish?" Melody asked. "She was supposed to come back with elephant ears fifteen minutes ago."

"It seems the redheads have made a run for it," Abe said. "They're probably plotting world domination."

A loud yell pierced the air, and I honed my hearing to discern where it was coming from. It was too muffled for human ears to hear because no one else besides my group reacted. This didn't sound like a couple of teenagers having fun. This was a scream of terror and I couldn't ignore it.

The sound had come from the bleachers near the rodeo arena. I handed Colton to Lela who understood what I was thinking. I rushed off with Kevin and Terrence close behind me. Lela was capable of helping, but Gallard made her promise to stay out of trouble since it seemed to find her. Melody didn't like violence, so the two men were my only other option for back up.

I smelled the blood before I saw anything. Everyone else was still trying to find the source of the screams, so we were the first ones to arrive there. I ducked under the bleachers and froze when I saw Nicola kneeling over a man. He was conscious and slightly shaking, but his throat was bleeding profusely. I didn't need to ask to know what had happened.

"I didn't mean to," Nicola said. "I was . . . so thirsty."

I couldn't move, so Terrence took initiative and ran off to alert someone that we needed an ambulance then Kevin rushed in to take him from Nicola. He carried him around the corner, leaving Nicola and me alone.

"I thought I was under control," she said. "I don't know what came over—"

"You don't have to explain, Nic. You slipped up, it happens." I heard footsteps coming our way. "You need to get out of here."

"Lucas, I'm sorry I—"

"Go! I'll handle this."

She hurried under the bleachers and disappeared then I let out a long exhale, raking my hands through my hair. This was a mess. It would be easy to explain to the police what happened without incriminating myself. I was still in uniform. But the only problem was there was a victim who saw everything and was still very much alive.

Once the initial shock wore of, I went to go help Kevin and found him standing there shaking. I took the man from him before he would drop him.

"I'm sorry," Kevin said. "There's too much blood. I don't trust myself."

"Don't worry about it. I'll get him help."

I hurried to the first security station and they called an ambulance. While we waited, the onsite medical response team put gauze on the man's throat and wrapped him in a blanket so he wouldn't go into shock. The sheriff arrived first and he started asking me questions. He had blonde hair and blue eyes, like mine, but he appeared to be in his forties.

I met Sheriff Tyler McPherson on my first day on the job. I'd immediately recognized his name from Lela's journal, and I felt guilty that I hadn't told her I was working for her ex. He was a great guy, just like she described and a great boss. We rarely ever spoke but when we did, he was always friendly. When he saw me, he reached out and shook my hand.

"I hear you were the first to respond," he said. "You're the new guy, right? Cadet d'Aubigne."

I tried not to act nervous. This man didn't know that I knew exactly who he was or that his son was kind of dating my aunt. Even more importantly, that his ex-girlfriend was here as well. There was no way he could connect me to Lela, or as he knew her, Diane Fontaine.

"Is he going to be okay?" I asked.

"Thanks to you and your friend, yes. Do you mind if I ask you a couple of questions?"

I cooperated and answered everything he asked. I had to lie of course, but I felt like I was convincing. I told him that he was lying on the ground bleeding and that the assailant had disappeared too quickly for me to see if it was a man or a woman.

Once all the commotion died down, the man was driven away in an ambulance. I stuck around in case there was anything else I needed to be asked. Taking off would appear suspicious and I wanted to be as unsuspicious as possible. Sheriff McPherson spoke with a few other officers then came back over to me.

"Normally I pay more attention, but I've had my hands so full with work that I hardly have time to get to know my new employees. How long have you been an officer?"

"Two months. I'm still in the training process and doing ride-alongs."

"I see. Did you go to college?"

"I have a bachelor's degree in criminal justice and was accepted into Yale but deferred for medical reasons. I did the police academy thing because I had family in the business, but I wanted to defend people instead. Changed back to my original plan after I moved."

"Hmm." Tyler grew quiet for a while then said. "These medical issues. Are they still a problem?"

"No, it was a fixable thing. I could have gone to Yale, but I have other priorities right now that require me to be close to my family."

"I'm sorry if I'm being intrusive. I promise there's a reason behind my questions. I've been speaking with Trooper Beau Hawes and he was raving about your heroism the other night. You saved his life. Anyway, I would like to offer you a new position on the force."

I raised an eyebrow. This man who had history with my family was offering me a job? I already had one. All he knew was that I'd gotten into Yale and that I saved a fellow officer, just like anyone else would do.

"What sort of job?" I asked.

"Why don't you stop by my office tomorrow and find out? What time are you free?"

"I drop my son off at school at eight. Does eight-thirty work?"

"That's perfect." He shook my hand again. "It was good to meet you again, Cadet. I look forward to our meeting."

Considering my mom's reaction to Robin going out with Erik, she probably wouldn't be too keen on my working with his father. I would keep this job interview to myself until further notice. In the meantime, I needed to speak with Nicola about what had happened and figure out how to help her.

"Hey," Kevin said. "Abe just told me that Robin is here as well. Do you know anything about that?"

"I thought you knew she was here. Oh well, I guess it doesn't matter either way. Go check on her, I'm going to talk to Lela and then head home."

16

Robin's thoughts were interrupted when someone wrapped their arms around her middle and gently squeezed her. She smiled in surprise and turned around to see Erik smiling down at her. He'd worked way past five o'clock, but she understood that he had to do his job. Their time apart was worth seeing him again.

"Miss me?" he asked.

She hugged him back then he lifted her off the ground and swung her in a circle.

"Yes, I did! Your family was really fun, though. Nadia kept winning the ring toss and won eight goldfish."

"They almost had to use force to get her to leave some fish for the other people," Amanda chimed in. "Why did your shift last so long?"

"Some idiots were jacked up on crank. We had to haul them to the station, and I was the lucky guy who got to debrief. I had to do a strip search and you don't want to know where some of them were hiding their stash." He shuddered. "But I'm back now."

He sank down to the blanket, taking Robin with him and slipped his fingers through hers. His family had just settled in their spot for the parade and now that Erik was here, everything was perfect. She loved being here with him, holding his hand and feeling close and protected by him. She hadn't seen a parade in a long time and was excited to see the floats.

She turned to see Tyler coming up the sidewalk and he whispered a few words to Amanda. He seemed on edge and worried about something. He then caught Erik's eye and started speaking to him.

"I think I found someone for that position today," Tyler said.

"Really?" Erik asked. "I thought you were waiting another week. Did you clear it with the city council?"

"I'm hoping to clear it with them tomorrow. Chase is on board, shockingly. It's about time it was done, don't you think? If everything goes the way I've planned, that vampire will be caught by the end of the month."

"Does he know what he's getting himself into?"

"Not a clue. I ran into him by chance. He was reporting a crime and I offered him a job. You may know him. Cadet Lucas d'Aubigne."

Robin turned to Erik who had a look of recognition in his eyes. Erik's dad offered Lucas a job? Why would he do that? There was no way he could know that he was her nephew, or rather her cousin.

"Hey, Robin, isn't that your cousin?" Erik asked.

"Brother-in-law, actually."

Tyler's phone rang and he answered it. Robin didn't listen to the conversation, but after he ended the call, he stood up.

"I'm really sorry, but I have to go. Duty calls."

"You need me?" Erik asked.

"No, you already put in your time today. I'll get someone else."

"Be safe, Ty," Amanda said. "I love you."

He leaned down and kissed her then pecked each of his daughters on the head before heading down the street. It must be hard for his family for him to have to run off unexpectedly. Robin knew the feeling since her dad and Gallard were often away.

Faint music started playing along with the beating of drums and everybody began cheering. Robin was glad their attention had switched to something else. The first group that went through was the Lyndon High School drill team. They did a synchronized march while the band played and parents cheered from the sidelines. The cheerleaders did back flips and fancy routines.

A horse-drawn carriage was coming up when she spotted people she recognized. Abe and Kevin were walking down the path, looking around as if they were searching for someone. She knew they were looking for her, so she pulled her hood over her head, which wasn't easy. Her curls made it fall, but she kept trying.

"You cold, beautiful?" Erik asked, rubbing her arms to create friction.

"No, I'm hiding." She glanced at Kevin and they made eye contact. "Don't look now, but my brother is here."

Kevin and Abe jogged over to her and she ignored them. She wasn't in the mood for getting scolded.

"Robin?" Kevin said.

"Go away. I'm on a date."

She prayed that Kevin wouldn't get into an argument or make a scene like he'd done at the bar.

"Is everything okay, Robin?" Amanda asked.

"He's my brother. And Abe is—"

"I'm her ex," he said with a smug smile. Kevin punched him in the arm, and the stupid smile left his face. "Okay, I'm not. I'm Kevin's ex."

Even Robin couldn't hold in a laugh at that one. But when she saw Erik's face, she stopped smiling. He was giving the two men an interrogative look. Did he really believe Abe?

"Well, if you're friends of Robin's you're welcome to stay," Amanda said.

"That's kind of you, but I only stopped by so I could speak with my sister for a moment," Kevin said. "I just need to borrow her for a minute and I'll let you enjoy the rest of the festival."

Robin sighed then stood up and followed her brother and Abe away from Erik's family. Kevin looked nervous and was keeping his distance from her. He had his hands in his pockets and she noticed he hadn't removed them at all since he'd approached her.

"Something's happened," he said. "Another person was attacked."

"Do you know who hurt him?"

"Yes. I'm not sure about the whole story, but we'll discuss it later when we have time. I only wanted to let you know what was going on and make sure you were safe."

"Kevin, my blood isn't appealing to vampires, remember? No one will hurt me." Not a vampire, anyway. An angry mortal might, though.

"I know." He kissed her forehead. "You're my baby sister. It's natural for me to worry about you."

"Erik takes care of me too, Kevin. Just like Gallard takes care of Lela and Solomon takes care of Cherish. You need to find your own girlfriend to take care of."

Kevin made a funny expression that confused Robin. What had she said that made him react like that?

"Amen," Abe said. "Why do you think we're here? We're scoping out the possibilities. Even though it's hard to settle for daffodils when you could have a rose."

"I'll let you go," Kevin said, eyeing Abe suspiciously. "You know Lela is going to kill you, right? You're supposed to be at home with Lucian."

"Are you going to tell on me?"

He crooked his mouth and shook his head. "I don't see the benefit in dragging you out of here kicking and screaming. Just promise you'll tell her yourself. We don't need any secrets between us."

She went to hug him, but he took a step back. When she questioned him with her eyes, he pulled his hands from his pockets and showed her. They were stained with blood.

"I carried the injured man," he explained. "I have blood all over me. Don't worry about all this, we'll handle it."

He and Abe left, and she watched until she couldn't see them anymore. Kevin hadn't hurt the man, but someone had. Two other people had been hurt the week before. There was another vampire in town and whoever he or she was, they needed to be stopped.

She sat back down next to Erik and leaned against him as the first float came by. He rested his chin on top of her head but didn't say a word. He'd started acting funny ever since Kevin and Abe showed up. She could have slapped Abe for joking about being an old boyfriend. She'd told Erik she'd never seen anyone else and now he might think she was a liar.

"Can we go for a walk?" she asked. "I never got to try one of those giant churros."

"I was just about to suggest that."

They stood up and informed his family where they were going, and they walked hand in hand down the sidewalk. Luckily, the churro stand was on the same street, so they wouldn't miss any of the parade. He bought her the treat and she split it in half to share because it was too big. He remained silent while they ate, and she grew even more worried.

"Erik are you mad at me?" she asked.

"No, of course not!" He held her hand with his free one. "I'm only curious about your brother." He stopped walking and locked eyes with her. "I didn't know he was a vampire."

Her eyes grew wide and she trembled. This was it — her relationship with Erik was over. He was a cop and he was probably going to have Kevin arrested again. She couldn't handle being separated from him anymore. She was constantly being torn from those she loved and those two months she'd spent worrying about him had been hell. She couldn't go through that again.

"Please . . . don't arrest him. He's registered, and he doesn't hurt people. He drinks from blood bags. He's already been in jail for saving me from a terrible man and —"

"Whoa, Robin." He reached up and touched her face. "Nobody is arresting anyone. My dad may be all for that vampire incarceration thing, but I'm not."

"But what about the recent attacks? You don't think he's responsible?"

"They have people on the case, but I say innocent until proven guilty."

She relaxed completely. Nothing was ruined. Erik wasn't going to take her brother away. She was falling for him even more, knowing that he wasn't on a mission to eradicate every immortal in sight.

"You don't hate vampires?" she asked.

"I can't really say. There haven't been very many in these parts since the John Slayer dropped off the radar almost thirty years ago. Your brother is one of the few I've met."

"Would you still like me if *I* was a vampire?"

Robin had to ask this question. It was the defining one that would help her decide whether they could be together. By choice or not, her family consisted of vampires. And if he was going to accept her, he would have to accept them as well. She longed for a day when the ones she loved didn't have to hide anymore.

He took one of her curls between his fingers and pulled on it until it straightened then let go so that it spiraled again. "I think I would prefer you with your blonde curls, but if they were black, I would find you equally as funny, and very beautiful. As long as you didn't try to make me or anyone else your dinner, it wouldn't be an issue for me. Don't tell my dad I said that."

Erik rested his hands on her waist and pulled her close to him. She was so sure he was going to kiss her now. The way he was looking at her made her stomach flip and the thought of his lips on hers caused her heart to beat faster.

"I'm not going to kiss you just yet," he said. "I want to, but I want something to look forward to." He removed his hands from her waist then took her hands in his. "I'm taking some time off next week. How would you like to come with me to Austin? We could spend time in the city or go fishing. My grandparents have a cabin there with all sorts of outdoor equipment. Our options would be endless."

While she was disappointed that he hadn't kissed her, the thought of being alone with him somewhere made up for it. He wanted to take her on an extended date. One where she wouldn't have to worry about sneaking behind her sister's back to see him. She couldn't imagine anything better.

"I would love to go away with you," she said. "When would we go?"

"We could leave Sunday and come back Friday."

She smiled up at him. "I'm in. Now." She started walking down the street. "Tell me about these drug dealers you probed."

17

J.D. carried the sleeping Colton into his room and lay him on the bed. He didn't wake, so she pulled a pair of pajamas out of his dresser and proceeded to undress him. After all the commotion with the injured man, Lela suggested they head home. Lucas was still down at the station giving his statement about what he saw and would be home soon. The weird thing was that Nicola was nowhere in sight. She'd been with Lucas all day and suddenly pulled a disappearing act, just like she had the previous Monday night. J.D. didn't think it was a coincidence that she jetted out of there just before the vampire attack.

She finished dressing Colton then tucked him under his covers and kissed his forehead. She left the room and started to go the living room when she looked down the hall towards Lucian's room. He said he would be home all night, but with Nicola's absence, he was bound to be missing as well.

That didn't stop her from heading in that direction and stopping in front of the door. She listened for movement then slowly pushed it open. It made a crack big enough for her to see inside and she was left breathless with what she saw. Lucian had just gotten out of the shower and his hair was wet. He had nothing on but a towel. His light was on, so she could see him very clearly.

Lucian wasn't particularly muscular or tall, but he was toned. From where she stood, his scar was clearly visible — the one he'd gotten when he was stabbed through with the sword. She forgot that she was supposed to be mad at him as she beheld this man that she undeniably loved.

He stopped moving around the room and she held her breath. Any sudden movement and he would know she was there. His back was to her and there weren't any mirrors around, so he couldn't see her. He turned his head slightly to the right and she continued to refrain from breathing. Then he yanked on the towel, causing it to fall on the ground and she gasped in surprise then hurried away. She was almost down the hall when he cut her off.

"Like what you see, darling?" he asked with a seductive smile on his face. She glanced down then quickly looked back at his face when she saw he was still naked. Her cheeks grew red and she folded her arms.

"Maybe," she said, trying not to sound flustered. He laughed then traced her lips with his thumb. She hoped that he wouldn't kiss her. If he did, she was afraid she would let her guard down and dismiss any lie he'd ever told her. She wanted him and he knew it.

He disappeared for a second then reappeared, this time with jeans on. She relaxed a little, but she still couldn't get the images of him out of her mind. She knew it was all she would be able to think about all night.

"Why did you come to me, darling? I doubt you were here to get a glimpse of me."

"I wanted to see if you were home. I need to talk to you."

"About?"

"Your lies. You said you were out with Cherish, but I think there's more to it."

He rested one hand on her back and signaled with another to follow him to his room. She obeyed and went in, admiring everything in sight. This was the first time she'd ever been there, and she'd always been curious about it. His comforter was grey with a white throw blanket folded across the front. His sheets were white and there were lights attached to the black, wooden headboard. There was a small chair in the corner with a lamp to the left and he had a rack with of his shoes on it. It looked very cozy. She wouldn't mind spending the night in there.

She sat on his bed and crossed her legs. Instead of sitting down, he stood in front of her and kept his hands in his pockets. She had to fight the urge to pull him onto the bed and tempt him into forgetting his conditions for being with her. It was killing her that she had to wait until Gallard got back. She'd almost called him on the phone a few times but decided to let Lucian take care of that.

"You said you have questions," he said. "Ask me anything, and I will give you an honest answer."

"Okay. What I want to know is where you were the night you called Gallard."

He sat on the bed next to her but didn't look at her face. This was his last chance to be honest before she would give up on him completely. If he lied again, then her feelings would mean nothing, and lust would only be the attraction she had for him.

"I was with Nicola. We went for a walk."

"And why did you do that?"

"She needed someone to talk to. I had just gotten off the phone with Gallard and saw her crying on Lucas' porch. There's a secret we've been keeping. We being her, Lucas, and me."

"What secret?" She took his hand and laced her fingers through his. "If you tell me, I won't say anything. I promise you that."

He grew quiet and her heart pounded as she waited for him to answer. Whatever this secret was, it had to be big. Nicola usually told her everything and no secret should have been too big to share with her friend. J.D. didn't have many friends growing up because she'd been tossed around between families. She spent her early childhood with her mother and grandparents in England before moving in with Lela and Gallard in her teens. After she finished secondary school, she went back and forth between the two homes before deciding that she wanted to settle down. More accurately, she wanted to settle down with Lucian.

"Something happened the day we rescued Kevin. While Lucas was busy taking care of that, I dropped Nicola off at the Wright house so she could see Colton. She told me she would have Lucas pick her up afterwards, so I left her there and headed for Solomon and the other women."

"I remember that. Lucas told me to call you and tell you to back him up."

"That is true. But I did not arrive in time to stop Henry from hurting anyone. He . . . shot Lucas and Nicola was behind him. The bullet went straight through them. That was when I got there and . . . I killed Henry. I was too late, though. The damage had already been done and Nicola was bleeding to death. That was when Lucas gave her his blood to save her."

J.D.'s jaw dropped. This entire time, Nicola had been a vampire and she never even noticed. It must have been so hard for her to hide the truth from everyone. Why didn't Nicola tell her? She would have kept it a secret. They were supposed to tell each other everything. Her, Robin, and Nicola all had secrets that they only shared with each other. Why did Nicola feel like she had to hide that she was a vampire?

"That's why you've spent time with her," J.D. said. "You're helping her try and adjust."

"I do help her sometimes, yes. She is a day-walker, like I am, and she can change her appearance. I have been helping her find a balance so she can appear as human as possible. Her natural look is white hair like Lucas and grey eyes. If she's relaxed, she can appear as her mortal self."

J.D. threw her arms around Lucian, and he embraced her. She felt terrible for assuming they were having an affair. She understood why he bonded with Nicola. The two of them were alike. It was the same reason J.D. bonded with Robin.

"You're a good man, Lucian Christophe," she said. She pulled back and kissed his cheek. "I love you. I won't doubt you again, I swear to you."

He must have noticed the hesitation in her expression because he asked, "What is it, darling?"

"If you were with Nicola that night, then where was Cherish?"

He looked down. "I do not know. I never saw her."

"There's more. Someone got hurt tonight. A man was bitten, and Lucas found Nicola there with him. Are you sure Nicola is really under control?"

"Nicola has no problem controlling herself around blood. In fact, she's having quite the opposite problem. I have been trying to get her to drink more, but she won't consume more than a few ounces. Blood still makes her nauseous for psychological reasons."

"She wouldn't be the first one to lash out after fasting from blood."

Lucian nodded in agreement and neither of them said a word. J.D. knew that he was equally as worried as she was. If Nicola was keeping secrets from the one person who she told everything, the problem might be worse. J.D. didn't want to think about Nicola being responsible for the other deaths. But if she was, J.D. would be there for her to get her through this rough patch.

She heard the front door open and close, so Lucian put a shirt on, and they went out to see who had arrived. Lucas stood by the door when they entered the living room. He looked exhausted, both mentally and physically.

"How is that man?" J.D. asked.

"He'll be okay. He said he couldn't see his attacker's face, but he knows it was a woman with dark hair."

"What did *you* see, exactly?" Lucian asked.

Lucas tossed his keys onto the coffee table. "I saw Nicola holding onto him while he was bleeding. She told me she lost control so I told her to run before more people would show up."

Lucas glanced at J.D. then back to Lucian. She took the hint that Lucas wanted to speak with him alone, so she grabbed her jacket and headed for the door.

"By the way, Colton is in bed," she said. "I'm going home to wait for Nicola and Robin."

"Thanks, J.D.," Lucas said. He then surprised her by giving her a hug and she returned it.

She left the house feeling relieved and confused at the same time. Lucian wasn't cheating on her, but her friend could be in trouble. She didn't doubt that she could help Nicola. She wasn't going to abandon her like she had Lucas. It would be different this time. She'd developed a habit of leaving people when they disappointed her because she was used to them doing the same thing to her. Now she was surrounded by the most devoted family she could ask for and she wanted to change.

When she approached the porch, she stopped in her tracks. Robin was on the porch with Erik and they were talking. J.D. didn't know if she should say something or wait and see if they would take their little conversation inside. If they chose the latter, Robin was better than J.D. gave her credit for.

"About this trip," he said. "Who do I need to go through to get permission for you to go?"

"We don't have to ask anyone. I could say J.D. and I are taking a road trip to cover for me. I could even get her boyfriend to cover too and maybe those two could have their own getaway."

"I'm not sure I'm comfortable with sneaking around. Yes, we're adults, but I'm big on family approval. Call me old fashioned." He took her hand and kissed it. "I should go. It's late and you've had a long day. We can talk more later this week."

Robin bit her lip. "Do you want to come inside? I'm not really that tired."

J.D. covered her mouth in shock. Robin had more moves than she did.

She was startled by footsteps coming up beside her. Abe didn't say anything at first but then she noticed he was staring at Robin and Erik. She knew why she was taking her time to go inside, but why was *he* here?

"What are you staring at, brother?" she whispered.

"Nothing. I'm wondering what she sees in him."

When it clicked, J.D. couldn't protest fast enough. The last thing she needed was her brother going after sweet Robin.

"Back off, Abraham, I mean it."

"I don't know what you're talking about."

"Whatever little scheme you have going through your head — you need to drop it. Robin isn't a one-night-stand."

"Exactly. I want to prove that I've changed, and this is how. It wasn't my intention to fall for her, believe me. But she's something else."

"Well, I won't have it. You can be her friend but let her get closer to Erik. He'll be good for her."

"Will he? Or will he leave her in the long-run."

She frowned. "What's that supposed to mean?"

"Nothing."

J.D. turned her attention back to the couple on the porch. They still hadn't noticed that they weren't alone. She could see how they were easily lost in each other's company. There were times when she would hold Lucian's gaze and everything else would disappear. It would only get worse when they would finally get Gallard's blessing. If he would give it, that is.

"I won't come in this time," Erik said. He wrapped his arms around Robin. "Until then, how can I earn more points with your family?"

"You should come over for dinner!" J.D. shouted. They turned their heads in her direction, and she went onto the porch. "Seriously, you should. We haven't had a real dinner together since we've moved here. Lela's house has a big dining table."

"Yes!" Robin said. "That's a great idea. J.D. and Lela are good cooks. And I really want them to like you. We can convince them together that you, and I are a good couple."

"Okay," he said. "I've always liked J.D.'s family. What day works for you?"

"How does Friday at six sound?" J.D. asked. "You can come over for dinner, woo them with your charms, and they'll have no choice but to let you date her."

She could feel Abe glaring at her from the side. He knew she'd done this on purpose. He then turned around and walked towards Lucas' house.

"Friday at six sounds great," Erik said. "I should go now. I will see you ladies on Friday."

He gave J.D. a playful punch to the bicep then walked down the sidewalk to his truck. Robin was a lucky girl. He was the perfect boyfriend in every way — polite, considerate, hot. He was the complete package. This great guy had once had his eye on her but because of something she'd been going through at the time, she'd turned him down. Things were awkward between them for a while but now that they were reunited, she was glad they'd crossed paths again.

"Damn, girl, you almost got lucky tonight," J.D. said. "Too bad he's an honorable guy."

"Yeah . . . too bad."

J.D. lightly smacked her arm. "Robin Shepherd! Were you seriously thinking about bonking Erik?"

"Maybe. I can't be afraid of intimacy forever. Might as well start with him, right?"

J.D. was taken aback by her seriousness. In the future, she would be happy to know that Robin was able to get passed her assault, but it seemed very soon. She didn't know if she should be worried or supportive.

The women linked arms as they went inside. Robin told her about everything they did on their date. She even admitted that Erik knew that some of her family members were vampires and that he was okay with it. That made J.D. a little wary. Even she hadn't told him that secret in high school. Either that could go south, or he could be the exception and prove to be very tolerant.

Robin turned on the light in the living room and they both flinched when they saw Nicola sitting on the couch with her legs hugged to her chest. Cherish was sitting next to her. J.D. hadn't known they were home and their presence startled her.

"This is where you ran off to," J.D. said to Cherish. "Melody's pissed you forgot her elephant ear."

"Tell her I'll make it up to her." Cherish hugged Nicola for a long time. "It'll be okay, I promise. Whenever you need me, you know where to find me."

Cherish then got up and smiled at the two women before leaving the house. J.D. almost asked what was going on, but she had a feeling she already knew.

"Hey guys," Nicola said. "How was the rest of the festival?"

J.D. stared at her. After everything that had happened, Nicola was acting like nothing was wrong. Either this was an odd coping mechanism or she was in denial.

"The, uh . . . that man is going to be okay. Lucas came home with the update in case you were wondering."

"Man? What man?"

J.D. and Robin exchanged a worried glance. If anyone was good at interventions, it was J.D. She'd successfully helped Lucas snap out of his depression and she convinced Melody to get hair extensions since she was always talking about wanting longer hair. But this was direr than a style change or an attitude adjustment. Someone was seriously hurt.

Robin went to her room then J.D. sat on the couch next to Nicola. She usually didn't care about coming off as pushy and blunt, but Nicola was the queen of bluntness and J.D. knew she wouldn't be offended.

"You don't have to pretend with me. I get it— mistakes happen. I should know having lived with vampires my entire life. When I was five, the kids in my primary school actually laughed in my face because I thought that Kiefer Sutherland was the good guy in *Lost Boys*."

"What does that have to do with anything?"

J.D. blinked. "You're right. I have a point." She crossed her legs on the couch. "Lucas covered for you tonight, so you don't have to worry. But we have agreed that you need to be on probation, meaning you can't leave the house."

"What the actual hell are you talking about? I came home because I wasn't feeling well. I—"

"Nicola stop. I know you hurt that man tonight. Lucas saw you. I'm telling you that I'm not judging you and I'm going to be here to support you while you learn to control your blood thirst."

Nicola didn't say anything for the longest time and J.D. began to feel a little stupid. An intervention was supposed to help the person in question admit they had a problem. That wasn't happening here. Nicola just looked confused.

"Who told you?" she asked.

J.D. looked down. "Lucian did. He admitted Lucas turned you the day Henry died. It kind of hurt that you didn't tell me. I thought we were closer than that. You, Robin, and me are supposed to be the Three Musketeeresseses. That was too many esses."

"I'm sorry. I wanted to tell you, but I've been dealing with a lot of things. My transition has been a little hard to handle, and sometimes I think I'm going crazy."

Nicola's eyes teared up and J.D. gave her a hug. She wasn't going to keep pushing her to talk about everything, but at least this was getting somewhere. Nicola liked to keep everything bottled up but eventually, she opened-up. J.D was determined to help her in any way she could.

18

I tugged Colton's last shoe on then started to tie it when I had an idea. He had yet to learn how to tie his shoes, and I thought it would be smart to teach him. He was a smart kid and I figured he should start doing a few things himself to establish some independence.

"Hey, bud. Why don't you give it a try?"

"Is it hard?"

"No, it's very easy." I took each of the laces in my hands. "First you tie them in a loop, then you make them into two bunny ears, then you tie the bunny ears like the first loop and tug on it until it's tight." I finished lacing it. "See? It's easy. Why don't you try the other one?"

He got excited as he started attempting to redo everything I'd shown him. Lucian came into the room and smiled when he saw what we were doing. We'd talked almost the entire night and were both in agreement that we needed to take action. I hated plotting behind Nicola's back, but he might be my only chance at helping her.

"Why are you in uniform?" Lucian asked. "I thought you worked nights."

"I have a job interview. I don't know when I'll be back. If you could, pass the message to Nicola that I need her to pick Colton up from school."

"Why don't I pick him up? I think it would be best if Nicola stay in for a while."

"If you don't mind, you would be a life saver. And I agree about Nic. We should make sure she's better before she goes out."

Abe came out of his room, trudging to the kitchen. His usually fixed hair was mussed in every way and he looked extremely depressed. He opened the cupboard, poured cereal into a bowl and then covered it in chocolate milk. I raised an eyebrow, shocked by this. Abe never ate anything fattening, let alone sugary cereal.

"Bad night?" I asked.

"You have no bloody idea."

He took a bite of cereal. That was when I realized that something even stranger was going on. Abe hadn't slept at our place in nearly two months and not only that, his room had been completely silent all night.

"No company last night?"

"No. I wasn't in the mood."

"Wow. That's eight days since you've had someone over. I'm shocked. Would a woman have anything to do with this?"

Abe sighed then let go of his spoon, causing it to clink against the bowl. "I think I'm in love, and I don't know what to do about it."

Lucian smiled. "We have all been there. Who is the lucky woman?"

"I'd rather not say just yet. Give me some time and then I'll get back to you on that.

He picked up his cereal and took it to his room, probably to mope. This day was getting weirder by the second. Abe was in love? I thought that would never happen. He was always catching the eye of a different woman, and I had a feeling being monogamous would be a challenge to him. I was curious to know what woman had him so hooked that he wasn't practicing his old habits.

Colton had figured out how to do his laces, so I grabbed his backpack as well as my wallet. I walked out the door with Colton skipping ahead. His lace came untied on the one he'd done himself and he slipped and fell.

"Careful there, bud. A trip to the E.R. isn't as fun as it sounds."

"I'm okay!" He gave me a puzzled look. "Lucas, are you my real dad?"

I held my breath. I should have known my comment wouldn't slip passed him. He was a perceptive little boy and picked up on things quicker than most adults. I hadn't expected this secret to get out in this way, but now that the seed was planted, it was best that I be honest with him.

"Remember when Regina told you that they adopted you from parents who couldn't take care of you?"

"Uh huh."

"Well . . . those parents are Nicola and me."

I grew quiet as I waited to hear what he would say. He seemed a little surprised but not confused or mad.

"You mean I was inside of Nicola's tummy?"

I chuckled. "Yeah, bud. She gave birth to you and then Scott and Regina took care of you. But now that we are more capable, Regina let us take you with us so we could be your mom and dad."

"Oh. Does that mean I can call you dad? You kind of act like a dad, except you're not old."

I smiled and pulled him into my arms. "I would love it if you called me dad. And I think Nicola would be happy if you called her mom. She loves you very much."

"I love her too. She's nice and takes care of me and brings me water when I'm thirsty at night. She's like a mom to me."

I looked up and saw Nicola on the porch. By the expression on her face, she'd heard every word. She was smiling just like I was and for a moment, I forgot about our problems. I gave her a nod of acknowledgment then helped Colton get strapped into his car seat. When I shut the door behind him, I went over to her on the porch.

"Happy birthday, Nic." I kissed her cheek. "How are you feeling this morning."

"I'm a little better, thanks. J.D. said you helped a man last night. Is he okay?"

"I think he will be. I told the police I didn't see anything, and the man never saw your face. You should be safe."

"Lucas, I don't understand why you did that."

I pulled her close to me. It was so strange having our roles reversed. In the past, I was the one who needed rehabilitation from my uncontrollable blood lust and now I needed to help her. I was determined to help her in any way I could.

"I would do anything for you, Nicola Hendrickson. You had faith in me even after I almost hurt Mona and after I pushed you. I love you and I'm never going to stop loving you."

I kissed her forehead then walked to the car. I dropped Colton off at school then headed for the station. I was curious to find out what job the sheriff had in store for me. He hadn't given me any information. It was probably a desk job since I didn't have many credentials.

When I got to the police station, I parked in one of the visitor spaces. There were two precincts in Euless and Sheriff McPherson's office happened to be in the one I wasn't stationed at. The building was across the street from the mayor's office, which I hadn't expected. Compared to the MITF precinct, it was microscopic. It couldn't have been more than the size of two one story houses.

The mayor's office, however, was very rustic in appearance, like it belonged in an Old West mock village. It had a porch and a wooden sign above the steps that was painting in green and had white hand-painted letters. The only part of it that wasn't old fashioned was the glass doors.

All conversation stopped the moment I went inside and walked up to the desk. The woman sitting behind it was staring at me funny. She took off her horn-rimmed glasses then fluffed her copper brown hair.

"How can I help you?" she asked. She had a strong Texan accent and smiled a little too much.

"I'm Cadet Lucas d'Aubigne. Sheriff McPherson asked me to come in for an interview."

"Oh, yeah, he told me to watch out for you." She pushed the swing door on the side of the desk. "You sit tight, honey. I'll let him know you're here."

"Thank you."

She smiled at me again and walked away, whispering to her other coworkers on her way down the hall. The women giggled then looked around their cubicle walls to stare at me and I could feel my skin growing warm from embarrassment. I wasn't used to being hit on like this. Back when I was ill, people would see how sickly I was and give me looks of pity instead of looks of interest. I attributed this new attention to the uniform.

I relaxed a little when I saw Tyler McPherson coming down the hall. He stuck out his hand and gave me a firm but friendly handshake. He looked different in uniform.

"It's good to see you here, Cadet d'Aubigne."

"Thanks for having me, Sheriff McPherson."

He chuckled. "Maybe we'll go by first names. Sheriff and Cadet sound too formal. Are you ready to know about your mystery job?"

"I am. So long as I'm not going to be a drug mule or something skeevy like that."

"Drug mule?"

"Sorry. I'm from Miami, if that explains anything."

Tyler laughed then clapped me on the shoulder. "Come on. Let's take a walk across the street."

I followed him out the door and he told me we were heading for the mayor's office. I chose to keep my comments to myself and see what he had in mind. Police still made me uncomfortable, though it was Immortal Task Force officers I didn't trust.

We were going through what looked like a break room and were greeted with a loud gust of laughter. One of the officers was standing on one side of the room while another was opposite him. The second guy was throwing chocolate covered raisins and the other was catching them in his mouth. This was the exact opposite of the atmosphere at the MITF precinct. The mood was light and carefree. The officers looked like boys from next door — like they wouldn't hurt a fly.

When they saw that the sheriff was present. They scrambled around the room and acted like they were working. The goofy smiles on their faces proved they knew they were busted and there was no reason to try and pretend they weren't screwing around.

"Hello, boys," Tyler said. "Not enough work for you over here?"

"I got two DUI's and a parole violation today," one guy in the back said. He was black and his hair was close-shaved. He was one of the more serious ones from what I could see.

121

"Thank you, Officer Craven. But I'm not here to bust you for your shenanigans." Tyler put a hand on my shoulder. "Everyone, I would like you to meet Cadet Lucas d'Aubigne. He's an officer over at precinct two where my son's stationed."

"Dooby what?" another officer said.

"Just call me Lucas."

Everyone in the room laughed.

"Hey, I know that name," one guy said. "You know a J.D.?"

"She's my cousin."

"No way. I haven't seen her in years. What are you here for? A transfer?"

"He's being considered for the Euless Immortal Task Force leader position," Tyler said.

Everyone's reaction was different. One third of the officers were surprised while another third was excited. The other few seemed bothered or maybe annoyed. All I could feel was sickness in my stomach. He'd recruited me to kill my own kind.

"The mayor never said anything about this," one officer said. He was one who apparently knew J.D. He had light brown hair with violet eyes. I could tell that he was the type to take business seriously.

"That's my next destination, James. Is your dad around?"

He nodded. "He's in his office doing paperwork."

Tyler nodded his head to the left and I followed him through the room. While I was walking, I heard some of the officers whispering to each other followed by the sound of something whizzing in my direction. I turned around as quickly as possible and caught the soaring raisin right as it was about to hit me in the head. The officers gasped in shock and I smiled.

"I believe this is yours," I said to the one Tyler referred to as James. I flicked the raisin with my thumb, and it landed in the empty cup next to his plate. I then turned around and followed Tyler to the Mayor's office. Tyler knocked and there was silence at first, but then someone yelled.

"Come in!"

Tyler opened the door, and I could immediately feel the tension in the room. The Mayor was a cocky looking man with thick biceps and his ash brown hair was receding. His eyes were a shocking violet and his resemblance to James was apparent.

"Who's the pretty boy?" the Mayor asked.

Why did everyone call me that? Was it because I was blonde with blue eyes? He probably called Tyler pretty boy back in the day.

"Chase, this *pretty boy* is being considered for the Task Force position. I thought you should meet him before I went before the council."

Mayor Chase raised an eyebrow. When I heard that name, I immediately remembered who he was. Lela told me about the Chase she went to school with and how she thought he was a douche. I couldn't believe I was standing in the same room as two men from her past.

"I'm Lucas d'Aubigne," I said, extending my hand. When he didn't take it, I subtly put it back into my pocket. He stood up and walked towards me until he was standing close. He furrowed his brown and stared at my face intently.

"Do I know you from somewhere?" he asked. "You look really familiar."

I swallowed before answering. "I don't believe we've met. I've only just moved here four months ago."

"From where?"

"Florida. I'm twenty-two years old, and I have a bachelor's degree in criminal justice. I also graduated from the police academy around the same time. I was accepted into the Yale law program on scholarship. I had to turn it down because I found out I was a father, and I wanted to be there for my son. My parents are deceased, but I live close with my brother and his wife. Both have lived here for a few years longer than I have. I moved over here so that my son could spend time with his extended family and get to know them." I paused so he could let my information sink in. Everything I'd told him was what Gallard had instructed me to tell people. We even had fake documents to back everything up. "Anything else you want to know?"

"You ever train in the field?"

"I'm currently in training. My ride-along partner is Corporal Beau."

Chase looked at Tyler. "What makes you think the council is going to hire him? He's not even off probation!"

"So what? He saved an officer's life on the job. He's very promising and has a degree in criminal justice. All we need is someone to take over this investigation. I can't handle that and be Sheriff at the same time. The law says that if we have more than two vampire attacks, we're required to put together a team."

"Why not hire James? He's been on the force for two years. Hell, your son is even a more reasonable candidate."

This was what they wanted me for? To find out who was behind the attacks? Why did he pick *me*? For all he knew, I could be the biggest vampire sympathizer out there, which I was.

"You know why I can't hire Erik. It would be a conflict of interest. As for James, he's too young. He's only been off probation for three months."

"This guy isn't even off probation! He just started!"

"I have to agree with him on that," I threw in. "Why me? What about me made you think I could do this job, other than I finished the academy?"

"Let's talk on the way to my office. Chase, thank you for your time. I'll see you in the meeting."

Tyler waved me over to the door and we left the room. I gave Chase a quick nod to try and say it was a pleasure to meet him then closed the door behind me. I was interested to hear what Tyler had to say.

"Lucas, I have to be honest. I hired you on a whim. You had the required training, you show incentive, and I was not in the mood to go through an interview process. Plus, I would rather not bring in anyone from San Antonio. They'd turn this case into a witch hunt. I was fortunate to run into you at the festival and my gut told me you would be perfect for the position. I need this case to be solved before our reputation as the safest town in Texas is compromised. And because I don't want to make another visit and tell expectant parents that their child isn't coming home."

"I understand. I'm sure that would be hard. Even after —" I instantly shut up. I almost said way too much and I couldn't let him know who I really was. It was Lela's choice whether or not she would approach him and I didn't want him to know that his ex-girlfriend was my mother.

"After what?" he asked.

"After the incident in San Antonio and the John Slayer. I know about those crimes. How did you get into this?"

"It's a long story. Maybe I'll tell you one day. For now, I would like you to look over what we have on the case."

We went across the street and back to the station. The lady at the desk was still there and she smiled big then waved when she saw me. I waved back and she acted like I'd just given her a million dollars. As soon as I went inside the mayor's office, I could hear her talking with the other women outside. It was flattering and embarrassing at the same time.

I sat in the chair in front of his desk and observed the office while he looked through some file boxes. It was a little smaller than Scott's, but less intimidating. Like Scott's, there were pictures of his children on the desk. He had two daughters, both who were a little younger than me and they were with Erik. On the wall was a picture of him and his wife at what looked like senior prom and next to it was a shot of them on their wedding day. Tyler hadn't changed too much, other than being a little more muscular and he had small wrinkles around his eyes.

"Your wife is lovely," I said. "You high school sweethearts?"

He looked at the picture and chuckled. "Not exactly. We both went through break ups right before prom and since we were friends, we decided to go together. We listened to our hearts rather than our heads and the next thing we knew she was pregnant with our son. I'd grown to really care for her, and now we're married with three children."

"I wish everything had turned out differently for me. I mean, I love Colton and I wouldn't give him up for anything. But I want him to have a normal life. That's why I moved him here to be with his family."

Tyler grabbed a file and sat down. "Is Colton's mother in the picture?"

"She is. We married young, mostly for our son, but we're solid."

"I'm glad to hear that. It's good for a child to be with both of his parents." He slid the file over to me. "All right, here is what I wanted you to see. It's all the information we have on this case."

I opened the file and looked through the papers. There was a drawing at the very top and I nearly gasped when I saw that the picture looked a lot like Nicola, only the hair was darker. It was unnerving me, so I flipped through everything else and looked at the crime scene photos. They were pretty gruesome, but I'd seen worse.

"To spare you the hours of reading, I'll fill you in," Tyler said. "The young man's name was Frankie Ramón. He was walking home from a school function with his girlfriend when he was attacked. The girlfriend ran off to get help but there was no way she could have saved him. She said that the attacker was a woman with red hair. That's all she knows." He flipped through his own file. "Victim number two— Claudia Sullivan. She was leaving a friend's when she was attacked by her car. A taxi driver found her outside the new art gallery in town. She lived long enough to tell the police it was a redheaded woman. She died from her injuries around two-thirty a.m."

There was no doubt that Nicola was out and about during the time of that attack, and I couldn't vouch for her for the other. Maybe the reason she was so miserable as a vampire was because she'd taken a life and felt guilty about it. It was the one thing I was afraid of ever experiencing.

"What do I have to do to get involved?" I asked.

Tyler smiled. "Let me talk to the council. I'll get them to agree to a trial run, and we'll see from there."

19

I pulled up to the house, already eager for it to be next week. I'd spent all afternoon listening to the city council debating whether or not I was the best candidate for the job, and they came to an agreement that I was. I would start work the next Monday. My precinct was informed, and I would be working from the same building as the mayor. I even had my own office.

On my way home, I'd stopped at an office supply store and got myself a briefcase. It was strange since I'd always stuffed my things into backpacks, and it made me feel like a real businessman. I also stopped to get a card to go with the gift for Nicola for her birthday.

I was walking inside when I heard Colton laughing in J.D. and Nicola's backyard. Curious, I set my briefcase on the porch walked around the side of the house. I stopped in my tracks when I saw the huge above-ground swimming pool in the middle of the yard. It was at least fifteen feet long and the outside was designed to look like it was made of wood. From where I stood, I estimated that the depth was four feet

Nicola was in the water with Colton, holding onto his waist while he paddled. He wore goggles and floaters on each arm. Abe was reclined on a body-sized float and drinking a beer. The hose was still draped over the edge and the pool wasn't quite full yet. I wondered whose idea it was to get the it because it was a great one. Now Cole had something to do while at her house.

I walked up to the edge of the pool and Colton smiled when he saw me. Nicola stopped moving and held him with her arms around his waist so that he was above the water and walked over to me.

"What are you guys up to?" I asked.

"We got a pool!" Colton said. "Mom surprised me when I got home from school."

He was already calling her mom? I could see in Nicola's eyes that she was beyond happy.

"It's a gift from Lucian," Nicola explained. "How did your interview go?"

"It went very well, actually. I'm the one in charge of the vampire case."

"Oh. Is that going to be difficult? Conflicting interests, I mean."

"I actually want to talk to you about that. Do you have a moment?"

Lucian and J.D. came outside just then, both dressed in swimwear. They were laughing and flirting like usual. I was surprised they were being open about their relationship. They probably figured we already knew about it. Robin came out as well and she looked happier than I'd seen her in a while. Maybe having Erik in her life was a good thing after all.

"Hey, Lucian. Do you mind watching the little guy for a while?"

"Not at all." Lucian got into the pool and took Nicola's place helping him swim and she got out. I grabbed one of the towels and wrapped it around her shoulders. We sat on the porch and she shook her hair on me so that I got wet.

"What did you want to talk about?" she asked.

"This case. While I am on it, I intend to protect you in any way I can. I know that you didn't do it intentionally and there's no way I'm going to let you be incarcerated for a crime you had no control over. We're going to help you through this. I'll find a way."

She grew quiet as she leaned against me. I had no idea how to lead the task force off her trail. However, I wouldn't lie and say I wasn't struggling with this morally. I was a firm believer in justice and those two people wouldn't get it if I kept their killer hidden. The police officer in me wanted to give the families closure and the boyfriend side of me wanted to protect her at all costs. I wished Gallard was there to give me advice.

"What time is it?" she asked.

I checked my phone. "Two-thirty."

She sprang out of my lap. "Oh shi . . . itake mushrooms. I'm supposed to decorate the cake before Melody gets back from town."

"Why are you decorating your own birthday cake Nic? Let someone else take care of it."

"I know it's not tradition, but I insisted. I was supposed to be in the shower five minutes ago."

"By all means, let me assist you."

I lifted her into my arms and sped into the house before she could protest. When we got to the bathroom, I set her down and wrapped my arms around her from behind and kissed her neck. If we weren't going to discuss what happened, I would much rather spend our time doing this. She turned around and her lips met mine. All our problems seemed to disappear with each intoxicating kiss.

She started unbuttoning my shirt. I wasn't sure what she had in mind, but I wasn't about to protest. Undressing me was a long process since I had on the uniform, a bulletproof vest, and a white t-shirt, not to mention my belt with my gun. She was wearing a one piece, albeit a very sexy one, so it wasn't very easy to undress her either. I managed to get it off and cast it to the floor then continued to kiss her as I turned on the shower. I nearly tripped as I slipped out of my pants and she laughed at me

"Klutz," she said.

"I may have a long way to fall, but at least I'll look good doing it."

We got into the shower and I kept planting small kisses on her shoulders while she went about washing off. Feeling daring, I took the loofa from her and picked up where she left off.

When I was sure I'd gotten every inch of her body, she turned around and kissed me. I backed her up against the wall then lifted her up. She wrapped her legs around me, kissing me more passionately than ever. I held onto her tighter but then I heard her moan and it wasn't a good moan, so I stopped kissing her.

"What's wrong?"

"Nothing. I'm just sore."

I took a moment to examine her, and I noticed there were several bruises on her stomach and near her ribs. They were purple and looked terrible.

"Nic, how did you get hurt?" I asked.

Nicola met my gaze and the terror in her eyes made me feel even more disturbed than the actual wounds.

"I was pushing myself to see how resilient my body is. I guess I pushed a little too hard."

She started to get out when I gently grabbed her shoulders and kept her so that she was facing me.

"Don't lie to me. You can lie about something you did or didn't do, and you can lie about being somewhere when you weren't. But do not lie to me about someone hurting you. Because I will go out and kill whoever did this and you know it."

Her eyes brimmed with tears and she wrapped her arms around me, resting her head against my chest. I couldn't hold her close enough to me. Someone had done this to her, and I wasn't there to stop it. It was killing me and made me angrier than I'd felt in a while. I hadn't been this angry since Henry forced me to feed on her.

"Please, Nicola. Tell me who did this to you."

"I can't. Not yet."

I was going to question her further when the door to the bathroom opened and someone started shouting.

"You better not be having sex in there!" It was J.D. Like she had room to talk. I didn't have to guess to know what she and Lucian were up to whenever no one was around.

"It's my birthday, isn't it?" Nicola shouted. "We did it in the kitchen and on your bed too."

I opened my mouth to correct her, but she covered it with her hand. I had to admit it was fun messing with J.D. She was like the sister I never had, and it was easy to tease her.

"You're disgusting, you know that? Anyway, Lela told me to tell you she's frosted the cake and it's ready for when you want to decorate it."

"Thanks. Tell her we'll be over in five minutes."

It grew quiet for a moment then J.D. said, "Ooh! Is this thing loaded?"

"Don't even think about touching my gun, J.D.," I warned.

She laughed. "Relax, I didn't even touch it. But I did take your taser."

After the door closed, we got out and dried off. During that time, I decided I would let Nicola talk when she was ready. She'd opened-up about what Ash had done to her and I trusted that she would tell me who had given her those bruises.

I went to my place to put on some more casual clothes and grabbed her gift then headed over to Lela's. Everyone else was already there except for Melody, so I pitched in to help decorate. It wasn't a particularly fancy party, but everything looked nice. Lela had purchased ivory and black napkins as well as matching plates and utensils. Nicola put an ivory fondant on the cake and used black piping to create an elegant design on the sides along with edible pearls.

Robin had just finished setting up the gift table when Melody returned. She informed us that she'd had the birthday dinner catered by some Mexican place in town and it was going to arrive within the hour. My family was a huge fan of Mexican food and it sounded extra good because I hadn't eaten since seven-thirty.

When we finished eating, we gathered in the living room to open gifts. Nicola received a gift card for a clothing store from Melody, some champagne glasses with her initials on them from Lela, and a necklace from Lucian. It resembled one he'd given his daughters when they had turned fifteen.

Colton handed Nicola a small, rectangular package and I wondered what it was. I hadn't taken him to buy her a gift, which I felt bad about. Someone must have unless he'd made it at school.

"What could this be?" she asked.

"Open it! Aunt Melody helped me find it for you today."

Nicola smiled then popped the lid. She stared at the contents then covered her mouth with her hand.

"If you look closely, the ends of the heart are two people," Colton said. "The boy on the right is me, and the lady on the left is you. Because even though Regina is my mom, you're my birth mom. So, you're my mom too, and I love you very much."

There wasn't a dry eye in the room. Nicola waved Colton over and they hugged each other for a long time.

"I love you too, bud. I've loved you from the day I found out I was going to have you. I'm never taking this off."

It was a beautiful sight to see and, without a doubt, one of my top ten favorite moments. After she'd composed herself, she had Colton help her put the necklace on. It was a gold heart with each of their birthstones as the head of the boy and woman. The Topaz stone for Nicola matched the gold of her eyes while the aquamarine matched Colton's. It was too perfect.

It came time for Robin and J.D. to give her their joint gift, and I held my breath while Nicola unwrapped it. When she saw the painting, she became speechless.

"Oh, my goodness." She started laughing. "I can't believe you guys bought this!"

Lucian, Kevin, and Terrence walked behind the couch to get a look at it and Lucian's face turned red as he quickly moved back to his spot. Colton wanted to see, but I held onto him to keep him from looking. He would never be old enough to see that painting.

"Do explain so I can gouge the eyes out of the man who painted this," Lucian said.

Cherish laughed. "Calm your tits, father. It's not really her, is it?"

"Hell no! I would never pose like this for a stranger." Nicola smiled. "Thank you, J.D. and Robin. I will keep this forever."

We ate cake afterwards and everyone broke off into groups to talk. While I was chatting with Robin about her date to the festival, I noticed that Nicola had made a disappearing act and so had Cherish. As soon as J.D. stole Robin away, I went looking for Nicola. The back door was open, and it was a safe bet that they'd gone out there.

I heard Nicola's voice first, so I stood by the door and listened to the conversation. She and Cherish were arguing about something. I knew that they often clashed because of similar personalities, but this didn't sound like a disagreement.

"I didn't say anything to him," Nicola said. "I can't. I don't want to hurt him."

"He deserves to know what's going on. I promise to keep your secret, but I don't think you should. What makes you think he's suspicious?"

"He followed me last week."

Cherish sighed. "You can't keep this from him. He's going to find out."

"I have to. You of all people should understand why I'm doing this."

"I do understand. But I also know the consequences. This is only going to end badly, and I don't want to see you or him hurt."

130

Nicola hugged her for several moments then headed for the door and I rushed away so she wouldn't know I was eavesdropping. I hated that their conversation had been so cryptic. It was like trying to learn about my family all over again.

Whatever Nicola was hiding it gave me some comfort that she was confiding in Cherish. I only wished she would confide in me too. She never used to lie to me and my hopes for us building our relationship were starting to crumble.

20

J.D. stirred in the bed then opened her eyes. She and Lucian had stayed up all night talking in his room before she'd fallen asleep. She wanted to stay awake so badly, but it had been a long night. Especially since Abe had gone back to his old habits. They'd had to tune out his moaning for a solid two hours.

She felt movement next to her and she turned around to find Lucian smiling at her. He'd changed out of his clothes since the night before and was in athletic shorts. She loved that he hardly wore anything less than his best, but what she loved more was that he would go casual for her. She leaned over and kissed him good morning.

"Your snoring is quite precious, darling," he said.

"I don't snore!" He gave her an accusing look. "I don't!"

"Tis all right. I don't mind it."

He pulled her close to him and kissed her once more. She could feel that he was trying to hold back, but she wouldn't let him. She deepened the kiss, holding him against her and he rolled over so that he was lying on top of her. She liked this side to him, and he didn't show it often. She felt that they earned a few moments of fooling around since they'd been good all night.

Lucian ended the kiss after a few moments, and they were breathless. She didn't want to stop there, but it was his rule. They couldn't go any further until he had Gallard's permission to see her. It was frustrating and romantic at the same time.

"You know, we can sleep together if we want," she said.

"I thought we did. You were asleep, I was asleep, and we were together."

She rolled her eyes. "It's not what I meant. Why can't we? Gallard wouldn't know."

"No, he wouldn't." He gave her a slow and intoxicating kiss. "But I would. And I promised I would not deceive him ever again."

He was still lying on top of her, so she began sliding the tips of her fingers up and down his back. He let out a content sigh and she hoped that she was getting to him. She was starting to run out of seduction ploys and her last resort was going to be calling Gallard herself.

"What is it with d'Aubignes and their magic hands?" he asked.

"Actually, it's *Christophes* who have magic hands. You didn't get the gift because you're a McCain."

He laughed. "I have always wondered what my name would have been had Rebecca Asper not been burned at the stake. I would probably be a gypsy."

"You'd make a sexy gypsy. A golden earring— colorful bandanas. But you would probably stand out since you have red hair. They'd put you in a freak show."

"That is very comforting darling."

She slid her hands down his back and rested them just above the band of his shorts. She wondered what he would do if she tried to take them off. It wasn't like she hadn't seen him before, and she wouldn't mind seeing him again. Maybe this time, she would give him a glimpse of what he was missing, or rather putting off.

Instead, she slid her hands down a little lower and gave him a little squeeze. His eyes widened with surprise, but he didn't stop her. Unfortunately, he didn't do the same to her. He never touched her. It frustrated her that he was being so honorable.

You slept over? Jordan suddenly said. *Are you crazy? I thought I warned you that getting involved with him was dangerous.*

Go away, dad. This is a private moment.

No, I'm not going away. He's going to grow tired of you after a while just like he did with all the other women. I'm trying to protect you, sweetheart. He'll only break your heart.

I don't believe that. I think he's changed. More than you think. What more does he have to do to prove himself?

"You seem troubled, are you all right?" Lucian asked.

"I'm only curious." She turned her eyes to him. "What was it about Florence that made you want to marry her? It couldn't have been purely physical. You had to at least like her, and yet you ended up hating her."

He sighed. "She was a different person when we married. She was a hopeless romantic, like Melody, and the unruliest of women. She would race with the boys during social gatherings. She let her hair down while everyone else pinned it up. She loved to have fun. You know, she was only sixteen when we married. I wanted her more than I ever wanted anything. She seduced me with her outlandish ways. Then I was obligated to marry her, and I did so to protect her honor. She was a Lady, after all."

"What changed?"

"She must have realized that I didn't love her, and she made my life a living hell because of it. When I got her pregnant, she never forgave me for that."

J.D. couldn't help but pity Florence. Her bitterness turned her into a terrible person, and she lost sight of who she used to be. J.D. couldn't imagine what it would be like if she married a man who didn't love her.

"No," he said.

"No what?"

"It is not the same with you. I can see in your eyes that you are concerned. What I felt for Florence was lust. But I am with you because I love you."

She smiled with unabashed joy, all her concerns disappearing with that short but powerful phrase.

"If getting my uncle's permission wasn't an issue, would you agree to be with me? Right here, right now?"

He turned his eyes from her for a moment. Her heart beat faster as she waited for his answer. Was his hesitation leading up to a no? He had a legacy of always getting what he wanted and not letting anything get in his way. She saw in his eyes that he wanted and desired her. Why wasn't he giving in when she was so willing to be with him?

"There are not many things I have done right in this life," he said. "I bound myself to Florence for honor, I failed as a father, and I ruined many lives for the sake of my vengeance. But I have been given a second chance. If we are to be together, it will be as it should.

"I plan to spend as much time with you as possible. I want to take you to dinner, and I want to hold your hand while we go for walks under the moon. I want to dance with you. I want to kiss you and hold you in my arms, as I do now. And when I know the time is right, and with Gallard's permission, I want to buy you a ring. I will get down on one knee and ask you to do me the honor of spending the rest of your life with me. And, if you say yes, I plan to marry you in front of all we know while you wear a white dress." He pressed his forehead to hers. "We'll go away on a vacation. Somewhere nice and secluded so we'll be alone. Then, and only then, will I make love to you."

He got up from the bed and went into the bathroom to take a shower while she lay there, speechless. After this speech, she was certain that he loved her. He wanted more than to just be physical—he wanted a relationship. He wanted to marry her. That was when she realized that she wanted to marry him too and she couldn't wait for the day when he would ask.

Lucian would probably be at least twenty minutes since he had a long shower routine, so she got up to get something to eat. She found Abe in the kitchen making one of his usual fruit smoothies. She hardly saw her brother eat anything other than fruit, chicken, and vegetables. He claimed it was how he maintained his physique.

"Morning, sis," he said. "I didn't know you stayed over last night."

"Yeah, I did. You must have had a good time last night."

Abe smirked. "Yeah, if you call watching WWE and eating pretzels a good time."

J.D. rolled her eyes. "Why bother pretending, Abraham. We heard you and whoever you were banging."

"Whatever, Jordin. It was totally you and Lucian making all that noise last night. I had to turn the TV up to block it out."

"Contrary to what you think, Lucian and I aren't sleeping together yet. I know you're a manwhore. There's no need to hide it now."

He chuckled. "I'm many things, but not a liar. If someone was getting it on last night, it wasn't me."

At that moment, someone else walked into the kitchen. A guy that J.D. didn't recognize. He had sweats on and a muscle shirt tighter than the ones Abe wore. He had a douchey haircut too with his obviously bleached hair longer on top and the sides buzzed with a cheesy design.

"Morning," he said, acting as if they were all good friends.

"Who the hell are you?" Abe asked.

"Chad." He started opening the cupboards. "Hey, Kev! Where are the K cups?"

This douche was here with Kevin? J.D. never would have guessed. By the look on Abe's face, he was equally as confused.

Kevin came into the kitchen at that moment. Lela had been giving him her blood the past few weeks since Lucas didn't know when he would be investigated. His hair was wet, and he had a towel around his waist. When he saw that he'd been caught, his expression became grim.

"Uh, Chad. Maybe we can grab coffee in town."

"But that requires spending money."

Kevin ground his teeth. "I'll pay. Now can you go back to the room, please?"

Chad glanced at J.D. and Abe as if he were sizing them up then walked passed Kevin down the hall.

"Sorry about that," Kevin said. "We'll go to his place next time."

"Since when do you have a boyfriend?" Abe asked. "Is that why you never want to go pick up chicks with me? You're gay?"

"I thought you knew." Kevin crossed his arms. "Anyway, he's not my boyfriend."

"Good," J.D. threw in, finally finding her voice. "Because you can do so much better."

Kevin shrugged, a clear sadness in his eyes. He didn't look like a guy who had just spent the night having the time of his life. His gaze was empty. Like he was disgusted with himself.

"Why do you think I'm always defending your brother? It's because we're the same. I'm just as much of a manwhore as he is. I'm just more discreet." He sighed. "I'd appreciate it if you didn't mention this incident to anyone. I'll go to Chad's place from now on."

Before J.D. could reply, Kevin disappeared back into his room. Unlike Abe, Kevin had a good excuse for his behavior. Her father told her what happened to his fiancé, and it broke her heart that he still hadn't recovered. She would be devastated if anything happened to Lucian.

"My head is spinning," Abe said. "Did you know Uncle Kev was gay?"

"Yes. And I think it would be very wise to abide by his wishes." She looked into her brother's eyes. "I'm sorry I assumed it was you last night."

He nodded. "You're forgiven."

Feeling a little emotional, J.D. did something she hadn't done in years and hugged Abe. He was just as stunned but hugged her back nonetheless. When she released him, she went out the door and headed for her house.

She was almost to the door when she saw Robin come out from around the corner. If she wasn't mistaken, Robin looked like she'd put on a little weight. Her shirt was a bit tighter than usual. She glanced around like she was afraid someone would see her. Curious, J.D. stopped and watched her for a bit.

Robin took her hands out from her pockets and something fell out and spilled onto the grass. It was cigarettes. J.D. could see them clearly from where she was standing. Robin frantically gathering them up and tried to stuff them into the box and doing a poor job of it.

"Busted!" J.D. shouted.

Robin flinched. "J.D.! Don't scare me like that!"

"Sorry hon, I couldn't help myself." J.D. bent down and finished helping her. "Not to sound like your mother, but you know smoking kills, right?"

"Not me, it won't. The blood pills help fight off illness and disease. Not that it's any of your business."

That was harsh. Robin hardly ever got mad, especially at J.D. Robin was a sweetheart and was even nice to strangers. Something was going on with her.

"You okay? You seem . . . on edge."

"PMS." Robin angrily put the cigarette pack into her pocket. "Please don't say anything to anyone."

"Robin—"

"I'm begging you. Because I've kept your secret about Lucian for months and I ask that you do the same for me."

There was no winning there. J.D. knew that she owed Robin for helping them hide their relationship. The only difference was that her seeing Lucian wasn't destructive behavior. Either way, she wouldn't betray her friend. Instead, she was going to try and help her with whatever was causing her to pick up the nasty habit.

"Deal. Hey, why don't we have a girl's day? I think Nicola is teaching her class today. We could sign up and see if we're talented or not?"

Robin smiled. "Sure, we can do that. Let me change into something ratty."

The two women threw on old clothes then headed for the gallery. J.D. was already aware that she was terrible at painting but thought it would be fun anyway. She was in the process of finding her calling in life. She'd tried everything from ballet to college to modeling. The modeling thing quickly went downhill when every interview she scored would end with, "Wait, are you Abe Christophe's sister?" Then she would get callbacks, not because of her merit but because of her name.

She parked the car then they got out. The lot was practically empty, and she wondered if anyone else had shown up. Nicola had mentioned most of her classes had at least four or five people at once. Judging by how bare the lot was, it looked like only two people were there. There was a limo parked by the entrance. Maybe someone rich was coming to buy art.

Robin opened the door for them and they listened for signs of life. It was eerily quiet, so J.D. checked her phone to make sure she had the day right. It was Tuesday, and Nicola always taught on Tuesdays from ten to noon. It was currently nine fifty. People must have been running late.

"Hello!" someone said, startling them. A tall man came out from the other room and he was wiping paint off his hands onto a rag. "I'm sorry I didn't hear you at first. I was lost in a piece I'm working on."

She studied him further. He was very muscular, though not as big as Abe, and had dark brown hair. Then her heart lurched. He had Lucian's eyes.

"You're not Ryan," Robin said. "Who are you?"

"Simeon Atherton. I'm—" he narrowed his eyes at Robin. "I'll be damned. You are the spitting image of Sheila Bledsoe!"

"She was my mother," she said. "How do you know her?"

"We went way back. Your father and me too. We went to college together. Pardon me for saying this but, I was under the impression that you were dead. The only explanation is that Jordan d'Aubigne brought you back, but he is dead as well."

J.D. shot her a sideways glance. He may have known Robin's parents and the existence of vampires but that didn't mean he could be trusted with vital information. There were two unspoken rules in her family — do not tell anyone that they were vampires and do not tell anyone who is a vampire about Lucas' abilities. She was extremely protective of her cousin. Especially when it came to Lucian's psychotic grandson.

Careful, sweetheart. That man is dangerous.

What did he do?

The list is too long. But you should know that he killed your mother with the intent of killing you and Abe. He was out to destroy the d'Aubigne line.

J.D. nearly fell over. This man had murdered her mother? She'd known her mother had died in a fire and that her father resurrected her on accident, but he never told her someone had murdered her. She felt even more protective of her brother now. If he found out who she was, he might try again.

"Jordan brought her back before he died," J.D. said.

"Interesting." He smiled. "And now here you are, in my art gallery."

"Excuse me, *your* gallery?"

"That is correct. I own it and Ryan runs it. He's currently taking care of something and he asked that I fill in as the teacher. I guess he and his assistant are out of town checking out a new piece he wants to buy. She's kind of a hit around here. When the students learned I would be subbing, a lot of them didn't show up."

"Well, we would like to take a class," Robin said. "Unless you're canceling due to low numbers."

He gave her a smile that made J.D. uncomfortable. The best and worst part of Robin was that she liked to see the best in everyone. She had a very low radar when it came to shady people and that was why J.D. took it upon herself to look out for her. She wasn't about to let another Ash incident happen. It would probably break Robin.

"I would love to teach you," he finally said. "For old time's sake." He chuckled. "Wow. You Bledsoe women are striking."

Robin blushed. "You're very kind."

The three of them went to the art room and Simeon gave them each a fresh sheet of newsprint. Thankfully there were available art supplies for them to borrow and he started out with simple shading techniques. For a while, J.D. set aside her leery vibes she was getting from him and paid attention. He was a good teacher and she caught on very quickly.

They moved on to colors and he told them to draw the first thing that came to mind as some sort of creative exercise. She thought of Lucian and how she'd loved spending the night with him. She'd never drawn a portrait before, so she did a vague silhouette type sketch, focusing mostly on his eyes and hair.

Simeon walked up behind Robin and stared at whatever she was drawing. It was a broken teacup and there was a small bird on it.

"You're a natural," Simeon said. "I love the way your hands move when you draw."

"I guess I draw the way J.D. taught me how to sew. Again, you're being too kind."

"No, I'm truly impressed." He put his hands on her shoulders. "You have the hands of a goddess."

J.D. raised her eyebrow and looked at him. Did he touch all his students that way? If so, he better keep his paws off of her or she would poke him with her recently sharpened charcoal pencil. She was surprised that Robin wasn't shrugging him off. She was too polite for that.

Simeon finally moved away from Robin and walked up to J.D. She stopped drawing and waited for him to give her a critique. She was well aware that the drawing looking nothing like Lucian, but she liked to think she'd captured his essence.

"Who is that?" he asked.

"He's . . . well, I wouldn't call him a boyfriend because he isn't a boy at all. Let's call him my lover."

Robin laughed and she shot her a glare, which made her stop, but she was still letting a little giggle out here and there.

"You're involved with Lucian Christophe?"

J.D.'s flinched. "Yes."

"Well I'll be! You're dating my grandfather. Does that make you my future grandmother?"

Ew, Jordan said.

My thoughts exactly.

"Yeah, no," she said. "Not happening."

"I didn't think he'd ever get over Lela," Simeon said. "However, I can see why he did."

To hide her discomfort, she continued drawing. The subject of Lucian's past feelings for Lela had always been something she didn't want to discuss. Sure, they talked about Florence, but he never loved her. Lucian dove in front of a sword for Gallard because he knew Lela would be devastated if he died. She often wondered if the switchback had never happened if Lela and Lucian would have ended up together.

They finished up with the class, and he insisted that they not pay — a family discount, he called it.

J.D. rolled up her drawing and Robin did the same. She planned to come back when Nicola was teaching to improve her technique. At least then she wouldn't spend most of the class making sure Simeon wasn't flirting with Robin.

She started to leave but Robin lingered behind. She was talking quietly with Simeon and he leaned over and whispered something into her ear. She smiled at him and then he slipped a piece of paper into her back pocket. His hand lingered there longer than necessary, and J.D. could have screamed but she didn't. She would save the lecture for later.

It was difficult, but she kept her opinions to herself until they were in the car. Immediately after they were buckled in, she spoke.

"What the hell was that?"

"What was what?" Robin asked, refusing to make eye contact.

"That whole creepy thing with the note? Show it to me."

"Again, it's none of your business."

J.D. grew quiet and started the car. Since when was Robin turning into such a grouch? She was usually a lot more cheerful. Especially after she started dating Erik. Now she was smoking, snapping at everyone, and taking secret notes from creepy guys.

"I'm not asking because I want to blab," J.D. said. "I just want to know. We share everything with each other."

"I don't see why you're freaking out. A guy gave me his number, so what? It's not like I'm going to call him. I like Erik. I want to be with him."

That perv gave her his number? Oh, hell no, you need to shut that down!

Working on it, dad!

"Well good. He's way too old for you anyway."

Robin smirked. "As opposed to the six-hundred-year difference between you and Lucian?"

Hah! Good point.

Shut up dad.

"All right, I'll drop it. Just promise me you won't meet with this guy, painting class or not. Erik is the better choice and the safer one. I don't trust that Simeon guy. I heard he attacked your sister when she was fourteen and guys like that tend to make a habit of not taking no for an answer."

They didn't speak for the rest of the drive home. Even though Robin played off the afternoon as nothing, J.D. was still worried. She hated to think that Robin was going through a rough time and she'd been too wrapped up in Lucian to see it. She was supposed to be her mentor and friend and she could feel Robin pulling away from her. One way or another, she was going to rebuild their tight relationship.

21

Robin grunted once more as she attempted to button her jeans. She'd been able to hide her growing belly for weeks, but this morning it seemed she'd doubled in size. A flowy shirt still covered her up, but her jeans had gotten too small. After trying on four pairs, it seemed she would have to wear either yoga pants or sweats.

How could she go on a date with Erik in sweats? Even worse, how much longer could she keep her pregnancy from him? She kept making the excuse of PMS bloat, but he was bound to notice sooner or later. Especially with her getting bigger.

When she first moved in with her Uncle Declan and Aunt Paula, Paula used to take her to her spin classes and her intense dance workout sessions. In four months, Robin had gotten into the best shape of her life and rock-hard abs. She still worked out with J.D., but not as intensely as she had with Paula. Soon, her abs would dwindle, and her baby belly would erupt full storm.

What worried her more was what she would do when it was time to deliver. Could she manage to hide it that long? She planned to tell Lela, but every time she built up enough courage, it would disappear the moment she faced her sister. At this rate, she would have to deliver the baby in the toilet like the women on TV.

The front door opened, and she listened to figure out who was there. J.D. and Lucian had gone into town, so it could be anyone. She hoped it wasn't Abe.

"Anyone home?"

It was Nicola. Robin wasn't so worried about her finding out. Nicola knew how to keep a secret, especially of this variety. She'd hidden her pregnancy for years. Only her mother knew.

"I'm here" Robin said without getting up. She'd admitted defeat and sat on the floor with her unbuttoned jeans.

Nicola came pushed open the door and smiled. "Hey, you. What are you doing on the floor?"

"Nothing." Robin looked down at her uncooperative button. "Just sitting here wishing I wasn't fat."

"Robin, you are anything but fat. Your hour-glass figure is something any woman would kill for."

Robin scoffed. "Yeah, right. I'm fat, and I'm only getting fatter."

Nicola sank down on the floor next to her. When Robin first met the woman, she could see in Nicola's eyes that she was sad. Her brother had the same look in his eyes after their parents were killed. Robin had wondered if she'd lost someone.

"What makes you think you're fat?" Nicola asked.

She shrugged then got up and grabbed some leggings from her drawer. She turned her back to Nicola while she changed, not because she was embarrassed but because she didn't want Nic to see her stomach.

"Robin, can I ask you something?"

"Sure." She turned back around and joined Nicola on the floor again.

"How are you doing? And I want you to be honest. You know you can tell me anything."

Robin dropped her gaze. She wanted to tell Nic everything – about the baby, the smoking, the insomnia. Keeping everything inside made her feel even worse but talking about it hurt too.

"I've been having nightmares," she admitted. "I used to dream about it every night. If I don't sleep, I don't dream."

Nicola put an arm around her. "I understand. I used to have nightmares too. About what happened to me. About Colton. The nightmares made me mean, and I didn't treat my family very well after that. Except my mom. She was the only one I didn't push away. I'm surprised Mona didn't hate me when I came home."

Robin lightly smiled. "Your sister never would have hated you. Just like how I could never hate Lela. I understand why she killed me all those years ago. I wouldn't want to be ten years old forever." She looked at Nicola. "Did the nightmares ever stop?"

"For a while." Her eyes suddenly became happy. "Whenever I sleep next to Lucas, the nightmares go away. He keeps them from haunting me."

Robin hugged her knees to her chest. "Do you think if I sleep next to Erik he'll make the nightmares go away?'

Nicola shrugged. "Maybe. Does he make you feel safe when you're with him?"

"Yes. He makes me forget about what happened to me. But what if he finds out and he hates me? What if he thinks I'm dirty?"

"Oh, Robin, he would never think that! You didn't want to be with those men. They were the dirty ones, not you."

Robin fought the tears as they stung her eyes. Maybe he wouldn't care that she'd been violated, but what if he found out her nephew might be the father of her baby? She wished there was a way to clear it up without having to tell anyone of her condition.

"Hey," Nicola said. "I hate to go, but I have class to teach. I just stopped by to grab a quick drink. You ever need to talk, you come find me, okay?"

She nodded. "Okay. Thanks for listening to me, Nicola. Lucas is lucky to have you."

Nicola shrugged. "I think I'm the lucky one. He made me part of this wonderful family."

"And I hope you two get married someday. You'd make a great sister-in-law."

Nic kissed her cheek. "Thanks, hon. Hang in there. We're all here for you."

Her friend stood up and Robin felt even more lonely as Nicola walked out of the room. She listened as the front door closed, leaving her alone in her sadness once more.

Nicola was right— she couldn't keep it all in. If she couldn't talk to her friend, there was one person she knew would make her feel better.

She pulled out her phone and dialed the number. It would be a long shot if she got an answer, but she had to try. She was running out of options and time.

"Hey, Robin bird! How are you?"

"I'm okay, Gallard." She teared up again but didn't try to fight them anymore. "It's good to hear your voice. I miss you."

"I miss you too. I miss all of you. Even Lucian, but don't tell him I said that." He chuckled. "How are you, really? You sound kind of sad."

She sucked in her breath in a poor attempt to stop herself from crying. Gallard knew she wasn't okay. She never could fool him. He knew her too well. She never thanked him for all the times he'd flown all the way from Las Vegas just to check up on her while she was grieving her sister's death. He made everything better then, and she needed him to make her feel better now.

"Gallard, I'm pregnant," she finally admitted.

It was such a relief to share this with the one person she really wanted to talk to. He didn't say anything for a long time, but she wasn't worried he would hang up. No doubt he was angry, like he had been when he found out what happened to her. She was afraid that this would upset him even more.

"Oh, Robin, no," he said after a while. "Are you sure? Please tell me there's a chance this isn't true."

"I'm sure. I thought I might be, but I wasn't sure until I took a test. I'm already six months along." She started sobbing beyond control, and she could hear on the other line that he was crying as well. "I don't know what to do. Tell me what I should do."

"I'm coming home."

She composed herself enough to answer. "No! You can't come home. You need to find people to help Micah!"

"Even if I did, it will still be months until we can carry out a plan of action. I've been gone for over a month and my sister-in-law needs me right now. I'll have Solomon and David continue to find people. I'm coming home."

"Okay." Robin wiped away her tears. "Please don't tell my dad or Lela. I want to tell them myself."

"It will be hard, but . . . I will keep this to myself. Stay strong, my Robin bird. I'll be home in a day or two."

"In time for the family dinner?"

"Family dinner? Sounds like one of J.D.'s schemes."

Robin laughed. So far only Abe and Gallard still had the ability to make her laugh. Once they were both in her life, she might finally be able to heal.

"It is. As if we don't eat together all the time already. This is a special occasion, apparently."

"You're funny, you know that? You and your sister have a way of being able to laugh when times are hard. I wish I was that strong."

"You are strong. Why do you think I like you so much?"

"I thought it was my good looks and great hugs."

She laughed again, her sadness quickly washing away. Talking to Gallard was exactly what she needed.

"Oh, and I have one last request. It might seem strange, but you're going to have to blame Melody for this one."

"Well, Melody is very persuasive so I better do as she asks. What is this mysterious request?"

"Could you . . . show up wearing a marine's uniform?"

There was silence again.

"I'm going to pretend that this isn't strange and just go with it," he said.

"Thank you, I really appreciate your blind faith. And um . . . you're going to have to cut your hair."

"What!"

"You won't look like a marine with shoulder-length hair. It'll grow back!"

He sighed. "I haven't had short hair since I was born. But if that's what she wants, it's what she'll get. She owes me big."

"Big? Like a wig? I'm sure Lela could find something for you."

"You read my mind. I always knew you were a smart girl." He chuckled. "Hey, I gotta go, but I'll see you soon." He grew serious once more. "I love you. Hang in there, okay? You don't have to go through this alone."

"I love you too. I'll see you."

She hung up, feeling excited and worried at the same time. Gallard was finally coming home after a month and he would help her make a decision. But he didn't believe that she had a boyfriend and she dreaded his reaction when he would find out she wasn't joking.

22

I tucked my shirt into my pants then buckled my belt. Thanks to Lucian's help, I was able to upgrade my wardrobe from that of a bachelor to a respectable businessman. My clothes weren't as expensive or fancy as Lucian's, but they were very nice in my opinion. My job allowed for me to wear street clothes, and I wanted to look a little formal. I was eager to start work and looking forward to what I would be doing.

My phone started to ring. I checked the I.D. and saw it was the school. I assumed Colton had gotten there okay with Nicola and I had a feeling this was about the investigation. It had gone well, and I had faith that it was all over.

"Hello?" I said once I'd answered it.

"Is this Lucas d'Aubigne?" the woman asked. I recognized the voice as Mrs. Archibald.

"Yes, this is. Is everything okay with Colton?"

"I'm not sure. I was just visited by the recess supervisor and she said that Colton was taken off campus by an unknown male."

As my anxiety level went from zero to ten in less than a second, everything in the room began to vibrate. Someone claiming to be his uncle had picked him up from school? Who was this person? Everyone in my family knew to call me before they made any decisions concerning Colton.

Even Nicola would send me a text to let me know he'd been picked up and dropped off safely, which she had. She wouldn't let anyone take Colton out of school without telling me.

"Did the supervisor happen to catch a good glimpse of him?"

"No, she only said the guy was some sort of officer. Maybe a Chief or a Lieutenant. Some sort of police rank I think."

It had to be Scott. Who else would Colton willingly trust and leave with? How did he find me here? I never mentioned to anyone in Miami where I was going, and I was so careful.

But why would he come for Colton? He'd promised taking Micah was the trade for Colton. That was when I remembered Henry. We'd made the agreement before Henry was killed and he probably knew that I was responsible in some way. And he wanted revenge. In a way I pitied him. If someone killed Colton, I would want revenge. But Colton hadn't violated women or forced them into an experiment they didn't want a part of. Colton hadn't killed anyone. He didn't kill Mona or threaten to murder Nicola.

"What about the car he was driving, did you see it?" I asked, going into cop mode.

"Let me transfer you to the principle."

The few milliseconds it took for me to be transferred cranked up my anxiety even more. Every second that I was gathering information, Colton could be getting further and further into the MITF's clutches.

"Hello, Mr. d'Aubigne. I'm Principle Alfred Gaines."

"Mr. Gaines, I was just told that my son was taken off campus without my consent."

"I was informed, and we are currently taking action. The man drove a black Cadillac Thorium. We were going to call you before we contacted the police in case—"

I hung up the phone then dialed the station. If Colton had just been taken, there was a chance they could stop Scott before he was out of Texas.

"Sheriff's department, how may I assist you?"

"Sheriff Tyler, it's Lucas. My son was taken by a man in a black Cadillac Thorium. I don't know the plates, but I doubt it would be hard to find it around here."

"We're on it. Come down to the station and we'll keep you filled in on the details."

"Thank you, I appreciate it."

I hung up as I got into my car and gunned it down the street. I probably broke the sound barrier as I screeched around the corners and made my way to the station. I kept my eye open for the car, weaving in and out of traffic. I couldn't believe this was happening and I wished I'd seen it coming.

I never even said goodbye to Colton before he went to school. I hadn't even said two words to him since the day before. I'd only ruffled his hair.

I should have gone over to kiss him goodnight instead of stewing over my relationship problems. He'd only just called me dad for the first time ,and I may never hear that again.

My phone rang again and I answered it without checking.

"Did you find it?" I asked.

"Better news. I was just told that a man driving that car was arrested five minutes ago for speeding and driving under the influence. They said he had a little boy with him.

"I'll be there in five minutes. Thank you, Sheriff."

Relief washed over me and I nearly cried. They'd stopped him from taking Colton away. No words could describe how I felt at that moment. Five minutes was too long to have to wait to hold my son in my arms again. I didn't even park straight when I got to the station and I had to catch myself before I used my superhuman speed to get through the door.

I looked around the room until I saw Erik and I went to him first. He was talking with Sheriff Tyler. When he saw me, they stopped speaking and turned their attention to me.

"Lucas, hey," Erik said. "I heard that the guy we brought in had taken your son."

"Yes, he did. Where is he?"

He pointed over to Officer James, and I saw that he was playing with Colton. He'd given him his handcuffs and Colton looked so intrigued. I hurried over to him and picked him up without giving him a greeting. I didn't say anything but held him as if I were never going to hold him again. I promised myself I would hug him like this every day and not take my time with him for granted.

Are you okay?" I asked him. I kissed the side of his head. "They told me you were taken, and I was worried."

"I'm awesome, dad." He leaned close to my ear and cupped his hand around his mouth, whispering quietly, "Grandpa is in town. I couldn't tell anyone, and he said to call him uncle."

I raised an eyebrow. Why was he calling Scott grandpa? Was it because he was my adopted father? And Sheriff Tyler had said that he was arrested for drinking and driving. Scott hardly ever drank, let alone enough to get drunk.

"Hey, bud. Why don't you play with the cuffs again? I'm going to talk to your uncle."

I set him down then rejoined Erik and Tyler. I wanted to clear up all these confusing facts and figure out what was going on. Colton didn't seem scared at all and I wanted to know who they had in custody.

"The man who took him— what does he look like?" I asked.

"Well . . . *you*, actually," Erik said. "He said he was on leave and that he wanted to surprise everyone. Keeps saying something about diplomatic immunity. He wouldn't give us his name, though."

Now I was really confused. Erik started walking down the hall and I followed him. We stopped in front of one of the two-way mirrors. I looked in and saw one of the other officers questioning a man in a marine uniform. I stared intently at the man, trying to figure out where I'd seen him before and then it clicked.

"Would it be possible for me to talk to him?" I asked.

Erik nodded then knocked on the window. The officer got up from the table and opened the door. Erik told him what was going on and then we went into the interrogation room. I figured he was supposed to be there in case there was confrontation. This unrecognizable man smiled at me and stood up. He staggered a bit then put his hands on the table for support.

"Lucas! How did you know I was here?"

I reached over and hugged Gallard. Despite the scare, I'd missed my dad this past month. It felt like something was missing and with him here, everything might start coming together. What I wanted to know was why he was impersonating a marine and why he'd scared me half to death by taking Colton out of school.

Something else wasn't right. He reeked of alcohol. I then remembered the DWI arrest. If he was a vampire, he shouldn't have been able to get drunk, nor would alcohol appeal to him. Everything about his being here felt off.

"You know this man?" Erik asked.

"Of course he knows me." Gallard gave me a firm pat on the back. "I'm his—"

"Brother," I interrupted. "He wasn't lying about being on leave."

Gallard held his hand to Erik who took it. "I'm Private Warren d'Aubigne. I'm also a Marquess. You see, my great-grandfather was a Duke and—"

"You took Colton out of school and didn't tell me?" I interrupted. "I thought he was gone for good! You of all people should understand."

Gallard sank into the chair and covered his face. "I know. I was hoping they wouldn't call you until after I got to the house, but then I got pulled over."

"You were speeding? And driving drunk with my son in the car? What the hell were you thinking? You could have killed him!"

Erik must have sensed that this was a private conversation because he left the room without a word and shut the door behind him. I hardened my gaze on Gallard and waited for him to give me an explanation.

"You're right. I was—I *am* drunk. I helped myself to the bar on the plane and I can't even remember landing. Or buying the car for that matter. Things started to clear up when I stopped by the school and then I saw the flashing lights."

I sighed then took a seat in the chair on the other side of the table and stared at him. I tried to understand what exactly was going on. The man in front of me, excluding his changed appearance, wasn't the same man that left me behind with the promise that he would return with a plan. He was drunk, irrational, and making poor judgment calls.

"What's wrong with you?" I asked. "You're not yourself."

"Actually, I am. This is me. Three hundred . . . days ago. I'll be fine, Lucas. I just needed something to help me forget. I needed to relax."

"Relax? You're not relaxed, you're drunk to the point of blacking out. You're putting your nephew in danger! What if mom saw you like this?"

He looked up at me with his slightly bloodshot eyes and that was when I noticed they weren't grey. They were blue, like mine. I nearly forgot that Arnaud had given him my gift. It must have granted him temporary mortality, at least mortal bodily functions. He was a mess and I didn't want my mom to see him like this.

"How is it that you are so friendly with these cops?" he asked. "That one who brought me in acted like he knew you."

"I do know him, *Warren*. I'm a cop now, remember? Unfortunately, my job description doesn't include defending drunk marines."

"You're right. You have no business trying to bail me out of things. I'm supposed to be responsible for *you*. I apologize."

Someone knocked on the window, and I stood up then left the room. I had no idea how I was going to get him out of this. He could be doing jail time and that was the last thing we needed. He'd already been broken out of jail in this state and I doubted it would go any better than the last time.

"I know this looks bad, but he's been through a lot. He was honorably discharged because of his PTSD and he's not acting like himself."

"I would try to compromise at this point, but driving while intoxicated is a serious crime," Erik said. "The best we can do is try and get him decent bail and hope the court is sympathetic." He paused. "Robin told me your family has regal background. Is your brother really a Marquess?"

I couldn't believe she told him that. I always knew this fact about the Christophe family line but none of us ever went by the titles we were technically under.

"Yes, he is. And I'm technically . . . an Earl."

"It's true! Lucas, what the hell is an Earl doing being a cop in this small town?"

"Because I have no land or estate to preside over, I guess. Unless you count my one-story house on Hawthorne."

"Hmm. Earl of Hawthorne." Erik gave me a teasing smile. "I like it."

A half an hour later, we went to his arraignment. Everyone agreed this should be dealt with as soon as possible so he could get home and I sat in the back with Colton in my lap. Gallard could barely walk into the court room and I shook my head in disappointment.

"On the charges of driving while intoxicated, how do you plead?" the judge asked his lawyer.

150

"Guilty, your honor."

"And on the charges of kidnapping, how do you plead?"

"Not guilty. Your honor, the child in question is related to my client. His brother is dropping the charges of kidnapping."

"Very well. Mr.—I mean Private d'Aubigne, because you were driving while intoxicated and had a minor under the age of fifteen in the car, I'm afraid your bail will not be the minimum. Bail is set at ten-thousand dollars."

"Your honor, while he is a military officer, he is also high ranking in diplomacy. He has diplomatic immunity."

The judge sighed. "Present documented proof and then he can be released. Court is dismissed."

Thankfully, I had said documents on my phone and ready to fax. I didn't really want to, but I did it for old time's sake. I ran into Tyler while I was waiting for Gallard to be released.

"I am sorry you have to go through this."

"So am I. It won't happen again. I'll make sure he doesn't get behind the wheel unless he's sober. I'll bring him in myself if he does."

I helped Gallard walk to the car and he had Colton's hand in his. I was grateful that Colton was too young to realize what was going on. Out of desperation, I called Lucian and asked that he fly down to the precinct and drive the Cadillac to the restaurant. I didn't tell him about Gallard just yet. I planned to do that when we would meet for coffee.

23

Since Colton only had an hour left of school by then, I brought him with us. People kept giving Gallard nods of approval and some even thanked him for his service. A hoard of teenage girls kept staring at him like a bunch of cats ready to pounce on their prey.

I dropped Gallard into a chair and helped Colton into a booster seat before ordering two black coffees. Both were for Gallard. I also ordered a grilled cheese for Colton and iced tea for me. Gallard wasn't as loopy, but he was still a long way from his old self. He hadn't said a word to me on the drive over but kept staring at me with such regret that it was hard to be mad at him. I was tired of being let down by people I cared about and I really didn't need it from him.

"Okay, tell me. What's going on with you? You're drunk for a reason and I want to know why."

He took a sip of the coffee and set it down, barely getting it far enough away from the edge.

"I remember the day you were born like it was yesterday. Lela was crankier than usual and Cherish had come into town with Melody because Lela was close to forty weeks. She and Cherish were arguing about something while Solomon and I were talking in the kitchen. We tried to tune out the conversation, but it was so loud that we listened in. That was when we realized that Lela had gone into labor four hours before and hadn't said anything. Cherish had been trying to convince her to go to the hospital.

"When I held you for the first time, I cried. You were the most beautiful baby I'd ever seen. You weren't wailing like I expected, and I could have sworn that when I smiled, you raised an eyebrow. You didn't look amused at all and I knew that peek-a-boo would not be your favorite game. You looked like your mother, still do."

I forced a smile and stirred my ice cubes with the straw. Lela had written about the day I was born in the journal, but I'd never heard it from Gallard's side. Hearing about it made me wish that I'd been there when Colton was born. At least I'd been around when he was barely a few months old. I was only a brother to him then, but I cherished those moments that I looked out for him and helped take care of him.

"What does that have to do with why you're drunk?"

The door to the restaurant opened and Lucian walked in. I waved him over and he came to the table, giving Gallard a wary glance. When he figured out who it was, he chuckled.

"Solomon must have told you what my Melody has been telling everyone around here," he said. "Did you return alone?"

"Unfortunately, yes. I would have returned in one piece had Solomon been with me."

"Why did you come back? Not that your presence isn't welcome."

"I was just asking him that," I said.

Gallard finished the first coffee and started with the other. His silence made me anxious and I already had enough anxiety in my life.

"I met God on top of Mount Sinai," Gallard said.

Lucian and I exchanged a glance.

"Is this the alcohol talking?" I asked.

"I'm serious, Lucas. I was so awestruck that I was literally brought to my knees. He showed me something that might be important to you. It explains everything— your gifts, our existence. Maximus' motives."

"Tell us," Lucian said. "If there is more to the story I want to know."

Once he'd sipped the last drop of coffee, he pushed it aside and took off his hat. I couldn't hold back the slight yell that escaped my mouth when I saw his hair, or lack thereof. He'd given himself a buzz cut making it shorter than mine. Erik was right—he did look like me. He resembled Micah more when he had longer hair, but now he was nearly my doppelganger.

"Maximus was born in eleven A.D., just before Caesar Augustus was murdered and succeeded by Tiberius," Gallard began. "He was born and raised in Philippi and was related to the guard responsible for watching over Paul and Silas in prison. After they escaped, his household was baptized and he began to heal and raise the dead, just like the other apostles.

"One day, he met a woman named Deborah. They fell in love, and he ceased his ministry so they could marry. But before they could, she was killed by a chariot. He tried to bring her back and couldn't. That's when the devil made a deal to imbue him with the power to do so. He dug up her body and took her out to the desert. He resurrected her, but it was apparent she wasn't the same. She craved blood. Fearing for her life, he kept her hidden and they spent several months — "

"Do *not* say copulating," I said.

"Why not?" Lucian asked. "You know so much about it. J.D. will not use her shower anymore."

"She told you about that? Does she not know how to keep a secret? Maybe I should put an ad in the paper about *her* activities. And tell her to give me back my taser."

Gallard raised an eyebrow. "I was going to say helping her adjust, but I'm sure they did that too. Anyway, you interrupted my story. Later on, Deborah attacked a lone traveler then to save his life, the devil told her to give him her blood, thus turning the first second-generation vampire. Then he gave his blood to others and so forth. Maximus realized he was deceived, and he didn't resurrect another person for thousands of years."

"That was when he turned me," Lucian said. "But since he didn't give it all, he didn't earn his place, right?"

Gallard crooked his mouth and nodded.

"What about Jordan?" I asked. "How does he fit into this?"

"That, I am not sure of. It all has to do with our souls. They're trapped here and you had the ability to have your soul take over someone's body rather than being trapped in a void. But since Lucian still wields Maximus' power, he's in danger of unleashing the darkest evil."

"Darkest evil? As in . . . the devil?" Lucian asked.

"Yes. Your gifts make you vulnerable to his influence, which means he could take over your body if he wanted. So long as you suppress the power and not let it in, you should be fine."

I let out an impressed whistle. It was amazing how everything seemed to work out. Everything that ever happened was all meant to be. We all had a purpose.

"What's the alternative?" I asked. "If immortals lost their souls when they turned, there must be a way to reverse it, right?"

Gallard leaned back in his seat and folded his arms. "There isn't. We lost our souls the moment we drank blood. All we can do is hope that we can fight for our rights and try to bring peace between the races.

This was disappointing. He'd gone all that way and learned all this information about Maximus for what? To clarify the story? None of it had any real purpose. He did all this for a woman, and it blew up in his face. But it didn't help us any. We just had to keep Lucian alive.

"Wait," I said, my wheels turning. "Jordan had to know that Lucian was susceptible to the devil's power. It's imprinted on his soul, and since he possessed you for a time, that meant your body could have been an easy target for the Devil. Jordan needed Lucian to be alive. That was why he brought him back." I thought some more. "He tricked Simeon into killing the wrong man. And then he gave his power to me. I don't see how that fits. Why, if killing Jordan wouldn't kill the immortals, did he transfer the power?"

"He must have allowed the vampires to kill him as a way to give us more time to try and stop Simeon," Lucian said. "And because of . . ."

Gallard shot him a glance and Lucian suddenly became tight lipped.

"Because of what?"

"Nothing. He gave you his power so we would have a way to defend our race. Simeon wasn't going to stop until Jordan was dead. He acted out of desperation."

None of this was making any sense. What I wanted to do was go to Mount Sinai and get answers myself, but now was not the time. I felt like I could really make a difference here in Arlington, starting with defending immortals. Going to Sinai would be my last resort if this army thing didn't work out. Until then, I would focus on the here and now.

24

Robin sat in the empty swivel chair and read her book while she waited for Lela. when Lela asked if she wanted to spend the day in the salon, she couldn't say no. She loved spending time where her sister worked. She watched as customers came in and got their hair done and even struck up conversation with some of them.

One of the other stylists, Kendra, kept raving about Robin's hair until finally she couldn't stand it anymore and gave Robin a free makeover. She took off about two inches, put light blonde highlights in it and smoothed it out with a flat iron. Robin liked her hair straight better than curly because it was easier to manage.

"You ready to go, hon?" Lela asked as she put on her jacket. Robin nodded then got out of the chair and stuffed her book into her purse. They walked out the door and Lela locked it behind her before they went to the car. Robin got excited when Lela said she could drive, so she hopped into the driver's seat and headed for Euless.

"Are you not feeling good," Lela asked.

"Huh? Why do you ask?

"You're keep touching your stomach. And you're . . . how do I say this without sounding rude? You look a little bloated.

She crossed her arms, glancing out the window. She loved her sister, but she was terrified of how she would react to the news of the baby.

"You're still mad at me." Lela stated. When Robin didn't answer, she said, "You know I'm only doing this because I care. I'm not trying to be the evil villain that keeps the hero and heroine from having their happy ending. I think you should wait a while before you try to have a relationship. Now isn't really a good time."

"Why not? I'm not a child. I'm old enough to understand that when you say Gallard has magic hands, it doesn't mean he can do card tricks." Lela gasped in shock when Robin said this. "I know I'm right, don't deny it. And I know that you weren't married to him yet when you made that comment."

"Robin Michelle, you are something else." Lela reached over and took Robin's hand. "I'm also thinking of your emotional health. You went through something terrible, and it takes time to heal. I admire that you were comfortable with Erik because if it were me, I would have stayed far away from men."

"But what about Simeon? Didn't he hurt you?"

"How did you—oh, I guess it doesn't matter. Yes, Simeon tried to hurt me, but he didn't. Gallard made sure of that. And I defended myself when Matthew tried the same thing. There are disgusting people out there, as you know. I just wish you never had to experience that."

Robin glanced out the window. There was something that she never told Lela, even when she was a child. She would rather forget it and hadn't even thought about it until Matthew was mentioned. The truth was that Ash wasn't the first man to violate her. Matthew was.

All these horrible memories were dampening her mood. Hanging out with Erik would always help her forget and for a while, she would be happy and content. But as soon as he would drive away, she would remember she was damaged and go right back to finding ways to cope. Lela probably would have understood but talking about it was worse. She'd hated having to tell Lucas when it happened. She'd hated having to retell it to the police, twice, and all she wanted was to forget and focus on her new life in Texas.

"I actually wanted to talk to you about something," Robin said.

"Okay, shoot."

She thought about how she would word this. She hadn't exactly told Lela that she'd invited Erik for dinner. As far as Lela knew, this was just a family only thing.

"Erik is coming over for dinner tomorrow."

"What? Robin, we already talked about this!"

"I know. We talked, and I disagree. Erik is a great guy and he wants to prove that to you and everyone else."

"I don't need proof. I've met him before when he was friends with J.D. I agree that he's a great guy, but hon you are *not* ready to be in a relationship. You were five years old when you came back seven months ago, and you still have a lot of growing up to do."

Robin frowned. "What would you rather me do? Go to preschool with Colton? Play on the swings? You may think I'm a child but I'm not. I want to live my life as if I had been alive for the past twenty-two years. I want to register to vote so I can have a say in what goes on in this country. I want to go to college. I want to stand by you and the rest of our family and fight for immortal rights." She paused for a moment. "I want to fall in love and have children. I'm nearly thirty, which means I have about ten more years before that option will be gone. I don't have the luxury of time like you do, Lela. I'm not going to be young forever. And I don't want to be either."

Lela leaned over and kissed Robin's cheek. She didn't have to say anything for Robin to know what she was thinking. Robin had come up with that speech while preparing for breaking the dinner news to Lela and she was surprised by how well it went. She never felt more empowered than in that moment.

"You're right. You're so right, Robin. I've lived with vampires for so long that I forget that some people are going to die eventually. It's just that . . . when I lost you, it killed something in me. And now that I have you back, I don't want to lose you again."

"You won't. The only way you'll lose me is if you don't let me spread my wings. I don't want to stay stuck in the past. I'm ready to grow up and I want to do that while getting closer to Erik."

Lela never protested to this, but Robin could feel that she wasn't on board yet. They had needed to have this talk, though. Robin hated that there was animosity between her and her sister and now that they both knew where the other person stood, they could work towards a compromise. Starting with this dinner.

When they got to the neighborhood, Robin dropped Lela off at the front of her house before parking two doors down. She went inside, feeling hopeful about her sister's decision.

Robin liked the scent of the hairspray the woman had used after straightening her hair and she kept taking her locks and smelling them. It was like candy or something sweet.

What changed her mood was seeing Abe on the couch. She was surprised that he hadn't found some girl to go out with yet. This was the longest time she'd ever seen him alone.

"I've been waiting for you," he said. "Can we talk?"

"About?"

He gestured for her to sit on the couch and she obeyed. The fact that he could have been waiting for quite a while worried her. She hadn't really taken his flirting seriously but his expression was so serious that it made her wonder. He had been avoiding her lately and she didn't like that. She missed his teasing and his infuriating attempts at trying to be her bodyguard.

"I want to apologize," he said. "I'm afraid I've ruined our friendship by hitting on you, and I don't want that."

This wasn't what she expected, but she was glad they were having this talk. She didn't want their friendship ruined either. She was closer to him these days than anyone else and she didn't want to push him away like she was J.D. She felt bad for snapping at her earlier when she was just showing genuine concern.

"You're forgiven," she said. "I've missed you. It's weird not having you stay here."

He smiled and his smile reminded her of Jordan even more. Abe had his brown eyes, but his mom's brown hair. She missed him since he'd been such a big part of her life before Lela was resurrected.

"I suppose I can come back. Since you miss me so much."

"Good."

Abe forced a smile. "How are you feeling? You know, with the baby and everything?"

Robin put a hand over her stomach. "I'm not throwing up anymore. But I'm growing, and people are starting to notice. Lela said I look bloated today. I about died."

His eyes dropped to her stomach. "I wouldn't have noticed if you hadn't said anything. You look great. You have plenty of confidence, Robin. You're smart, stunning, and have a laugh that could make any man fall for you."

The smile left her face and she stared into his eyes. His tone hadn't been teasing like when he usually flirted with her but serious and genuine. He thought she was stunning? It made her giddy and happy when Erik called her beautiful. But when Abe had called her stunning, she felt warm and alive. Kind of like how she did when Simeon said she was gorgeous.

What was wrong with her? She'd specifically told herself that any man like Abe would be a definite no to be attracted to. She respected Gallard and Lucas for their integrity and devotion, which was why she cared for Erik. He had the qualities that reminded her of them, and she'd known from childhood that was the kind of man she would want to end up with. Abe was the opposite—arrogant, pushy, promiscuous. If Lela was worried about Erik and her dating, what would she think if Robin was seeing a man like Abe?

"You shouldn't say things like that," she finally said.

"Why not? It's the first thing that comes to mind whenever I see you. You're all I think about lately and it's driving me crazy."

He slid his fingers down her arm and her body grew warmer. She should have pulled away, but instead she sat there, gazing into his eyes. She hadn't even noticed that is his face had gotten closer to hers until they were less than two inches apart.

Finally, he closed the space between them and kissed her. She never thought her first real kiss would be with her best friend, but it was so enthralling that she couldn't do anything but respond.

Abe started kissing her more passionately and she tensed up as she felt his tongue slip past her lips and then touch hers. She expected it to be horrible like the first time, but he wasn't forceful about it, and it somewhat excited her. She relaxed and kissed him back the same way. Her arms slid around him and she fell back on the couch, taking him with her.

His hand traveled over her leg and her heartrate picked up. This was what she'd wanted. What she'd been afraid to admit out loud. Ever since she first caught Abe sneaking a woman out of his room, it had piqued her curiosity about what it would be like to hook up with him. She wanted to experience being with someone when it was her choice. Abe was the perfect candidate because he was her best friend and she knew he wouldn't tell anyone. Maybe then she could be with Erik without worrying about having a panic attack or freaking out on him.

She stopped them for a moment and tugged off her shirt. She waited for him to put a stop to it, but he didn't. Instead he removed his own then he pulled off her leggings she had borrowed from J.D. from when they did the art class.

"Are we alone?" she asked between kisses.

"Yes." He pressed his lips to the base of her throat. "J.D. is at your sister's and Nicola is out of town. Just the same, we should —" he kissed her collarbone — "Be careful. Neither of us have super hearing."

His fingers trailed down her stomach then slowly slipped into her underwear. This startled her at first but then he began to touch her, and worry was replaced by pleasure. Simultaneously, he kissed the side of her neck and she could feel her body responding to him. Why had she been so afraid of this? It was wonderful. If it was like this with Abe, she could be comfortable with getting closer to Erik.

He pulled her underwear down more and he shifted back then put his mouth on her, pleasuring her in ways she never knew were possible. She lost track of time and for a while, her heartache and pain was forgotten. All she felt was pleasure.

"We should take this elsewhere," he said after a while. "I feel too exposed out here."

She gave him a sneaky grin. "Then let's go to your room."

Robin got decent then took his hand, leading him towards the guest room, or rather his second room. She was going to go inside when he stopped her.

"No, not there. I've brought several women there. With you, it's sacred."

His words touched her, but she didn't waste time dwelling on the sentimental. She kissed him once more and he picked her up, carrying her to her bedroom. Once inside, he closed the door and lay her on the bed. He nibbled on her bottom lip and she giggled. This was a lot of fun and she wanted him to touch her again. She was also curious about him.

As he kissed her, she let her hands wander over his body. They found the waistband of his sweats and she slowly slipped her hand down the front. When she felt him, she suddenly grew timid and pulled her hand back. He chuckled and stopped kissing her.

"It's okay, babe," he said. "I don't mind."

"Does it feel as good as when you touch me?"

He nodded. Curious, she went back to what she was doing and this time, she didn't pull back. He let out a moan as she softly stroked him, and it was very intriguing. He started rolling his hips as she continued and then he grabbed her hand.

"You have to stop," he said.

"Why?"

"Cause I can't hold out much longer."

She smirked. "What if I don't want to stop?"

Ignoring his suggestion, she continued stroking him until he let out a long moan and she felt something odd. She quickly took her hand back.

"Did you just . . . pee on me?"

Abe looked her in the eye then burst out laughing. It startled her and she glared.

"It's not funny! Why did you do that?"

"Robin . . ." he chuckled. "I didn't . . . oh, babe, you're so adorable when you're clueless."

She rolled her eyes. "Glad I amuse you."

Abe stood up and led her into the bathroom and helped her wash her hands. He still hadn't explained what had just happened, but he'd stopped laughing. He looked sad now. After she was cleaned up, he shucked his pants and got in the shower.

Robin sat on her bed and waited for him to come out. She was starting to feel awkward. Did he not like it? Maybe she was bad at doing whatever it was they had just done. She had no experience when it came to fooling around. He was probably used to women who had done this before.

When he came out of the bathroom, he just stood and stared at her. She couldn't take the silence anymore, so she spoke first.

"Abe, is something wrong?"

"What are we doing?" he asked. "You have a boyfriend."

She sighed and sat with her knees hugged to her chest. "That's never stopped you before, has it?"

"No. Are you going to tell him?"

"Tell him what? That I fooled around with my best friend? Of course not! It didn't mean anything."

The hurt in his eyes made her realize that she'd hit a nerve. This whole time, she thought he was just flirting with her like he did the other women he brought home, but she had been wrong. Maybe he did have feelings for her.

"You did this for, what? Fun?"

"Yes. We had fun, right? You do it all the time. Why can't I?"

The hurt expression turned to sadness and he reached over and pulled her into a hug.

"Oh, Robin. What have I done to you?"

He got up and went into his room, leaving her stunned and confused. Since when did he suddenly develop a conscience when it came to hooking up? Was it because he saw her as innocent too? Then again, they wouldn't have done what they did if he'd thought that. A harsher realization set it. He thought she felt the same way about him. That made her feel worse than ever.

25

Robin heard the familiar engine rumbling and looked out the window. Erik's truck was parked in front. She quickly got dressed then went out to see what he was doing there. He was leaning against the door of his truck and he had on his uniform. It didn't even bother her anymore and she thought it made him even sexier. Her encounter with Abe gave her a new confidence.

"Hey, beautiful!" he said when he caught her eye.

He pulled her into his comforting embrace, and she took in the scent of his cologne. He smelled wonderful, like how she imagined Texas would smell if it had a scent. It was a mixture of something spicy and the scent of hay. Being in his arms and seeing the kindness in his eyes, she knew he would never hurt her like Matthew and Ash did.

She needed to kiss him. She'd mostly kissed Abe back because she was so curious and now that she had some practice, she might be able to show more finesse when kissing Erik. Plus, she'd been thinking about it for days and couldn't wait any longer.

Robin stood on her tiptoes and pressed her lips to his. His lips moved softly against hers, sending a thrill of excitement through her. It wasn't as lurid as Abe's kisses, but she liked it nonetheless. When he finally pulled back she took his face in her hands and tugged him closer for another kiss. He chuckled and ended it once more.

"You liked it that much, huh?"

She nodded. "Better than the movie and our walk in the garden. I think I want to kiss you every day for the rest of my life."

He let out a laugh that gave her butterflies. She could listen to that laugh every day as well.

"I know you were waiting for the right time, but I couldn't stand it any longer," she said.

"Well I'm glad you took charge because I was going crazy too."

Robin kissed him once more and he responded to her kiss, lifting her completely off the ground and twirling her in a circle. When he set her down, she nearly lost her balance from being dizzy and he reached out to save her from falling but was too late and they both ended up falling onto the grass. She laughed at their clumsiness and he turned red.

"That's embarrassing," he said. "I'm a cop. I should be more graceful than that."

"I doubt you'll be kissing the criminal when you tackle him." She sat up so that she was supporting herself with her hands behind her. "Why are you here?"

"I'm on lunch break. Well, dinner actually. I'm working nine to nine today."

"Are you hungry? We have cake leftover from Lucas' wife's birthday."

He moved so that his arms were on either side of her. "I already ate before I came here. Granted, I had to take big bites and I almost choked. It got me here faster."

She cast her eyes down as her cheeks grew hot. She was growing more and more comfortable with him, but he still made her feel shy whenever he would complement her or say how much he loved seeing her. She felt the same way and she wanted to be as open and comfortable with him and she was with her family. Because he was the right man to be with, not Abe, no matter how much she'd enjoyed their fooling around. Or how thinking about him touching her made her blood warm at that second.

"I talked to my sister today. She's still not on board with our dating, but she's letting you come for dinner, so that's a start."

"I talked to my parents too. I brought up the cabin idea and they weren't too happy either. They think we're moving too fast." He looked into her eyes. "Do *you* think we're moving too fast?"

Robin often wondered this herself. She had only known Erik for two weeks, but she really liked him. He'd never been inappropriate with her and she felt completely safe with him. If she moved too fast with him, her family might see it as a sign of immaturity.

"Can I be honest?" she asked.

"Please. Whatever it is, I can take it."

"We should wait to take that trip. We could go on dates instead and stay in town." She fiddled with his badge. "Maybe we could hang out at your place sometime. Around here, there are too many people."

He laughed. "I agree. I know what it's like to always have eyes on me. Okay, so we won't go away. But I do want to cook you dinner sometime."

She leaned forward and kissed him. He was so great to her that she couldn't believe he'd chosen her. If she hadn't gone to the store with Abe, she never would have met him. She loved that he didn't call her Broom Girl, even if he'd started that trend. She wanted him to always be in her life. More importantly, she wanted her family to accept him. She was determined not to let what happened between his dad and her sister to happen to them.

Robin let herself fall back on the grass as she continued to kiss him and he went with her. She got lost in the moment and forgot that she was supposed to be taking things slow with him.

Then she found herself comparing the kiss to kissing Abe. There was a significant difference, but was it a good different or a bad different? What she needed to do was try something with Erik that she had done with Abe to prove she could get the same reaction from kissing Erik as she did with him. That would have to wait until they were really alone.

Feeling bold, she let her hand slide down until it was resting on his backside and then gave it a small squeeze. J.D. had told her that Lucian liked it when she did that and Robin was curious to know if Erik would too. Immediately after, she regretted it. He stopped kissing her and stared at her in shock.

"Robin Shepherd, did you just grope me?" he asked, laughter in his voice.

"I'm sorry! I don't know what I was thinking."

"I knew it! You and that kid were working together, weren't you?"

She laughed. "How did you know? I guess you have to arrest me after all."

He dipped his head and kissed her again. It was strange and exciting at the same time. Her tongue slid over his lip and he parted his lips, welcoming her. She started touching him the same way she had before, letting her hand roam a little. Her fingers found his belt buckle then traveled lower and she stroked him with her thumb. Her heart skipped a beat when she heard a low moan in his throat as she continued.

They were interrupted when a car pulled up to the curb and Erik immediately backed away and helped her stand up. When she saw that it was Lucas' car, she hoped that he hadn't seen what she and Erik were doing. He got out then unstrapped Colton from his car seat. By the look on his face, she could feel a lecture coming.

"What the hell are you doing?" he asked when he'd come towards them.

She rolled her eyes. "Kissing my boyfriend. What does it look like I'm doing?"

Lucas glanced at Erik then back at her. Was he going to give her a hard time too? It was bad enough that Kevin was always on her case.

"It looked like a lot more than kissing to me," Lucas said. "You're lucky I caught you and not Lela."

"I apologize, *Earl Hawthorne*," Erik said, stifling a chuckle. "We got caught up in the moment. I promise it won't happen again."

"No, you don't have to promise him anything," Robin said. "It's not like we were showering together."

Lucas's expression filled with guilt, and his shoulder's relaxed. He must have realized that he sounded extremely hypocritical. He sighed then turned to Erik. "All right, I'll stop being a pain. But if you hurt her, you'll have a lot of angry people coming after you."

"Understood," Erik said. "You don't have to worry. I will treat her like she's the queen of England. Or maybe the Dowager Duchess or something. All these terms are confusing."

Robin was about to comment when another car pulled up. It was a very expensive looking one and she wondered what it would be like to drive it. The passenger side door opened and a man wearing a marine uniform stepped out. Robin didn't recognize him at first but when he spoke, she knew who he was.

"How's my Robin bird?" Gallard said.

She practically sprinted over to him and jumped into his arms. He hugged her tightly but as gently as he always had. He then kissed her forehead and set her down. "Wow. I wish I could get greeted like that every day."

"I'm so happy that you're home! How did you get here so quickly?"

"I caught a red eye. I missed you. And I missed Lucas, Colton, and most of all, I missed your sister. Is she here?"

Not a second later, Lela came out of the house and it also took her a moment to recognize Gallard. When she did she walked over to him and Robin reluctantly released him from her embrace so Lela could take her place. Lela took Gallard into her arms and gave him a long and tender kiss. Robin's heart warmed at the sight of their reunion and she reached over and took Erik's hand.

"What a homecoming," Gallard said. "I missed my girls."

While Lela, Gallard, Lucian, and Lucas all spoke, Erik took Robin to the side.

"I should go. I don't want to take you away from your family time."

"Okay. I'll see you tomorrow night."

Erik was about to leave but Gallard stopped him. Robin grew nervous because she had no idea if Gallard knew about her having a boyfriend.

"You here to check up on me?" Gallard asked Erik. "My friend drove me here, I swear."

"No worries, I'm actually here for Robin."

Gallard chuckled. "What did she do?"

"She stole my heart." Erik lifted their joined hands and kissed her knuckles, just as he had on their first date. "It was a pleasure meeting you, Warren. I'll let you go now. And congratulations, Captain Lucas. There are many who are eager to work with you."

"*Captain* Lucas?" Gallard asked. "And what did he mean Robin stole his heart?"

As Erik got into his truck, Lela rubbed Gallard's chest and told him that they would talk about it later. Afterwards, everyone else headed for Lucas.' They were eager to hear about what Gallard had learned while he was away and the whole walk over, Lela kept touching his nearly bald head and trying not to cry. Robin thought he looked okay no matter what length his hair was, but this wasn't really his best look. Melody was almost twice as upset as Lela was and Cherish practically had to console her.

Then the conversation became serious and he told them what he learned about Maximus and how why vampires were created in the first place. The story was very intriguing to Robin, especially when he spoke of the woman Maximus once loved.

Gallard finished the tale with Lucas' theories about what really happened the night Jordan died. Robin had never been told about everything that happened after she died. All she knew was that Mark had been behind the plot and that Aaron had tried to kill her sister. Lela graciously filled her in then they both resumed to listening to Gallard.

"Ivelisse said she has friends interested in our cause. She isn't coming to Texas but told me to call her when we are ready, and she will come. As for David and Solomon's progress, they have recruited twelve people. We're kind of doing a pass it on type thing. Every person they recruit has to try to recruit at least one other person and so forth."

"By the time we're ready for war, we'll have more than enough," Ramses said. "If needed, I know a few people in Egypt who will gladly join my side, including my brother Ammon. Ask and I will return to my country to gather forces."

"That would be helpful, Ramses, thank you. And Terrence, I would appreciate it if you could go to Orlando and find some more of those who used to frequent the bar. I'm sure they would want to be part of this as well."

"Will do. I could go do that next week. It is getting rather cramped living here. Besides, your wife keeps picking on me."

Lela flipped him off again and the room erupted with laughter.

"I have another theory about that night," Gallard said. "Lucas informed me of his other abilities, it got me thinking. I don't believe Jordan only gave Lucas the ability to heal and raise the dead."

"What else can you do?" Abe asked Lucas.

"I can move things with my mind. I can also access people's memories and dreams just by touching them. And I can fly without being in animal form."

"That's incredible," Lucian said. "What are your theories, Gallard?"

"Remember how there was an earthquake that night? Well, if Jordan gave his power to Lucas, then that earthquake wouldn't have occurred. I think Lucas caused the earthquake that night. Lela had just been stabbed and as you know, Lucas died for a few short minutes. When Jordan brought him back to life, moments later he was killed, and we'd mistaken the earthquake to be caused by Jordan's death when in reality it was Lucas' resurrection that caused it."

"Okay, and what of the theory about our souls?" Ramses asked. "Obviously some of us here know from experience that when we die, we're stuck in a black void. How does that fit in?"

Gallard grew quiet and he didn't answer right away. Robin had a feeling that he was about to deliver bad news. He'd had the same expression when he'd come to Virginia to tell her that Lela was dead. Whatever he was going to say couldn't be good.

"I'm afraid it doesn't," he said. "If Lucian loses control, the Devil himself will take over his body. As silly as it sounds, we have to make sure that doesn't happen."

Lucian chuckled. "Just be sure not to piss me off, and we'll be fine."

The room erupted with laughter. The conversation then shifted to less serious matters and Cherish and Lela caught him up on everything he'd missed, save for Robin's relationship. But Robin couldn't shake the suspicion that Gallard wasn't telling the whole story. And this whole thing was stressing her out. She slipped outside and closed the door behind her.

It was a warm night, and she had to take off her jacket. She sat in one of the chairs on the porch and watched as a few cars drove by. To distract herself from her worried thoughts, she recalled her moment with Erik in the yard earlier. They were going to slow down the relationship. Somewhat. What they'd done had been far from slow.

"Mind if I join you?" she heard someone say. She turned and smiled when she saw Gallard had come out on the porch. He'd changed into some clothes he'd borrowed from Lucas.

"You can join me anytime," she said.

He kissed the top of her head before sitting down. He kept silent for a while and she enjoyed his company. From the moment this kind and loving man walked through the door, she knew she wanted him in her life one way or another. Lela told her that she could trust him and it only took her a second to know she could.

"I've missed Texas," he said. "It's the only place that has ever felt like home to me."

"To me, home is wherever you and Lela, and Kevin are. So, I agree — it feels like home here."

He smiled. "Do you remember when Lela and I got married? Melody was filming us while we were getting ready and you told me you wanted to marry me so I could give you McDonalds every day."

She laughed. She had treasured every moment of that day because it was her last happy memory.

"You said you would give it to me anyway," she said. "I knew that you would, too. You've always gone above and beyond for me."

168

"And I will now." He reached over and took her hand. "I've kept my promise and haven't told anyone about the baby. How are you doing? Have you seen a doctor?"

"No. No one ever leaves me alone long enough to go to town. And I'm too scared to ask someone to take me."

"I'll take you. Just say the word, and I'll take you to a clinic. The sooner the better so you can make sure you stay healthy." He paused for a moment. "You are . . . carrying to term, I assume?"

She shrugged. "What other choice do I have? I'm almost seven months along. Besides, I couldn't have an abortion. The baby didn't ask to be conceived, no matter who the father is."

Gallard sighed. "Lucas should know. If this child is his, he would like to know. But if it's not . . . what do you plan to do?"

"What do you think I should do? Keep it? I'm not capable of being a mother. I want children someday, but . . . I don't know the first thing about being mom."

"You'd be surprised at what you're capable of when life throws a curveball. I thought I would have a few years of being married to your sister before being a father. Then Lucas came along, and I couldn't believe I'd missed out on fatherhood for so long. I love every minute of it." He paused for a moment. "Robin, was Officer Erik serious about having feelings for you?"

"He was. We met last week and he's so wonderful. I like him and I hope you like him too because he really wants my family's approval."

"Dating a cop isn't really the best idea considering our situation. He could get nosy."

"Then how come Lucas can work with the police? Isn't that just as bad as sleeping with the enemy?"

"Sleeping? Oh no, you are not —"

"Calm your tits, Gallard. Nobody is sleeping with anyone."

Not yet, anyway. She was determined to change that. One way or another, be it with Abe first or Erik, she was going to have a redo of her first time. Preferably sooner than later.

The serious look left his face, and he started laughing. It was infectious and soon she was laughing too. The people around her didn't realize that she heard every word they would say, and she was picking up on phrases. Cherish liked to say that to everyone, especially Lucian. Robin hadn't meant to say it and it just came out.

"You're so much like your sister, you know that? Back to the point — I can't believe she didn't tell me you were seeing someone. That you have a . . . I can't even say it."

"Boyfriend? Gallard, are you upset because you're worried I'll get my heart broken?"

"As always. And because of your condition. I would hate for him to take off when he finds out. Then again, I don't know him well enough."

At least that was the reason and not because he saw her as a child.

"It's not going to be like that with me," she said. "I think you should give him a chance. He's coming over for dinner tomorrow so you can get to know him."

She put on her best pathetic face, one that Kevin had taught her to do when she was young. He said that with that look, she could get away with anything, including murder. It was working because Gallard's scowl disappeared and he smiled again.

"Oh, Robin. How can I say no to that face? You and your sister have too much power over me."

She laughed. "Abe said it's a Shepherd thing. Lela said that was why Melody fell for David."

"That and his dance moves. I think your sister is the only one in the family who can't dance. Don't tell her I told you that."

She rested her head on his shoulder and closed her eyes. Talking with Gallard was just what the doctor ordered. She wanted to tell him about everything— her relationship with Erik, how she had had her driver's license.

The content smile left her face. She also wanted to ask about Abe and advice concerning what she should do about him. She'd used him and it hurt him. But what she wanted him to know was that she hadn't used him entirely. She'd fooled around with him because she trusted him more than anyone. Would she ever trust Erik like that?

"What are you thinking about?" Gallard asked.

"It's a secret."

"Okay. Why don't we make a deal? If you tell me what you're hiding I will tell you what *I'm* hiding."

She sat up and looked at him. She'd had suspicions about his not telling the whole truth. He always got shifty eyes whenever he was leaving something out and she'd picked up on that trait when she was a child. She, on the other hand, had learned at a young age how to keep secrets.

"I will make that deal but you have to promise you won't yell or get mad."

He laughed. "Have you ever known me to yell? All the same, I promise I won't. Now what's going on with you?"

Robin took a deep breath then looked into his eyes. She couldn't talk to the person she usually did because it involved him. Her only choice was to talk to the man she looked up to the most.

"I hooked up with Abe."

26

I woke up to the sensation of someone stroking my back. I smiled because I knew who it was and. After I'd dropped Colton off, I went back to bed and took a much-needed nap. Everyone was up late talking the night before with the rest of our family about plans concerning gathering the troops while I had my last day on the night shift. I was exhausted, but her touch was waking me right up. I was glad she'd decided to drop by.

"Oh, good, you're awake," she said.

"I am now." I turned over and kissed her. "Wanna fool around?"

"Tempting, but I actually wanted to ask you something."

Whatever it was she wanted to ask I had a feeling I would like it. Unless she was thinking of shaving her head like Gallard. That was a definite no.

She looked away for a moment then smiled at me. "I know you said that we aren't ready for another child, but I disagree. I would love to have another baby. Maybe a girl this time."

My mouth hung open. That was miles from what I thought she was going to say. I thought she would want to move in or even get our own house with Colton. Even marriage was on my list of possible topics to discuss.

"You want a baby? Right now?"

She shrugged. "If I happened to get pregnant, I wouldn't be upset. I've always wanted a family, and I think Colton would love a brother or sister so he isn't so alone all the time. I mean, I'm twenty-four. Most women my age have at least two kids already."

I had to agree that it was hard seeing Colton alone. He said he had some friends at school but he'd never been invited to anyone's house nor had he invited anyone to ours. He needed someone his own age to bond with so he wasn't stuck with just Kevin or me all the time. But this was not the best time to have a baby. We still had so much ahead of us — rescuing Micah, raising awareness for immortal rights. How could we do that and tend to a newborn?

"Nic, are you serious? We're not equipped to be parents of a baby right now. What brought this on?"

The smile left her face. "I disagree. We still don't know exactly when it will be safe to return to Miami. We could be here in Texas for another year or even longer."

"Yeah, but you would be carrying that child for most of that year and when it's time to move on, the baby would be a few months old. You're still adjusting to being a vampire and a mom to a four-year-old. Have you even held a baby before?"

She pressed her lips together. "Just because you got to take care of Colton when he was a baby doesn't make me less capable. I used to babysit. I actually babysat a lot of my college friends' kids when I was in New York."

"Babysitting for a few hours and tending to an infant twenty-four seven is completely different. My mom was exhausted when we adopted Colton. It's rewarding but time consuming. Babe, I love you, but we can't do this right now. I have too many obligations to give up the mission just to start a family."

A tear escaped her eye. "I'm not asking you to give up the cause. You wouldn't even have to be around. I would wait for you."

"And leave you behind to raise a baby and Colton on your own? Hell no. I wouldn't do that to someone I hated, let alone my girlfriend."

Someone knocked on the door and we looked at each other. Again, everyone we knew was comfortable with walking in. We both got up and I answered it. The moment I opened the door, I was startled by Gallard's appearance. He looked as messed up as he had at the police station the day before. He had on sunglasses and he was supporting himself with the doorframe.

"Are you okay?" I asked.

"Far from it. I'm drunk and it's only eleven in the morning."

I thought that his being here and telling us about Maximus was a sign that he was done with this kind of behavior. Apparently, I was wrong. Another thing that was bothering me was that he never told us why he came back.

"Care to explain?" I asked.

"Not really. I'm the dad. I don't answer to you."

"Well, when someone drives your kid while they're wasted, then you can understand why I'm pissed."

"Someone did hurt my kid. The man drove him over the edge of a cliff and made me think he was dead. And then another man took my other kid and is now probably doing experiments on him."

His words hit me like a punch to the gut. He was right about what he did not comparing to what he'd gone through with me and was still going through with Micah. It didn't excuse his behavior, though.

Gallard took off the sunglasses and rubbed his eyes. "Damn, I'm screwed up, aren't I?"

"Very. It might be the healing power. I was kind of a dick too up until Arnaud took it away."

He laughed. "Now you're calling me names. It's true, I'm an angry drunk. If you can forgive me for my actions, I will forgive you for calling me a dick."

"Done. Now get in here before someone sees you. Coffee's in the cupboard to the left of the microwave. Sober up."

He came inside just as Nicola came into the living room. She wasn't looking as sad as before, but I knew better. She was disappointed in how our conversation went. I wanted to discuss it more, but as always, we were being interrupted.

"Hey, how are you?" Gallard asked. "I heard you turned the big two-four recently."

"I did! That makes me only a year younger than you now." She gestured to his head. "I never had the chance to tell you, but I like your new look. It's pretty sexy."

He laughed. "You're the only one to think that."

While they talked, I made him some instant coffee. I eavesdropped on their conversation, and I could hear in his voice that he was wasted. He was talking strangely and stammering his words. I hoped that Lela didn't know about his being drunk. She had to. Where would he have gotten the alcohol?

"By the way, I'm going to give you your gift back," Gallard said to me. "Just let me know when you want it."

I'd nearly forgotten about his having my gift. I wasn't in a rush to get it back, but I could see the toll it was taking on him. Finding him drunk one time was forgivable, but a second time was concerning. If anything, I wanted it back so he would stop drinking. I also had the feeling he was hiding something. Kevin said the same thing when we'd spoken later that night. But no one was willing to call him out on it. I would save that discussion for later. "Sure, how about now?"

He cast his gaze to the floor. His hesitation was even more confusing than ever. He told me that he'd thought about physically maiming Arnaud in order to convince him to give the gift back and now Gallard was the one who didn't want to part with it.

"How about tonight? Cherish is excited that we can finally drink together. She wants to take me out later."

I couldn't believe what I was hearing. After endangering Colton and getting wasted early in the morning he was going to go out and party? He wasn't just crazy, he was psychotic.

"Gallard, were you cloned?" I asked.

"What?"

"Do you have an evil twin who kidnapped you and took your place? Who the hell are you? Because you're not my dad."

"Lighten up, Lucas. You're too uptight! Let loose every once in a while." A huge smile formed on his face. "Hey! You and Nicola should come with us tonight! You're both over twenty-one."

"I've had enough of this." I handed him the cup of coffee and took Nicola's hand. "We're going to pick up our son then take him to the park or something. I'm done trying to reason with you. When the real Gallard wants to talk, let me know. I don't care about when you give me my gift or not, but if Lela starts asking questions I'm not going to lie."

Nicola let go of my hand for a moment to get her supplies then followed me out the door. I'd forgotten about her class that was later that day, but I didn't mind. I wanted to get out of the house and spend time with Colton.

I drove rather quickly because I was so mad and we arrived at the school fifteen minutes early. I parked the car in our usual spot and killed the engine. We hadn't spoken much on the way over and I was waiting for her to ask questions. I hadn't told her about the scare I'd had the day before and she deserved to know. She was his mother.

"Things are very tense between you and your dad," she said. "What's going on?"

"I don't know. He's been weird ever since he got here. It started when he took Colton out of school without telling me."

"He took him out of school?"

"That's not the worst of it. He was drunk and he got pulled over by none other than Erik McPherson for speeding and his blood alcohol level was 0.13."

"You're kidding me! He drove drunk with Colton in the car? I could punch him!"

"He was lucky that they didn't can his ass. His lawyer got the judge to release him on diplomatic immunity. I should have let him spend the night in jail so he could learn his lesson."

Nicola covered her face with her hands for a moment then let out a long exhale. I hated telling her all of this, but we'd agreed to be honest with each other when it came to our son. I took her hand in mine and we sat in silence as the bell rang from inside the school.

"You should spend some time with him," Nicola said. "After you drop me off at the gallery, you should have a family day with your dad and Colton."

"But I thought the three of us were going to have family day."

"I have to teach all afternoon. Ryan upped my pay and gave me an extra day. I think it would do both of you some good, and once Gallard is sober, maybe he'll open up."

I wasn't too thrilled about that idea, considering the words we'd exchanged before I left. But she was right. If I was going to get answers from him, I would have to spend time with him and convince him that I could handle whatever he was hiding.

The kids began flooding the front area, and Nicola and I got out so we could watch for Colton. I spotted his blue baseball hat first and when he saw me, the smile on his face warmed my heart. He ran over to me, slightly faster than a five-year-old should be able to. No one seemed to notice. I held out my arms to him and lifted him off the ground when he was within reach.

"Hey dad!" he said. "Guess what happened today!"

"I don't know, bud. I'm dying to know."

"I saved a boy from falling. He slipped on the jungle gym, and he almost fell when I ran over to him and grabbed him. He's in first grade, so he's bigger than me but it wasn't that hard."

Nicola raised an eyebrow. She was probably as concerned as I was, but we hadn't gotten any calls from the school about this incident.

"That's great, honey," she said. "But be careful, okay? People can't know that you're stronger than the other kids."

He nodded. "Okay, mom. I'm sorry if I didn't do the right thing. I didn't mean to."

"Oh, baby don't be sorry. It's always the right thing to help people. Never forget that."

He smiled then I opened the back door and strapped him into his seat. I thought we handled this pretty well and Colton always did as he was told. I trusted that he would be careful as we'd asked. It was also comforting to know that he was using his abilities for good and not to try and impress people.

I got to the gallery and Colton and I helped her carry everything in. We successfully dropped off her stuff, and I gave her a quick kiss before putting Colton onto my shoulders and heading for the exit.

"Dad, can I see mom's paintings?" Colton asked.

"I don't think any of her work is hanging in here, but we can look around."

I gave him a little tour of the place. Colton seemed genuinely interested in every piece. He was like his mom in that way. I thought he would get bored after the first couple, but he would stare at each one we stopped at. He even asked questions and we made a game of it where we would take turns making up a story about the pieces.

When he was ready to move on, I sent a text to Gallard asking if he wanted to meet. We were nearly out the door when I happened to see Ryan out of the corner of my eye, and I slowed to a stop. He was standing behind one of the displays and having an intense conversation with someone. I saw the long auburn hair first and that was when I realized he was talking to Nicola.

"You are going to blow this," he said. "He's already starting to ask questions."

"You think I don't know that? I'm doing the best I can here. I can't please everyone all at once."

He sighed and stroked her side with his hand in a way that made my blood boil. "How are the ribs?"

"Sore as hell. I can take a hit, though. You know that better than anyone."

"Have you spoken with the family yet?"

"No. Why bother? They're never going to believe Cherish hurt me."

I couldn't believe my ears. All this time, I thought it was some unknown enemy that was hurting Nicola and she was confessing to Ryan that Cherish was responsible? Cherish didn't hurt those close to her. What reason would she have for hurting Nicola?"

"Nic?" I said, making my presence known.

She turned her head to me, and I saw she was wearing sunglasses.

"Lucas, hey!" She came over to me and gave me a hug. When she looked at Colton, she slightly lowered her sunglasses. "What are you still doing here?"

"Colton wanted to look at the art. I think he might be a little Picasso in the making."

She smiled and patted Colton's leg.

"Mamma, why aren't you wearing your necklace?" Colton asked.

"Oh? I have it in my pocket, honey. I don't want to get paint on it."

"Can I talk to you about something?" I said.

Nicola glanced at Ryan then followed me further into the gallery so we could be alone. I sent Colton off to go look at the paintings. I couldn't wait until later to talk to her about what I'd heard. This was too serious.

"Is it true?" I clenched my teeth. "Did Cherish give you those bruises?"

Nicola looked around then back at me. "Lucas, could you do me a favor and not tell anyone? It was all a misunderstanding."

"A misunderstanding? Your ribs were pretty bruised. If Cherish is hurting you, I think our family should know."

"I need time. Please, just let me figure this out." She looked around again. "I have to get to my class. Can we talk later?"

"Yeah, of course."

I leaned down and kissed her. I meant for it to be a quick peck, but she got more into it, pulling me close to her by my belt loops. Her hands slid over my butt and then up my back before they snaked around my neck. I hadn't expected her to get so enthusiastic since we still hadn't resolved the whole baby discussion. I was afraid she was going to try and do me right there with Colton and all her art students present.

"Ew," Colton said.

Nicola chuckled and stopped kissing me. "Sorry, Cole. I just find your daddy so irresistible."

I gave her a nervous smile. "I'll see you at dinner tonight."

She gave me a flirtatious wave and walked away, swaying her hips as she did. I took Colton's hand and we left the building. That whole encounter gave me chills and I was contemplating what I should do with this information. On one hand, I trusted Nicola and on the other, I trusted Cherish too. I was torn.

While I was strapping Colton back in, I noticed he looked very morose.

"What's up, bud? You okay?"

He shook his head. "Something's wrong with mom. She made me feel bad."

"You mean you had a bad feeling?"

He nodded. "Mamma was acting funny."

I had to agree with him. Nicola was acting strange and it sickened me to think that Cherish had hurt her. The way they were acting so affectionate with each other had made me so happy. How could they go from that to Cherish hurting her?

27

J.D. laughed as Gallard downed yet another shot of vodka. When he'd suggested they go partying, she thought he had something else in mind. Lucian tagged along to be the D.D. and J.D. made Robin come with her. Abe was only there because she'd given him a grace period for staying away from Robin. Lela and Melody stayed home to get ready for the dinner and Cherish was due to show up later after running an errand.

"That's eight shots!" J.D. said. "Shouldn't you be passed out by now?"

"I'm immortal. I can handle about eight more."

He ordered more drinks and J.D. shook her head as she sipped her margarita. Lucian looked utterly dumbfounded, and she didn't blame him. Gallard wasn't exactly an uptight person, but he never partied. In fact, he hated parties yet here he was, downing shots and challenging random strangers to drinking contests. He'd won about three of them back to back.

The music changed to something faster and he slammed his glass down on the table.

"We need to dance."

"Dance?" J.D. said. "You dance?"

"Hell yeah, I dance!"

He grabbed her hand and she had to stealthily set her glass down before she dropped it and he dragged her onto the dance floor. Once they were in the center, he started moving with the music and forcing her to dance. She looked back at Lucian who was equally as confused by Gallard's behavior. She decided to go with the flow and dance with him.

Soon, Robin joined her and the four of them were thrown into a crowd of random dancers. J.D. was impressed with some of Gallard's moves and never would have guessed he was a dancer. She knew that he could tango, but not the kind of sexy dancing he was doing. He had to be completely wasted.

J.D., something is wrong, Jordan said. *He's out of control.*

I think it's funny. He's letting loose for once in his life.

Letting loose? He's drunk out of his mind! Gallard never danced when he worked at the night club.

He's turning over a new leaf. He met God, for crying out loud. He could be inspired to enjoy life.

Enjoy life? He could enjoy life when he's sober too! I know I'm not one to judge, but I was never a great example. He inspired me to be a better man. That man is still in there somewhere and he's crying out for help.

J.D. stopped dancing and watched her uncle. It may have been funny that he was drinking and dancing, but it was disturbing. Her father was right—this wasn't Gallard. The Gallard she knew had the ability to have a good time without getting crazy. He stopped dancing as well then went over to the bar to get another drink. If she calculated right, he'd had about twelve shots. They'd only been at the bar for a half an hour.

He was about to drink when Lucian snatched it away from him. They started arguing and Gallard nearly fell over. She hadn't noticed how tipsy he was until then and it upset her. He tried to take the drink again and Lucian drank it himself. Gallard looked extremely pissed and their argument escalated into shouting.

"What's going on?" Robin asked J.D.

"I'm not sure. Let's ignore them and keep dancing, okay?"

Robin took her advice, but J.D. kept an eye on them while she pretended to be into the music. Lucian gently pushed Gallard back as he started to get closer and Gallard reacted by taking a swing at Lucian. Thankfully, his motor skills were greatly impaired, and Lucian stopped his fist before it collided with his jaw.

That was the last straw. Gallard was escalating to trying to start a fight. He was getting way out of hand and she didn't think Lucian could get him under control by himself, sober or not. She took Robin's hand and pulled her through the crowd until they were outside. She then pulled out her phone and dialed Cherish's number.

"Hello?"

"Aunt Cher, where are you?"

"On my way. Why, what's wrong?"

"Gallard is tanked. And I don't mean sort of drunk, I mean Girls Gone Wild kind of tanked. He got into a fight with your dad and he's trying to punch him."

"What? But they just got there a half an hour ago! Never mind. Sit tight and I'll take care of it. I'm two minutes away."

J.D. hung up and suggested to Robin that she wait outside with her. She didn't need to witness Gallard getting crazy like that. J.D. knew that Gallard was her favorite person in the whole world. It was already bothering J.D. because Gallard was her favorite person too, aside from Lucian.

Abe came out a few minutes later.

"What's the problem?" he asked.

"The problem is that our uncle is going over the deep end. I called Cherish."

"He got a little drunk, so what? That's an average day in London. Oh, wait, you wouldn't know because you left."

"I had good reasons for leaving, Abe. I wouldn't have if I didn't have a choice."

"Really? What choice, J.D.?"

You still haven't told him? After all these years?

He'll only blame himself and make it all about him. What's the point, it was years ago.

He's your brother! He should know why you left. Why you had to live with Lela and leave him behind.

"You want to know why I left?" she asked. "Aunt Abigail's boyfriend raided my room looking for money and found my journal. There were personal things in there about our family. He told her about our dad being a vampire, and she said I was crazy and made it all up. She tried to have me committed and her boyfriend dragged me to an institution. I was there for three weeks before Gallard came and rescued me. That's why I went to live with him and Lela."

Abe stood there, stunned and she wished she'd said it a little more delicately.

"Aunt Abigail said you ran away," he said quietly. "She said that you called Gallard and dragged them into a custody battle because you didn't want to live there anymore."

"Well, she lied. I didn't run away. They took me while you were at your karate lesson. I was bunked with a woman who thought she was a cat and ate her own hair. They had me on antipsychotics. Gallard had to get custody or else he couldn't get me out."

Cherish showed up at that moment and J.D. met her in the parking lot. She would have to finish her conversation with Abe later, but now she needed help with Gallard.

"Hey, J.D. Has he calmed down?"

"I don't know. We've been waiting outside. Something's wrong, Cher. He's not himself."

"He's going back to his old habits. If he's as bad as you say, he's acting like he did when we first met."

"We should tell Lela. She should know what's going on."

J.D. took out her phone but Cherish grabbed it away. "No! You can't tell her. She's been through enough. We'll sober him up and hide him at Lucas' until he's well enough to go to dinner."

J.D. disagreed. Keeping secrets about her relationship was one thing but hiding Gallard's behavior from Lela was another. Lela had always been honest with J.D. and in return J.D. was honest with her aunt. Whatever was going on with Gallard, Lela needed to know because she may be the only one he would talk to.

"Give me my phone, Cher."

"No, let me handle this. Let Gallard tell her when he's ready."

"He's been drunk since eight o'clock this morning! Lucas texted me earlier and told me. I told him he was overreacting but when I saw Gallard try to hit Lucian, I realized it was worse than I thought."

J.D. started walking back to the bar and Cherish followed. Abe went ahead to check on Lucian and Gallard and see if they'd escalated into a fight. If Cherish wasn't going to give her the phone back, J.D. had no problem using the one inside. She wasn't going to hide this from Lela, and it was time to plan an intervention.

Before she could go in, Cherish grabbed her arm and yanked her back onto the sidewalk.

"You're not saying anything. I helped him before, and I can help him now. Lela doesn't have to know."

"I disagree. Now let go of me!"

"Hey!" someone shouted. She turned to see Lucas had showed up. "What the hell is your problem?"

"Why are you mad at *me*?" Cherish asked.

"You're manhandling her. Don't you think that's a bit much?"

Colton remained silent and stood timidly to the side of the building while all of this was going on. J.D. was equally as confused as Cherish was. She knew for a fact that Cherish hadn't been more excessive than usual. She was trying to keep her from going into the bar. Lucas was overreacting.

Cherish let go of J.D.'s arm. "I'm sorry if it came off that way."

"Yeah, I'm sure you are."

She scoffed. "Okay, I don't know what your problem is but you're blowing this way out of proportion."

"Just like Nicola's bruises are way out of proportion, right?"

Moments later, Lucian and Abe came out of the bar with their arms around Gallard's shoulder. Gallard was struggling to walk but at least they weren't fighting. Lucian stopped walking and kept looking between the two of them.

"What is going on?" he asked.

"I have no idea," Cherish said. "According to Lucas, I'm a little too rough."

"Well, you've maimed me a few times, I know that," Gallard said. She glared at him. "What? Cher, you have to know that you're kind of hands on. We love you, but it's true."

"But I don't beat on people I care about! Lucas claims I was manhandling J.D."

"Colton saw it too," Lucas said. "When I showed up, you were standing roughly jerking on her arm."

"Colton?" She turned to the little boy. "Honey, do you think that too?"

He looked nervous. "Um . . . I don't think you hurt J.D., but you hurt my mamma. She said you did."

That made two people who were convinced that it happened. Even still, she was starting to have her own doubts. Cherish had been more forceful than usual. But hurting Nicola? J.D. couldn't imagine Cherish doing something that cruel. She was a female version of her father — rough around the edges but a compassionate person underneath.

"Since when is Nicola claiming I hurt her?"

"She said that Cherish hit her," Lucas said.

"I have no reason to hurt her! Especially now that — oh, never mind."

Everyone grew quiet again and J.D.'s stomach turned. Nicola never told her that Cherish had beat her up. She hasn't even said anything to J.D. about being hurt in the first place.

"Cherish, Nicola never told me that you hurt her," Lucas said. "I heard her admit it to Ryan at the gallery. She said she never told anyone because she thought no one would believe her."

"I need you to hear me out," Cherish said. "I know about the bruises, but it's not because someone hurt her. Think about it — why would I hit her?"

"She might have seen something," Lucian said. "Darling, I do not want to gang up on you, but you have been disappearing a lot as of late. You go out at night when you think no one is watching and you don't come back until early morning."

"And that night at the festival," J.D. said, her wheels turning. "You went AWOL just before that man was hurt. Later on, Nicola found the man and then she wouldn't talk about it. She kept acting like she had no idea what we were talking about and that she wasn't even there."

"So, you assume because I left at that time that I'm the one who hurt the man and knocked her around to keep her quiet?"

J.D. wanted to believe that the others were making her paranoid, but all the facts were pointing towards Cherish being guilty. The thought was making her nauseous and she couldn't hear anymore.

"I'm not doing this anymore," Cherish said. "I'm going to hit the gym and vent for a while and hopefully you all come to your senses at dinner time."

She took off in a flash and they watched as she drove away in her car. J.D. still felt sick with guilt and she hated that they'd ganged up on her. If

Cherish really had been hurting Nicola, she needed help not a lecture. They were supposed to be lecturing Gallard, for crying out loud and it had turned around on her in less than a second.

"What just happened?" Gallard asked, suddenly less drunk than before. "The way you were talking sounded like this was the culmination of a previous problem."

Lucas filled him in on the killings and attacks that had been happening. Lucian admitted that Nicola claimed to be responsible and his doubts behind her confession. Lucas also told them about the bruises and cuts he found on her and then ended with what he'd heard Nicola say at the gallery just before they'd arrived.

"And nobody cared to call and tell us this why?" he asked. "Solomon should know what's going on."

"And put the mission in jeopardy?" Lucian said. "It's already at risk with your being here. As soon as you give Lucas his gift, you need to return to Solomon and help him find more supporters."

"It's nice to know you want me out of here so soon."

"It's not just that," Lucas said. "We're worried. You're drunk and unruly. Frankly, you're not very fun to be around right now. I need my gift back so you can get your common sense."

Gallard rolled his eyes. "Okay! I'll give it back to you tonight. That way I can at least enjoy one last meal from your mother before I go back to a strict blood diet."

Lucian hauled Gallard into the parking lot and Lucas helped him get in the Cadillac and closed the door. J.D. and Robin had taken her Vanquish so everyone was set for rides. The entire way home, J.D. kept looking in the streets, hoping she would see Cherish's car. They always fought and she knew just how to get under Cherish's skin, but J.D. loved her like crazy. She wished that she'd stood up for her and now it was too late.

28

Robin tapped her foot to the music from her phone as she chopped carrots. Ever since everyone got home, things got weird and awkward. Lela noticed right away that something was going on but she didn't say anything. Robin and J.D. went over to help cook while Lucas, Abe, and Lucian were trying to help Gallard get sober in less than four hours.

Old Britney Spears albums weren't putting her in a good mood like they used to. She couldn't get Cherish's hurt expression out of her mind. She had no idea what was going on with everyone or why they thought she'd hurt Nicola. She'd been so wrapped up in her relationship that she hadn't realized her friends and loved ones were hurting.

She did understand why Gallard was coping by getting drunk, though. She'd promised him she wouldn't say anything and it was difficult keeping her mouth shut when everyone expressed their concern for him. She couldn't believe it when he'd told her and it made her heart break all the more.

"You okay, hon?" Melody asked her.

Robin flinched, startled by her voice. She took the ear buds out and stuffed them in her pocket.

"I'm fine. Just nervous about the dinner."

"It'll be fine. Lela and Gallard already know Erik and there's no reason the rest of us won't love him as much as you do."

That wasn't what she was worried about. She was worried that the tension between her family members would blow up into something ugly. And she was worried that Erik would find out that she hooked up with

Abe. Twenty-four hours later and she still felt guilty. Guilty because she'd gone behind his back and guilty because part of her wanted to do it again. At least Gallard had kept his promise and hadn't told anyone. Melody had been right—romantic relationships were messy.

She finished with the carrots then went onto the porch to wait for Erik. He was always ten minutes early and she wanted to greet him when he arrived. Seeing him again might sort out her feelings and confusing thoughts. He should have been the only man she wanted to be with. Hopefully this dinner would clear that up for her.

The car Melody and Cherish shared pulled up in front of her house and she watched Nicola get out. She spoke with Cherish for a few seconds then ran into the house. Cherish didn't drive away but got out instead.

"Cherish! You're back!"

"Of course I'm back, hon." She approached the porch and sat next to Robin. "I wanted to thank you for earlier. You were the only one who didn't rush to blame me."

"You're welcome." Robin rested her head on Cherish's shoulder.

"I'm going away for a while. It seems that people are angry, and I have a few things I would like to sort out."

"Please don't leave. Melody would be sad and so would I."

"You're so sweet. You don't have to worry about me. I've been taking care of myself for centuries. Tell my sister that I'll be back before she knows it."

Cherish stood up and kissed Robin's forehead. Robin was going to miss her. Wherever she was going. J.D. said that she wanted Robin's help in proving Cherish's innocence and she was all for it. Lucas was going to be on the case as well and she hoped he would find out she had nothing to do with it so Cherish could come home.

"Look out for Nicola okay?" Cherish said. "Something is going on here and I am going to find out what. She may not open up to anyone else, but she might listen to you."

As Cherish walked to her car, a shiver went up Robin's spine. Cherish was right—something was wrong. That whole night where Nicola denied being there when the man was hurt and now she was apparently accusing Cherish of hurting her. The pieces were there but they weren't fitting.

Nicola came out of the house not five minutes later. She'd showered and changed into some nice dark skinny jeans and a black, loose-fitted shirt that hung off of her left shoulder. Robin stood up to greet her.

"You look nice," Robin said.

"Thanks! So do you, hon. Your boyfriend is going to flip when he sees that dress."

Robin smiled shyly and glanced down at her clothes. It had been J.D.'s idea to dress up and she'd picked a black and green high-low dress with a brown belt. Her hair was straight, but Lela had helped her make waves with one of her hot tools.

"Hey now. You need to turn that frown upside-down," Nicola said. "You look sad."

"So do you. You were happy this morning but when Cherish dropped you off, you were sad."

"I'm mostly sore."

"Sore? Why?"

Nicola's eyes widened for a moment. "No reason. I'll be fine when I take some aspirin."

Nicola tried to walk by, but Robin stopped her. Everyone was saying that Cherish hurt her, but Robin had never seen any proof. Without warning, she lifted Nicola's shirt and gasped in shock. Her ribs were horribly bruised.

"Nic! What happened?"

"I made someone angry. Please don't tell Lucas. He has enough to worry about with his dad."

Robin gently hugged her so she wouldn't hurt Nicola then watched her go into the house. Why did every ask her to keep their secrets? Soon she was going to explode from everything she was keeping bottled up.

Erik arrived ten minutes early, as Robin predicted. Her melancholy mood left in an instant and she took in the sight of him as he approached her. He was in a white button up and black slacks. He had a bouquet of dark pink roses.

"Those are beautiful," she said. "For me?"

"Actually, they're for your sister. It's my way of saying thank you for giving me a chance, for inviting me to dinner, and for letting me see you."

She took his free hand and they went inside. The house smelled amazing and the scent of food wafted throughout the living room. Lela made Gallard's signature beef stew and J.D. made some delicious apple cake for dessert. Melody oversaw the décor and they were using the best China.

"Oh, hey, it's the Popo," Terrence said. "Since you're off duty, I hope you don't mind if I smoke a little something."

"Terrence!" Robin said, appalled. "He's joking, Erik."

To make the dinner less awkward, Lela had given Kevin, Terrence, and Ramses some of her blood. They all looked like completely different people with their natural hair and eye colors. Apparently, Terrence was curious about modern hallucinogenic drugs and had gotten high with Kevin earlier that day. Robin couldn't believe how uncivilized her family was acting. J.D. and she got high sometimes, but not when they had company.

She pulled Erik away from Terrence and they sat in the living room. Melody came in with two glasses of champagne and handed one to him and one to Robin. After they made introductions, he thanked her and took a sip.

Gallard and Lucas showed up eventually, and everyone pitched in to set the table. Gallard was looking a little more like himself, minus the hair, and he even greeted Erik warmly, to Robin's relief and so did Lela who loved the flowers and even put them in a vase on the table.

Everyone else sat at the table with Abe sitting to Robin's right and Erik on her left. Altogether, there were fourteen of them and it was a good thing the table was so big. Lucas was clear on the other side and about a jaunt away. The only place that was empty was next to Melody.

"Where's Cherish?" Lela asked.

"That's a good question," Melody said. "Has anyone heard from my sister?"

The room grew awkwardly quiet. Not everyone was in the know about what happened earlier that day and Robin hoped they could keep it that way. Only everything changed when Cherish decided to go out of town without telling anyone but her.

"She said she was going to the gym," Lucian finally said. "She promised to be here in time for dinner."

"The gym?" Lela said. "I thought she was joining you for some time in the city."

"Wow, this food looks great!" Gallard said.

He started serving himself and nobody questioned his maneuver. Lela gave him a funny look but didn't say anything. Once he was served, he passed the food to the left and soon everyone had their plates filled. The chatter was sectioned off based on who was sitting closest to whom and Erik struck up a conversation with Gallard.

"Your . . . I'm sorry, I don't know what she is to you, but Melody said you were stationed in Africa. What were you doing there?"

"I spent about a week in Egypt trying to put an end to civil war in Sinai."

"I heard about that. It was successfully thwarted, right? It must have been terrifying. They said about thirty U.S. soldiers were lost in that battle."

"It was terrifying. But it earned me honorary discharge. I'm home for the duration." Gallard stared intently at Erik. "Why do you look so familiar?"

"I was friends with J.D. in high school. I came over a few times. That was about five years ago."

"Right, I remember now. You graduated two years ahead of her. So how did you meet Robin?"

Erik went into the story and Robin focused on her beef stew. While they continued to talk, Lela started asking Robin questions.

"Hey, you were with J.D. and Gallard at the bar, right?"

"Yeah. But I wasn't drinking all that much. I only had one cocktail."

Lela chuckled. "That's not what I was going to ask. Did you see Cherish there?"

187

Robin hesitated before nodding.

"Well, what did she say?"

"Robin! I hear you're a real hero in this town," Gallard said, interrupting Lela again. "I think you and Lucas should both join the task force and kill all the vampires in Texas. You can stake them with a broom and he'll levitate them to another city."

Robin kicked him again, harder this time. If he was sober, why was he acting like this? He was giving away private information. It was one thing for Erik to know about vampires and another to know about Lucas' abilities. She pretended to pick something up from the floor and that's when she saw the tiny bottle of alcohol in Gallard's hand. He'd been secretly pouring it into his drink.

She sat back up and tried to subtly hint to Lela what was going on. Lela frowned then bent down to and when she came back up she looked as appalled as Robin did. She had a feeling this dinner was going to go south. People didn't know where Cherish was while she did, Gallard was drunk again, and Lela was starting to figure out that people were keeping secrets.

"Husband, can I see you in the kitchen?" Lela whispered to Gallard.

"No, you can talk to me right here."

Robin gasped in shock. Gallard could be rude and snappy with everyone, but not Lela. She was his wife and the love of his life. He was never mean to her and even though Robin knew why he was acting strange it didn't justify his being mean to her of all people.

"Erik, why don't you come with me to get more champagne?" Robin suggested. She needed to get him out of there before it got ugly.

"No, no, stay here," Gallard said. "I'll get it for you."

He tried to stand up, but he stumbled, and Lela caught him before he fell. All chatter ceased at that moment and every gaze went to Gallard. Robin wished she could sink between the floorboards and disappear. This was supposed to be a nice dinner but all the lying and the secrets were keeping that from happening. Instead of cowering, she decided to take charge.

"This ends now," she said. "Everyone at this table is keeping secrets and acting strange. We're going to settle this."

"Robin —" Lela said.

"No! We are supposed to be a family and we can't be one if we're all lying to each other. Everyone is going to say what they are hiding, and you can't leave the table until you're honest. It's Two Truths and A Lie time, minus the lying."

"I have something I'd like to say," Abe said.

"Not you! Sit down," she said with clenched teeth. He gave her a smug smile then returned to his seat. She was safe, at least for a little while.

She waited for everyone to tell her to sit down, but no one spoke. Melody was the first one to stand and she took a sip of champagne before setting it down and clearing her throat.

"Robin is right. We have been keeping secrets and it's tearing us apart. This dinner was supposed to bring us closer together but obviously there's tension. So I will go first since I am the third oldest at this table." She grabbed onto the chain around her neck and pulled it out from inside of her shirt, revealing a small diamond ring. "David and I are married. We exchanged vows in the justice of peace two days before he left. Cherish was the witness."

Everyone murmured in surprise. So this was why she kept telling everyone she was Lela and Robin's step mother. It was because it was true. David had said she didn't want to get married, but something must have changed.

"Congrats, Mel!" Lela said nervously. "I'm happy for you. Welcome to the family, not that you weren't already part of us. Let's give a toast for the new Mrs. Shepherd."

Everyone raised a glass then took a sip except for Gallard. Lela had stolen his bottle and removed his champagne. The next person to stand up was Kevin. The room grew quiet once more as he began to speak.

"Ever since Curtis died, I've been on the verge of a breakdown. Losing him . . . killing my brother, Robin's assault. All these events have pushed me closer and closer over the edge. I've tried to numb the pain by hooking up with random strangers. Doesn't matter the time or place. While I was in prison, I reached an ultimate low. I started sleeping with one of the prison guards for a blood fix. One day when he was supposed to bring me the bag, there were other officers there. He told them I was a prostitute and that I should be punished for offering my services to a police officer. They but a dog collar on me and beat me until I passed out."

Kevin paused and Lela got up, wrapping Kevin in her embrace. Robin wanted to cry for her brother. Everything he suffered in prison was because of her. If he hadn't come to see her, none of what they'd gone through would have happened.

"You were with a man?" Robin asked. "Does that mean you're . . . gay?"

"Yes, I am. Do you have a problem with that?"

"Not at all! You're my brother, Kev. I love you no matter what. I just want to know why you never told me."

"I'm telling you now. It's not that I didn't trust you or think you were old enough to understand. It's just hard talking about it."

Robin felt a tear slide down her cheek. Her brother never talked about what he went through and hearing this broke her heart. All this time, he'd plastered a smile on his face just like she had and he'd been amazing at hiding his pain. A hand slipped into hers and she turned to Abe, smiling with gratitude. His touch was comforting and just what she needed.

After Kevin sat down, Terrence stood up. Robin thought he was going to say something stupid, but he shocked her with his words.

"I'm still in love with you, Celeste. I've had many a woman in my life, but you were always the best I ever had. I loved you then, and I know why you betrayed me. I never thought I'd get another chance with you, and I don't want to miss this opportunity."

Celeste blinked and nobody else said anything. Robin didn't pay much attention to Celeste because she was always quiet.

"I . . . I don't know what to say."

"Say you'll give me a chance. I've hated myself all these years and it was my fault you were killed. I should have put aside my ambition and accepted that you would love me whether or not we had money. But I was so set on making sure you were as privileged as you were before you met me that I forgot to make you my priority. I lost you because of it, and . . . I failed our son. I don't know what happened to him or if he ever had a family, but I should have stuck around to find out. I didn't."

Terrence sat down and the room went quiet once more. Robin was curious to know his story, but this wasn't the time to discuss it. She would have to ask Gallard later.

J.D. stood up next. "I would give a long, heartwarming speech like the rest of you, but I would rather not make anyone vomit. So, here it goes. Lucian and I are dating. Well . . . not really dating because we haven't actually been on a date, but we are involved."

"What!" Melody, Lela, and Gallard said in unison. Robin was surprised that J.D. was admitting this. She'd fought to keep their relationship a secret for so long. Apparently, everyone was taking her advice about being open.

"Is this true?" Gallard asked Lucian.

"Yes. It's true. We were going to say something when you came back, but there have been too many distractions."

"Anything else I should know about?"

"I think everyone has been honest enough," Lucas said. "I think *you're* the one who has some explaining to do."

Before anyone could say anything, Nicola stood up. Robin could see from her spot that Nicola was trembling and she hoped she was going to be honest about her injuries. Robin couldn't stand by and watch her friend suffer abuse.

"I'm having an affair with Ryan Aspen," she said. She then turned to Lucas. "I met him when he first came to town. He told me about his gallery, and he's been giving me painting lessons at his apartment since September." She paused. "I lied to all of you about that painting. That woman—she doesn't just look like me. She is me. Ryan painted it two months ago and we made a deal. If someone bought it, I would have to tell Lucas about our relationship. I never thought J.D. would be the one to do that." Nicola looked at Lucas. "I'm so sorry."

Robin couldn't have been more shocked if Nicola dumped a bucket of paint on Lucas' head. She was having an affair? That didn't make any sense at all. She was either lying to cover up the abuse or Ryan was the one she was being abused by. Robin's head was spinning, and she stole Abe's glass of champagne and gulped it down.

Gallard stood and walked out of the room. Lela followed him and so did Lucian. Robin wanted to be with them but was distracted when Erik's phone started ringing. Everyone at the table was murmuring and talking amongst themselves about the huge bombshells they'd been hit with and she could barely process her own thoughts. Erik answered it and spoke quietly with the person. By the look in his eyes, it was a call about his job. He hung up then put the phone in his pocket.

"Hey, beautiful, I gotta run. Something important has come up."

"Really? But we were having so much fun!"

He chuckled and kissed her cheek. "This was by far the most interesting experience I've had so far. You're always surprising me. I'll call you tonight, okay." He got up from the table. "Lucas, I think you should come with me."

Lucas, who now looked like death, slowly turned his gaze to Erik. "Why?"

"I just got a phone call. They've caught the killer, and we need as much back up as possible. You want to start that job early?"

Lucas dropped his napkin on the table and got up. He ruffled Colton's hair before following Erik out the door. The rest of the table sat awkwardly in silence and Robin then stole her sister's glass and gulped that down too. This whole secret revealing thing hadn't gone as planned, but it was a start. Soon, everything would be out in the open.

Abe, whom she had forgotten was on the other side of her, leaned close to her ear.

"You're lucky everyone left before I could share my secret."

She groaned in annoyance. "How polite of you to not humiliate me in front of my boyfriend."

He reached over and took her hand under the table, startling her. "All right, I won't tell anyone what happened. However, I want you to know that I made a decision. I'm not doing the friends-with-benefits thing. I refuse to touch you until you're no longer seeing him. I'm determined to win you, Robin."

Abe downed the rest of his champagne then got up from the table. She was more confused than ever now. She didn't want anyone fighting for her or any reason. All she wanted was to be with Erik and enjoy their growing relationship. How could she do that when another's man's kiss burned in her memory? She'd seen the look on Lucas' face when he found out Nicola had cheated. She couldn't bear to do that to Erik, and she didn't want to be considered a cheater. There was only one thing left to do. She would have to avoid Abe at all costs. Even if it meant never going to Lucas' house again.

29

I rode with Erik to the station where he switched to his squad car and we took off at a fast speed into town. The others hadn't really given him much details but I couldn't help but worry that they'd gotten to Cherish. She was missing at dinner and had been since earlier that afternoon. I kept praying over and over that it wasn't her.

I was also trying to process what Nicola had revealed at dinner. She'd been having an affair for almost three months, and I'd never even suspected it. Either that or I never wanted to see it. She had been hiding something from me and this was not what I expected it to be. My heart felt like it was being ripped out of my chest.

"Sorry about earlier," I said, trying to get my mind on something else. "We usually don't expose our darkest secret at dinner."

"No need to apologize. There isn't enough excitement at my house. I found it very amusing."

That was one of us. When Robin demanded everyone reveal their secrets, I hadn't expected anyone to actually do it. The problem was, I hadn't heard from the people who really needed to speak up. Gallard was still drinking to cover up whatever it was he was hiding, and Nicola hadn't told us if Cherish really hurt her or not.

"I'm sorry about your wife" Erik said after a while. "That's gotta be tough."

"Yeah." I clenched my teeth. "I'm sorry too."

The sea of red and blue lights shone up ahead and Erik parked as close as he could. When he got out, he unclipped one of his guns and tossed it to me.

"You ever use one of these?"

"Several times. What's it loaded with?"

"V.S. darts. You're going to need them in case this person is dangerous."

I shoved the gun into my belt and followed behind him. I didn't feel comfortable being in possession of V.S., let alone thinking about having to use it but if I was going to do this job I had to pretend I was okay with it. Erik ran towards the crowd of police officers and I saw that they were all standing in a circle with their guns aimed in the direction of a wall.

"Erik," Sheriff Tyler greeted him. "You came just in time. Did you bring it?"

"Yes, and I gave it to Lucas as you asked."

Tyler turned to me. "I know you're technically starting on Monday, but I wanted you to take credit for this. The suspect was seen here, and Craven happened to be patrolling the area. There's a man protecting her, and he's believed to be hostile. He couldn't have gone far."

I wasn't in uniform, but I had on good shoes. He gave everyone instructions then sent us in different directions. Erik had partnered up with me and we ran, guns locked and loaded, down the alleyways. Erik was in good shape and could no doubt stop a normal person on the run, but frankly he was slowing me down. I needed to use my abilities in order to find this guy.

"We should split up," I said.

"What? You can't go in alone. He's a vampire. You won't stand a chance."

"I'll look for him and then let you know when I find him. I promise I'll call you in for back up."

He gave me a brief nod then I rounded the corner, checked for witnesses, then took off at a high speed. I could smell blood and that meant the suspect probably had some on his clothes. I followed the scent for about five blocks then jumped onto the roof of a restaurant so I could get a better view. I couldn't see anyone suspicious yet. I closed my eyes, honing my senses.

Moments later, I heard it. The sound of quick footsteps — too quick for a mortal. It didn't take long for me to locate them and I jumped off the roof, racing towards the sound. My night vision kicked in and I saw the man just as he disappeared down the alley. I chased him down, cutting him off from the other side, and shoved him to the ground.

"Look, man, I don't want any trouble. If we could talk this —"

Before I could finish, the man bounced back up and bit onto my neck. This was the first time I'd ever been bitten and hopefully the last. It hurt like hell and I couldn't push him away fast enough.

194

"Ugh," the man said. "You're disgusting. Must be a B negative. Doesn't mean I won't have fun killing you."

He lunged at me, but I grabbed onto his throat and slammed him back to the ground. He got up and pushed me into the wall, but I managed to knock him in the mouth with my elbow. He lifted me into the air, which was an awkward feat because I was so much taller than him and he tossed me about ten feet away. I hit the ground and rolled. Because of my blood diet, I was able to recover quickly.

"What the hell are you?" he asked.

"Not someone you want to piss off. Now look, you could either tell me who you are or I can shoot you with V.S. and haul you into custody."

"I am Ishmael. I work for Simeon."

What a surprise. I had a feeling that rat was behind this. The question was why would he try to frame Nicola for a crime she didn't commit? It had to have something to do with Cherish and why she was acting funny lately.

"Lucas!" someone shouted. I recognized the voice immediately and turned around to see Cherish approaching me. She was wearing her favorite work-out tank top that said *I run because I eat.* I hadn't expected her to be there since she was absent from dinner. What was she doing here?

"Aunt Cherish, what's going on?"

Ishmael lunged at her, but she was quicker. She kicked him away then rushed up to him, grabbing him from behind then separated his head from his body. I helped her move the parts further into the alley to be burned by the sun later. I wasn't sure if helping her was the best thing. I had no idea what Ishmael stood for or what he wanted. Cherish had killed him before I could get more answers.

I heard a car approaching, and by the sound of the tires against the pavement, the car was at a crawl. The police were starting to search the area. Cherish remained with me.

"Cher, if you stay here, I'm going to have to arrest you."

"I know. At this point, I believe arresting me is the only way to protect Nicola. They're catching on and it's a matter of time before the crimes are tied to her."

"Cherish." My shoulders sank. "You don't have to do this."

"Yes, I do. She didn't do this, Lucas. Please trust me when I say that. She's being framed. However, I'm not going to force you to choose between your job and your family. Let me do this for her."

As the car grew closer, I gave Cherish a silent message and she understood. If this was going to look legitimate, I would have to use force. Once the squad car was in sight, I shoved Cherish against the wall and proceeded to cuff her. More cars swarmed the area and then several officers got out. I led her towards one of the squad cars. The officers clapped the entire time and I tried to act like I was flattered. Inside, it made me sick that I had to arrest my own aunt. I gently put her in the back of the car and let out a long exhale.

"That was incredible!" Sheriff Tyler said. "I have never seen a vampire cooperate like that. We usually have to put up a good fight and sedate them. What's your secret?"

I shrugged. "I told her I could either do it the easy way or the hard way. She chose the easy way. There was another man with her, but I wasn't able to catch both."

"And I'm sure you'll find him. You did a good job, son. You've lived up to your position. Welcome to the team, Captain Lucas."

I didn't say a word as we drove to the station. The other officers kept giving me approving pats on the back and handshakes, but I didn't feel deserving of them. I felt like I'd betrayed everything I stood for. I watched as they took her mug shot photo, fingerprinted her, and then took all of her personal belongings, including her wedding ring.

Afterward, Tyler invited me to watch outside the window while they interrogated her as a way to show me how it was done. They asked for her whereabouts the nights of the first and second murders and the night the man was attacked at the festival. She gave them convincing answers but I knew she was lying.

"She's so unique," Tyler said. "I haven't seen a vampire like her since . . ."

I turned to look at him. "Since what?"

"Nothing. I'm just being nostalgic is all. Usually vampires don't dye their hair or wear contacts. No wonder she blended in so well."

I cleared my throat. "Did she say what her name was?"

"She said Charity Tophé. She's a drifter from Chicago. Doesn't have I.D. on her, and she won't tell us where she lives or how long she's been here."

Cherish had given her old alias. Maybe she wanted to protect my family. If they knew she was connected to me, we wouldn't be able to stay in Euless. The only thing not blowing her cover out of the water was Erik's silence. He could say anything at any time and that scared me. I knew it was too risky for Robin to date a police officer. I should have put a stop to it before it even started and now we could be in trouble.

"I have never seen a guy take down a vampire that easily. You had to have had training or experience."

I pressed my lips together. "Guilty. I applied at the MITF. I went through the training but didn't make the cut. It sucked, but I moved on."

"They turned you down? What for?"

I was going to answer when Erik came into the room. I was glad that I'd been saved. If I was honest and said I failed the drug test, it might compromise my integrity. Cherish said that Nicola was being framed so that meant the real culprit was still out there, and I was going to find out who this person was.

"Lucas, you don't look so good," Erik said. "Why don't we have your bite looked at?"

I nodded then followed him down the hall. I couldn't take watching Cherish anymore and I was dangerously close to losing my dinner. The anxiety was too much and if I didn't relax soon, everything was going to start floating around the room.

Erik and I went to the break room then got the first aid kit. He handed some gauze and medical tape to me and I cleaned off my neck with alcohol wipes then covered my already healed wound with the gauze. I couldn't let him see that I wasn't hurt anymore and would have to wear the gauze for a while. I could feel bile rising in my throat, but I remained under control. What I really needed to do was call my family and tell them what was going on. I couldn't do that with so many eyes on me.

"I didn't say anything about your friend," Erik said. "Or whatever she is to you."

I chuckled. "Cherish is married to Kevin's Uncle."

"Is he Robin's uncle too?"

"No. Robin and Lela have a different dad than Kevin. Solomon is really close to the family, though."

Solomon. What was I going to tell him? That his wife was in jail for a crime and that she was taking the blame for Nicola? That was the last thing he needed to hear. Gallard was already a mess and we didn't need the next most stable person to lose it as well. Solomon and Gallard were the rocks of the family and with one rock about to crack, we were in serious trouble.

"You should go," Erik said. "You look like you could use some rest. Arraignment is Monday and you can officially start your job fully recuperated."

"Are you sure? Your dad doesn't need me?"

"I already talked to him earlier. Go home. There's nothing you really can do at this point. We'll do a lineup on Monday and bring all the witnesses in. Until then, the DA is just going to be doing paperwork and getting ready for arraignment." He put a hand on my shoulder. "I'm sorry about your relative. It must not have been easy for you to bring her in. Like I said, I'm not going to say anything. You have my word."

I took him up on his suggestion and walked out of the station in slow motion. That was when I realized that I hadn't driven there so I took out my phone and called the only person I really wanted to talk to.

"Lucas? I wanted to call you, but I wasn't sure if you were free. Are you okay?"

"I'm fine, mom." I let out a sigh. "Actually, I'm not fine. Everything is falling apart and I'm not sure how to fix it."

I told her everything that was going on. About my suspicions around Nicola and that they'd been proven wrong when I'd heard Cherish's confession at the gallery. I then told her that Cherish was in custody and that she was most likely going to get jail time.

"I'm coming to get you. Stay put, okay?"

"Mom, it's fine. I could fly home."

"No, I'm coming. Your dad is coming too. You need to talk to him and we can figure out how to help Cherish together."

I hung up and waited over at the park next to the station. I saw Lela's car pull up and I got into the backseat without saying a word. I was startled when I saw that Lucian was in the back seat as well. He must have wanted to come since it was his daughter who was in trouble. I was glad he was there.

"If this is about Cherish, I don't really know much. She's —"

"No, Lucas, this isn't about Cherish," Gallard said. "Cherry Pop can handle herself. There's something I need to tell you. What I should have told you when I first arrived."

Lela drove down the street then parked the car at another park. The four of us got out and sat around one of the stone bench and tables. Their silence wasn't doing anything for my nerves, and I wanted to get this talk over with. On the other hand, what Gallard had to say couldn't possibly be as bad as what was happening with Cherish.

"First off, I want to apologize for everything," Gallard said. "I'm not good at coping and my actions were a result of that. I'm not justifying them at all. Driving drunk with Colton and drinking as much as I have been was completely stupid and irresponsible."

"Well, because you're my dad, I suppose I can forgive you."

He smiled. "That means a lot to me because I don't deserve it. Lucas, what I wanted to tell you is what I've been hiding. Why I've been having such a hard time lately."

Gallard paused for a moment and I waited expectantly for his answer. By the expressions on everyone's face, I was getting even more worried. What could possibly be worse than what had happened that night? I was starting to come up with a million scenarios.

"Please tell me this isn't about Micah."

"No, no. Nothing like that. Sadly, I haven't heard anything concerning him. This has to do with what I learned at Sinai. It's about your gifts."

"My gifts? What about them?"

Gallard looked at Lela then back at me. "You mentioned you could move things with your mind? That you could fly? It's puzzling, considering you supposedly gave them away. And you mentioned feeling an earthquake the night Mona died."

I nodded. "Yeah. That was the first time I'd ever done anything like that. But you're right. I shouldn't have been able to do anything if I'd given my gifts away."

"Exactly. I thought the same thing until the guy on the mountain brought it to my attention. The healing powers you had are only an edition to the powers you already harness. Lucas, the powers you gave away weren't meant for you."

This was not what I'd expected him to say. How could the gifts not be mine? I felt so incomplete without them. Whenever I healed my friends and family, it gave me purpose.

"If they're not for me, then who are they for?" I asked.

"He wouldn't tell me. He said you would understand in time." He sighed. "I'm afraid there's more. When I said that there was no way to save the vampire race, I was lying."

This got my attention. If there was a way, I wanted to know so we could work towards it.

"How can this be done? Whatever it is, I'm up for it, no matter what it takes."

Lela's eyes misted and she took my hand. Gallard let out a hard exhale and I could see he was struggling to hold himself together.

"Years ago, Bodoway saw a vision from Maximus' future. He foresaw that two men would save the vampire species from destruction. That being said, I finally learned everything when I went to Egypt. In order to curse vampires to a life trapped between Heaven and Hell, Lucian has to die. You know that already. But . . . if we were to save them — return their souls and make them all mortal again, someone else has to die."

"Someone else as in who?"

When no one made eye contact, the truth hit me. This was the reason why Gallard had gone off the deep end and drank until he was well past intoxicated. It was why he'd gone all nostalgic on me at the restaurant and why he was even here in the first place. The realization made me sicker than ever.

"It's me, isn't it?" I said. "I'm the one who has to die."

"We've known for a while that you were different," Lela said. "Bodoway predicted your birth long before your father and I were even romantically involved. And . . . I had these dreams. They were messages about your purpose. We never thought it was so extreme." She wiped away her tears. "Nobody knows this information but the four of us sitting at this table. As far as we're concerned no one else has to know."

"But, it would eliminate the problem." The initial shock had passed and now the idea was starting to sound genius. Our plan was to start a war and fight for our rights, but what if we didn't have to fight at all? What if no one had to risk their lives and we could free them of the blood lust and the pain and suffering that came with being immortal?

"What are you saying?" Gallard asked.

"Don't you see? This is even better than what we planned! If we made all the vampires mortal again, the government would have no reason to keep them in custody. They wouldn't need an army to try and fight against them. Micah could be released and you, mom, Solomon, everyone would be able to finally have a real life. No more running, no more hiding."

"Lucas, think about what you're saying. You would have to *die*. What about Colton? Do you really think you could leave him behind without his father?"

"He's young. He would get past it. Besides, he would always have you and Lucian and several other men who could take my place."

"It's easy for you to say," Lucian said. "You're not the one who has to live without you. I told you before, you're like my own flesh and blood. I would sooner offer myself up for the slaughter than let you die."

I didn't want to admit it, but they were right. It would be easy for me because I would be dead. Everyone else would have to live with the aftermath. I thought back to when I'd seen them all grieving when they only thought I was dead. How much worse would it be if I were actually in the ground?

"Sweetheart, please give this more thought," Lela said. "There is so much at stake here and there isn't a person you know that won't be willing to fight for our freedom. We always have that option. Your sacrifice should be a last resort."

"Okay, I'll think about it. And I will let you know when I decide. I promise I won't off myself on a whim."

Lela punched my arm. "That's for all the times I never got to spank you."

I chuckled then hugged her close to me. This had to be a tough thing to talk about. I would have said the same thing if it were Colton trying to sacrifice himself. She was right. I needed to consider how this would affect everyone before I jumped to making decisions.

Gallard stood up and Lela released me from the embrace. I was going to speak when Gallard took her place in hugging me and I felt a surge of energy pass through me. My body hummed and I could feel the warm, electricity spreading through my arms and legs.

When he finally let go of me, he supported himself with the table while he clutched his chest. He gasped for air while Lela gently rubbed his back. The transition back to being dead had to be more difficult than what I'd just gone through. Soon, his hair, what was left of it anyway, was black once more. He looked like my father again and I knew that he was his old self on the inside as well.

"Thank you," I said. "I feel whole again for the first time in months."

"So do I. That gift wasn't meant for me, and I'm glad it's back to its original owner."

We got back into the car and drove home. It was so strange having all my power at once. I could feel it surging through my fingers as if it were ready to be used. I was ready to use it again. It would come in handy at some point.

I said goodnight to my parents then Lucian and I went into our house. Apparently, Terrence was out with Celeste somewhere and Kevin went for a walk to clear his head. It was very quiet.

Before going to bed, I went into Colton's room first and smiled when I saw him sleeping. I thought back to what Lela had said about how my decision would affect him. It was easy to say that the other men in his life could replace me, but was that possible? Nobody could replace Gallard in my heart. Colton already suffered enough separation, and I didn't want him to break and have episodes like I had.

I softly kissed his forehead before leaving and I went into my room. I was going to change when I saw Nicola lying on my bed. How long she'd been there, I didn't know. She was actually the last person I wanted to see. She sat up and looked at me when I closed the door and I sat next to her on the bed.

"Lucas, hey!" She got up and hugged me tightly, but I didn't hug her back. "Did they catch the killer?"

"I'm not so sure. Cherish turned herself in in your place and now she's pretending she doesn't know me. It's pretty bad and I don't know how we're going to get her out of this."

Her head rested on my shoulder. We didn't speak for about ten minutes and I used that time to take in everything that had happened.

She moved away from me and crossed her legs. Her revelation at dinner had slipped my mind for a few hours but now that I remembered, I felt sick. Robin was right — once everything was out there, we could come together and be stronger than ever as a group. We would need all the strength we could muster. But Nicola's confession had pushed us apart.

"Lucas, I am so sorry about dinner. I really wanted to enjoy the family time, but —"

"Save it, Nic. You're not sorry." I gave her a cold stare. "You made me out to be the biggest idiot. How could you stand there and let me admire that painting when you knew that Ryan had painted it?"

"Lucas, what do you —"

"Let me finish. I just want to know why. Why did you leave me for Ryan? What happened that I wasn't enough for you anymore? Is it because I don't want another child? Or is it because I'm a reminder of everything you've lost?"

Tears flooded her eyes and she turned her head while she wiped them away. I couldn't believe she was crying. *I* should have been the one to cry. Instead, I was trying so hard not to comfort her like I used to. She'd broken my heart, and this was ten times worse than what I did to her in the summer.

Reaching over, she took my hand. I didn't shy away from her, and I started digging into her mind. I had to see for myself what she was trying to tell me. I saw some images from the week before. She was with Ryan and they were painting and drinking champagne. Then it jumped to the previous day when she and Ryan went to Austin to look at a painting. Ryan was flirting with her and showering her with compliments. I then went back several weeks to around the time she said she started seeing him.

Finally, I found it. The specific moment I was looking for. It was from that afternoon while she was at her class. I let go of her hand and I could see in her eyes that she understood that I'd figured it out. I knew what I had to do.

"I'm sorry Lucas. I cared for you, I really did. But Ryan gives me what I need."

"If that's how you feel, then get out of here, Nic. I've had a long night and I don't want to do this right now. Just go."

She walked out of my room. I closed my eyes, falling back on my bed and tried to keep from turning into an emotional mess. But it also got my mind turning with ideas. I wasn't sad or depressed—I was angry. Everything I'd gone through in the past week culminated into this moment and now I was more determined than ever. I wasn't going to let our life here be ruined, no matter what.

30

TWO WEEKS LATER

Nicola turned over in her bed and instinctively reached over to her right. When she found the space empty, she opened her eyes and her heart sank. The wonderful moments she'd thought were real had only been a dream.

Every morning, she would reach for the right and every morning she would forget Lucas had broken up with her. When the realization would come back to her, she never felt more alone. She was so used to waking up next to him and that may never happen again.

More than anything, she wanted to stay in bed and have a pity party. It was Saturday, so Colton didn't have school. Thanksgiving had long passed, and it was early December. There was no art class and she had nowhere to be.

On that note, she nestled into her covers and got comfortable. Her fingers found her phone and she opened one eye and started scrolling through her photos. The first one she saw was of Lucas putting Colton on the pony at the festival. The next was of Colton on his first day of school and then there was one of her and Lucas that J.D. took at the bar.

Seeing these pictures made her want to cry and she clung to the pendant Colton had given her. Why did she listen to the threats and let them control her? She was supposed to be stronger now that she'd told the police about what Ash had done and when she turned into a vampire, she thought maybe she could gain more confidence in herself. Then someone stronger than her made her feel like the weak and helpless woman she used to be. She hated herself and she hated that she was forced to break up with Lucas. Her only hope was that she could somehow get herself out of this whole mess.

She flinched when her phone started ringing then groaned when she saw the caller I.D. Ryan was the last person she wanted to talk to and she wished he could give her a moment of peace. It was bad enough that he was constantly texting her to ask where she was and what she was doing.

"Hello, Ryan. To what do I owe the pleasure of this call?" she said in the most cheerful voice she could muster.

"I wanted your voice to be the first I heard this morning. Did you sleep well?"

"Yes, thank you. You're so sweet, you know that?"

Nicola wanted to gag on her own words. Ever since Ryan revealed the real reason why he'd kept her close, she'd had to fake interest in him. She was even forced to lie to Lucas for him and she resented Ryan.

According to him, he'd been chosen to be her blood mate — the Romani coven's version of arranged marriage. Every female in the coven was paired with a man of good, strong background and they would be joined in a ceremony.

All this time she was spending with him was the courting stage. Not that she would be able to decide not to be his blood mate. It was a required time for them to get to know each other.

"I'm calling to confirm your appointment," he said. "The limo will pick you up in a half an hour."

"Appointment?"

"The fertility tests. We discussed this, remember?"

Right, the check-up. Every female member of the coven had to take tests to ensure fertility since each couple would eventually conceive a child. Those who couldn't were cast out, no exceptions.

She forced herself out of bed and took a shower. When she got out, she looked in her closet for something comfortable. One of the women in the coven had forced her to go shopping, saying that she needed to start dressing like she was important. She liked the way she used to dress, and Lucas liked it too. She didn't need silk shirts or five hundred-dollar shoes to feel confident. Again, they wouldn't listen and had to control every aspect of her life.

The green off-the shoulder top seemed like the best choice. She finished off the look with black skinny jeans, her black flats and, of course, wore the necklace. It gave Nicola a reminder that of why she was doing this. Colton's safety depended on her cooperation.

She had fifteen minutes to spare, so she drank some blood then waited on the porch. J.D. had left a note to say they were having breakfast at Lela's to spend more time with Gallard. Due to recent events, he decided to stay in town longer. Nicola wanted so badly to join them and forget about her problems. Their family had taken her in so willingly and she cared for them as if they were blood related. Now she had to distance herself from them to keep Colton safe.

The door opened at Lucas' house and she was stunned to see him standing there. He was dressed semi-casually, the way he always did for work, and wearing the jeans that made his butt look amazing. She realized that she was staring at him too intently and quickly looked away. He'd already noticed she was there, and he came over to her.

"You look gorgeous," he said. "Date with Ryan?"

"Maybe." She'd replied coldly. If this was going to work, she had to pretend she disliked him. That way if anyone was watching, they wouldn't know they'd faked the breakup.

"What do you guys do, exactly? Paint all day in the nude?"

She glared. "No, we have other interests. He's a very intelligent guy. He's passionate about preserving ancient cultures and he has a lot of depth."

"I see. Well, have fun having deep and passionate conversations."

To be more convincing, she decided to turn this into a fight. She was already having difficulty not grabbing him and kissing him right there on the porch. She missed the feel of his arms around her and his heart racing kisses. His touch always made her legs feel weak and even his gaze made her dizzy.

"Really?" she said. "Are you really going to be like this?"

"Like what? I was trying to be nice."

"No, you were being sarcastic. Just like you always are. I can never have a serious conversation with you!"

He chuckled then leaned against the pillar next to the steps. She couldn't look at his face any longer or she would fall apart. Why was he here? He'd ended things two weeks ago and they'd rarely spoken except to discuss Colton. He was supposed to be avoiding her.

"By the way, I want my painting back," he said.

"What painting?"

"The one you did of me. I don't think I want that floating around for just anybody to see."

Nicola put on her best angry look. "No, it's mine. Besides I haven't finished it yet."

"Oh! You plan on finishing it? What for?"

Her cheeks grew red thinking about that day. When he'd suggested she paint him, she had been a bundle of nerves. She didn't know about him, but it took a lot of self-control to sit there and paint when all she wanted was to drag him into the bedroom.

"You're so sexy when you're mad," she whispered. He raised his eyebrows. Realizing she broke character, she continued saying, "I finish everything I start. I'm going to finish it and add it to my portfolio. It's mine and you have no claim over it."

"Okay, fine. I would like to see the finished product, though." He stepped away from the pillar and moved until he was standing in front of her. "You really do look beautiful by the way."

He gave her the sexiest smile that she'd ever seen from him and then he walked down the steps and headed for his mom's house. She was left breathless and could feel her eyes changing color. She always knew if her eyes were not her natural color because she would see a tint before they would change. Right now, they were as green as her dress. She took a few deep breaths until everything was back to normal. This was going to be harder than she thought.

Five minutes later a white SUV limousine pulled up to the house. Apparently, the coven leader required that she be escorted in style. She had yet to meet the guy, but she didn't look forward to it.

The limo stopped in front of the gallery, and the driver led her inside. She had to give it to them—the coven was stealthy. They'd purchased several buildings in Euless and used them as secret locations. There were tunnels underground that hadn't been used in years, and these buildings were connected by these tunnels. It was how they were able to make quick exits.

She and her escort got into the tunnels through a trap door in the janitor's closet then he lit a torch to light the way. She didn't need it. Her night vision kicked in the moment they'd plunged into darkness.

"Where are we going?" she asked.

"The temporary clinic is in the old hatchery. Ryan is unable to attend, but I promise you will be taken care of. I am to escort you to the next location afterwards."

Nicola didn't question him further. She'd learned long ago that asking questions never got her anywhere. She'd fully submitted to the coven, and yet they kept her in the dark.

They finally stopped about half a mile in, and her escort knocked on one of the doors. Someone opened it and they spoke to each other in Romanian before allowing her to go inside.

"I'll be out front in the limo," the escort said. "Go on ahead."

She went into the building and had to shield her eyes. The transition from dark to light was drastic. The building didn't look like a hatchery, but a clinic. The floors were tiled and it smelled like the place had recently been sterilized.

The female coven member who had answered the door was wearing a nurse's uniform. She had a friendly face, unlike the limo driver. Nicola trusted the frowning members over those who smiled. Those who were happy to be there were even more deluded.

"Have a seat here," the nurse said, gesturing to the room on the right of the hall. "Dr. Atherton will be here shortly."

Nicola thanked her then went inside. The exam room looked exactly like a real doctor's office complete with the blood pressure cuff, exam table, and a biohazard disposal. She took the liberty of sitting on the table since she'd end up there anyway.

The door opened and she smiled when she saw a familiar face. It was Ezekiel — Ryan's slightly nerdy yet lovable brother. She'd hoped she could run into him again.

"Ezekiel? You're a doctor?"

"Yes, I am. Well, technically a nurse. The coven duties haven't allowed for me to go to med school." He adjusted his glasses then crossed his arms. "I hope this isn't awkward. I am the only person trained for this."

She felt her cheeks grow red. "Oh. It didn't even occur to me that you'd be, uh . . . examining me."

"I assure you this is completely professional. I am the primary physician for all members of the coven — men, women, and children."

"I believe you. You don't strike me as a perv anyway."

Ezekiel's cleared his throat. "I suppose we'll get stared."

After going through normal procedure of checking blood pressure, temperature, and heartrate, he left the room so she could put on a gown. Truthfully, she was slightly nervous about this exam. She hadn't had one since Colton was born. Her aversion to being touched played a major part. She was getting better, but the idea of being examined by someone she barely knew filled her with dread.

He came back with a couple of tools. He wore gloves and had a mask on his face. She sat with her legs crossed, dreading this whole thing.

"Before we begin, I must ask a few questions. Just know that what you say will stay between you and me, and there's no judgement."

"Good to know."

He sat down on his rolling stool and prepared some of the tools.

"Are you sexually active?"

"No."

"Have you ever been?"

Her stomach tightened. "I was . . . assaulted five years ago. I haven't been with anyone since."

The compassion in his eyes made her feel less ashamed.

"Are you currently on birth control?"

"No." She hesitated then said, "I've been taking fertility shots. I haven't had a period in three months. I . . ." A tear fell down her cheek. "I wanted to have children with my boyfriend. My ex-boyfriend, I mean. We haven't had a chance to try."

Ezekiel touched her hand. "It's okay. Like I said, what you tell me stays here."

"But I thought your loyalty was to the coven."

"I was born into it. I had no choice. I do what I do to keep my loved ones alive. Just like you."

Nicola smiled. "Would it be incredibly inappropriate if I hugged you right now?"

He blinked. "I suppose. I don't hug people much. But I read somewhere that hugging releases endorphins. I think if everyone hugged each other every day, we would have less murder and crime. Maybe I am the way I am because I wasn't hugged enough as a child. Children thrive on physical connection, especially with their parents. The first few years of their life are critical. Those who are deprived of affection at a young age tend to grow up with emotional problems, depression, they act out—"

"Zeke?" Nicola chuckled.

"Sorry. I was born with a mild case of Asperger's. I try my best to maintain it, but I occasionally run my mouth."

Instead of replying, Nicola gently put her arms around him. She had a feeling he had some form of Autism, but it made him more lovable. It was why she knew he wouldn't hurt her—why she felt comfortable with him. Not that she pitied him or saw him as handicap. He was just different. He saw the world differently.

When she let go of them, they both took a deep breath.

"Okay, let's get this over with, huh?" he said. "Just make yourself comfortable and I'll be gentle."

Though the exam was uncomfortable, Nicola found it surprisingly bearable. Ezekiel did his thing and finished up by taking a blood and urine sample. Afterward, she had to sit in a waiting room while he went through the tests. These days, a person didn't have to wait a week to get results. They could find simple problems in a matter of hours.

Thankfully, he came to get her only an hour later. She spent that time reading through old magazines they had on the coffee table. Some of them were ten years old.

"What's the prognosis, doc," she asked when they were back in the exam room. "Am I fit to put my birthing hips to use?"

Ezekiel sat on the stool and folded his hands in front of him.

"Nicola, you said you saw a physician before?"

The teasing smile left her face. "Uh, yes. Planned Parenthood."

"And did they do physical exam?"

"No. They just did blood and urine tests." She bit her lip. "What is it?"

He sighed. "As you know, we have equipment that can see the ovaries. I'm required to check everything." He fiddled with his glasses. "Nicola, your eggs are dormant."

She inhaled deeply, holding the air in her lungs until they burned, then breathed out.

"What do you mean dormant?"

"Women secrete a hormone from the pituitary gland that alerts the ovaries to release an egg. It seems your body is failing to create that hormone, which is why you haven't had a period. I'm so sorry, but you are barren."

Nicola choked on a sob but didn't cry. She'd known all along. Ever since she first realized she was late, she had a feeling in her gut that something was wrong. She wanted nothing more than to have a family with Lucas, and now that would never be. Colton would never have siblings.

"You have to tell the coven leader, don't you?"

"That information is required of me, yes. I'm so sorry, Nicola."

She forced a smile. "It's not your fault. Just the same, thank you for everything. I'll always remember your kindness."

Neither of them said another word, and she walked out of the room and to the front door. As promised, her escort was waiting for her outside. She couldn't believe this was happening. All her hopes and dreams were shattered in an instant.

"Ah, Casper," Ezekiel said to her driver.

"Zeke."

"He has you driving the limo?"

"His driver is currently . . . receiving payment."

Nicola frowned but didn't inquire. She knew from experience that asking questions never meant she would get an answer. Ryan kept a lot of the coven's secrets to himself.

"We better be off," Casper said. "I'll see you at dinner."

They left the tunnel and made their way back to the car. Casper drove for quite some time then came to a stop at a shady looking building, no bigger than a small shed. The escort didn't get out, and she wasn't sure what they were doing there.

"Is this their torture chamber?" Nicola asked.

"Not sure— they don't tell me everything. You've been instructed to go inside."

Nicola rolled her eyes then got out. She hated that they were so cryptic. At least she wasn't wearing heels, or the trek would have been a real bitch.

Nicola went inside the building and the door slammed shut behind her. Her eyes adjusted to the darkness and she saw that there was a flight of stairs a few feet away from the door. She inhaled to see if she could recognize any scents but nothing was familiar. It was stuffy and smelled of rotten wood. They descended the stairs one at a time then stopped at the hallway at the bottom. There were about three rooms to the right and left.

"Hello?" she said. "Ryan, are you here?"

No answer. She decided to check the first door on the left. She went inside and found that it contained a bed frame and a single lamp on the floor. Everything was dusty and the particles tickled her nose. She coughed then left the room to check out the others. The second door led to a bathroom where the tile had been stripped out. The toilet didn't have a lid and the mirror was cracked.

Then she heard movement. She turned her head slightly to the right and listened. Someone was in the room next to the bathroom. She hurried to the door, jiggling on the handle. It was locked. Whoever was in there, she had a feeling they weren't there by choice. She looked down the hall and couldn't see anyone, so she used her strength to knock in the door with her shoulder. It only took two tries and she was inside.

She didn't see anything at first, so she went further into the room. It was darker than the other and had a bed as well. Her eyes adjusted and she scanned the area for whoever was in there, checking behind her in case. When she found what she was looking for, her breath caught in her throat. The woman was chained to the wall and the chains were probably long enough for her to reach the bed and the personal toilet on the other side. She was dressed in nothing but underwear and a ripped shirt.

Nicola was so shocked that she couldn't move or speak. The woman finally looked up at her and her eyes widened in surprise. Her mouth was covered in duct tape and it was torn as if she'd been trying to get it off. By the looks of her, she had probably been there for at least ten days. Nicola was going to step forward and free her when someone's hand clamped over her mouth and he held her so tight that her air was cut off.

"Don't say a word," Ryan said. "We're leaving now."

She tried to protest against his hand, but she couldn't articulate her words. He dragged her out of the room and up the stairs. Once they were outside, he closed the door and locked it behind him. She could see he was shaking, and she knew he was equally as shocked as she was. She pressed his hands against the door and breathed heavily in and out.

"Were you here the whole time?" she asked.

"Yes. I had Casper bring you here to meet me."

"We have to go back there! We can't just leave her there!"

"Oh, yes we can. That's only a taste of what they can do to you if you break their rules, Nikita. That's why I need to know for sure that you are going to go through with the ceremony."

"What makes you think I won't?"

"I saw you today. You were flirting with that boyfriend of yours. Now, you may not have to convince me that you're over him, but if they find out you still have ties to that family, they'll do worse. Our leader has no mercy, not even for his own children. You don't want to know what he did to his own son. He'll do much worse to yours."

His words did nothing but pique her curiosity. They had yet to reveal the name of their leader. What had happened to his son? Whatever it was, it had her terrified.

31

Robin sat on her bed, chewing her thumbnail while she waited for Gallard to come over. She had been getting ready for a date with Erik when her stomach started to hurt. The baby moved quite a bit, more than she was used to, and she began to panic. Not knowing who else to call, she'd texted Gallard and told him what was going on.

She heard the front door open and Gallard said a few words to J.D. before knocking on her door. She stood up and winced as she felt the cramps and walked over to the door taking ginger steps. She opened it and immediately burst into tears when she saw him.

"Oh, Robin!" he came into the room and shut the door before pulling her into his arms. "Hey, it's okay! I'm here now."

She cried for a few minutes then tried to compose herself. They went over to her bed and sat down. He was kind enough to wipe her eyes with his sleeve. She'd probably ruined her makeup, not that it mattered. She couldn't see Erik after this.

"Tell me what's going on," he said after a while. "You said you had pain?"

"Yes." She sniffed. "I have cramps, and it's m-m-moving a lot. I think I'm going into labor."

"May I?"

She nodded, and he lifted her shirt, putting a hand over her belly. She'd grown significantly in the last few months, and thanks to the colder

211

weather, she could pile on layers of clothes to hide it. She'd started hugging Erik from the side as much as possible and not hugging her family at all except for Gallard.

"Ooh!" He smiled. "Baby just kicked."

Robin couldn't bring herself to enjoy it. Every kick she felt reminded her of what had happened to her. Who had put this baby in her. She wanted so badly to be excited but all she felt was sadness.

"Is the baby coming?"

"You're how far along now?"

"Eight months, I think."

"Hmm." He felt her stomach for a bit. "Are the cramps constant or do they come and go?"

"They're constant. I've had them before but never this bad."

Gallard lightly smiled. "I think your body is just making room for baby. The female body isn't designed to hold it, so it has to stretch over time so the baby isn't smashed." He pulled her shirt down. "Just the same, I really think you should see a doctor. I've kept your secret as you've asked, but you're a month away from delivery. Lela's going to kill me enough as it is."

Robin bit her lip. She didn't like asking him to keep secrets from her sister, but she didn't want to hurt Lela. She didn't want her to have a breakdown like she had after she was forced to kill Robin all those years ago.

"I suppose I can have J.D. take me," she said. "I'll tell her I want to get birth control."

Gallard winced. "I guess that works." He paused. "By the way, you and Erik aren't . . . you know."

"No, we're not. Believe me, I want to, but I couldn't let him see me like this."

The pained expression on his face made her laugh.

"What?" he asked.

"Your face. You look so disgusted."

Gallard smiled. "Sorry. I'm still getting used to the idea of you being a grown woman. You're having a baby for crying out loud. Just yesterday you were playing with your toy Spock and doing a happy dance when I got you McDonalds."

That had her laughing. "I still do a happy dance when people get me McDonalds."

"Don't ever change, okay?" He kissed her forehead and stood up. "By the way, you need anything just call me. And go to the clinic. That's an order, young lady."

"Yes, Gallard. Love you."

"Love you too, Robin Bird."

He winked before he walked out of the room and Robin put her hands on her stomach. She was glad she wasn't in labor, but having this scare made her realize this was happening. She was going to give birth sooner or later, and she couldn't keep pretending.

More importantly, she needed to tell Erik the truth. He might not want her if he knew she was having a baby with another man. Another man who was dead and had forced her into it.

She found J.D. lying on the couch. Her face was tight in a grimace, and she had a heating pad on her stomach.

"J.D, you all right?"

"Not really, hon. Bad cramps. They're worse than usual."

Oh boy. At least her were from PMS and not a going-into-labor-scar.

Her expression softened a bit and she opened her eyes. "What were you and Gallard being all hush hush about."

"We were talking about Erik." Robin hated lying, but she was still too scared to say it. "Gallard wants me to be careful. That's what I wanted to talk to you about. I want you to go with me to the women's clinic."

J.D. sat up. "Say what?"

"Erik and I are getting pretty serious. We've talked about it, and I want to be prepared. You know, for when we decide to be together."

J.D. set the heating pad down then sat up. Robin thought that she would be thrilled to take her. She was always joking around about her and Erik getting together and now that Robin was seriously bringing it up, J.D. was a clam.

"Okay, we'll go. But I'm not telling anyone. If they ask where we're going, say we're going roller skating."

Robin waited for her to pop some more pain pills then they prepared to leave. They went outside and her heart palpitated when she saw Lela and Lucian on the porch talking to Celeste. The three of them looked at the women and Robin tried to hurry and get in the car.

"Where are you headed?" Lela asked.

"Out," J.D. said. "We thought we would go roller skating."

"What is roller skating?" Celeste asked.

"It's only one of the most fun things to do on this planet," Lela said. "If you girls don't mind us cramping your style, we might expose her to some modern-day pass times."

J.D. groaned. "Okay, fine, we're not going roller skating. We're going to the women's clinic."

Robin could have kicked her. Why was she telling her this? At least she could have come up with a boring activity instead of being honest.

"Why are you going there?" Lela asked.

"Because J.D. wants condoms," Robin blurted out.

Celeste started laughing and J.D. looked like she didn't know who she should be more annoyed with. Lucian, however, had nearly choked on his drink. Robin then realized that wasn't the smartest thing to say because everyone knew about J.D. and Lucian's relationship.

"Care to explain?" Lela asked Lucian.

"This one is all her," he said. "I have nothing to do with this, nor do I intend to compromise your niece. If I did, I would not send her on such an errand with Robin."

"I'm so sure. You better not be lying, but if you are, I will personally beat you if you get her pregnant."

He laughed. "You act like I'm this rake who's out to impregnate every woman I meet. I am more responsible than that."

"Uh huh, sure. We all know Cherish was an accident."

He stopped laughing, but he still had a mischievous grin on his face. This conversation was awkward for Robin and she couldn't believe her family was talking about condoms and pregnancy prevention so casually in the front yard where all the neighbors could hear. It was embarrassing.

"You can rest assured that I'm not with child," J.D. said. "These raging cramps are proof of it. We're going now. You all have fun here getting knocked up while I take responsibility."

"It's not called getting knocked up when you're married," Lela argued. "I like to think of Lucas as a miracle and not an accident."

"Well tell your little miracle that he needs to let me make *his* little miracle lunch for school. Colton comes from a long line of chefs and it's a disgrace that he's eating P.B. and J."

"Will do. We'll let you girls go. Have fun buying contraception while we're having a better time roller skating."

J.D. rolled her eyes before getting into the car. Robin wanted some driving practice, so she got into the driver's seat and started the car. She safely got them to the clinic and she reluctantly got out of the car. They went in and J.D. sat in one of the chairs while she approached the desk

There were other women in there, some pregnant and others that appeared very young. She never got to experience being an awkward teenager — to celebrate her sixteenth birthday — to go to high school. She nearly missed it all and now she was nearly thirty.

"Your name, miss," the receptionist said.

"Robin Shepherd."

"Date of birth."

"December seventeenth, two-thousand and nine."

The receptionist clicked away at her keyboard and Robin looked around at the posters on the wall. They were about STD's, sex education, and abortion. She wondered if those pamphlets would tell her all she needed to know so he could just skip the whole examination and question process. She didn't want to go through what she did for the rape kit. It had been painful, embarrassing, and nearly worse than the actual assault.

"All right, Miss Shepherd. The doctor will be ready to see you in twenty minutes."

She nodded then went to sit with J.D. She didn't say anything, but pretended to read a magazine. It was filled with smiling babies and diaper ads. She couldn't take it, so she switched to *Highlights*. It reminded her of her childhood and remembered the countless issues she'd read. Her mom had subscribed to them and it was the best part of her day when they would come in the mail.

As the receptionist promised, the nurse came and got her twenty minutes later and J.D. stood up as well, but she stopped her.

"I want to go alone."

"Are you sure, hon? You don't have to do this alone."

"I want to. Please, let me do this."

Without letting her argue further, Robin followed the nurse to the back. She was weighed and then taken to an examination room. The tools in there reminded her of before and she averted her eyes. She took a seat next to the desk and folded her hands in her lap.

"Hello, Miss Shepherd," the nurse said. "I'm Laney. What are you here for today?"

If she was going to do this, she needed to be honest. She hadn't spoken of what happened in a long time. J.D. and Nicola never brought it up and neither did anyone else in her family. She expressed a long time ago that she wanted to move on and pretend it never happened. But her pregnancy was preventing that.

"Back in May, I was raped by a police officer. I was late, so I took a home pregnancy test. It was positive."

A sympathetic look swept over the nurse's face. "I'm sorry to hear that. And what is the next step you would like to take? I would recommend an ultrasound, considering the timeline. You are well overdue for one by now."

The nurse crossed her legs. "Miss Shepherd, do you have a support system right now? Family, or friends?"

"I do. I have a huge support system. I wouldn't have recovered without them. But only two people know about the pregnancy. I've managed to hide it, but I won't for long."

"Well, let's get you checked out then, shall we? I'll get you a gown then we'll go to the exam room, okay?"

Ten minutes later, Robin was lying on a table and waiting for the technician to come in. She was wearing nothing but a blue hospital gown, her underwear, and her socks. She didn't like being this exposed, but she'd only seen one man among the other doctors, so she wasn't too nervous. There were more pictures of smiling babies on the wall and they were making her uncomfortable.

Another woman walked in this time and she was older than Laney. She had grey hair and thick glasses. Her friendly smile instantly put Robin at ease.

"Hello, Robin. How are you today?"

"Pregnant."

The woman looked taken aback by Robin's blunt answer, but Robin couldn't think of another answer. She wasn't okay, she wasn't *not* okay — she was just pregnant, and she didn't want to be anymore.

"If you could lie back for me then we can begin the procedure."

Robin obeyed and the woman draped a modesty blanket over her then took a bottle from the shelf and squeezed a warm, blue gel onto Robin's stomach. It reminded her of art supplies she used to use. In fact, many things about the clinic brought her back to her childhood. It was her deep-set desire to turn back time — she knew it, but it only made everything that much harder.

The technician moved the tool around on her stomach for a while then stopped. Robin made sure to keep her eyes away from the screen. She was afraid if she saw anything, she would change her mind.

"Oh, there it is," the technician said. "It appears that you are thirty-two weeks along. You're near the end of your third trimester. I'm surprised that you barely have a bump. Must be good genes."

"How big is the baby?"

The technician eyed Robin over her glasses. "At thirty weeks-two, your baby is at the size of a squash but about as long as a cucumber."

Robin forced herself to look at the screen. The picture wasn't grey as she'd expected but almost like the ultrasound was taking a video of the inside of her stomach. Technology had significantly progressed since she was a kid. Back in her day, sonograms were usually black and white — barely visible. She could see everything — the baby's curled fingers, the tiny legs, it's little face. The infant on the screen moved and at the same time, she felt a flutter in her stomach. She let out a small gasp and the woman smiled.

"Would you like to know the sex?" the nurse asked.

"Yes, please. I've been dying to know."

"It's a girl."

A tear rolled down Robin's cheek and she wiped it away. She couldn't see this anymore. It only made everything so much harder. She should have felt an emotional attachment to the child, but she didn't. The baby didn't even seem like hers but someone else's child.

"I would like to do an extensive exam," the nurse continued. "Since you haven't had any previous appoints, I think you would benefit from it. Just to be safe. It may be a little wait since we're a busy today. Would you mind waiting in the lobby for a bit?"

"Not at all."

The woman left and Robin got dressed once more. As much as she wanted to get out of there, she couldn't put her health at risk. She hadn't been taking very good care of herself these days. She smoked, she drank, she ate a lot of fast food. It was a wonder her baby didn't have two heads.

32

While Robin waited for her second exam, she went back to join J.D. who was reading an article called *When Your Man Stops Speaking to You.* For a moment, Robin forgot about why she was there. J.D. hadn't talked about what had happened after revealing her relationship with Lucian and since they were acting less affectionate, Robin sensed something was wrong.

"Why are you reading that?"

"They won't talk to me." She put the magazine down. "Not since that night. They won't even look at me. My uncle and Lucian are the two people I care about most and they're avoiding me."

"They'll come around. If Gallard can accept that I'm dating Erik, he'll warm up to the idea of you being with Lucian. Lela has."

"No, Robin, you don't understand. He and Lucian may be friends but there's still bad blood between them. The whole Lela thing was pretty twisted and now Gallard probably is taking it personally that Lucian went for me. My father slept with Cherish to make Lucian mad and Gallard might think Lucian is trying to do the same, which he's not. We are abstaining until we're married."

Robin understood. She hated everything that was going on. Family members weren't speaking. One had been in jail, and another was acting funny. What was supposed to be a nice dinner turned into a disaster in less than ten minutes.

The entrance door opened, and Robin froze when she saw Amanda McPherson come in. On her list of people she didn't want to run into today, Erik's mom was one of them. She didn't want her making assumptions about their relationship. It was embarrassing enough that J.D. had dragged her there and actually told Lela where they were going. She tried to turn her head to keep from being spotted.

"Robin?" Amanda said. She looked at J.D. and gave a big smile. "J.D! It's so good to see you again! I haven't seen you in years. Erik mentioned you were in town."

J.D. suddenly appeared to be uncomfortable. "Yeah, we've run into each other now and then. Family okay?"

"Family's fine. You should stop by! Imogen and Nadia saw you as a big sister."

"And Ty? I mean . . . Tyler is Sheriff now, I hear."

"He is. He loves his job. He's busier, but he makes sure to come home to us."

Robin sensed the conversation desperately needed changing, so she asked, "What brings you here?"

"I work here! I'm a women's counselor."

"I didn't know that. Well, I'm here with J.D. to get a check-up."

Amanda laughed. "You don't have to tell me why you're here. It's none of my business. But I am glad I ran into you. We want to have you, J.D., and your cousin over for dinner."

"We would love to come to dinner. I miss Nadia and Imogen. All of you, actually. We had a lot of fun during game night last week."

"Then I'll see you tonight. Have a good rest of your day."

After Amanda disappeared around the corner, J.D. grabbed Robin's hand and dragged her outside.

"Why are we leaving?" Robin asked.

"I just remembered I have to do something. Don't worry, they have your contact information and insurance. You can reschedule your appointment."

Robin opened her mouth but never said anything. Instead, she got into the car and drove them away. J.D. suggested they go shopping and Robin didn't object. She wanted to do anything that would get her mind off the awkward run-in with Amanda. She had to have an idea of why she was there. Women's clinics were for three things: abortion, STD screening, and birth control. She didn't want to even consider which option was going through Amanda's mind.

"What was that awkwardness between you and Mandy?" Robin asked while they drove.

J.D. chuckled nervously. "What awkwardness? Mandy's great. We were always close."

Robin raised an eyebrow. "Sure. The minute she walked in you got all weird. And I thought *I* had an excuse to be nervous."

J.D. looked out the window. "You can't tell anyone. I mean it. I won't say anything about you and Erik if you promise to keep this a secret."

"I promise."

"Back in high school, I was being harassed by these guys in my class while walking home. Tyler McPherson happened to be patrolling the neighborhood and scared them off. That was back when he was just a regular cop. Anyway, he gave me a ride home and we struck up a conversation. Of course, I didn't know at the time that he used to date Lela."

She paused. "We started meeting a lot. At first it was innocent but then our encounters started getting intimate. Talking led to kissing. Kissing led to more than kissing. We never slept together, though. We did get pretty carried away sometimes, and I regret giving a part of myself to him. We even had nicknames. He was Mai Tai and I was J.J. Long story short, I found out who he was and when I confronted him, he admitted he was attracted to me because I reminded him of Lela. I was the same age they were when they met. He got nostalgic and used me to recreate old memories. I didn't know he was married either. I felt terrible and I didn't want to be responsible for him losing his job or breaking up his family. We mutually ended things."

"J.D.!" Robin was shocked. "I don't believe this. He used you!"

"But it was mutual. He didn't seduce me or anything. I liked him. That was before Lucian came into my life, and I regret it so much. I would take it all back if I could." She wiped away a stray tear. "I was friends with Erik at the time. I had this subconscious need to make up for nearly destroying his family, so I became his friend. We got close, and I learned to forgive myself as well as Ty. Tyler. Anyway, that's in the past. I'm with Lucian now, hopefully. And I love him with all my heart."

Nothing more was said on the matter, but Robin couldn't stop thinking about J.D.'s story. She used to really like Erik's dad because he was so nice to her and kind to everyone he met. Now she saw him in a completely different light. How could a man who was so devoted to his wife and family have an affair with a young girl like that? And it had all been a fantasy. It would be hard acting normal around him at dinner.

The store they picked happened to be down the street from the art gallery. They hadn't gone back since Nicola revealed she was having an affair and the place brought up bad memories.

While they looked through the racks of clothes, Robin thought about Nicola's new boyfriend. Something about the whole thing didn't sit right with her. Why would Nicola admit to having an affair around the same time that Cherish was arrested for a crime she didn't commit? There had to be a connection.

"What are we going to do about aunt Cherish?" Robin asked. "Everyone thinks she is guilty, and we know she's not."

"We don't know anything, R. Nothing is making sense. All the evidence says that she's guilty and my heart says that she's not."

She really wanted to do something about this instead of going out and shopping. She was Broom Girl after all and she would gladly hit someone else with a broom if she found out they were framing her aunt. She went over and sat on a stool next to the shoes and gave it more thought. J.D. and she had stayed up that night talking about how they were going to fix this but hadn't really gotten anywhere.

"Hey, J.D. I'm going to the bathroom," she said. "I won't be long."

"Okay, hon. Wait! Before you go, how does this look? Mona wore a similar dress to that party, and I've been on the hunt for something like it."

She held up a black halter top dress that was t-length. Robin thought it was pretty, but she was also anxious to get going so she could hurry up and get back.

"Lucian will love it on you."

"Really? Then I'll get it."

Robin forced a smile then nonchalantly walked towards the bathroom. When she was sure J.D. wasn't watching, she skirted the wall until she got to the front door and hurried out. It was a good thing she was wearing walking shoes or she wouldn't have been able to jog. She got to the parking lot of the gallery then looked around before going to entrance. The sign on the door said it was closed but that wasn't going to stop her.

There were two cars parked out front which she discerned as someone being there. She opened the door and she went inside. Thankfully, it didn't have a bell on it. She made sure that the door closed quietly and tiptoed through the room. She checked every corner for signs of Ryan. She remembered that Nicola mentioned that the gallery was supposed to be closed on Saturdays. What was Ryan doing here?

She heard several steps towards the back room and she leaned against the wall. She probably looked ridiculous trying to play Nancy Drew, but nobody could see her anyway.

"Well where the hell is she?" a familiar voice said. "I told you to keep an eye on her after Ishmael was killed. You need to do something about this."

"She can take care of herself," Ryan replied. "She knows what she's doing."

"I don't care. I know what she's capable of, and I want her back here."

"Okay, I'll work on it. I'll talk to her or —"

"What about Nicola?" the mystery man asked. "Is she finally cooperating?"

"She is. Took some convincing, but she is going to do everything we ask. I promise you that if she doesn't, we'll take out the kid."

Robin was going to leave but a hand came over her mouth. A hard body pressed up against her from behind and she began to panic until the man spoke.

"Don't scream," Abe said. "Come with me."

ELLE BRICE

He removed his hand off her mouth then took her hand, quietly leading her out of the gallery. What had he been doing there? Did he have the same idea of casing the place as she did? If so, she was slightly grateful for his arrival. If she'd been caught alone, she wouldn't have been able to fight off the two men.

Once they were outside and well across the parking lot, she addressed him.

"Why are you here?"

"Lela told me that you and J.D. were at the women's clinic getting condoms. Is that true?"

She frowned. "And if it were? I don't think that's your business."

"I don't think you should be sleeping with Erik. It's too soon."

"Says the one who can't keep his hand out of my pants. It's my choice, Abe!"

His nostrils flared, and she half expected him to yell at her. But he didn't. He kept calm.

"I can't think about you and him," he finally admitted. "It breaks my heart."

Her anger softened a little, but she was still annoyed. She didn't like people telling her what she was and wasn't ready for. Only she could possibly know that. On the other hand, it hurt her to see how much her relationship with Erik was affecting Abe.

"He's my boyfriend," she said calmly. "I care about him and he cares about me."

"But I love you." He took her face in his hands. "There, I said it. I love you. I've been falling in love with you since I spent time with you at the beach in Miami. And at that party — you've never looked more beautiful than you did in that *Sleeping Beauty* costume. I want you. I want to wake up to you in the morning. I want to hear your laugh." He rested his hands on her hips and pulled her against him. "I want to make love to you until we're both so exhausted that we can't move. And when it's time, I want to be there when you give birth to your baby. You're the first woman I've wanted a future with, and I will do everything to make that happen."

The door of the gallery burst open and Simeon came out. He looked at her, scrutinizing her with his gaze. Abe released her and she almost backed away but remembered her promise to herself that she was going to be brave. Plus, she wasn't alone. She stood her ground as he went towards her.

"What are you doing here?" Simeon asked.

"We were here to check out the art," Robin said. "I heard Ryan got some new pieces in."

This wasn't a bluff. Nicola had been raving about this one painting of a river the week before. It was hard listening to Nicola talk about her new boyfriend, which wasn't often. J.D. practically had an ulcer when she'd found out and didn't speak to Nicola for several days. "Well,   we're

221

closed today, so you can see them on Monday." He crossed his arms and looked at Abe. "You're Jordan's boy?"

Abe nodded. "Yes."

"Figured. You d'Aubigne men have always had a thing for Bledsoe women." To Robin, he said, "Why haven't you called me?"

Abe gave her a side glance but she ignored him.

"Because I have a boyfriend."

"Yet you are here with a different man who just professed his love to you." The smirk left his eyes. "I hear you're close with Nicola."

"Yeah, she used to date my nephew," Robin said. "Just to let you know, I'm not happy about Ryan seeing her. Stealing her from Lucas was a lousy thing to do."

He smiled. "Sometimes feelings take you by surprise. I am sure a beautiful woman like yourself would understand that." He flickered a glance at Abe. "You're seeing that cop, right? Officer Erik McPherson? Nice guy. We had ourselves a chat when I called the police about seeing the murder suspect. He has a lot of potential, that young man. It would be a shame if his career were cut short by an accident."

Robin stopped breathing. He knew that she was listening and now he was threatening Erik. It was one thing to plot Cherish's death and another to openly threaten her boyfriend. She wasn't afraid, she was angry. Too many times had those she cared about been threatened and she was so over it.

"We have a lot of dangerous people in our family," Abe said. "Piss me off, shame on you. Piss *them* off and you face them. Threaten Erik again and I might send someone over for a visit."

Simeon laughed at him. "Send someone like who? Gallard? He's so drunk he can't even walk in a straight line. And Lucas? He gave up Nicola without a fight. And I'm not afraid of the infamous Lucian Christophe. I have eyes on everything. Watch out. Because you're about to see what we're capable of."

He went back into the gallery and Robin calmed down a bit. This man knew way more about her family than Robin was comfortable with. She believed him when he said he had eyes on them and that frightened her. But he was nothing compared to the past threats. If he decided to strike, they would be ready.

"You're coming with me," Abe said.

"But J.D.'s going to wonder where I am."

"Then I'll drop you off at the store. Either way, you're not walking there alone."

She opened her mouth to protest but didn't. Instead she followed him over to his car and got in. He drove out of there and took off down the road. She could barely type her message to J.D. because she was scared. Scared for Cherish and scared for Erik.

"Abe, what if he wasn't kidding? What if he really hurts Erik?"

"I know Simeon's type. He'll bark all he wants but he'll never bite."

Kind of like you? She wanted to ask. His words weren't comforting and hadn't eased her anxiety at all. For all she knew, Simeon had several dangerous friends on his side who could go after Erik. And what had he meant about seeing what he was capable of? Was he going to go after someone else?

Abe reached over and took her hand. She almost pulled away but didn't. His touch was gentle and comforting, somewhat like Gallard's but how she felt about it was different. Gallard's comfort was like that of a brother or uncle and Abe's touch was intimate.

Robin let her fingers tangle with his and he looked at her. His confession had taken her by surprise, and she didn't know how to respond to it. He loved her. His words were so convicting, and it made her wonder if she felt that way about Erik. Did she love him? Was she even ready to be in love? It was probably too soon. They had only been together for a month. But one thing was certain. She was deeply cared about him and she was afraid for his life.

"Robin, Erik is going to be fine. Lucas and I will make sure nothing happens to him."

"How can you promise that when you want to steal me from him?"

"Because your happiness is more important. You want him safe so I will do everything in my power to do that."

Her heart warmed to his words and a smile crept onto her face. He rarely ever showed this tender side and she'd missed it. Avoiding her best friend was hard and she hated it had to be this way.

He parked the car in the parking lot, but she didn't get out. She hadn't let go of his hand either and he wasn't making an effort to pull away. She knew she would need to tell Gallard and Lucas about what they'd heard and she would. After she talked to Abe. She wanted to catch up on everything she'd missed in the past two years.

"I heard J.D. finally told you why she's mad at you."

"Yes, she did. When she moved out, she asked me to come, and I refused. In truth, I was afraid to go with her. I didn't want a life of hiding and worrying about my family getting caught. I wanted to be human."

"But you are human."

"No. And neither are you." He let go of her hand and trailed a finger don't he side of her throat. His touch made her anxious and enchanted at the same time. "All it would take would be for me to snap your neck and you would be immortal. For me, I could get shot or have a car accident. I live in fear every day of my life because I don't want to be immortal. I don't want to live on blood." He let go and tightly gripped the steering wheel. "Remember when I told you about the guy I fought? The one who hid razors in his gloves?"

"I remember. You said he really hurt you."

"That fight was what made me quit. I nearly bled to death and the reality that I could die hit me harder than ever. I was scared out of my mind and it spooked me enough to stop fighting. I know that probably isn't a good enough reason to avoid my sister and my family, but I was terrified. It was difficult coming back and getting involved."

She took his hand again and held it in both of her own. She understood what he was going through. She hadn't wanted this life any more than he did. The difference was, she hadn't tried to escape it. Instead, she tried to make the most of it. Running away wouldn't make her family mortal again. Denying her heritage wouldn't bring her mother back or change what had happened to her.

"Don't be afraid," she said. "If you're scared all time, you're going to miss out on life."

He chuckled. "Smart and sexy."

"You're not so shabby or incompetent yourself, Abraham. Any woman would be lucky to have you."

"Just not you. And yet, you're still holding my hand, so I must be making progress."

Robin stared into his eyes for a moment. She could feel her self-control slowly creeping away. Once again, she was giving in to his seductive eyes and his ability to make her stomach flip with his heartfelt words.

"You should go inside," Abe finally said. "If I spend one more minute alone with you, I'm not going to stop myself from breaking my rule and having you right here in this car."

Robin forced herself to leave and go back into the store to find J.D. She had to get away from him because for a fleeting moment, she was thinking the same thing and that scared her more than anything.

34

Staring at my computer screen, I was very tempted to throw it out the window. I had been chasing leads all day and none of them were leading anywhere. That forced me to spend several hours doing research on past crimes. Without Cherish, I wouldn't be able to know who was behind all of this. I had some suspicions but none I could carry out with my task force. I would need to do some off-duty sleuthing.

Since everyone had been working their butts off all week, I let them go home early. There was one lead I hadn't followed through with. Ryan Aspen. By prying into Nicola's mind, I saw what he had been doing. Tricking her into taking art lessons and then trying to get her to leave me for him. When that failed, he'd given her no choice. Unfortunately, her memories never showed me why this was going on and because we were supposedly being watched, she couldn't tell me face to face.

My door opened and I looked up to see Abe come in. I was a little stunned since my family never came to my job. Probably the only time was when I'd forgotten a lunch and J.D.—instead of merely bringing it to me—cooked up a curry dish with chicken and rice with a side of sautéed zucchini. I hadn't forgotten my lunch today, so this was probably a social call.

"Hey cousin!" he said. "Wow, real swanky abode you have here. You even have a nameplate on your desk."

"Abraham. What brings you here?"

"I brought a visitor."

He opened a small athletic bag that was hanging on his shoulder and a bat flew out. It transformed into Gallard. I quickly stood up and shut the door, locking it.

"Are you two crazy? Tyler McPherson could be around here!"

Gallard pretended to be offended. "You underestimate my stealth. Abe checked around ahead of time. The Sheriff is on lunch break."

They pulled up a couple of chairs and sat on the other side of my desk. Though I was a little nervous about having Gallard there, it was nice to get a break from work. We hadn't had a chance to redo our father-son time since he'd been drunk and I was always busy. Now that he was sober and more agreeable, I welcomed his company.

"We have a lead," Gallard said. "I know you're probably tired of dead ends, but we can help."

"Wow. And here I thought you wanted to see me because you missed me."

Abe laughed. "It is rather lonely waking up and not seeing you in the kitchen cooking breakfast. How long are you going to be on a fast food diet?"

"How long are you going to be celibate?" I raised a curious eyebrow.

"Not as long as you are. Your breakup has gotta be rough."

This was the second topic I would rather not discuss. I couldn't let on that the breakup had been staged. The more people who knew, the more dangerous the situation could get for Nicola and possibly for my family.

"I still can't believe she cheated on you," Gallard said.

"Neither can I. She hid it for so long, and I was too blind to see it."

"Who is this douchebag that is apparently more worth her time than you are?"

"Ryan Aspen." I picked up the clay ball with the turkey on it that Colton had painted for me at school and tossed it into the air. "He's her art teacher. The one J.D. bought Nicola's picture from. She didn't feel like there was enough passion in our relationship and she gets that from Ryan."

His name felt like a sour grape in my mouth. It would be so easy for me to be the crazy ex and go off on him but I wanted to be civilized and handle this calmly and let the situation play itself out.

"Oh, please," Abe said. "If it's passion she wants, I can give you a few ideas."

"No!" Gallard and I said in unison.

"At least tell me you hit it before you quit it."

"Abraham!" Gallard said. "And here I thought your father had no tact."

I sighed. "The only thing I'm hitting right now is my head against this desk while I try to figure out who killed those people."

"Well, like we said. We have a lead," Gallard said. "Robin, being your mother's sister, decided to spy on Ryan Aspen. She got caught but not before she overheard him talking with Simeon Atherton."

"So, he is involved in this. What else did she hear?"

"That was it," Abe said. "But after she was caught, Simeon hinted that if we didn't stay out of it, he was going to target Erik."

"What! That bastard! I can't believe him!"

With my burst of anger, I made the furniture rise a little off the ground then slam back down. Gallard stared at me in amazement.

"Sorry. I usually can control that. But if Simeon goes after Erik, nothing will stop me from going *Carrie* on his ass."

"I still don't think I should leave," he said. "What if Erik decides to say something and mentions her connection to you. Our whole family would have to pack up and leave before they investigated further."

"It's a risk putting our trust in him, but I think he'll pull through. He cares about Robin too much to betray her, not to mention his friendship with J.D. In return, we'll protect him as well. I'm not letting anything happen to Erik."

I noticed the physical change in Gallard and Abe's demeanor and furrowed my brow. At the mention of Robin's name, they'd suddenly gotten quiet. I then remembered Abe was going to say something at the dinner and Robin had shut him down. What had that been about?

"That boy is as smitten with her as his father was with your mother," Gallard said. "Whether or not it will last is a mystery."

"Why wouldn't it last? She's loyal, he's a great guy. I think it could work."

"We'll see," Abe said.

I crooked my mouth in thought. I hated the idea of uprooting her from a happy relationship. There was no need for her to stay with us when we did eventually leave. She couldn't fight anyway. Would leaving her here to build a real life for herself be all that bad?

Familiar voices echoed in the hallway and I stood up. Erik and Tyler were coming and were at least twenty steps away. I thought Erik had gone home for the day.

"Bat!" I said to Gallard.

"What? Where?"

"No, *you* need to bat!"

He transformed and then Abe stuffed him back into the bag. He must have squeezed Gallard too hard because he started chirping loudly and Abe apologized before cinching it closed. At that moment, someone knocked on the door. Abe nonchalantly sat back in the chair while I answered it.

"What an honor to run into the Earl of Hawthorne," Erik said once he and Tyler came in.

"Earl of what?" Tyler asked in confusion.

"He's an Earl, remember? His brother had diplomatic immunity."

Tyler laughed. "I'm impressed. You're an Earl, you have task force training, you arrested a vampire without backup. What other secrets do you have?"

Gallard chirped again and Abe had to cover it up with a weird cough. Erik looked at me funny but didn't say anything. I knew Gallard was just trying to make this situation difficult for his own entertainment. Gotta love dads.

"Who's this?" Tyler asked.

"Tyler, my cousin Abe. Abe, this is Tyler McPherson — Erik's dad and my boss."

"This is the Duke," Erik said, still using his teasing tone.

"Pleasure to meet you," Abe said, looking a little too happy to be addressed by his formal title.

Tyler rested a hand on Erik's shoulder. "My son was just telling me what a great time he had having dinner with your family. And I've kind of been raving about you to mine. I'm glad we ran into you because my wife insists that I invite you and your sister-in-law over for dinner."

I didn't really see that night's arrest as anything to rave about, but I could see the pride in his eyes. What would it be like to have dinner with my mom's high school boyfriend? Probably very weird. If Robin was there, the weirdness might be lessened.

"I would love to have dinner with your family," I said.

"How does tonight sound? Unless you have plans with your own family. I know you mentioned your brother leaving for rehab."

"Oh, no. He's actually doing it on his own and just going to therapy. He wants to be near the family since he's been away for so long."

"That's good to hear. I hate to see young people with so much potential throw their lives away. So, tonight works for you? She makes a really good macaroni casserole."

"Tonight is perfect. I will be there."

"I will text you directions," Erik said. "Well, we'll leave you be, now. See you tonight."

They left, and I waited until I couldn't hear them anymore before I took Gallard out from his hiding place and I stared at him with exasperation. I could see the smirk in his eyes, and it made it hard to be annoyed at him.

I tossed him into the air, and he flew around for a while before swooping close to the ground and transforming back into his human self. I hadn't transformed since the day I'd hidden in the room while waiting to reveal to Nicola that I was alive. Colton loved it when Kevin, did and he would act as excited as if he was at Disneyland.

"Dinner at the McPherson's? That should be fun. But shouldn't you be focusing on helping Cherish?'

"Who are you, my father?"

He laughed and slung one arm around my shoulder and another around Abe's as we walked out of my office. We'd bailed Cherish out of jail anonymously the day after her arraignment and she was staying in a hotel until it was safe for her to be moved back to our neighborhood. In the meantime, the task force was working on a new case. There were rumors of a vampire hoard somewhere in the city and we were trying to see if they were true.

"I do need you to do one thing," I said. "If you're willing."

"As long as it doesn't entail stealing anything or getting naked."

Abe snorted and I shot him a look. He would probably jump at the chance to get naked if a woman was involved.

"What's that funny look on your face?" Gallard asked.

"Nothing. Abe made me lose my train of thought. Oh, right. I need you to bring Cherish home and keep an eye on her. I'm worried about her."

"Well, whatever you end up learning, don't include J.D.," Abe said. "She'll just get caught and you'll have to rescue her."

I laughed, not because it was harsh but because it was true. She always got caught whenever we would try to be stealthy. Lucian plucked her right off the sidewalk and then Henry nearly hurt her when I tried to sneak out of the house with Colton. Not to mention she'd been caught when we were trying to break Kevin out of jail.

"No, I'm still thinking of something. Cherish knows more than she's letting on and I think she's the best bet for getting any information. Nicola too. This all started with Nicola. She's not speaking with me, but I know she admires you. Maybe use some good ol' d'Aubigne charm and get her to talk?"

"Will do. And don't include your mom either. She's a trouble magnet."

"You really think I can stop her from participating? You might have to bribe her with your magic hands."

Gallard closed his eyes. "I can't believe you know about that."

"Blame Robin. When she thought I was you, she asked me to do a magic trick."

He laughed and soon I was laughing too. It should have been awkward to talk about since I knew the real story behind the magic hands thanks to Cherish. Now it was an ongoing joke among everyone in my family.

"Fine. I'll trust you," he said. "Whatever you choose to do, I'll do whatever you need to help."

We got to the Cadillac, and I got in the driver's seat. He hated that his license had been suspended, but we couldn't risk his being caught driving. We already had one family member in trouble and we didn't need two.

"I need to say something," Abe said out of the blue.

"Okay, speak, *Duke*," I said.

He hesitated before continuing. "I'm only saying this because Gallard already knows. Robin and I . . . we've been spending time together."

I snorted. "No, duh. I know you're her bodyguard. No mystery there. What's this about?"

I glanced over at Gallard and he had a pained expression on his face. I looked at Abe in the rearview mirror and he shared the same expression.

"I mean more than that," he continued. "We hooked up."

My foot slammed on the break in the middle of the road. "You're hooking up with Robin?"

"Yes. Well . . . one time."

"Are you insane! I can't believe you would be so desperate to get laid that you would go after her!"

"To clear that up, we're not sleeping together. We just fooled around. And for your information, she participated just as much as I did. I didn't turn her away because I care about her. If you must know, she's the woman I told you I was crazy about."

Gallard looked back. "I didn't know you felt that way."

"Well, I do. I'm in love with her. The problem is she has a boyfriend, and I'm afraid that even though we did what we did, she might love him."

"Robin is in a lot of pain. She's really good at hiding it, but I can tell. For that reason, Abe, I think you need to put a stop to it. I have zero tolerance for infidelity, and I don't want to see her get hurt. Not after what happened with her mother."

I wanted to put in my two cents but chose to keep my mouth shut. I was livid. I didn't care that Abe was in love with her or whatever. He shouldn't have touched her, no matter who started it. My entire family was going crazy and if we didn't stop making awful choices, we were going to crumble. We couldn't continue with this cause if we weren't united.

35

Gallard moved the curtain aside when he heard a car door close. Nicola had finally come back from wherever she had been and was going into her house. He hadn't been waiting long but he wouldn't lie and say he hadn't constantly checked to see if she'd arrived. He wanted to catch her alone so he could try and get her to open up.

Soft footsteps came up behind him and without looking, he reached down and lifted Colton into his arms. He still couldn't believe he was a grandfather. Twenty-two years later and he was still trying to grasp that he was a father. A father of two, even. Now he had an amazing grandson whom he loved fiercely and cherished every moment he got to spend with him.

"Is mamma home?" Colton asked.

"Yeah, she just got back. Do you want to go see her?"

Colton shook his head. "No, that's okay. I just like to know when she's home. I feel scared when she's gone."

Gallard's shoulders sank. "Why do you feel that way bud?"

He didn't answer right away. Whatever was bothering the little boy, Gallard didn't like it. He knew Nicola was a great mom and always took care of Colton. Why he would have separation anxiety was clear, though. He'd been separated from the woman who raised him and connected with Nicola to fill that space. That's what Gallard thought, anyway.

"I'm afraid someone will hurt her," Colton said. "She is too. Mamma is scared a lot."

"Well, I'm going to find out why." He set the little boy back down. "Why don't you see if uncle Kevin will play with you? I'm going to talk to your mom."

Colton's eyes lit up with excitement, and Gallard took his hand as he walked out the door. Colton let go once they were in front of Lucas' house then Gallard waited for him to go inside before he headed for J.D.'s. The women had gone roller skating and Lela had let him know that Robin and J.D. went to town. There wouldn't be anyone to interrupt their conversation.

He knocked on the door then waited. As he stood on the porch he looked around and admired the decorations the three women had done. There were beautiful red flowers in the window sill and a wrought iron table and chairs set to the left of the door. The doormat was brown and in white font said *No Wine No Entrance*. He knew J.D. had something to do with that.

The door opened and he blinked when he saw that Nicola was wearing a towel and her hair was wet. She folded her arms then leaned against the door.

"I'm sorry," he said. "If I'd known you were busy, I would have come by later."

"It's no trouble at all." She straightened up. "Come in."

She walked away and he followed her in. While she went to get dressed, he sat on the couch. He wasn't exactly sure what he was going to talk to her about. He was here as a favor to Lucas.

As much as he was saddened by the whole breakup, he would still be there for her. For Colton's sake, mostly. Cheating was something he felt strongly about, though. It was why he'd had a very long talk with Robin after she admitted to fooling around with Abe. It was a bad tendency among the people close to him and he wanted the younger generation to not make the same mistakes as the elders.

Two minutes later, Nicola came back into the living room and sat next to him. Probably a little too close and he almost scooted over. He hadn't thought her to be an invader of people's space. That was always J.D.'s thing.

"What can I do you for?" she asked.

"Actually, I wanted to talk to you." He thought for a moment. This wasn't supposed to be confrontational, so starting off with asking about Cherish wouldn't be the best way. He decided to work up to that, starting with pleasant conversation. "How have you been?"

Her lips curved into a teasing smile. "You came all the way over here to ask how I've been?"

"Yes. And no. I haven't really talked with you much since I've been back. You're Colton's mother and that makes you family and I care about my family." He smiled. "So, are you doing okay?"

"I was a little down in the dumps until you showed up. You really know how to brighten a girl's day."

He laughed. "Well, I'm glad. I've been worried about you. Colton has too — we all have. You mean a lot to us, and your wellbeing is important to me."

"And yours is important to me too." She reached over and rested her hand on his shoulder. "I never found out why you were going through that drunk frat boy phase. Do you want to talk about it?"

Gallard hated discussing that topic. Ever since he told Lucas about what his death would do for immortals, he decided not to bring it up anymore. As far as he was concerned, it wasn't even an option. Lucas may have been for it but he wasn't going to let it happen.

"That's all right. I was having a hard time but being back with the family has helped. I would rather talk about you. Is there anything you would like to talk to someone about?"

She smiled. "You're so sexy when you're concerned. Lela is a lucky woman."

If he could breathe, he knew he would have stopped. He thought maybe he'd imagined those words coming out of her mouth but as she continued to give him that seductive smile, he knew he'd heard her correctly. He was used to her complimenting him as a joke but this time it sounded completely serious.

"Uh . . . thank you. But, Nicola I really am worried. Lucas said that Cherish hurt you and I want to know why."

The smile left her face. "You know why. Cherish killed that girl and that boy. I had my suspicions, so I followed her at the festival and when I saw her attack that man, she took off. I confronted her about it and she struck me several times and said she would hurt me again if I said anything."

"Why would Cherish kill them? She feeds on vampire blood and while she is rough at times, she doesn't kill for fun. Especially not mortals."

Nicola leaned close to him and he froze. She then whispered. "She's doing it for *them*."

"Them?"

"The Romani coven. The same coven that Lucian's mother was from. They want to initiate her and by doing that, she had to kill three people. She hurt me because she doesn't want you to know what she's up to. They probably threatened someone in this group. Hell, they threatened me if I said anything."

Gallard's anger began to grow. There was always a threat to his family, and he was tired of it. Tired of complying with mad men to save those he loved. Tired of running and making sacrifices. Tired of living in fear.

"This coven. They must be following someone. Do you know who their leader is?"

"Do you want me to get killed? I can't tell you that. They could hurt Lucas or Robin or worse. They could hurt Colton." She started to get emotionally distraught. "Please, don't make me tell you. I don't want anything to happen to my son."

He put an arm around her to comfort her as she began to cry. He would abide by her wishes and stop prying. He wanted to know more but Colton's safety was more important than any information she could give. He was also beginning to think that she hadn't really cheated. Someone must have threatened her into ending things. Why else would she suddenly betray Lucas?

Her sobs quietly some and she wiped her eyes then looked up at him. He thought back to the first time he'd ever met her. She was six months old and her mother had handed her to him without warning so she could greet Lela. Nicola had been a cute baby and he never would have guessed she would end up with his son. He should have known since the Taylors had been linked to Lela for years.

"I'll protect Colton," he said. He wiped away her tears and smiled. "I promise you that. I don't make promises I can't keep, so you can trust that I will follow through."

She smiled. "You're such a good man. Good men are hard to come by these days."

Leaning over, she kissed his cheek. It was an innocent gesture and he didn't protest, but then she kissed him again, this time on his neck and a red flag went up.

"Nicola —"

Before he could react, she had crawled into his lap. She pressed a firm kiss to his lips, and he was stunned. He quickly but gently pushed her away and she stared at him with wide eyes as if she were equally as shocked as him by her actions. He was so stunned that he couldn't even form a sentence.

"I'm so sorry. I don't know what came over me. I have to go."

She got up from his lap and ran towards the door and went outside. Once he'd had a chance to recover from the strange incident, he got up and followed her.

"Nicola, wait!"

Without a second glance, she got into the car and drove away. He was wanted to keep this incident a secret, but, how could he? Something was completely off about the entire conversation, but he couldn't figure out what. He decided to only tell Lela and Lucas. Whatever had come over her, he would have to figure it out before her behavior escalated.

My hands were tense on the wheel as I coasted through Arlington. I'd wanted to cancel the dinner plans in light of everything that had happened, but Gallard convinced me otherwise. Robin wasn't too thrilled either and I felt terrible that she'd gotten caught up in this.

When Gallard told me that Nicola had kissed him, I was furious. It was one thing for her to pretend to be interested in Ryan, but Gallard wasn't part of the whole charade. I hated thinking that maybe she was playing me, but I couldn't think of a valid explanation. She had to be crazy. She joked all the time about how hot she thought my dad was, but that was always innocent. A kiss wasn't.

Then there was the fact that Simeon had threatened Erik and Robin was fooling around with Abe behind Erik's back. I wasn't going to tolerate any of this. I had wanted to keep this issue contained but it was spreading and spreading like a flame to a river of gasoline.

"Are you mad at me?" Robin asked, breaking the silence.

I forced a smile and shook my head. "No, of course not. I could never be mad at you, Robin Bird. I'm angry at Simeon for making threats to you."

"He probably would have hurt me if Abe wasn't there. I can't believe Erik might get hurt because I was spying."

Thinking about Simeon made power within me throb throughout my body. He'd been crossing so many lines that I was ready to confront him face to face. Only I couldn't. I needed to pretend I wasn't onto him so I could help Cherish and that wouldn't work if I punched him in the face.

I was glad she kept this incident a secret from Erik, however, he would have to know sooner or later because he was on my task force. I'd been given the list of my team members the previous Monday and there were a total of five of us. James, Erik, Officer Craven, and a woman named Talia. She was there mostly as a secretary and would give me DNA evidence results or any other important documents.

The first week on the job had been intense. I was under a lot of pressure and felt like all eyes were on me, waiting for me to screw up. James turned out to be a pretty cool guy, despite the raison incident. He started calling me Raison Boy and joked that I should team up with Robin, Broom Girl. Learning that she was doing her own investigation had me flirting with the idea of hiring her after all. At least that way I could keep an eye on her and make sure she was staying away from Abe.

"Robin. Listen to me—I'm not going to let that happen. Gallard is bringing Cherish home tonight and we'll keep her safe. And I'm going to keep an eye on Erik. No one is going to get hurt on my watch."

Robin's shoulder's sagged, and I hoped I had brought her peace of mind. It had to be hard for her to keep this information to herself. She would be safe and then I would work on finding the people who were out to get her.

"I don't know what they have planned, exactly, but we will figure it out," I said. "In the meantime, don't do anymore spying. I need you to be safe too."

We found the McPherson's address and I parked behind Erik's truck. We were about ten minutes early but we wanted to allow for time in case we got lost. They lived on the outskirts of town in a beautiful, two-story home. The siding was tan and each window had black shutters. The trim was white and there was a magnificent tree in the front yard.

I let Robin knock on the door, and we waited for someone to answer. We'd agreed that we would dress a little nicer than if we were having barbeque at Lela's, but not as nice as we would dress for a public outing. Thanks to Lucian, I had more clothing options. Robin was in a navy jumper that was a little short for my liking, but she said she would tell Gallard about the nude painting if I bothered her about it. How she learned about the painting was a mystery to me.

"By the way, I know about you and Abe," I said.

"What? Oh my gosh. Why does everyone feel the need to blab about my personal life?"

"Because we care. By the way he was the one that told me. I don't like it, and I don't think it's fair to Erik either."

She cast her gaze down. "It only happened once. It's over, though. I want to be with Erik, and I'm done going behind his back. I really care about him, Lucas. Please don't say anything. I messed up and I want to change."

The door opened and we were greeted by a smiling woman. I recognized her as Amanda from the photo on Tyler's wall. She was older than the teen from the prom picture, but I could still see hints of the girl she once was.

"Robin, it's wonderful to see you again," she said. "And you must be Lucas."

"It's nice to meet you, Mrs. McPherson."

"Mandy, please. Come in, everyone is in the living room."

Robin linked arms with me as we stepped into the house. It smelled like freshly baked cinnamon rolls. It reminded me that I'd skipped all meals that day. I wouldn't pass up on home cooking. I was getting tired of canned soup.

We went into the living room and everyone stood. James and his wife Emily were there as well sans their baby and it was weird seeing him out of uniform. Tyler said that because we were now a task force, we could have the option of wearing street clothes.

"Hey, beautiful," Erik said to Robin. He kissed her cheek then shook my hand. "I'm glad you came.

"Where's J.D.?" Mandy asked.

"J.D. was invited?" I asked.

"We ran into each other yesterday. I invited both her and Robin."

That was news to me. Neither Robin nor J.D. mentioned it.

"She's not feeling well," Robin said. "She asked me to say hello for her."

That was a complete lie. J.D. was in great health. There had to be another reason my cousin was avoiding this dinner. Maybe she had something up her sleeve in regarding Lucian.

Erik and Robin sank onto the couch and began flirting with their gazes. James groaned loudly in annoyance then laughed.

"Can you believe those two?" he asked me.

"Jimmy, leave them alone," Emily said. "We were just like that when we first started dating."

"Glued to hip? Not even close."

The five of us talked until Tyler came home with his two daughters. They were dressed in gymnastic uniforms and had a lot of make up on. Tyler introduced me to them, and they headed upstairs to change. Amanda told us not to worry about waiting and we went into the kitchen to serve ourselves. The macaroni casserole looked and smelled heavenly.

James dished up a ton and Amanda scolded him and forced him to put some back. Seeing this reminded me of how I used to be with Nicola's family. Gabby treated me like her son and I often shared a lot of laughs with her and her parents. Riley was always telling stupid jokes and making up stories about his college experience that were clearly over exaggerated. I missed those days.

The two sisters joined us just as we were about to be seated and the older one, Nadia, sat next to me. She didn't have as much makeup on, but she was still fairly decorated. She resembled her mother while Imogen looked more like Tyler. Erik was a mixture of both.

"Tyler tells me you're a father," Amanda said to me. "You have a little boy?"

"I do. Colton—he's four. He started his last year of preschool back in September."

"Aww!" Amanda ruffled Erik's hair. "I remember when my boy was in preschool. Even then he wanted to be a cop. He was a cop every Halloween until high school."

"Then I put on a real uniform," Erik said, trying to save his dignity.

Everyone laughed. Colton had been different things every year. When he was a baby, Regina dressed him up as a bumble bee. The year before, he was Spiderman. This year, he was an alien while Nicola and I were Mulder and Scully, at his request.

"Wait, you're twenty-two, right?" Nadia asked me.

"That's correct."

"And he's four. You had him in high school?"

"Nadia . . ." Tyler cautioned.

"What? Everyone knows you and mom had Erik your first year of college."

"No, it's okay," I said. "Yes, I was in high school. My girlfriend — I mean my *ex*-girlfriend is a year older than me and had just graduated at the time. She went away to get her accounting degree while I went to a private college in Miami. We finished school and we moved here so we could raise him together."

"Cute, single, good with kids, and a Captain? Erik, why didn't you tell me about him?"

Erik shot her a stern look. "Four syllables. Stat-a-tor-y."

Everyone laughed but Nadia turned red from embarrassment. She was a pretty girl, but she was five years my junior. Besides, my heart would always belong to one woman.

"What is statutory?" Robin asked.

The table went quiet.

"Uh . . . it's illegal activity between an adult and a minor," Tyler said. "It's laws to prevent older individuals from engaging in inappropriate relationships with teenagers."

"Ah." Robin poked at her plate. "What are the laws in Texas?"

"Oh! I know this one!" Imogen said. "The age of consent is seventeen, but also it's illegal to sleep with anyone who is more than three years older than you if you are under the age of fourteen."

"Seventeen? Interesting. What is the punishment?"

I glanced at Robin from the corner of my eye. Why was she asking these questions? I knew she had some interest in police business because of Erik and the case, but this had nothing to do with either.

"Um. You are fined, forced to register as a sex offender, and you could spend up to twenty years in prison," Tyler finally said.

"Very interesting."

"Don't worry, Robin," Nadia said. "Erik is well beyond the age of consent."

Some people groaned while others laughed. I was glad someone lightened the conversation. I would have to ask her later why she'd grilled him on the topic.

"You moved from Miami to Euless?" Imogen asked me. "You're an Earl, why would you do that?"

I looked at Erik and he had a guilty smile on his face.

"Blame Robin," he said. "She's the one who told me your grandfather was a Duke."

"I don't mind."

"Wait, if you're related to J.D., does that mean she's like a Duchess or something?" Imogen asked.

Tyler looked up. "J.D. is in town?"

"Yes, daddy. We already told you that."

Robin glanced over at Tyler and they made eye contact. Erik started poking at his food, stirring it around, his mood suddenly changing. This situation was getting weirder and weirder.

"To answer your question, Imogen," I said, "J.D.'s brother is a Duke, so that makes her a Lady. Only the wife of a Duke is considered a Duchess. You should have seen my little brother when he found out he was a Lord. He spent all sorts of money and acted like —"

I cut off that sentence. It wasn't very often that I talked about Micah except for with family and talking about him now was making me miss him like crazy. I wanted so much to go back and get him but Scott had been clear — return to Miami and he would kill Micah. I would have to come up with a solid plan first.

"You have a younger brother?" Erik asked. "Where is he?"

"Still in Miami. He didn't want to come with me when I moved."

The conversation changed for a bit and James told the funny story about how the Grocery Store Groper and how he'd burst into tears in the interrogation room. It was funny but I could understand it. Though James was a great guy, he could be really intimidating.

"Speaking of interrogation, I was just thinking that Broom Girl would be useful on the task force," James said.

"I agree," Tyler said. "Talia actually came to me and said she would rather not work on the task force. She's afraid that whoever is working with Charity Tophé is going to come after her."

I stopped chewing and shot a quick glance at Robin. We hadn't called the police about Ryan's threats or what she'd heard him discussing. The last thing I needed was for my coworkers showing up on my family's doorstep.

"How does Talia know someone is working with her?" I asked. "That hasn't come up in the investigation."

"Talia said that a man approached her and started asking for information," James said.

"Man?" Robin asked. "Do you happen to know what he looked like?"

"Dark brown hair, blue eyes, tall and muscular."

This man had to be someone else. That description didn't match Ryan. However, it did match Simeon. If he was working with others, I wanted to know just how many people we were dealing with.

"You should try to find this man. He may have answers."

"Oh my goodness," Nadia said. "Can we not talk shop? It's making me paranoid."

"I agree," Amanda said. "Why don't we talk about something happier?"

The conversation grew lighter after that and we finished the meal on a happy note. Amanda then brought in a plate of cinnamon rolls, which James devoured half of on his own. We then took a few lawn chairs into the front yard and talked while we looked up at the stars. I wished that my family could relax like this. We had too much stress in our lives

We left the McPherson's house around ten and Robin fell asleep on the way. I'd hoped she would keep me awake but now I had to rely on the radio. Somehow, my thoughts went back to what Tyler had said about a man trying to bail out Cherish. I knew Gallard had beaten the man to it, but the mystery man's description sounded a lot like Simeon.

I pulled into my driveway and Robin didn't wake up. I gently unbuckled her and carried her into her house. J.D. opened the door for me and Robin became lucid enough to go to her room without help. J.D. and I exchanged a few words then I headed for my own home.

I went inside, feeling extremely exhausted. This day had been long and stressful. I did want to be with Colton, though. I stole him from his bed and carried him to mine. I tucked him under the covers and he opened his big blue eyes.

"Dad?"

"Yeah, I'm here bud." I kissed his forehead. "How are you doing?"

"I'm okay. Mamma didn't say goodnight to me. I think she's sad about something"

Not as sad as I am, I thought to myself. I would have to talk to her about the Gallard incident at some point, but I was still trying to limit my contact with her. We'd had a private agreement that we would make the enemy believe we were at odds and I had to follow through or someone could get hurt. That was the last thing I wanted.

"Your mom is fine. Don't worry about her, okay?"

"Okay." He closed his eyes for a moment then opened them. "Dad, could I have a glass of water?"

"For you, any time."

I handed him his favorite stuffed animal then went into the kitchen. After I filled a glass for him, I took a blood bag out of the fridge and guzzled it. I didn't even bother putting it in a cup. I knew I would feel fidgety in the morning, but I needed a hit. I planned to spend the day with family anyway.

I was headed back to the room when I saw movement over on the couch. I turned the light on and exhaled when I saw who it was.

"Cherish, hey!" I went over to her and gave her a tight hug. She hugged me back with equal intensity and didn't let go for a long time.

"I'm sorry," she said. "Melody is mad at me, and it's too awkward over at J.D.'s I didn't know where else to go."

"I don't mind at all. Feel free to crash here as long as you want."

I took Colton his water and just as I entered the hall, the door to Abe's room opened and he came out.

"What's up?" he asked.

"Cherish is staying here."

"Oh. Hey, Cher, take my room."

She grimaced. "Is that such a good idea?"

He rolled his eyes. "I just changed the bedding, and I haven't brought anyone home in two months. And I shower daily. I insist."

Cherish touched his cheek. "You're a good kid, Abe. Thanks."

"You need something to sleep in?" I asked.

"If you don't mind. I forgot to bring some with me. I'm so used to wearing an orange suit that I'm not used to having options."

I found a pair of shorts and a shirt for her and she changed in the bathroom. I saw Lucian staring at me from the crack in his door but neither of us said a word. I was surprised he hadn't given his daughter a warm welcome. He'd been the most worried when he found out she was arrested.

Cherish came back out and noticed Lucian staring. He quickly closed his door and I could see the disappointment in her eyes. I pulled her into another hug, and she rested her head against my chest.

"They'll come around," Abe said. "We're going to prove your innocence, I promise. And then they'll see that you're not the person you've been framed to be."

"Once a reputation is tarnished, it's impossible to get it back."

"Well, you have me convinced," I said. "Someone else is involved and my task force has been working almost nonstop to solve this."

"I believe you." She forced a smile. "Until then, do you mind if I hide out here?" I shook my head. "Good. Because you owe me for all those diapers I changed." She poked Abe in the ribs. "You too, Abraham."

I chuckled. "You're welcome here as long as you want, Cherry Pop. Now get some sleep. Enjoy your first night on a real bed."

She kissed my cheek before going into the room and I went back to my own. Colton had passed out again. I changed into my night clothes then slid in next to him. All my exhaustion seemed to go out the window after drinking that blood because I lay on my back the entire night, staring at the ceiling.

36

Nicola threw the wiffle ball towards Colton and he hit it with the bat. He giggled in surprise since it was the first time he'd been able to do it and she cheered for him. Playing with her son was exactly what she needed to get her mind off the woman from the warehouse. If she thought about it too much, she would freak herself out. She was afraid that one wrong move would put her in chains.

"Nice one, bud!" she said. "With a hit like that, you'll be in the World Series."

"Really?"

She shrugged. "Could happen. I bet Ichiro didn't think it was possible now look where he's at. Baseball Hall of Fame."

Lately, Colton was the only person who was willing to spend time with her. Robin was civil, but she could feel the tension. Cherish's arrest wasn't making anything less tense either. Lucas told everyone about her claims that Cherish was the one that hurt her and surprisingly, everyone believed her. However, that didn't stop a rift from forming between her and his family.

Nicola tossed the ball again and Colton missed. He was bummed but determined to go again. While she continued to play catch, she thought back to the incident at the abandoned house. Ryan hadn't elaborated on what he meant about her not wanting to end up like their leader's son. It made her wonder how many children he had. She wanted to meet the S.O.B and find a way to escape.

The black Cadillac pulled up to the house and Colton immediately lost interest in batting practice at the sight of his grandfather. He dropped the bat and when Gallard got out of the car, Colton went running towards him. Gallard scooped him up from the ground and took him in his arms.

"Grandpa guess what! I hit the ball very far, and now I'm going to be in the world serious!"

The World *serious*?" Gallard smiled at Colton with pride. "Well you better score me some free tickets because I'm going to every game."

Gallard set Colton down and he grabbed his ball once more and began tossing it in the air and catching it. Since he was entertaining himself, Nicola took a moment to sit on the steps. Gallard walked over to her and sat next to her. She hadn't spoken to him much in the past few days and his company was welcome. Ever since she'd met him, she'd immediately warmed up to him, just as she had with Lucas. There was a comforting air about him that made it easy to talk with him. That had probably changed after everything that happened.

"He's getting bigger every day." Gallard said. "He's like his dad. Growing like a weed. Lucas was twenty-two inches when he was a newborn. Was Colton long?"

"No. He was so tiny he could fit in a shoe box. He was two months early. I didn't sleep much after he was born because I was afraid he wouldn't make it through the night. I couldn't bear it if I was asleep while he was taking his last breath."

Gallard put a sympathetic hand on her shoulder for a moment then let go. That was another thing she liked about him. He didn't crowd people. He was there if he was needed but didn't push people to talk. His touch was gentle and comforting.

"I'm sorry you had to go through that alone," he said. "I know for a fact if Lucas knew about the situation, he would have been at your side."

Hearing Lucas' name made a tear escape her eye. When they first started playing this game, they would subtly flirt through their fake fights. Now he wasn't even fake fighting with her anymore. Something was wrong but she couldn't ask him in fear of getting caught in her lie to Ryan.

"You don't have to be nice to me," she said. "I know that you're upset with me about . . . well, everything. I wouldn't blame you if you made me move to another neighborhood."

He chuckled. "No, I'm not going to do that. And I'm not going to treat you like a pariah infected with smallpox."

She raised an eyebrow.

"Sorry. I grew up in the eighteenth century, if that explains anything."

"You're so old. Must be great being old *and* hot."

The smile left his face and he looked away. She wondered if her comment had made him uncomfortable. She joked about his attractiveness all the time, but she never thought it bothered him. She was going to apologize when he spoke first.

"Nicola, this can't happen. Despite everything, you're the mother of my grandson. Broken up or not, that makes you family for life and I care

243

about you. But the flirting has to stop. I'm a married man, and I take my marriage seriously."

A laugh escaped her lips. "Gallard, seriously? *Flirting*? If you think that's me flirting, then you really don't know me. I'm like a little boy on the playground who throws rocks at the girl he likes. If I was attracted to you, I would insult you instead of flatter you."

He finally made eye contact with her again. "I see. So then why did you kiss me?"

Another laugh erupted, only louder this time. "Does Lela know you're drinking again? That's the most ridiculous thing I've ever heard!"

"Nic, please. I'm not going to make a big deal out of it. You were emotional and sometimes we act out of character when we're upset. I know because I've experienced that several times. But I can't pretend it didn't happen."

She started to say something but then her phone started buzzing and she lost her train of thought. She pulled her phone from her pocket and checked the I.D. It was from an anonymous number. The message said, *Let's play a game called 'Can you outrun my zero to sixty in two-point five. For Colton's sake, I hope you can.'*

An unfamiliar car came down the street and stopped about three houses down. The windows were too dark to see through. Meanwhile, Colton had wandered over to the sidewalk and was still tossing his ball. He threw it in the air and missed it. It rolled over the curb and into the street. He went after it, looking both ways as he'd been taught and stepped into the street.

Then the car started. Nicola immediately understood what was going on and she opened her mouth to call out to Colton, but her voice cut off. The car roared and started driving towards him at about fifteen miles an hour. On instinct, she got up and ran as fast as she was capable of. She managed to push Colton out of the way, but the car hit her instead. She rolled over the hood, smashing the windshield then landed on the pavement.

The driver tried to speed off when Gallard got it them first. He ripped the door off then yanked the culprit out. Nicola recognized the man as someone who had been at Ryan's gallery the night Cherish was arrested. The man was a vampire and as soon as he was exposed to the sun, his skin started to burn. Gallard took action and threw him back into the car.

"Who are you?" he demanded.

"I will never tell you!"

Gallard exposed his face to the sun and the man yelled. Before he caught on fire, he shoved him into the shade.

"I'll ask again— who are you?"

"I am a follower."

"Of who?"

"I cannot say. I was only instructed to act if we were compromised."

Nicola got up from the ground and hurried over to the two men. She wanted to hear what he had to say. Ryan was keeping her in the dark and she wanted to know why she was being forced to lie to those she loved.

"Compromised how?" Nicola asked. "I haven't said a word about anything! I've kept my promises!"

"I know for a fact that you revealed confidential information to this man not two days ago. It doesn't matter to me. My work here is done."

He pushed past Gallard so he was in the middle of the road once more and he caught on fire. He yelled in agony as he burned alive and Nicola averted her eyes. Gallard gently took her arm and pulled her away from the scene and she came back to reality when she saw Colton crying in the road. She ran over to him and picked him up, holding him tightly.

"Are you okay baby?" she asked, the tears falling once more.

"I'm fine, mamma." He sniffed. "He was so fast. I didn't have time to move."

"I know, I know. I'll always be there to push you out of the way, okay?"

Gallard came over to them and stroked Colton's hair. She was so glad he was there. She wouldn't have known what to do and the man responsible could have gotten away. She hated Ryan even more for this. He'd tried to kill Colton just because she was having a conversation with Gallard. If he could kill a child just to shut her up, she didn't want to know what else he would do.

"Nic, how did you move that fast?" Gallard asked.

"What do you mean?"

"You were at least fifty feet away from Colton and you got to him in less than two seconds. You were hit by a car going fifteen miles an hour and you don't have a scratch on you."

Her eyes filled with fear. She'd been able to keep her vampirism a secret for so long and she'd forgotten he didn't know when she'd rescued Colton. She had no regrets, though. She would give away any secret for his sake.

"Gallard, something happened the day Henry died and I've been keeping it a secret."

Gallard's shoulders sank in realization. "You turned. But . . . you still have your natural hair and eye color. You have a heartbeat. Not even Lucian can create a warm-blooded vampire."

She sucked in her breath then kissed Colton's cheek before handing him to Gallard. She was wrong about honesty being the right thing. She couldn't tell anyone what was going on. Not if it meant Colton could be killed. People would resent her for her silence, but it was for the best.

"I'm sorry," she said. "I can't say. No one can know about me, please don't tell anyone." She rubbed Colton's leg. "Take care of him for me. You're the only one who can."

Nicola ran off down the street, moving too fast for eyes to see. She had her destination in mind before she even started running. It was going to be a giant risk doing this, but Ryan had crossed a line. He kept talking about family and loyalty, but she was done with him.

After she got into Arlington, she made a quick stop at a gas station and bought a small pack of bottled water, plastic forks, deodorant, a toothbrush, six packages of Wet Ones, an entire box of protein bars, beef jerky, a razor, and shaving cream. It was all a spur of the moment thing, so she'd gone overboard. She then went to a nearby clothing store and bought a pack of underwear, a pack of Hanes t-shirts, three bras, and some leggings. The last purchase was a bag big enough to fit these items and she threw it over her back before heading to her destination.

It was dark before she finally got to the warehouse. She honed her hearing to make sure no one was nearby then she approached it. She'd broken the lock earlier and this enabled her to go inside. She descended the stairs quietly in case someone else had decided to make a visit there. For safety's sake, she listened one more time and when she was convinced she was alone, she hung a left at the bottom and opened the door at the end.

Her eyes adjusted quickly so she looked for a light switch. There was one but the light was burned out. She wished she'd thought to bring a flashlight. She would have to settle for the light from her phone. She clicked on the flashlight app then shined it across the room.

"Hey," she said. "I haven't forgotten about you. I brought food and clothing."

She forgot about the duct tape, so she sat on the ground and gently pulled it off. She then opened the bag and went for the wipes first. She used it to clean up the hostage's face and once all the dirt was gone, she gave her a bottle of water. The woman thanked her and guzzled it down quickly. While she did, Nicola opened a protein bar. The woman took that as well and ate it in small bites.

"I know you're probably wondering why I'm making your stay here comfortable instead of getting you the hell out. The answer is that something happened today that opened my eyes to how dangerous of a situation we are in."

The woman nodded as she chewed on the bar. Nicola thought she was mad but when she smiled at her, all her worry washed away. She could see in her eyes that she was grateful for the food, water, and toiletries.

"Someone tried to kill my son today. I got to him in time, but it was a close call. I never want that to happen again, so they have to think I'm on their side. I have faith that someone will figure out what's going on and that will save me the danger of being caught distributing information. Until then, I promise to replenish your necessities and visit as often as I can, but I need your help in return."

The woman cast her gaze down and Nicola fiddled with her hands while she waited for an answer. Nicola knew that she owed her much more than just necessities. It was all she had to offer at the moment. Too many lives were at stake.

Finally, the woman set the bar down and brought her gaze back to Nicola's.

"What can I do to help?"

37

J.D. paced back and forth on Lela's porch. It had taken her all night to build up the nerve to confront Gallard, but she was still too nervous to knock on the door. It wasn't that she was afraid to talk to him. She was afraid of the answer she would get. Also, she wondered if this was a good time, considering what had happened with Colton. Lucas had freaked out and pulled him out of school. Colton wasn't to be left unattended under any circumstances.

Out of curtesy, she'd given everyone some time to recover as well as react to the news of her and Lucian dating. She thought that fifteen days was more than enough time. If he wasn't going to talk to her, she would approach him. She didn't want her relationship with Lucian to always be two steps back and no moving forward. Not discussing it was doing just that.

The door opened and Gallard came out alone. She could tell that he was borrowing Lucas' clothes again because Lucas was the only one who wore True Religion jeans. Gallard never wore anything that expensive. That brand seemed to make d'Aubigne men's butts look really good. She'd tried that brand and it made her look flat.

"Hi, J.D.," he said. He gave her a warm hug. "How are you?"

"Been better. I'm pissed about little Colton and frustrated with the whole thing. But I'm sure everyone feels that way." She released him from the hug and tried to think of what she would say. "Can we talk?"

He nodded and they both took a seat at the small table on the porch. He seemed calm, but then again, he was a calm guy. She hadn't seen him as angry as she had when he'd found out about Robin or when he'd tried to start a fight with Lucian. He wasn't an angry guy.

"What did you want to talk about?" he asked.

"I think you know. You haven't said two words to me since I told you about Lucian and me. I tried to wait, but your silence is killing me."

He sighed and folded his hands on the table, keeping his gaze away from her.

"I haven't spoken with you because I've already spoken with Lucian. Well, he spoke with me. I'm surprised he hasn't said anything."

She was surprised too. If Lucian had already pled his case, why wasn't he coming to her with the news? He should have been excited.

"What did he say?" she asked reluctantly.

"I think you should ask him. But anyway, J.D., I will be honest and say I'm not exactly jumping for joy over this. It's not that I'm still holding a grudge, but I am still learning to trust him when it comes to these matters. For years, I had to spend time with him while in the back of my mind I wondered if he was still in love with my wife. We were often apart and leaving him alone with her made me uncomfortable. I was happy to learn he'd moved on."

She hung her head. "Just not happy that he moved on with me?"

He nodded his head honestly. She appreciated that he wasn't holding anything back. He was always kind and honest with her, but he never tiptoed around her. He always told her exactly what he thought of something and they'd had a great relationship when she'd lived with him and Lela. She didn't want that to change just because she was a grown woman now.

"Does that mean you didn't give him your blessing?"

"I told him that I would never do anything to stand in the way of your happiness. I also told him that if he ever hurt you, I would castrate him."

J.D. laughed. She couldn't imagine Gallard doing something that violent, but she didn't want to push his buttons either. It would never happen, though. Lucian loved her and wanted to marry her. He wanted an actual future and she wanted the same. She couldn't picture herself with anyone else.

"Thank you, uncle." She threw her arms around him and gave him a tight embrace. "I love you."

"Love you too, Jordin Anastasia. Now go talk to him. He said he was going to visit with Cherish, so he should be at Lucas.'"

Leaving the porch, she practically skipped over to the house next door. Gallard was okay with their relationship which meant they could finally go out on dates. They could kiss and hold hands in public. They could introduce themselves as a couple. And someday in the future, they could get married.

She opened the door to Lucas' house and closed it behind her. She was about to look around when she saw Cherish standing in the kitchen. She was wearing one of Lucas' shirts and stirring something in a coffee cup. Cherish turned around and stopped stirring when she made eye contact with her. She smiled.

"Hey, you. I didn't get to see you when I came home. How are you?"

"I'm fine." J.D. looked everywhere but at Cherish's face. Things were still awkward because of Lucas' claim that he'd heard Cherish admit to hurting Nicola.

"You looking for my father?" Cherish asked.

"Yes. Is he here?"

"He's in his room."

She gave Cherish a friendly smile before going down the hall. This time, his door was wide open so she wouldn't have to worry about walking in on him while he was changing. She caught him as he was putting on a jacket. He smiled at her, but his eyes were sad. She felt for him and his having to worry about his daughter.

"You talked to Gallard?" he asked.

"Yeah. How did you know?"

Lucian walked over to her and stroked her cheek with the back of his hand. "Because you have that same look in your eyes that you get when you're incredibly happy."

He knew her too well. She also knew things about him, like how he smiled differently around her. With everyone else, he would have a crooked smile with his lips slightly turned up to the left. With her, he would smile with his full mouth. Lucian usually showed his feelings in small gestures while he would tell her how he felt about her.

"I think we should celebrate," she said. "Cherish is out of jail, we have Gallard's blessing. I think everything is going to be okay." She lightly punched his arm. "Why didn't you tell me you had Gallard's blessing?"

"Because, darling, I wanted to be sure that you and he were still on good terms. I would rather not have his permission than for you to have a broken relationship with your uncle. And . . . I also needed time."

"For?"

He smiled and took her hand, leading her outside. She had no idea what was going on, but she couldn't stop her heart from pounding in anticipation. He didn't stop until they were by the tree where the punching bag was usually hanging. It was gone today. He then took both of her hands in his.

"Jordin, when I first saw you, I had no idea what to think. As you know, your father and I never got along and I thought, '*Perfect, it's a female version of Jordan. I should keep my distance.*' I was so sure you would drive me crazy and we would end up hating each other. Quite the opposite happened. I fell in love with you. From the moment we met, life became an exciting ride. You're always making me laugh, and your mind is so busy that sometimes I cannot keep up with you. We're opposites, but also you're my other half. The balance to my soul. I met you at a young and awkward seventeen and now you're an amazing and beautiful woman of twenty-two. I do not want to go another day without you being mine. I love you, Jordin Anastasia d'Aubigne."

Lucian got down on one knee, and she finally figured out what was going on. She covered her mouth with her hand to keep from breaking out in girlish giggles. She couldn't believe this was happening and she could hardly contain herself.

He opened a small leather box and she stared in awe at the radiant ring with a diamond that matched her eyes. That was when she could feel the happy tears escaping her eyes.

"Will you do me the honor of being my wife? I may be a crotchety old man sometimes, and I am positive you will have to put me in my place on many occasions throughout our marriage, but this clueless ass face would be the happiest man on earth if you —"

"Yes!" she finally said. "Yes, yes, yes! I love crotchety old men, and I love you!"

He laughed then slid the ring onto her finger. She didn't even wait for him to stand up and she tackled him onto the ground and kissed him. He kissed her back and held her in his arms. She adored this man and now he was her fiancé. She was going to spend the rest of her life with him, and she couldn't imagine being happier.

I'm getting married!

Wait, he proposed? Without asking me?

He asked Gallard. That's good enough, right?

Well, there's not much I can do about it. Congratulations, sweetheart. I hope he makes you happy.

Finally, she allowed him to stand up and they went inside, hand in hand. She wanted to shout her news from the top of the house but decided to be civilized about it instead. Cherish was still in the kitchen and J.D. showed her the ring first. Cherish took her hand and studied the shiny piece of jewelry.

"Well, congrats you two!" she said. "Are you planning to elope like my sister?"

"Not a chance," Lucian said. "I want the full-blown church wedding and I want Solomon to marry us."

"Good answer. We need a normal wedding around here. And father, thanks! Now Lela owes me a hundred dollars."

"What for?" J.D. asked.

"She bet Lucas would propose to Nicola first. But I guess now that they're broken up it was inevitable. Anyway, I am happy for you. I better be a bridesmaid."

J.D. hugged her and then Lucian said he wanted to speak with his daughter for a bit. They planned to tell everyone their news that night when everyone was home and that gave her something to look forward to.

To keep herself occupied until then, she wanted to see what everyone else was doing. Melody was with Celeste and they were shopping in town and Lela was at work. Then she saw the door to Lucas' house open and he and Robin came out. They were both dressed casually. Robin wore one of Gallard's sweatshirts, and it was way too big. She'd been wearing baggy clothes a lot lately.

"Where you are two going?" she asked, trying not to sound overly cheerful. She'd hidden the ring so it would be kept a secret until later on.

"My task force is getting together for some recreational basketball. James felt we need a break from the case and honestly, I can't sit in my office anymore. Robin is coming to be a cheer leader. Want to join?"

Spending time with Robin and Lucas was exactly what she needed. If she could pretend to be excited about a basketball game, then maybe she wouldn't be tempted to blurt out her news. She needed a distraction.

"Yeah, I'm in."

A huge, black Escalade pulled up to the house and the driver honked obnoxiously. The driver's side opened, and a muscular specimen of a man got out. He was no body builder, but J.D. could see from far away that the gym was probably his friend. He wasn't the same short kid she remembered from high school.

"Yo, Raison Boy. We have a problem," he said to Lucas.

"And that is?"

"Craven backed out. His dad is dragging his family into Dallas for a football game. He couldn't say no to the Cowboys, so we're short one guy. Know anyone?"

"My brother would probably like to play," J.D. said. After talking with Robin that morning, she'd decided she would make a better effort at getting along with her brother.

James laughed. "Well I'll be, it's my very own Brit!" He hugged her tightly and swung her in a circle. "How have you been? I haven't seen you since graduation!"

Somebody's popular.

What can I say? I'm a dude magnet. It's a d'Aubigne thing.

"It's been too long, James. Didn't Sexy McPherson tell you I was in town?"

"No, Lucas did. Erik's too busy sucking face with Broom Girl. Nadia mentioned it at dinner, which you were supposed to be at. Why did you ditch?"

J.D. exchanged a glance with Robin then looked back at him. "Headache. We should have lunch sometime, the three of us. I'd like to hear what you've been up to besides vampire hunting."

She heard the door open and Lucian came outside. He was giving James a scrutinizing look. It amused her, but he didn't have anything to worry about. She was his forever and always. Plus, Lucas had told her James was married with a baby.

252

"It's great to see you again," she said. "Let me go get my brother."

She blew Lucian a kiss before going off to Lela's house. Abe spent most of his time with Gallard because they hadn't seen each other in so long so he was bound to be there. Sure enough, they were sitting on the couch and talking. Both men grew quiet as she approached them.

"What can we do for you, sis?" Abe asked.

"Lucas and his band of merry men need an extra basketball player. You free?"

"Definitely. You don't mind?"

"No, I don't. You promised to stay here and so far you've kept your promise. In return, I'm going to try and repair our relationship." She gave him a genuine smile. "Robin and I are going to be the cheerleaders."

He couldn't have stood up fast enough. She knew by the excitement in his eyes that he wasn't eager to join for sibling bonding time. He wanted to be around Robin. She'd warned him that Robin was off limits and that he should let her be happy with Erik but he wouldn't relent. Once he put his mind to something, he never gave up.

"What was that about?" she asked Gallard.

"I think your brother is in love."

J.D. saw that one coming. She'd been afraid that her brother saw Robin as some conquest, but she was starting to realize it was more than that. Abe never put this much effort into pursuing a woman so he must have really cared about her. It was hard not to. Robin was a sweetheart and loved by everyone. The problem was that Robin was with Erik and she was really into him. She was afraid someone was going to get hurt because of this triangle.

Abe returned from changing and came back down wearing black sweats and a grey t-shirt. He then followed J.D. outside. This was going to be interesting. She'd never seen Abe play any form of sports besides mixed martial arts, let alone basketball.

"Whoa," James said. "Are you who I think you are? Abraham Christophe?"

Abe smiled humbly. "That would be me."

"J.D.! You didn't tell me your twin is an MMA legend! I watched you all the time in high school!"

"Abe, this is James Newberry," Lucas said. "My second in command and apparently your biggest fan."

James rolled his eyes. "We're a task force, not a bunch of pirates. But you should have seen him when he arrested that vamp. He charmed her with his good guy routine all the way into the squad car. Didn't even have to shoot her."

J.D. flinched and she hoped James didn't sense the discomfort that had settled over her and her relatives. She may have had suspicions surrounding Cherish, but she was still family. The thought of her being hauled away like a criminal unnerved J.D.

"Well, we should get going," Lucas said. "This game isn't going to play itself."

Everyone piled into the Escalade. Lucas introduced the rest of his task force, which consisted of two other men and Erik was there as well. Robin climbed into the back with him. J.D. sat between Abe and Lucas. They arrived at the gym five minutes later and the men went ahead, save for Abe. He walked with J.D. and Robin, visibly out of his comfort zone. J.D. knew that he would be more like himself if this was a photo shoot. She would have invited Lucian, but he looked too much like Cherish for comfort. As much as she wanted to spend every waking minute with him, she cared about his safety and her family's.

J.D. followed Robin to the top of the bleachers and plopped next to her. She watched as the men split off into teams and Erik unloaded a bag of basketballs. They each took one and started taking practice shots. Abe threw one and missed and J.D. snorted. He'd heard it because he gave her an exasperated look and it made her laugh even more. She knew he wasn't trying.

"I'm glad you convinced him to come," Robin said. "He stays at home too much."

"You're right. My brother has never been a homebody. I think with time we can get close again. We'll have to be if I want him to be in my wedding."

"Wait, what do you mean?"

J.D. took her ring out of her pocket. "I wasn't going to say anything until tonight, but I have to tell you. Lucian proposed today."

Robin laughed excitedly then threw her arms around J.D.

"I'm so happy for you!" She then looked around and lowered your voice. "I can't believe you're getting married!"

"Me neither! But I don't think it will be anytime soon. We still have a lot of important matters to deal with. Until then, I'm going to plan everything so I'm ready when the time comes."

The game started and she found herself getting into it. Abe and Lucas were on opposing sides and she smiled at their attempts at outdoing each other. They didn't do anything that would compromise their identities, but they were really pushing it. Lucas moved too fast for the other team members and if he got too cocky, he was going to slip up.

"Careful," she said in a low voice. "Can't have them thinking you're a mutant."

Lucas looked at her and then laughed. Without missing a beat, he continued playing the game.

"Erik invited me over tonight," Robin said, breaking J.D.'s trance.

"Ooh, for what? Something that involves being in his room?"

Robin's cheeks flushed. "I think so. This is the first time he's ever invited me to his place. He's been busy with work lately and wants to make it up to me. He wants to cook."

"Oh, he wants to get in your pants all right."

"J.D.!"

"Hon, they can't hear me."

"You have a very loud voice. It carries, and I don't want that to carry."

J.D. forgot about her happy news for a while and went into prep mode. She wanted to make sure that whatever would happen on this date that Robin would be ready. They had been dating for about a month now and she wouldn't be surprised if Erik had something special planned. Cooking dinner at his place was a romantic idea. It was the kind of gesture that led to other things.

"Are you prepared?" J.D. asked. "You never got those pills last week."

"I think we'll be fine without pills. And I haven't told him about what happened to me. I don't want him to be afraid to touch me. I'm fine. More than fine."

J.D. sighed her head. "I can't believe you might go further with Erik than I have with Lucian. Sure, we fool around, but never any skin-on-skin contact. He's adamant that we're married first."

"Well, Erik isn't that old fashioned. I do want to be with him, J.D. He's a great guy and let me tell you, he has a great body."

"You're so naughty. Maybe I shouldn't have let you read my romance novels."

They both jumped when the gym doors suddenly flew open. Five men and two women walked in wearing black cloaks. This didn't look good and she tried to get Lucas' attention. The men stopped playing and turned their gazes to the surprise guests. The one in front took off his cloak and J.D. could see from far away that the man in front was Simeon. Lucas stepped forward as the spokesperson and approached him with caution.

"Can we help you?" he asked.

"We are looking for Cherish. We have unfinished business and we wish to speak with her."

"You mean Charity Tophé?" James asked. "The hell should we know? She made bail."

"We have personal interest in her. Tell us where she is and we will leave you to your game."

"The bail was posted anonymously," Lucas said. "It's up to the courts to know her whereabouts. You're talking to the wrong people."

"I am not fond of liars," Simeon said to Lucas. "I expect you to give us information." He turned his head and J.D.'s heart skipped a beat when she discerned that he was looking at Robin. "Or her, either one. You see, I like to collect beautiful women. It's a hobby of mine and I have yet to have a blonde."

Erik stepped closer to Simeon. "That's my girlfriend you're threatening. Lay eyes on her again, and I might just burn you on the spot."

Simeon shoved Erik back so hard that he flew across the gym and landed with a harsh thud on his back. Robin screamed and James ran over to check on him while Lucas grabbed onto Simeon's throat. J.D. wasn't worried . . . yet. Lucas could easily take on two night-walkers.

"Get out of here before I do to you what my father did to that messenger of yours," Lucas snarled. Simeon tried to fight off Lucas, but Lucas body slammed him onto the ground so hard that the floor cracked. The entire gym began to shake. Lucas was getting upset and if he didn't calm down, the gym could crumble down on everyone.

J.D. grabbed Robin's hand and they hurried down the bleachers as fast as they could without tripping. They got to the bottom just as Lucas let go of Simeon. The other four cloaked people opened the door then the five of them ran out. Lucas then ran over to the rest of the officers who were gathered around Erik.

"Are you okay?" Robin asked him.

"I . . . I don't know." His eyes filled with fear. "I can't feel my legs."

Lucas exchanged a glance with Abe and J.D., and she knew what he was thinking. Erik was more than likely paralyzed and the only way to keep him from living the rest of his life in a wheelchair was to heal him. But he couldn't do it with James and the others watching.

"I called an ambulance," James said. "Hang in there, big guy. You're going to be fine. We're going to get the bastard who did this to you."

Lucas' expression became wary and J.D. frowned. She thought that he was as surprised by this visit as she was but that moment said otherwise. He knew something that he was refusing to share.

The ambulance came and Robin rode with Erik while the rest of them rode in James' Escalade to the hospital. J.D. could sense Robin's unease when it came to doctors, but she wanted to be there for Erik. They sat in the waiting room and J.D. looked over at Lucas. He was tapping his feet as if he were nervous and she could see his hands were shaking. She reached over and took his hand.

"You okay?"

"I'm pissed. Simeon carried out his threats against Erik and my son's life and now he's making threats against Robin. I can't let him hurt another member of my family."

"You won't. You'll figure this out. But you can't do this alone, so you're going to have to tell me what's going on."

"I can't tell you. It's why Colton was almost run over. They thought someone was talking when they weren't."

"You're letting them win? That doesn't make sense. Since when do we let people push us around?"

"I'm handling it. Nobody is pushing anyone around. Trust me, okay?"

She didn't ask any more questions. She did trust him, but she also worried for him. The last time he tried to solve something on his own, Mona ended up dead and Nicola nearly lost her life as well. She hoped that he would get help when it came to finding out what these men wanted and taking the necessary steps to protect Cherish. If she wanted to be protected.

James stepped out of the elevator and everyone stood up. He looked incredibly sad and Robin grabbed J.D.'s hand, squeezing it tightly.

"It's not looking good," he said. "Doctors say his spine is broken and there's severe nerve damage. They won't know the extent for a few days but . . . Erik still can't feel anything below the waist."

Robin started crying and J.D. hugged James while Lucas remained silent. He wasn't shaking like before, but J.D. could feel he was still fuming. It must be a terrible burden to feel out of control when he had the potential to protect people. Hiding his identity was wearing on him and she was afraid he would have to throw the rules out of the window to do what was necessary.

"We're going to find those people," Lucas said. "They aren't going to get away with this."

"I agree," James said. "I just got off the phone with Tyler. Talia was found dead in her apartment. Gunshot wound to the head. We're going to have to get another person on our task force. The city council said we have to have at least six field officers to keep the task force going, especially now that Rick is on desk duty."

"We'll find someone on Monday. In the meantime, please watch your back. All of you. I can't be there to body slam every crook who shows up. We're not going to sleep until he's found."

All the men clapped Lucas on the back. Since there was nothing more they could do for Erik, they took off to work on the case. Robin wanted to stay behind and wait for Erik's parents to arrive and wait with them. Abe called Gallard and he was due to pick everyone else up.

When everyone was gone, Lucas pulled J.D. aside.

"I need your help with something."

"Anything. What do you need me to do?"

"You and Abe need to guard the door while I heal Erik. I'm not letting this happen while I have the power to stop it."

She nodded and then her brother followed him down the hall. So far, most of the nurses probably assumed they were just visitors and didn't give them a second look. Abe looked around then nodded and Lucas quickly slipped into the room. J.D. wished she could watch. She loved seeing Lucas heal people. She admired him for it and was glad that he didn't use his gift to obtain fame or notoriety. He simply used it because he cared.

Four people started coming down the hallway and Abe nonchalantly knocked on his door. J.D. recognized them as Erik's family. Tyler and Amanda looked worried. The two sisters had tear-streaked faces. Imogen and Nadia recognized her and she hugged them both. They sure grew up. Nadia was only ten when J.D. last saw her.

"Hello, J.D.," Tyler said. "Is this our son's room?"

"Yes," she said. "We were there when it happened. Lucas is in there right now."

The doctor showed up again and Amanda went with the girls to speak with him. Tyler stayed behind, and She had hoped they wouldn't have any conversation beyond hello and goodbye.

"I had no idea Lucas was related to you," he said.

"Yup. Last name didn't give a clue?"

He flinched. "You were always J.J to me. Anyway, James said Erik was attacked by a cloaked man who had five others with him. That Erik may have suffered a spinal injury." His taut shoulders relaxed. "Distract me. How have you been?"

"I'm good. I'm engaged actually."

He smiled lightly. "That's wonderful. I'm glad you're happy."

She forced herself to look into his eyes. "Are *you* happy?"

He looked over at the door then back at her. "I am. Been fighting my demons and now I got to a good place. My wife and I are closer than ever."

The door opened and Lucas came out with a smile on his face. His skin had a glow to it, and his hair had gotten even whiter. J.D. could feel relief wash over her. His expression could only mean one thing.

"How is he?" Tyler asked.

"He's fine. He had a compressed spine, but he slowly regained feeling. He was actually asking for you."

He stepped aside so that Tyler could go in. Robin, who had already been in there started to leave but they insisted that she stay so the three of them went downstairs to wait for Gallard to come pick them up. Erik's life was not ruined, but that didn't mean the threat wasn't still there.

They arrived at the house and J.D. quickly got out and headed for Lucas' house. She needed to speak with Cherish and get answers from her. The men had tried to threaten Lucas into telling them where she was, and J.D. wanted to know why. She closed the door behind her and turned on the first light she reached. Thankfully, Cherish was in the living room reading a book. She'd changed into some of her own clothes and had her hair piled up on her head in a halfhearted bun.

"Hey, you," she said. "How was the outing?"

"Kind of bad. Some crazy vamps showed up and hurt Erik. He's going to be okay, but they're pretty shaken up."

Cherish set her book down and folded her hands, resting them on her knee. "What did they want?"

"Well, *you*, actually."

She sighed. "I was afraid of that."

Cherish waved J.D. over to the couch and J.D. sat next to her. Cherish had lost some weight over the past several weeks. J.D. used to be so jealous of her body until she shot up about two inches taller than her. Cherish and Melody had always been about being healthy. J.D. used to go to the gym with Cherish when she'd lived with her and Solomon. J.D. missed those days.

"J.D., I'm not sure what is going on. Nicola said that I hit her even though I know the story behind her bruising. And they have this idea that someone is giving away information when she swears she didn't talk and neither have I."

"We can protect you, Cher. But I really think we should call Solomon. He should know what's going on. We need him here to help us."

"No, please don't do that. He has more important things to worry about."

"More important than protecting his wife? Cher, he needs to know!"

"I said no! Leave him out of it."

If J.D. wasn't mistaken, Cherish was more snappy than usual. She was known to be the grouchy one of the group, but this was a new level of grouchy. And J.D. felt like she was lying. She wanted Solomon in the dark for a reason.

"I don't get you," J.D. said. "You act all secretive and then you get pissed when we ask you what you're up to. If you're innocent, why can't you just say so?"

"Because it's bigger than me!" she shouted. "I'm not the only one who is in danger here."

J.D. heard someone step into the room and saw Lucian standing behind her. He looked as upset as she felt and she could have cried. She hated seeing her strong aunt so terrified. Hardly anything scared Cherish and whoever had her hiding away like a hermit was probably incredibly dangerous.

"You can't keep secrets anymore, Cherish," he said. "A man almost died tonight by Simeon's hand. You either tell us why he's suddenly interfering with our lives again or we'll find out for ourselves."

"Go ahead, figure it out. But father I can't say anything. The life of someone close to me depends on it."

Cherish stood up and left the room, going into Abe's. He wasn't there tonight and it was probably the only place she could have privacy without having to leave the house. Lucian didn't follow her but rather suggested J.D. stay with him. He was just as shaken up by this new threat as she was and she didn't protest to spending the night safely at his side.

38

I'm fine, mom," Erik said for the hundredth time. His sister had driven his truck to the hospital so Robin could drive him home. His parents had arrived at the same time and his mom wouldn't stop babying him. Robin was concerned but she knew his mother was probably ten times as worried.

"Honey, you're not fine," Amanda said. "You suffered a serious fall. Now you better lie down and rest. Don't do anything over-strenuous and let Robin help you with anything she can."

"Like bathe you and change your diaper," Imogen said. Erik groaned but Robin laughed. She knew he wasn't hurt anymore but the idea was comical. She would be there for him, though. He was given a mandatory two days off and she wasn't going to be anywhere but at his side to make sure no one else would show up and try to hurt him.

Robin had one of Erik's arms around his shoulder to support him and Tyler had another. Together, they were able to lower him onto the couch. Amanda tried to cover him with a blanket, but he waved her away.

"Mom, really. I'm bandaged up and I have Robin here with me. You don't have to hover. I'm fine."

Amanda's eyes teared up and she kissed his forehead. "I know you're okay. But I hate seeing my baby boy get hurt. I know you're a man and can take care of yourself, but I still worry."

Erik patted her arm in understanding then she and his family left the apartment. Robin took this time to look around. His place was about the same size as Lucas' other apartment but with a different layout. He had one couch and a love seat, both with matching brown interior and a twenty-one-inch TV resting on top of an oak entertainment center.

"Finally. I thought they would never leave." He got up, moving normally now that he didn't have to feign an injury, and hugged her from behind. "What do you think of my cave?"

"It's really nice. I expected there to be a lot of sports memorabilia or cop stuff."

He laughed. "Cop stuff, huh? Well at least now I don't have to worry about catheters and wheelchairs, right?"

The smile left her face and she leaned into him. He was very lucky to have Lucas around to heal him. Very few ever crossed an angry vampire and lived to tell about it.

She couldn't help but feel that this was her fault. If she hadn't approached Simeon and made him angry, this wouldn't have happened. She'd heard talk about the Sharmentino curse and how it touched everyone who knew them, and she began to wonder if there was truth to it. Was anyone she attached herself to in danger of dying because of who she was?

"Robin, hey? What's wrong?" Erik asked.

"It's my fault," she said. "Everyone dies."

"What do you mean?"

"No one is safe. My mom, Curtis, Lydian, Jordan, Mona — everyone dies and you could have died too!"

She left his side and started heading for the door. She needed to leave. She couldn't be here anymore if it meant Erik would be in danger. The curse had followed them all the way to Texas and was only going to keep following them unless they stayed away from every human being they came across.

"Robin, wait!" Erik ran and cut her off before she could open the door.

"Please let me go. It's safer," she said.

"What's safer? What do you mean everyone dies? Does this have to do with Lucas and his gift? He's a vampire too, isn't he? But how can he walk in the day? It's not possible!"

She started crying and covered her face with her hands. She hadn't allowed herself to cry in so long and all her emotions were flooding her at once. She cared about this man. He was kind and good — he didn't deserve to be put in danger because she could no longer imagine not being with him. He needed to know the truth so he would know why she needed to leave.

He took her hand and they both went back to the couch. She waited until she'd stopped crying so hard then used the tissue he gave her to dry her tears. Once she was composed, she began telling him everything. She started in the beginning with what happened to Lela when she was fourteen. A lot of what she knew was from what people had told her so she made it clear that some of it might not be accurate.

She told him of Lela's alias, Diane Fontaine. She told him about what had happened to cause her to finally be honest with Tyler and why she was forced to leave town so suddenly. She told him of what happened the night her mother was murdered and what she went through while in captivity. She told him about the strange events surrounding Lela's possession and how she'd come back a year later. She revealed everything up until when the attacks in Orlando occurred and then explained why she and her family were forced to leave Miami back in July and ended with telling him everything that was currently going on with Cherish and the mysterious men who wanted her dead.

He never said a word while she spoke. He kept his eyes on her for the first half but then gradually looked away as if he were trying to process everything. To give him some time, she got up and went into the kitchen to get him some water. She was going to fill the glass when he put a hand over hers.

"I'm going to need something a lot stronger than that," he said. He took the glass and poured some scotch into it. He didn't guzzle it like Gallard had at the bar but finished it in three small sips.

"Please say something," she said. "Even if it's that you're terrified or overwhelmed, I would like to know what you're thinking."

He set the glass down. "Every bone in my body is telling me to run. To get out of this before I'm in too deep and I really do end up dead."

"You should. Because if you did die, I would never forgive myself for putting you in danger or taking you away from your family."

He turned to her and gently took her face in his hands. "I wasn't finished. What I was going to say is that my common sense may be saying that, but my heart is telling me that if I don't fight for you or for us, then I will always regret it. My father has spent the past twenty some years living with his mistakes. He's haunted by what might have been had he not turned away Dia—I mean your sister. And I don't want that to happen to me. Yeah, your world is scary, but I accept your world. I accept you."

She couldn't imagine being happier than she was in that moment. She threw her arms around him and kissed him. This wasn't how she'd imagined this date going, but it was way better. He knew everything about her and there were no secrets between them. Almost.

"I can't believe your sister euthanized you," he said, stroking her cheek. "Did that ever come between you when you came back?"

"At first I was hurt. I understand now that it was the best decision. If she hadn't done that, I would be trapped in the body of a ten-year-old right now."

Erik frowned. "Well that wouldn't do. If you were ten years old, I couldn't do this."

He rested his hands on her waist and pulled her in for a kiss. It was a simple one, but made her melt nonetheless. His lips moved softly against hers and she put her hands on his chest.

When he went to remove her sweatshirt, she stopped him. She wasn't ready for him to see her just yet. She still hadn't told him about the baby, and he hadn't questioned when she stopped dressing cute and piling on the layers. She claimed she got cold easy since she was used to the Miami heat, and he'd believed her.

"What is it?" he asked.

"Um . . ." she swallowed. "Before we continue, I have to warn you." She thought about another convincing lie. "I'm fat."

He laughed. "Fat? You're anything but! I've seen you in that outfit you wore to the club. And that dress you wore to the festival."

She bit her lip. "I've gained weight since then. I'm embarrassed, and I don't know if I want you to see me."

Erik smiled and drew her lips to his again. "Robin, I like you more than for just your looks. I love your laugh, your kindness, your sense of humor. Your caring heart. Yes, I think you're the most beautiful woman I've ever met, and I don't think that will ever change."

Robin's heart jumped in her chest, and she suddenly didn't feel so self-conscious. She took off her sweatshirt then boldly removed her shirt as well. She was well aware her belly protruded, but she was still quite small despite how far along she was.

"You're so beautiful," he said. "Are you sure you want to?"

"Yes. It is why you invited me here, isn't it?"

He gave her wry smile. "Well, yes. But after everything, I didn't think you would want to."

"Oh, I do."

Her honest answer made him laugh and he surprised her by picking her up and carrying her out of the kitchen. He opened one of the doors in the hallway then set her down. The room was so homey and she loved it. The walls were white, like the rest of the house but they had pictures of his family as well as some photos of him and James from vacations.

He had two nightstands on either side of the bed and the lampshades were simple cream color. The bedspread was black and soft. She couldn't resist running her hands over it and imagined what it would be like to curl up underneath it. The bed itself was low to the ground but not too low to be like just a mattress on the floor.

She turned around and smiled. "It's cozy. I could live in here for weeks."

Erik tugged off his shirt then stepped closer. "I'm kind of gross from basketball earlier. I'm going to take a quick shower. You sit tight, okay?"

He tossed his shirt into a hamper by his dresser and left the room. Her pulse slowed a bit but she was still a little breathless from seeing him. He wasn't buff like Abe, but healthy. She admired his lean physique. She held him to his promise and finished getting undressed before taking the liberty of getting under the covers. The blanket was as soft as she'd guessed, and she buried herself beneath them.

An idea came to her. Simeon had nearly killed Erik and she wasn't going to let that slide. Her family now knew he was behind everything and they were going to go after him. But she wanted to throw in a few words of her own. So, she slipped out of the bed with one of the throw blankets around her and found her purse. She'd kept Simeon's number in there for reasons unknown. Taking a deep breath, she dialed it. It went straight to voicemail.

"Hello, Simeon. This is Robin. I think you know why I'm calling you. Just so you know, Erik is going to be okay. You failed. And you're going to keep failing because me and my family are done with you. I don't care that you knew my parents, I don't care that you want me. You're a dead man. If you're smart, you would walk away because if you don't, you're going to be sorry."

The water shut off, so she hung up and quickly tiptoed back into the room. He came back two minutes later wearing a towel. He smelled amazing and she didn't resist inhaling his scent. It was like pine, or some kind of fir tree. She giggled to herself when a funny thought entered her mind.

"What is it?" he asked.

"You smell like Christmas."

He laughed. "I love the way you think. It's so down to earth and so you. I love that you compare everything to Christmas."

"Well, it's the best holiday of the year. You can't get any better than Christmas, so I put that on the scale with Arbor Day being the worst."

He went over to his nightstand and put deodorant on. "Why Arbor Day?"

"Because there's nothing special about it. You don't get to miss school, there's no decorations. You just go on doing what you normally do, except a few people plant a tree. At Christmas, everyone gets together and eats good food and partakes in family traditions. And Christmas lasts all month long and sometimes even a few days after New Year's."

"You're so adorable." He winked at her.

"Thank you. And I'm going to talk to the man who did this to you and I'm going to make sure he regrets it."

"I'm touched, Broom Girl, but I don't want you fighting my battles. I can take care of myself."

"I'm sure you can, but I'm still going to beat him up with my broom. I'm going to take care of you. Got it?"

He sat on the bed next to her. "Yes ma'am."

They both grew quiet, and the look in his eyes suddenly became very tender. He was still wearing the towel but that didn't make her nervous. She'd seen him before and he'd seen her.

Erik dimmed the light then got something out of his drawer. He sat with his back to her for a moment then removed the towel and got under the covers. For a while they just lay there, staring at each other and

264

smiling. He stroked the tendrils of hair that framed her face. She was glad he wasn't immortal or he would hear how hard her heart was pounding in her chest. How was he so calm? She was a nervous wreck. Then it occurred to her that this was probably not first time he had done this.

"Erik?" she nearly whispered.

"Yeah, beautiful?"

She didn't know how to ask delicately, so she decided to say it straight forward. "How many women have you been with in the past?"

He lightly chuckled then lay on his back. "Uh oh. Here's the dreaded conversation." He turned his face back to her. "I'm not going to lie to you. You deserve to know about my past since I know yours. I have only been with two women. The first was older than me and offered to be with me so I could get it over with."

"Was she pretty?"

Erik shrugged. "Nah. She was a real shrew. I had to keep my eyes closed the whole time."

Robin swatted his arm, laughing uncontrollably. She knew he was kidding because Erik never talked badly about anyone. It was what she liked most about him.

"What about you?" he asked. "I know you haven't been back for very long. Is this your first time?"

"No," she said nonchalantly. "I'm not a virgin, if that's what you're asking. The first guy, I didn't know his name until after. Let's just say I'm not too proud of that."

He nodded. "I guess we've had similar experiences. That doesn't change how I feel about you and I hope you still feel the same. Because I'm crazy about you."

She could feel herself falling even harder for him in that moment. He was the complete opposite of, Ash and she couldn't believe how lucky she was to have met him. She wished so much that Erik could have been her first and that it had been her choice. Either way, she would never forget this night.

Erik kissed her, starting out slow then getting more and more passionate. She shifted so that he could accommodate her better and the moment they came together she was astonished by how amazing it was. Her insecurities melted away and she found herself coming out of her shell in ways she never thought possible.

Every movement he made, every touch he gave deepened her affection for him. She felt so many sensations and emotions all at once that it was overwhelming, yet she didn't want it to end. She finally understood what the songs and the movies all talked about. Being with him made her finally feel like a woman and not a child who had become a woman in a few short hours.

He gave her one last kiss before moving away from her but kept her in his embrace. She had one arm around his waist and her head was resting on his chest. Neither of them spoke, but rather basked in the moment, enjoying the emotional high of their passionate bond.

Erik played with one of her curls while she listened to the sound of his heartbeat and she let all her worries float away while she was in his arms. He may have thought he could take care of himself, but at the end of the day, he was only a mortal. He was no match against the vampires who had it out for him and she was determined to keep him safe. He wasn't going to end up like her mother or Curtis or Mona. As far as she was concerned, he was going to live, even if she had to die to keep him safe.

"You doing okay?" he asked after a while.

"Yes. You were right to wait." She turned so she was looking at him. "Tonight was way better than any nooner."

He laughed and gave her one soft kiss before letting out a content sigh. She knew how he was feeling because she felt it too — like she was in heaven. She was also feeling a little hungry. Their dinner had ended before it even started because they had other things on their minds.

"Are you hungry?" she asked.

"Starving." He picked up his phone to check the time. "It's only six. Want take-out or should we stay in and cook? My mom has a spare key for emergencies, and she went grocery shopping for me yesterday." He rolled his eyes. "My parents are always encouraging me to get out and be on my own but then they do stuff like that."

"I understand. My family is the same way. Why don't we stay in? I like being alone with you here."

He got up and walked over to the dresser to get some clothes. Curious, she watched him as he did and smiled. Never in her dreams would she have thought she would get to literally see him out of uniform. And she definitely liked what she saw. He quickly dressed and then she did the same.

Together, they went into the kitchen and started seeing what they could make with the ingredients that he had. Spaghetti sounded great to, so they went with that. He wanted to cook for her, but she wanted him to teach her how to make it. The recipe was simple enough. She loved doing this with him. It assured her that their relationship went beyond the physical stuff. He liked spending time with her and she felt the same way. She could cook next to him every night for the rest of her life.

They ate on the couch while watching a Christmas movie marathon on the Hallmark channel. She couldn't believe how much time had gone by. When she came back, it was barely summer and now it was almost wintertime. The weather had gotten colder but it hadn't snowed. She'd never seen snow before and hoped that this year would be her chance.

Erik twisted the noodles on his fork then put something red from a small bottle on it. "You have to try this. It's spaghetti with buffalo sauce."

She laughed. "Erik, you put buffalo sauce on everything. But I guess I could try it." She opened her mouth and he fed it to her. Normally, she didn't like that sauce but mixed with the beef, noodles, and Italian sauce it was delicious. "Wow. Tastes better than Christmas."

"Get out of here!"

He started laughing harder than she was. When he stopped, he took her chin in his fingers and gently pulled her face close to him until his lips met hers. He then smiled at her.

"I love you," he whispered.

His words caught her off guard and she stared at him in shock. They had only been dating for a month. Did he really feel that way already? If so, she wasn't sure if she felt the same way. Even worse, the moment he'd said that, she thought of Abe. He'd said the same thing. This night with Erik had given her clarity about who she wanted to be with and she thought she knew for sure. Until now.

Instead of answering, she kissed him again then cuddled against him. She couldn't say the words back. Not until she knew for sure that she felt the same way. She finished her meal then after they cleaned the kitchen, they returned to his room and continued expressing their feelings without words and she fell asleep in his arms.

39

Nicola held her arms in front of her in a defensive stance, eyeing the enemy before her. It remained unmoving, but she was ready. She'd been going over the moves in her head all night had when she couldn't bear to lie down any longer, she got up at five in the morning and began practicing. She was finally learning how to defend herself and with each perfected move, she felt more empowered.

She took a deep breath, allowing the strength within her body to build and build. She balled up her fists and positioned them in front of her face, continuing to keep her heart rate down. She imagined the enemy making the first move. Analyzing what it would do and which way it would move. Likewise, she envisioned which maneuvers would be necessary to block each blow.

Then, she was ready. She crouched down then twisted her body to the right then allowed for the momentum to send her in a three-sixty turn. She stiffened her right leg and held it out and when she'd finished the turn, her foot collided with the Styrofoam filled enemy, causing it to swing wide. She landed on her feet but didn't stop there. Once the bag swung towards her, she returned to her original stance and socked it with a punch. Her next blow came from her forearm and then she finished with a side kick with her left leg.

She was so wrapped up in the movements of the bag that she didn't hear the footsteps from behind her. She caught the person's scent first and being caught up in the rush of her fighting, she turned around and prepared to kick whoever was sneaking up on her. The person caught her foot just before she hit him square in the chest.

"Whoa!" Lucian said. "Quite impressive, darling. You nearly sent me across the yard."

He let go of her foot and she rested her hands on her knees, trying to come down from her adrenaline high. She was thankful that it had been Lucian and not Colton who had arrived without warning. If she'd kicked her son, she wouldn't have forgiven herself. Her fear was beginning to take over and she was in danger of kicking anything and anyone in her vicinity.

"Just letting off steam is all," she said, trying to downplay what just happened.

"Letting off steam? Those were some serious moves. I have not seen technique like that since . . ."

"Since what?" she asked, breaking the silence.

"You remind me of my daughter. When she was young, younger than you even, I taught her how to fight. I did not want her to be in a situation where she was vulnerable and unable to defend herself as I was. My parents nearly succeeded in killing me and I swore I would never let that happen again."

Her expression became sympathetic and she found herself feeling for him in ways she could never have imagined. He was family. "But people still hurt you, right? Solomon killed you and then your own followers killed you again."

"Not to mention my father killed me the first time. Fate had a different idea for me or I would not be here today."

And neither would I, she thought to herself. Cherish wouldn't have been born and she wouldn't have had an affair with Byron Atherton. She wouldn't have had a son and that son wouldn't have seduced Nicola's mother in college. She wanted to tell him these things, but she couldn't. She had to hide her knowledge and pretend that she didn't know she was his great granddaughter.

For weeks, she'd imagined what she would say upon speaking to him. She wasn't sure how to act around him or how she should treat him. Of course, the wise thing to do would be to treat him as she always had — as her mentor and friend. But everything was different now. She knew the truth about who he was to her.

"Why don't we both blow off some steam?" he suggested. "I could help you perfect that kick."

She didn't protest to this idea at all. She wanted to get better and it was hard to improve when all she had was an inanimate bag as a partner. Plus, she wanted to spend time with him. It was like she was seeing him for the first time now that she knew who he was to her.

He took off his shirt and then his shoes. "It is best to learn with less weight. The shoes restrict you from gaining full momentum on your kick."

"All right."

Nicola removed her own shoes then stretched a little before taking a defensive stance. He gave her a refresher course over the basic fighting techniques and then went into new material. He was good and she was impressed. There was one move she couldn't seem to get down, but she refused to give up. Her life depended on it and she wanted to be able to defend herself and her son. She couldn't do that with a defeatist attitude.

When she was sure she wouldn't be able to execute what he'd asked her to, she decided to use a different tactic. She waited for the signs that he was going to move and then she changed her hair from auburn to as red as his. He hesitated his move, visibly thrown off by the change and that was when she struck. She hit him square in the chest sending him back and onto the ground.

"Impressive," he said. "You are very resourceful. Where did you learn to strategize so well?"

"I hear I get that from my paternal grandmother." She had to keep from chuckling when she said that.

"I would love to meet the woman."

She held out her hand and helped him stand. Neither of them was tired but they decided to take a break. They sat in the chairs on the patio and sat in silence. Nicola was proud of herself for successfully taking him down and it gave her hope that she could improve. She had to. At this point, there was nowhere to go but up.

"Thanks for working with me," she said. "I'm sure you really came here to see J.D. and not spar."

"I actually wanted to catch you out here because I have to ask you something."

Why was everyone trying to ask her questions? Gallard asked her to be honest and that resulted in Colton nearly getting run over. She decided she wasn't going to talk to anyone or else someone was going to get hurt. Erik had nearly become a paraplegic thanks to Simeon.

"What do you want to ask me?"

"'Tis about Cherish. I want to know why she hurt you."

Resting her hands on her hips, she sighed in frustration. This whole thing was getting blown out of proportion and she needed to clear it up. There were several things she was sworn off speaking about, but this wasn't on the list.

"Cherish never hurt me, Lucian."

"Darling, please. You don't have to hide anything from me. If you say she hurt you, I will believe you."

"Except she didn't. I never said she hurt me, and I have no idea where people got that idea. Yes, I had bruises, but she didn't cause them. I didn't kill those two kids either and I didn't kiss Gallard."

"Then who did?"

Nicola thought back to the message she'd received after Colton's near accident with the car. The same person had texted again, saying *I won't miss next time. Keep your mouth shut or you'll be seeing your son in a coffin.* She was so frustrated that she could cry. What else was going to happen before they were pleased with themselves? She had done everything Ryan had asked of her and more.

"It isn't safe for me," she said. "I don't know anything about Cherish and I don't know what's going on."

Frustrated, she started to leave but he grabbed her arm. "You are lying. I can see it in your eyes. What has you so terrified that you are running at every rustle in the breeze? What are you afraid of?"

She tensed under his touch and tried to wrench herself from Lucian's grip but then his frustration left his eyes and was replaced with realization. He instantly let go of her and dropped his hand.

"Darling, I apologize. I would never hurt you. You know that right?"

Hugging her arms around her, she cast her gaze to the ground. She did trust him, she really did. But she was going right back to how she used to be — the broken girl who was afraid of being touched. This wasn't how it was supposed to be. She was supposed to be over her fear and yet she was cringing every time someone touched her unexpectedly.

Lucian pulled her into his embrace, and she held onto him, experiencing comfort she hadn't felt in so long. Somehow, it made up for the years that her real father wasn't around. Ryan claimed that her mother had kept her hidden and probably for good reason. He was somewhat delusional and very frightening. She couldn't decide if she preferred that over Edison's cold shoulder. Either way, she would choose Lucian's comforting embrace over both.

"Why don't we go grab dinner?" he suggested. He put on his shirt and then started tying his shoes. He hadn't even broken a sweat during their workout and he still smelled amazing.

"Dinner?" She started speaking in a British accent. "Don't you have more interesting people to dine with, like your fiancé?"

He laughed. "J.D. is spending time with her brother. Besides, I think you are fairly interesting enough."

"Well, good sir, I suppose I shall freshen myself and then join you for supper. Say . . . seven-thirty?"

"Seven-thirty it is. I will be outside by the car."

She excitedly went inside to hurry and shower. It had been too long since she had a pleasant outing, and meeting with Ryan didn't count. They were forced to go to lunch and appear before the coven as a happy couple. Neither of them were happy about it, but Ryan wouldn't lay off.

Since this was a friend date, she wore something semi casual but not too nice. It was so refreshing getting to pick what she would wear without someone instructing her. She chose a sleeveless blouse and dark skinny jeans. Her hair usually was fine when it air dried, so she used the blow drier for five minutes then headed outside. He was waiting as promised, dressed twice as formal as she was. He never wore less than his best.

"Where shall we go?" he asked as they went into town.

"I'm craving something greasy. Have you ever had a burger at that one place by the fabric store?"

"Can't say that I have. I am willing to try new things, though. If it's a burger you want, it's a burger you shall get."

He parked the car down the street from the place and linked arms with her while they walked. Out of the corner of her eye she studied him. He wasn't similar to her father at all, though she'd only seen a photograph. Spencer was tall and had angular features while Lucian's face was less harsh. The only characteristic they shared was the cyan blue eyes. Her mom had green eyes, which made Nicola curious about where she'd gotten her amber hue. Maybe from Byron's side of the family.

"What was your wife like?" she asked.

"You want to talk about my late wife?"

She laughed. "Bad topic?"

"Not bad, just not something I usually discuss. She was a very strange person. Kind sometimes and then cruel the next. I never knew what I was going to get with her. Melody is much like how my wife used to be before our marriage went sour. Resembles her so much as well."

"I don't know who I look like most. I have my mom's hair, only a little darker but I don't really share any characteristics with the rest of my family. I never met my father so maybe I look more like him."

They purchased their food then ate in the food court outside of the restaurant. She watched in amusement as Lucian took a bite.

"That is a very interesting flavor," he said. "What is that red sauce?"

"It's called Ketchup, Red Coat. People put it on almost everything. Burgers, eggs, potatoes. Even hot dogs."

He frowned in confusion. "I've never asked, but are hot dogs made of dog meat? David told me they were, but I'm not sure I believe him."

She laughed until there were tears coming out of her eyes. He was sometimes clueless about the modern world and she found it endearing. He didn't act offended by her laugh but rather laughed with her.

"What is it?"

"Hot dogs aren't really dogs. They're this long sausage made of a combination of different meat, usually beef."

"Ah, I see. That is a relief. Speaking of dogs, I've been thinking Colton would benefit from having a pet."

She hadn't expected him to say that. Truthfully, the idea never crossed her mind. As a child, she'd been denied a pet by Edison several times until finally her grandmother got her a fish when she was ten. When she went away for a camping trip, she came back to find that no one had fed it while she was away. It hadn't been her fault, but Edison refused to let anyone buy her another.

"I think Colton would love a pet. What did you have in mind?"

"How about a dog? A small breed, perhaps. But none of those that bark constantly. A pit bull would be perfect."

She raised an eyebrow. "A pit bull Don't those dogs tend to be aggressive and mean?"

"Not if you raise them right. With the proper care, pit bulls can be quite wonderful companions. From what I've heard."

This comment made her smile as a thought came to her mind. People probably thought the same thing about him. He'd been aggressive and mean in the past but with the help of those around him and the right influences, he'd turned out to be a great man.

"You loved taking care of Lucas, didn't you?" she asked.

"Indeed, I did. It was sort of a second chance to be good father. Sometimes I wish . . . I don't know."

She stopped chewing. "You want another one, don't you?"

"Truthfully I would love to give fatherhood another try. I envy Lucas when I see how good he is with Colton. I also wish that Jordan had a chance to see how wonderful his children turned out to be."

"I think you and J.D. would make very beautiful children."

He laughed. "Oh, really?"

"Totally. Your eyes and her hair. Or even your hair and her eyes. No matter how they came out, they would be very attractive. After you get married, you should seriously think about producing spawn."

He laughed harder this time and she laughed too. This was the weirdest conversation to have with him, but she found it easy to be her real self. Ever since she met him, she found they were similar in personality, quiet and very honest. She was glad she decided to go to dinner with him and couldn't wait for the day she could reveal their familial relations.

"Can I tell you a secret?" she asked.

"You can tell me anything. What is on your mind?"

All this talk about children brought back the sadness she'd had all week from learning the news about her health. She hadn't told anyone except for her new friend in the warehouse. Most of all, she wanted to discuss this with Lucas. If she could escape this life and finally reveal to him what was going on, they may have a future together and this would change everything.

"Two months ago, I found out that I can't have any more kids."

"Oh, darling." He sat back in his chair. "I am so sorry. How did you come to know this?"

"I had a checkup. You know, one of those exams women are supposed to get once a year or whatever. I guess I should have known since I'm a vampire now. Plus, I had so many complications when I had Colton. Having another child would have been risky anyway."

Out of nowhere, she started getting chills and began to look around. She was almost always able to sense when eyes were on her, especially when they were Ryan's. He often spied on her to make sure she wasn't lying about breaking up with Lucas and she had to avoid him at all costs except for switching custody of Colton. She couldn't be around Lucas without looking longingly into his eyes or flirting with him on accident.

"Is everything all right, darling?" Lucian asked.

"I'm not sure." She frantically looked around.

Finally, she spotted Ryan standing across the street. He looked livid and her heart skipped a beat, but then she remembered she was with Lucian. Ryan was still mortal and would be until well after their bonding ceremony. He didn't stand a chance.

Ryan waited for the traffic to cease then made his way towards them. She couldn't pretend she hadn't seen him because they'd already made eye contact. Still, she turned away and took a bite of her burger so she wouldn't have to talk. Lucian turned to see Ryan then they shared the same animosity.

"What are you doing here?" Lucian demanded.

"I saw my girlfriend and wanted to say hello." Ryan leaned over and kissed her cheek. "How are you?"

"Fine. Having dinner with a friend. Lucian, this is Ryan Aspen. Ryan this is Lucian Christophe."

Ryan held out his hand, but Lucian refused it. Nicola chuckled, thinking back to how she'd done the same to Lucian when they'd first met. Ryan then turned his attention to Nicola.

"I called you this afternoon. Where were you?"

"I never got a call, sorry. I've been with Lucian. I am allowed to have friends, right?"

She watched his fist tighten and his jaw clench. He was beyond pissed because she'd been ordered not to consort with Lucian. Ryan hated him and wished him dead. If only she could round kick Ryan like she'd almost done to Lucian. Nothing would give her more satisfaction.

"Yes, but—"

"But what?"

His nostrils flared. "Can I have a moment with you? Alone."

Lucian stood up from the table. "I do not think that is necessary."

Nicola sighed in defeat. If she didn't adhere to Ryan's wishes now she would only be punished later. She put a reassuring hand on Lucian's before following Ryan towards the alley.

"Why are you following me?" she asked.

"Simeon talked to me. He said Ezekiel won't shut up about you. He also said if I don't get my act together, he's going to mate you to Zeke!"

Nicola smirked. "Let him. You obviously don't want to be with me anymore than I want to be with you. Besides, he's nicer."

"You want me to be nice to you? We're both being forced into something we don't want. Why bother?"

"We're only going through with this ceremony because Simeon wants me to join the coven. Does it really matter how that happens?"

"Yes, it does. We had a deal, and if you don't go through with this ceremony, my ass will be on the line! This is my chance to escape this nightmare, and you're going to screw it up!"

She sighed. "Then why don't I talk to him? I'll tell him Ezekiel is a better match, and maybe he'll cut you a break. I'll tell him you recommended the match."

Ryan chuckled. "Oh, he would love it if you two got together. You have no idea what you're saying. Such a match . . . trust me, you don't want to mate him."

"Why, because he's autistic? That's cruel and you know it."

"That among other things. Besides, he's already been mated. He has a son as old as Colton."

Zeke was a father? That made so much sense. He had been so sympathetic when she learned she couldn't have any more children.

"If he's already mated, why would Simeon recommend we get together?"

"Let's just say Simeon has ways of making problems disappear. In your case, the problem would be Zeke's wife."

Nicola's heart skipped a beat.

"He wouldn't."

"Oh, he would. He's done it before with his own wives. I can't tell you how many times he's been married. Your mother got lucky. But I suggest you quit with your chilly behavior and pretend you like me a little. If you cooperate, I may decide not to make this blood match a living hell."

Unable to control herself, she grabbed his jacket and shoved him against the wall with great force. For emphasis, she extended her fangs and bared them to him. His eyes widened in shock and she did her best not to smile. She'd wanted to do this for weeks.

"Listen here, doucheface. The only reason I'm doing anything you say is because I want my son to be safe. I have no loyalty to you or this damn coven. I'll pretend to like you, I'll go through this ceremony, and I'll do it with a smile on my face. Order me around like that again and I just might do worse than throttle you. Got it?"

He nodded quickly. "Yes. Understood."

"Good." She released him and put on a sweet smile, circling her arms around his waist. "I am excited about the ceremony. I can't wait for you to see my dress. Now be a good boy and go give Simeon a positive report."

He then stepped away, allowing her to leave the alley. He crossed the street and she hurried over to the table and returned to her seat across from Lucian. Her burger no longer sounded appetizing, so she finished her drink instead. Lucian kept staring off in the direction Ryan had gone in.

"What ceremony were you talking about?" he asked

She stopped drinking and locked eyes with him. She should have known he would be eavesdropping and now she would have to explain everything, or at least somewhat inform him.

"I'm going to be his blood mate."

He raised an eyebrow. "I see. Is that like some form of marriage?"

"Yes. First there's a banquet, then the couple's first dance, then the bond is sealed with a consummation ceremony."

His eyes widened. "Nicola, tell me you're not doing this."

"I am. I have to. I wish you could understand."

"I do understand. I understand that you are so terrified that you've stooped to breaking up with the man you love. Nicola, please let me help you. We can stop this before it escalates into something dangerous."

She dropped her gaze to the table and a tear slid down her cheek. She was so tired of crying, but she couldn't help it. She was so unhappy with lying to everyone and not being with Lucas. Most of all, she hated how it was affecting Colton. He could see she was unhappy, and he was always doing things to try and make her feel better. She loved him so much and hurting him with her secrets.

"Lucian, there are eighty elders in this coven alone. Eighty. And we don't stand a chance against them if they get pissed off. I'm sorry, but I can't tell you anything."

Nicola got up from the table and ran off, hoping he wouldn't follow. She was going to go back to the warehouse and talk to the one person who she felt the same way as she did about the coven. Someone who wasn't in danger of telling someone that she'd been speaking about what she was sworn to secrecy about. Maybe she could come up with a plan.

40

I closed out of the tab and moaned as I stretched my back. I had been seated in the same position for several hours the past couple of days while trying to dig up information about the Romani covens. While there were several interesting articles about the people, themselves, there was nothing about the vampire covens.

I could pick up where I left off tomorrow. For now, I wanted to get into comfortable clothes and forget about all my troubles for a few hours. I'd sent everyone else home, save for James, and he hadn't had much luck either the last time we touched bases.

We'd worked with a sketch artist to see if the man who had attacked Erik was in the system and we were currently waiting for our guy to search through several photos. James couldn't even find any record of a Ryan Aspen. Like my family, he'd probably used fabricated documents.

Someone knocked on my door and then stepped into my office. James had come back from working with the sketch artist and he had his tablet in his hands.

"Any luck?" I asked.

"Yes. There was a facial recognition in the system." He handed me the tablet. "The man is believed to be a one Spencer Hendrickson. Someone did a sketch of him from a witness back in two-thousand nine when he was under suspicion of statutory rape. But get this. He graduated from the New York Academy of Art back in two thousand fourteen. The guy ages well. He should be in his late forties, but this photo was taken a little less than twenty years ago."

NYAA? If I recalled, Gabriella had graduated from that school the following year. It was too much of a coincidence that she attended the college the same time as Simeon. What was the connection?

"Great, we're getting somewhere."

"Actually, there's more."

I raised an eyebrow. "Oh?"

"I decided to go back even further, and I found records from his enrollment at Saint Leo University. Except then, he went under the name Simeon Atherton. He was in some club called the Ladies and Gentlemen Society. There were five members and guess who was in it."

"Will Smith?"

James rolled his eyes. "No, Mark and Sheila Sharmentino."

My stomach went in knots. It finally happened. This stupid case had managed to link itself to my family. If James did any more research he might get too close.

"What's so special about them?"

James then launched into a story that I knew all too well. His version was extremely exaggerated and completely wrong, but I pretended to be intrigued.

"Their daughter is wanted for murder in San Antonio and she hasn't been seen in twenty some years," James said. "My dad and Tyler went to high school with her and she disappeared just after the murders happened. I think she might be back."

"We'll see. We should have a meeting tomorrow. We still need another member if we don't want SAITF taking over."

"Sure thing, Captain. You should go home. It's nearly eleven o'clock."

I smiled. "I was actually just out the door. You should head out too. Spend some time with your wife and son."

"That sounds wonderful." He grabbed his jacket and shut off the lamp. "I'll see you tomorrow."

We left the precinct together then went our separate ways to our cars. The whole way home, I struggled to stay awake. I'd been invited to go on some sort of family outing, but I wasn't really up for it. My lack of progress was making me discouraged up until James' little discovery. Still, I was exhausted. If this was what Scott did every day, I had no idea how he'd stayed sane. Or he hadn't, which was why he'd resorted to evil scheming with the clinic.

I parked inside the garage then slugged into the house. It was dead quiet, and I was slightly disappointed that I didn't have Colton there to greet me enthusiastically. He was with his grandparents and with my new job, I hardly ever got to see him except to take him to school and kiss him goodnight. I promised myself that on my next day off, we would spend the entire day together.

I was getting a drink out of the fridge when I was startled by movement in the hallway. I turned around just as Cherish came into the room. I'd forgotten she was still staying with us and it made sense that she hadn't gone out with everyone else. She was supposed to be on the down low.

"Hey, Cherry Pop," I said. "How was your day?"

"Very interesting. I went from the couch to the bed to the couch and then I might have gone into the kitchen. No, I went to the couch. My mistake."

I chuckled. "I'm sorry that you're confined to the four walls of the house." I thought some more. "Cherish, what is your son up to?"

The smile left her face. "I don't know what you mean."

"I think you do. Ever since he showed up last month, you've been acting distant. And then people started dying and Nicola broke up with me for some guy she's taking art lessons from. Not to mention my son was almost run down by a car. My suspicions were confirmed when he nearly paralyzed Erik two days ago. I don't know the entire story about Simeon, but I think it's time that you opened-up. One of my men is starting to connect this case with our family and I can't abort the situation if I'm going in blind."

Cherish forced a smile. "When your father found out your mom was expecting you, he suggested I have a child as well. We joked that if I did, the child would be a mixture of Aaron Sharmentino and my mother." She looked up at me. "I was wrong. Simeon is ten times worse. I wouldn't even call him a sociopath. He's a monster."

I reached over and took her hand. "I'm sorry."

"The sad thing is that I still love him." She shrugged. "He's my son. My flesh and blood. I have tried everything I can to get through to him. You know what he said? He said if I slept with him, he would go away. What kind of a sick person does that? I'm his mother!"

I gave her a hug that I knew she needed. I used to think Henry and Ash were deplorable, but Simeon was on a different level.

"So, that's why he's harassing us? Because he wants you?"

"No, he wants something that I have. And I'm afraid that he's close to getting it."

She then began the long task of giving me the history of the Romani coven. It had first begun back in the early fourteen hundreds. Originally, they consisted of real Romanian people but after Simeon took over as leader, it slowly became more of a cult than a familial coven. He recruited people who had no one who would miss them and brainwash them into doing his every will. It was why he was here now — to recruit Nicola.

I finally knew what our attackers were up to. However, I couldn't bring myself to feel relieved. Every moment that Nicola was in their grasp, I was worried sick. Cherish told me about the ceremony traditions and all the requirements that were still in effect hundreds of years later. She was expected to wear a ball gown and dance with all the founding fathers of the coven and then end with a dance with Ryan. They would adjourn to dinner and sit at the head of the table. Then, at the very end, she would have to change into a different dress and they would drink each other's blood, thus making them blood mates and the ceremony would be complete when they consummated the bond in front of the elders of the coven.

The thought of Nicola doing that with Ryan made me cringe. It would be a cold day in hell before I would let that happen. I was determined to find a way to rescue her before that part of the ceremony. The question was how.

"Why did you hurt Nicola?" I asked, trying not to sound hostile.

"I didn't." Tears filled her eyes. "I swear to you, I never laid a hand on her. Those bruises have nothing to do with what's going on."

"Then what happened?"

"I can't say. It's her secret and she'll tell you when she's ready."

I wanted to press it but chose not to. There were more urgent things I could learn.

"How did all of this start anyway?"

"For about a month now, I was starting to feel uneasy — like someone was watching me. I would go out in the middle of the night and try to search for whoever it was. When Simeon showed up, I knew something strange was going on. I decided to play along. I would go and meet him, pretending I was on his side. I thought if I pretended long enough the real culprit would come forward. I wanted to know why she was saying I did it. There had to be a reason.

"After the incident with you getting mad at me and claiming she said I hurt her, I realized something was very wrong. According to you, she was in the presence of that man who was injured at the festival while she was with me at her house. And then Nicola told you that I hurt her when the previous day, she'd asked me for advice concerning her bruises. Then there's that whole thing where she kissed your dad. That was when my suspicions were confirmed."

"What suspicions?"

"I have some ideas. But first, I have to tell you something that is probably going to blow your mind."

"Did you win the lottery?"

She laughed. "Lucas, you are so much like your mother. Always telling corny jokes. No, I didn't win the lottery. It has to do with Nicola."

My phone started ringing, interrupting us. I didn't recognize the number but I answered it anyway. It could be important.

"Hello?"

"Lucas. It's Nic. I'm calling from a payphone."

I mouthed to Cherish who it was then put it on speaker.

"I'm here, what's up?"

"You need to tell Gallard to stakeout Erik's apartment. Robin called the guy who hurt Erik and now he's pissed. She threatened him and I'm afraid he's going to retaliate."

How the hell had Robin called Simeon? How did she even get his number? Either way, I was afraid for her. He'd already gone after Colton and he could easily go after her again.

"I'll send people over there, Nic. Thanks for the heads up. Why are you calling from a payphone?"

"They bugged my phone. If they knew I was passing this message, they would kill me. They might even be watching me right now."

"Where are you?" Cherish asked. "I'm coming to get you."

"No, don't. He's mad at you too, Cher. I'm not letting him hurt you. So far they're convinced that I'm on their side and we need to keep it that way for as long as we can."

"Nic—" I started.

"Please, Lucas. Just take care of Cherish for me. Don't let them know that she's at the house."

Before I could say anything else, she hung up. Her request that I look out for Cherish confirmed Cherish's claims. Nicola wouldn't have been protective of her if she'd been hurt by her. I also wanted to make sure Robin was being watched. That made two people I needed to monitor and I couldn't be in two places at once.

"You think Kevin and Terrence would be able to watch her?"

"Why not Gallard and my father?"

"Because they want you dead more than Robin. I need the stronger man-power here."

41

Y es!" Robin protested.

"No," Lela said.

"Come on, you know it's a good idea!"

"I know that it's not."

Ever since she learned there was a spot open for the task force secretary position, Robin desperately wanted to have the job. She wanted to be in on all the action and help Lucas and Erik take down the evil coven that was causing so much havoc in not only her family's life but those in Euless as well.

She'd been arguing with Lela for the past hour, but her sister wouldn't budge. Robin had stopped by Lela's job to have lunch and to tell her sister about her idea. She'd practiced everything she would say and the moment she started talking, she threw her speech out the window and came up with a spontaneous argument.

"Abe taught me some self-defense tactics. I'm not helpless. I don't have to use a gun or anything, I just want to be a secretary. All I would do is sit at a desk and read articles."

"That was all the previous secretary was doing and look where she is now."

That was a good point. The difference between her and Talia was that she had a bunch of people to protect her. Talia had been a single woman living alone in an apartment. It was easy for someone to break in and kill her. Robin had faith the same thing wouldn't happen to her.

"I have Gallard and Lucas to protect me. Even *you* could protect me. I'll be fine."

"I think she'd be a great secretary," Marcelle said. She was the head stylist and was always giving Robin advice on her relationship. She was a pretty, middle aged blonde and had known Lela for years. She knew all her secrets and didn't have a problem with Lela's identity.

Lela gave Marcelle a stern look who took the hint and returned to the perm she was working on. Lela finished trimming Delores' — a frequent customer's — hair then plugged in a flat iron.

"For arguments sake, let's pretend I agree to let you do this," she said. "How can I do my job when I'm worrying about you?"

"Choose not to worry. I learned my lesson about doing solo missions, and I feel responsible for Colton and Erik's injury. From now on, I will always have a partner."

"Like who? Erik?" Delores said. "Good luck getting any work done. You'll be too distracted by each other."

Almost as if he knew they were talking about him, the front door opened, and Erik came inside the salon. Robin smiled at him, surprised by his visit. She'd told him she would come back to the apartment later that afternoon. He wasn't supposed to be up and around just yet, but he was in uniform.

She rushed over to him gave him a soft kiss while the women in the salon whistled and cheered for them. It was embarrassing but funny at the same time.

"What are you doing here?" she asked. "Not that I don't mind your company."

"I uh . . . I'm not actually here for you."

The smile left her face. That was when she noticed for the first time that he wasn't smiling or acting excited to see her like she was with him. Something was wrong and she had a bad feeling.

"Why are you here then?"

His gaze shifted to Lela and she began to get even more worried.

"I'm sorry, but I'm going to have to arrest your sister."

The women of the salon gasped, and Lela stiffened. Robin realized what was going on here. It had to be related to the secrets she'd revealed to him only two days ago. He said that he accepted her world and hadn't given any indication that he was going to do anything with the information she'd given him. Why was he here now?

"On what charges?" Marcelle demanded.

"The murder of a police officer, aiding and abetting a criminal, resisting arrest, and for the several murders of Johns across the state of Texas."

Several other officers, including Tyler, entered the salon and two held a gun on Lela as another cuffed her. Her coworkers protested and demanded an explanation from her, but she remained silent. She didn't even try to defend herself. Robin could only stand there in shock, unable to accept what was happening.

"Hey, Ty," Lela said.

"Don't you even start," he said coldly. "You should have stayed away, Diane."

"Lela!" Robin finally said. "Tell them you didn't do it! Tell them you're innocent!"

Lela gave her a weak smile. "I can't, hon. Call Gallard and tell him what's going on then call Abe. Whatever you do, stay with him. He'll keep you safe."

The officers escorted her out of the salon. Robin came to her senses and realized that James was present as well. She grabbed his arm to stop him from leaving.

"James, please don't do this!"

He jerked his arm away. "Why shouldn't I? I know all about who you really are, Robin Sharmentino. You lied to me and you lied to Erik. He could have been killed because of your secrets!"

"James, please let me explain," Robin said.

"No! I don't want your explanation! I want to know why you've deceived us all. I trusted and respected Lucas and now I find out he's been hiding vampires away in his home? Your words don't matter. My best friend was nearly killed because of his ties to you. Death follows you wherever you go."

She turned to Erik. The man that she adored and the man she trusted with almost all of her secrets had betrayed her. She felt sick to her stomach and the room swirled around her. Lela was going to prison because she'd stupidly trusted him. Everyone had warned her that dating Erik was a bad idea and she hadn't listened.

"I'm sorry, Robin," Erik said. "I had to. I take my job very seriously. Your sister is wanted for murder in San Antonio and Miami. I couldn't just ignore that."

"You said you wouldn't tell! You said that it didn't matter that my family was made up of vampires!"

"I've known long before you told me who you really were. When I learned Kevin was your brother, I made sure to stay close hoping you would willingly give me information, which you did. I recorded our conversation at my apartment, and I told my dad yesterday. He agreed that this situation is out of control and we've called in backup. They're putting an APB out for Lucas, Terrance Fox, Melody Davis, and Cherish Christophe."

She wiped away the tears that were streaming down her cheeks. She should have known this would happen. He'd played her this entire time. He acted like the dutiful boyfriend and the understanding man whom she'd laughed with and shared secrets with. She thought he cared about her when he only used to her get information about her family so he could arrest them.

"What about me?" she asked. "Do I have to go to jail too?"

Erik shook his head. "Considering your past, I believe you're innocent of anything but association. We're telling SAITF you made a deal — information on your family in exchange for your freedom. That wasn't exactly the situation, but no one has to know."

"What's say-tiff?"

"San Antonio Immortal Task Force."

Robin looked at Erik one last time to see if maybe this was all some huge mistake, or even a nightmare. But the cold look in his eyes told her otherwise.

"I made love to you," she said. "Did it mean anything? Was our relationship all a lie? Is this because I didn't say I love you when you said it?"

"No. It has nothing to do with our relationship." He looked her right in the eye. "And it meant nothing. I'm sorry."

Everything, all her anger, her pain, and her heartache that had been building since her assault flooded her at once. She'd sworn to herself that she would be in control and she'd let herself be used yet again. Before she could stop herself, she lashed out at him.

"Well it didn't mean anything to me either! I was hooking up with Abe while we were dating. Yeah. Why do you think I was so experienced when we were together? Everything I did with you, I learned from him. Now who's the fool here?"

Something flashed in his eyes, but she couldn't read his expression. Hurt? Anger? She didn't care anymore. He'd done the unthinkable and broke her heart. She would never forgive him.

He and James left, and she sank into one of the open chairs. Marcelle told everyone that they would get free styles and was going to close-up early for the day. Robin helped her clean up since Lela wasn't there and waited for Abe to show up. Texting him everything had taken a while, but she couldn't call him. Not if she didn't want to fall apart.

The bell at the front door rang and Robin dropped the broom she was pushing and ran to Abe. He enveloped her in his big arms and let her sob for a while. She cried for at least two minutes before she was able to breathe properly again.

"I'm sorry. I got your shirt wet."

"Don't apologize. You can cry on me anytime."

Marcelle put the broom in the closet. "You go on ahead, hon. We can take it from here."

"Yeah, we're not letting this happen," one of the customers said. It was a woman about the age of Marcelle. She had rollers in her hair. "Your sister has been doing my hair for fifteen years. She has her secrets, yes, but we see her for who she is — a kind and loving soul. We'll do everything we can to make sure she doesn't get prison time."

Robin smiled, thanking her and said her goodbyes then took Abe's hand and left the salon. She felt as if she'd floated down the street because everything was a blur. This was what a broken heart felt like. She'd hoped that she would never experience this, but it had to be inevitable. She'd jinxed herself by dating a McPherson.

She got into Abe's car and he drove back to the house. On the way there, he explained everyone's plans. Gallard had shuttled everyone into Arlington and half were staying in the house he used to live in with David and Lela. The other half were in the house he'd lived in with Lela for the past twenty years. Abe was to take her to the second so Kevin could keep an eye on her.

While Abe waited in the living room, she scurried around her room trying to pack as much things as possible. Not long after, he walked in and she continued to pack while he looked around. She was proud to show him her room because she'd put a lot of work into decorating it.

The color scheme was grey, black, white and pink. Her bed frame was covered in cloth and resembled that of a couch and her comforter was white. She had two fuzzy pillows meant for decoration and the rest were black. There was a pink throw blanket at the end and in front of her bed was a bench with grey material made of the same design as her bed frame. On either side of the bed were green lamps with black shades and a mirror behind them on the wall. She was sad that she may never be able to enjoy it again. Most likely, they would have to move again and as always go on the run.

"I never paid attention to the layout before," he said. "It's so you. I like it."

"Thanks. I don't really like it anymore, but it's better than my old room. I had pink walls and glow in the dark stars on the ceiling."

"Wow. That bad, huh?" he said.

"I was only five then."

"Right. I keep forgetting about that."

"I think my next room will be black. This stupid room is too cheerful for my taste these days."

He moved away from the door and took her hands in his. "How are you doing?"

She bit her lip to keep from crying. She didn't want to cry over Erik anymore. It wasn't worth her time and there were more important things to worry about, like her sister and her family. After all that was resolved, then she might allow herself to get over the breakup. At least she had Abe with her. She would hate to be alone right now.

"I'm fine. I only feel stupid for not listening to everyone. None of this would have happened if I'd just listened instead of going off trying to claim independence."

286

"Hey." He cupped her chin with his hand. "It's not stupid to give someone a chance. You cared about him and he used you. That's not okay with me, not on my watch. He hurt the woman I love and that means he's dead if he so much as looks at you ever again."

She smiled. "Thank you."

His gaze lingered for a bit then he dropped his hand and cleared his throat. "You about ready?"

She zipped her suitcase shut. "Ready."

42

For emergencies, Robin grabbed a couple of the larger sleeping bags from Lela's house as well as two blankets and some pillows. They stuffed it all into his trunk and they were just about to leave when a couple of police cars pulled onto the street. Abe barely had time to start the car and drive out the there. The lights flashed and the sirens blared behind them and he continued to pick up speed.

"We'll have to change our destination," he said. "If we can't get them off our tail, we'll just lead them to their location."

"Then where will we go instead?"

"I don't know. Just sit tight, I'll figure something out."

He made a sudden left turn and they plunged into darkness as they entered a parking garage. The squeal of his tires echoed throughout the lot. He finally parked three levels down and he told her to grab everything and throw it into the truck they were next to. Stealing a vehicle wasn't exactly something she was comfortable with, but this wasn't the best time to argue with Abe. She did as she was told and then he hotwired it.

While he drove, she dug in one of her bags then tossed the item she found at him.

"Put this on."

He picked it up. "Is this a wig?"

"Lela always kept them for emergencies."

She tied her hair into a low bun then tugged a black bob over her scalp. It was snug, but necessary. Since he was trying to concentrate on driving and watching for police, she helped him get into the ugly man wig. It looked like he belonged in an Asian music video. He slowed to the correct speed limit as two cop cars approached and she held her breath until they'd successfully passed by.

Once they were out of the parking garage, he got on the freeway. It was safe for them to remove the wigs, so she put them back into her bag. Going to her family was out of the question now, so he suggested they head for Bedford instead. She didn't really have any objections. It would be hard not to be with the rest of her family, but Gallard would want her safe.

Feeling antsy, she took a cigarette out from her bag and rolled down the window before lighting it. She took in a long drag, letting it burn for a bit then blew out the smoke. She'd missed it. It had been two weeks since she last had one.

"You're still doing that?" Abe asked.

"Don't." She took another drag. "I can do whatever the hell I want."

"Not if it's going to hurt the baby. I'm not going to try to be your boss, but I will be your friend. As your friend, I think you should stop. It's not healthy and it's not going to heal your broken heart. Only time can do that."

She looked at him. This man had taken her by surprise from the moment she met him. He was the opposite of everything she wanted in a partner and yet the very person whom she was supposed to be attracted to had betrayed her. It proved that *meant to be* wasn't exactly accurate. She'd pushed Abe away because she was afraid. Afraid of making the wrong choices and not living up to her sister's legacy. It was then that she realized that she needed to start making choices based on who she wanted to be and not who she wanted to be like.

"I think I've had it all wrong." She tossed the finished cigarette out the window. "As a child, it was my dream to be just like Lela. To be brave and fearless. To have a man as amazing as Gallard at my side through every adversity. But I'm not her. I'm *me*. I may have to figure out what that means, but I'm not going to try and live up to an idea anymore. I think we have a choice in who we are and we shouldn't let what other people think dictate that."

"I think you know what I'm going to say."

She chuckled. "Let me guess— *smart and sexy*?"

He kissed the side of her head and held her hand while he continued to drive. His touch didn't make her uncomfortable anymore. Not because she and Erik were over but because she wasn't afraid to welcome his touch. She needed him right now— her best friend and the person she trusted to always be at her side when needed.

Robin fell asleep along the way and when she awoke, it was nearly dark. She checked her phone and saw that Gallard had texted her to say that Nicola and J.D. were MIA. Robin wouldn't worry just yet. Most likely they were together, and Nicola could take care of J.D.

Her phone rang and she saw it was the clinic. She'd tried to tell them to get lost but for some reason, they wouldn't stop hounding her. She let it go to voicemail then listened to it. They said they wanted her to come in for more tests. What for? She'd come up with a clean bill of health and she knew Lucas had healed her injuries. She should have been fine.

They arrived at some cabin around five o'clock and he parked under the wooden car port. Apparently, while she was asleep, he'd stopped and booked some vacation resort place. She forgot how rich he was and didn't mind at all. She would rather stay in a house than a hotel anyway.

Together, they hauled their luggage inside and because they were both exhausted, mentally and physically, they didn't bother to put it in the rooms and sank onto the couch.

It was a very homey cabin. The outside gave the appearance that it was entirely made of wood, but inside it was insulated and looked exactly like any other house. The floors were hardwood and the walls were a light green. There was a staircase that led to the bedrooms and the kitchen had a gasoline stove. There was a table big enough to fit five and a small fireplace was in front of the couch.

"Great place, huh?" Abe said. "It was the first place that came up when I Googled *resorts in Bedford.* It has a great view from the back and there's a beautiful lake down the hill that's perfect for fly fishing."

"If we're here long enough, you should teach me how."

"Oh, there are a lot of things I would love to teach you. How to drive a boat, how to cook a fish—"

"Can you teach me how to *gut* the fish too?"

He raised an eyebrow. "Really?"

"Oh, yeah! I want to know everything. I want you to teach me everything you know."

"Unfortunately, I don't know how to do any of those things. I don't even know how to bait a hook. I was just trying to sound all backwoodsy."

She laughed. "Abe, you don't have to sound like anything but yourself. That's my new motto— be yourself. That and *They can't fine me if they can't find me."*

The smile left his face and he looked down. She wondered what she'd said to change his mood. He was holding something back and she wanted to know what it was.

"Robin, you've seen how I really am. If I were you, I would have dumped me as a friend long ago. I don't blame you for not taking my affections seriously when you see me with different women all the time."

This was true. Abe was a player who'd slept with dozens of women while in the modeling business. J.D. was even able to pinpoint some of them just by looking at a magazine he'd featured in. Robin read into it as J.D.'s attempt at turning Robin off from him and it had worked at first. She even had a taste of what it was like. Now that she had experienced hurt and betrayal, everything was different.

"Then show me," she said. "Show me the real Abraham."

"I don't think you know what you're asking."

He was right, but oddly she didn't care. He'd said he would never turn her away and though she never thought she would take him up on his offer, she suddenly found herself wanting to. She wanted to forget every moment she'd shared with Erik. Every touch, every laugh, and every smile he'd given her. All of it had been a lie. If she sat around and pondered on it, each memory was going to rip her heart to pieces. She needed to forget, and she wanted to do that with Abe.

"I don't care who you used to be or about your past," she said. "I want you for who you are now. So, please. Kiss me."

Abe pulled her close to him and pressed his lips to hers, holding her tightly. The kiss deepened and he gently swept his tongue across hers. He leaned her back so that she was lying on the couch and lay on top of her. His hands roamed down her sides and rested on her hips. After having spent significant amount of time with him and Erik, she was more experienced, more aware of what men liked.

Robin sat up, exchanging places with him and pushed his shirt up then began kissing his stomach. His abs were rock hard, and she liked how smooth his skin was.

"Robin," he whispered.

"Sh." She stopped kissing him for a moment. "Just relax."

She unbuttoned his jeans then pulled down the zipper. Her movements felt robotic, but she continued. She wanted to feel something other than the pain in her heart. If doing this with Abe could make her forget, then she was willing.

She started to touch him when he sat up and grabbed her hand.

"Robin, don't." He got decent then swung his legs over the side of the couch.

"Why not? It's not like we haven't done this before. It's what you want, isn't it?"

He closed his eyes then held her hands in his. "There is nothing I want more than to be with you. But I can't do this. You should wait for someone better. Someone who won't betray you and doesn't have a history of scorning women. I may have feelings for you but that doesn't mean it would be right."

"It doesn't matter anymore. I . . . I slept with Erik."

The hurt expression on his face pained her, but she had to be honest with him.

"You did?" He swallowed. "And then he betrayed you."

He walked away and she was afraid he was going to punch the wall. His muscles were so tight she could see them bulging through his shirt and the veins in his forearms stuck out. She'd seen him this pent up while he was fighting in his videos but seeing it in the flesh was another thing. She wondered what would happen if he ever truly lost his temper.

"I could kill him," he continued. "If I could get my hands him, I would —"

"No, you wouldn't. You may be a fighter, but you're not a killer. It wasn't like it was with Ash. Yes, he lied, but it was my choice." She got up as well and took his hands in hers. "You said you wanted to be with me and only when I wasn't in a relationship. It's over. We can do this."

Abe turned around to face her and she could see the anger in his expression slowly softening. In the dim light, he looked even more like Jordan and she didn't know if that bothered her or made her feel more for him. Like his father, she trusted him to look out for her and that allowed her to be able to approach him like this with no fear.

She led him over to the couch and undid his jeans once more. He didn't protest but removed his shirt and everything else. Not wanting to bother, she only removed the bottom half of what she was wearing and left her shirt on. Slowly, she coaxed him into sitting on the couch then sat with her knees on either side of him.

His lips met hers and she took his face in her hands as she returned his kiss. His hands slid over her thighs then over her butt until they were resting on her hips. Slowly, they found their way to her most sensitive spot and he started touching her. It drove her wild and made her want him even more.

After a while, he stopped and when she was sure he was ready, she eased herself onto him. A moan escaped his lips and he held onto her tighter. They fit perfectly almost like a puzzle. Like he was her missing piece and she'd finally found him. Neither of them moved for a while, both taking in the magic of the moment. That was the only word she could use to describe this. Magical.

Gently, she rocked against him, and she was overwhelmed with pleasure and ecstasy. He put his hands on her shoulders as they continued moving together. This man was her best friend and now her lover. She wondered if this was what it was like for Gallard and Lela. She trusted Abe completely and she knew there would be no judgement on his part for this. As far as she was concerned, they could carry this secret to their graves.

"You have no idea how long I've wanted this," he said in a breathy voice.

"I wanted you too, but you had a criterion. Wishing you hadn't?"

Looking into her eyes he said, "No. It was worth it."

He picked her up and moved so that they were on the rug and he continued rocking against her. Gradually, he removed the rest of what she was wearing, and she didn't protest.

So, this was what it was like to sleep with Abraham d'Aubigne. She could see why so many women had been unable to resist him. She was unable to, herself. She complemented every movement he made, not want it to ever end.

Once he was spent, his body relaxed, and she rested her forehead against his. They remained joined for a few moments before he moved away and lay next to her. After the fact, she couldn't believe she'd done that. Lela never would have casually slept with someone. Then again, she wasn't Lela. This whole finding herself thing was going to be fun.

"I have no words." Abe smiled at her. "Except I'm glad you're already pregnant. Otherwise I probably would have knocked you up three times."

Robin laughed. "Oh stop. I'm trying to forget about this whole pregnancy."

He gently rested a hand over her stomach. "You're still barely showing. I often forget."

She kissed him. "I know I don't have much time left. It's too hard to think about."

"Just promise me something. Stop smoking. Take care of yourself for the baby's sake."

Robin sighed. "Fine, I'll throw out the cigarettes tomorrow."

He cleared his throat. "Okay, I'm holding you to that. But we should go to bed. I know you're exhausted."

"Can we stay here by there? It's warm enough, and I want you next to me."

"Of course. Let me get you a shirt."

"No." She nestled closer to him. "I want to stay like this."

Abe draped an arm around her, and she closed her eyes. She'd really played it down, but he was right. She needed to start living like she had a human being inside of her. She wouldn't forgive herself if the baby was sick.

She hadn't realized she'd fallen asleep until her phone started ringing. She had to take a moment to wake up and slipped out of Abe's arms. She went into the bathroom so she wouldn't disturb him. Gallard had called her but she hadn't answered in time. She immediately called him back.

"Robin?"

"Yeah, it's me. Do you have an update?"

"I still can't find J.D. or Nicola. Neither of them are answering their phones and Lucas said they weren't arrested. Did you speak to either of them today?"

"Yes . . . I just remembered J.D. went looking for Nicola because she wanted to ask her about what was going on with Cherish. Gallard, what if something happened to her?"

"I'm sure she's fine. We'll find her."

"How? She could be anywhere!"

"Lucian and I are on it, Robin. You and Abe just worry about staying hidden. Don't leave his side. You're safer in twos. And by the way, don't mention this to Abe. I don't want him to worry."

They exchanged a few more words before she hung up. Staying at Abe's side would not be a problem. He made her feel safe. However, she did worry about J.D. Everyone else could take care of themselves but J.D. was helpless. Wherever she was, Robin prayed that Erik would find her before the police did.

She grabbed a blanket from the couch then draped it over them and lay next to Abe once more, hugging him from behind. She was glad that he was there with her and she was worried that something would happen to J.D. She didn't want to lose anyone else, but she trusted Gallard to take care of everyone.

43

J.D. gasped when she saw movement out of the corner of her eye. It was just some stray cat and she felt silly for being so paranoid. If only she hadn't gotten a flat tire, she wouldn't be wandering around the outskirts of town. Not to mention she'd accidently picked up her phone while in a hurry to get out of the house, only to find that some trickster had put her case on Nicola's phone. Stupid, stupid, stupid.

Please tell me you have some sort of weapon, Jordan said.

I do. I have my mental prowess and my handy, dandy pocketknife.

Hah! Your mental prowess?

Shut up! I am very capable of talking myself out of things.

She took out the phone and held it in the air in hopes that the status of her signal had changed. She had zero bars and no way of contacting anyone to tell them where she was. She couldn't even receive texts, and people were probably worried. She hoped that the GPS locater was still working so they would figure out where she was. It was probably not wise to keep walking, but the area next to her car was in the middle of nowhere and she would rather not find out what was hiding in the never-ending fields of sagebrush.

A car drove by and then stopped a few feet ahead of her. She clutched onto her purse, hoping it wasn't some thief out to rob her, or worse a cannibal rapist who wanted to cut her up and keep her parts in a jar. She should have taken her chances with the critters in the sagebrush. The man got out of the car and he looked friendly enough. She put her hand in her pocket and curled her fingers around the pocketknife Gallard had given her.

"Howdy" the man said. "You need a ride, sweet thang?"

His accent was stronger than Erik's, and she found it cheesy. He was wearing jeans and a t-shirt, but he had on cowboy boots.

"No, I don't need a ride, honey buns," she drawled. "I'm enjoying the fresh air."

"That's a shame. Pretty girl like you shouldn't be in these parts alone. There's coyotes and other nasty little critters that can git to ya."

She smiled. "Listen here, Randy Travis, my entire family is made up of vampires, so coyotes are not even remotely frightening to me."

The smile left his face and she knew she'd succeeded. He scratched the back of his neck while he slowly moved closer to his car.

"Well, good luck with wherever you're going. I'll git out of yur hair."

He drove off faster than necessary and she huffed in frustration. If the guy was afraid of vampires, then maybe he wasn't a creep like she initially thought. Her attitude had lost her a chance of getting a ride to the nearest gas station or even a chance to borrow his phone.

You get your mouth from your mom. She isn't afraid to tell people off.

Well, I wish I was nice like you. I also that my best friend would just tell me what was going on with her instead of keeping everything a secret.

Her spirits rose when she saw lights up ahead. It looked like it might be a small diner or restaurant. Since she was in good walking shoes, she picked up her pace and slightly jogged the rest of the way there. She was right about it being a diner. A truck stop, no doubt. There were several semis parked in the lot nearby and there was an old-fashioned gas pump.

When she walked through the door, all eyes fell on her. Everyone was in flannel and cowboy hats while she was in boot-cut jeans, a baseball T, and black Dockers. She hadn't really given thought to her attire like she usually did because she was in such a hurry to leave. There wasn't a single man in there under the age of thirty-eight.

She pretended she wasn't feeling out of place and held her head high as she walked over to the bar. The bar tender slung a towel over his shoulder then leaned against the counter.

"I.D.?" he said.

"Actually, I wanted to use the phone."

"Ah, a Brit. Can't say that I've ever met one before. Here for some tea and a bicky?"

She scoffed in shock. "Stereotypical much? What if I assumed all Texans rode horses to work or went to school in a log cabin? Or I could assume y'all and all y'all swim in the creek up yonder for some mighty fine times. Well Yippy-ki-yay! Sign me up for the next hoe down."

The man blinked. "Phone's by the bathroom. It's by card only. You got one?"

"Yes, thank you."

J.D. hurried over to the phone and took her credit card from her wallet. She hardly ever carried cash on her but was glad this dive had modern phone booths. She quickly dialed Lucian's number. It only rang twice before he answered.

"Jordin Anastasia, where the hell are you?" he asked, without saying hello. How did he even know it was her?

"Hey, babe. Sorry I haven't been answering my phone. I accidently took Nicola's, and I don't get a signal out here and —"

"Do you have any idea how worried we are? Lela was arrested this afternoon and they're looking for the rest of us."

"What? What happened?"

Lucian filled her in on everything that was going on and she wished she hadn't taken off like she did. She needed to get answers and she hadn't really stopped to think. She felt awful about causing everyone to worry.

"Please tell me Nicola is with you," he said.

"No. She got into some car and I followed her but then lost track. I think she's here in Arlington, though."

Lucian mumbled a few expletives. "J.D., where are you?"

"It's some dive called Dickson's Beer and Burgers. It's just off highway 180."

"Alright, don't go anywhere. I'm coming to get you and then both of us are going to try and find Nicola. Stay put until I get there, I mean it."

"Okay! Be careful, Lucian. I love you."

"And I love you. Stay out of trouble."

He hung up and she walked with slouched shoulders back to the counter. Her poor aunt was in jail again and this time, it might not be so easy to just break her out. If Nicola wasn't going to give her an explanation, she might have to resort to teeth pulling.

She ordered a martini then started looking through Nicola's text history out of boredom. Most of them were messages between her and Ryan that made her want to barf. There was wifi in the restaurant, so she used the map to try and figure out where she was. She knew she'd been somewhere in Arlington when her tire blew out, but she didn't know where.

While she was waiting for the GPS to turn on, she noticed there was an address that was already typed on the search box. Curious, J.D. tapped on it to see if maybe it led to the secret hiding place of the coven. This information could be useful to Gallard and might help them stop Ryan and his followers more quickly. The address loaded then a pin dropped in its location then it created a route from her location to the other one. If the computations were right, she was only fifteen minute's walking distance away.

"Excuse me, miss," she said to the waitress.

"What can I do for you, sugar?"

"A gentleman is supposed to pick me up here, but I need to run an errand. I don't know if I'll make it back in time, but could you give him the address of where I'm going?"

"Sure thing. Just write it down so I won't forget."

J.D. found an old receipt in the bottom of her purse and scribbled the address as well as the directions on there then handed it to the woman. "The man's name is Lucian Christophe. He has red hair, blue eyes. Basically, the epitome of gorgeous. You can't miss him. Tell him his fiancée gave you this note."

She paid for her drink then hopped off the bench and rushed out the door. Thankfully, there were written directions for how to get to the other location and she followed them. Her energy had suddenly returned, and she no longer felt drained from walking so much. She jogged down the road, scanning up ahead for the outline of a building or a house. It could be a farm, for all she knew.

After twenty minutes, she almost gave up and turned around when the blue dot on the map lined up with the red one. She stopped walking and did a three-sixty turn. Her eyes adjusted and that's when she saw the warehouse about two hundred feet off the road. She used the light of the phone to look for a path and then quieted her steps as she approached the warehouse. Up close, it was extremely ominous, and she wondered if she should have waited for Lucian before playing Nancy Drew.

She was about to put her hand on the doorknob when her father's voice blasted inside of her head.

Jordin Anastasia! Are you out of your mind?

Dad, I have to know what's in there. What if it's the coven's hiding place?

Exactly! It could be their hiding place and then you'll be all alone without anyone to save you!

What am I supposed to do? Miss this opportunity?

Turn around, go back to the diner, and wait for Lucian.

Oh, so now you want me to be with him.

It has nothing to do with romance. I want you to be with him so you can be safe. You are in dangerous territory.

I'm sorry dad. I feel like I need to do this.

Without further ado, she tuned out his voice and opened the door. It smelled strange inside, like dampness or like it had just finished raining. Everything was dark. She took a few steps forward then turned the phone on for light, but she'd done it a moment too late.

She didn't see the descending stairs and missed the first step, tripping and falling. She rolled about six times before landing at the bottom with a splash. She moaned in pain, clutching at her leg. She'd rolled her ankle and it hurt so bad she wanted to cry.

"Hello?" someone said.

J.D. stopped moaning and looked around. She realized she was sitting in about a foot of water and stood up, struggling to walk. Each step felt like knives were in her foot and she had to slightly drag her ankle behind her as she hobbled down the hall. Someone was down there.

"Is someone there?" J.D. called.

"Nicola, is that you?"

The voice was coming from the room at the end. It didn't sound threatening and she could have sworn she'd heard it before. She pushed open the door and tried to see inside. She took the phone from her pocket and swore when she saw it was broken. The screen light wouldn't even come on.

"Who's there?" she said again.

"Can't you see me?"

J.D. stepped forward until she saw the outline of a woman against the wall. With further adjustment to her vision, she saw the chain on the woman's ankle and that it was attached to the wall.

"Who are you?" J.D. asked. She shuffled through the water then plopped down on the ground, no longer able to stand.

"Dominique. My father put me down here as punishment. Who are you?"

"I'm J.D. I found this place on my friend's phone."

The woman looked up. "You're J.D.? I know you. Nicola spoke of you often. She said you were a great friend."

J.D.'s heart sank. She'd been somewhat frustrated with her friend for weeks, but maybe there was more going on than J.D. wanted to see. Had Nicola been forced into all of this? She had to be. Why else would she visit this poor woman who was locked in here?

"How long have you been down here?"

"A few weeks. She was supposed to be here before sundown. I'm afraid something's happened to her."

J.D. looked around and saw that the water had risen at least four inches in the past five minutes. "Has it always been so wet?"

"No. The pipes are old, and they burst about a half an hour ago. I'm so glad that you came because at the rate the water is rising, I would probably be dead in a matter of hours."

J.D. forced herself to stand up and began looking around. She didn't know how she would get Dominique unchained, but she needed to find a way. If not, her only other option was to wait and hope Lucian would get her message in time. There was no way she could make it back to the diner with her injured ankle.

She went over to the bed and unhooked one of the bars from the frame. It wasn't much, but at least it was something. She struggled to carry it over to Dominique and then looked for a spot of weakness on the chain.

"You think that will work?" Dominique asked.

"Not sure, but I am willing to try."

J.D. struck the chain over and over until her arms burned from exhaustion. She was running out of steam, but still she struck it. She wasn't going to let this woman die here, stranger or not. Her adrenaline kicked in long ago, so she no longer felt the pain in her ankle.

The water rose up to her knees and it suddenly hit her. She wouldn't be able to break the chain. The water would restrict her from getting enough momentum behind her strikes. Out of desperation she held her breath then went under and began pulling on the chain, trying to slide it over Dominique's foot. She tugged and tugged with no results. Dominique finally had to pull her up from the water.

"You need to go," she said. "If one of us is going to make it, it should be you."

"No, I'm not leaving you! We can do this!"

Dominique gave her a smile. "Nicola was right about you. I wish I could have gotten to know her better. Both of you are amazing women."

"Who are you?" J.D. asked.

"I go by Dominique Atherton, but my birth name is Dominique Taylor. I'm Nicola's sister."

J.D.'s eyes widened in shock. Another sister? Why hadn't she said anything? Then again, she hadn't told Nicola about Abe either so she had no room to judge.

"That's cool," she said to make light of the situation. "I wish I had a sister. I do have a brother, though. Why did Nicola keep you a secret?"

"Nicola didn't know about me. Our mother gave me up for adoption after I was born. We figured it out when we learned we had the same father. She said I have her mother's eyes. Someone clued her in to my whereabouts and she found me. She's been bringing me food and clothing."

J.D.'s heart began to break. Nicola may have made her angry, but she was still her friend. How could she leave Nicola's sister behind to die? It would be the cruelest thing J.D. could do. She wasn't about to give up just yet. Nicola would get to know her sister one way or another.

J.D. raised the bar above her head and prepared to bring it down when Dominique gasped. J.D. turned around and saw Nicola standing in the doorway.

"Thank God! Nic, I need your muscle. I can't break this chain!"

Nicola looked at Dominique then back at J.D. She didn't move and J.D. was confused. Her sister was going to drown if they didn't act quickly. Why wasn't she rushing to help?

"I didn't think it would be this easy to get you here. Switching our phones was too easy." Nicola smiled then stepped forward. J.D. was going to speak when Nicola pushed her down. "You're too nosy for your own good, J.D. When are you going to learn to stop playing hero?"

"Nic? What's going on with you?"

"Oh, no . . ." Dominique said. "Baby sister, please stop!"

Nicola ignored her sister's pleas and stepped on J.D.'s injured ankle. J.D. cried out in pain. She started to get dizzy but maintained consciousness. Her ankle hurt beyond measure but nothing hurt more than her friend's betrayal. J.D. looked up at her and saw a hatred that she didn't think was possible.

"Why are you doing this?" she asked, trying not to cry. Nicola pressed harder on her ankle and J.D. yelled again.

"I have nothing against you, personally. I'm just making sure you're completely helpless. It's someone else who has beef with you."

Ryan into the room and J.D. glared at him. He had a smug expression on his face, and she wanted to punch it right off. If only her ankle wasn't busted three times over, she would have gotten up and kicked his ass.

"Thank you, my love," He said. He then kissed Nicola on the lips. "You did well. Now go wait for me in the car. I'll be right up."

Nicola nodded then left the room and with her, went all of J.D.'s hope that she would make it out of there alive. Nicola hadn't even given her own sister so much as a glance.

"So. You are the one Lucian loves," Ryan said. "Isn't this your lucky day?"

"What do you care who he is to me?"

"Oh, I care. He killed my mother and I feel he should pay for his crime."

J.D. frowned. "Your mother? Who was your mother?"

"Ajala. You see, she was chosen by Melody Christophe to give Lela Sharmentino the last bit of Lucian's blood. When Lucian returned, he killed her based on association for her ancestor's part in killing him and his daughters, leaving me motherless."

"I'm sorry you had to go through that. But he feels remorse for what he's done. He hasn't taken a life in years. Not without just cause."

Ryan closed his eyes. "Just cause. *Just cause!*" He stepped towards her and she tried to hit him with the bar, but her injured ankle kept her from being able to stand. He wrenched it from her grasp. "Just cause would be to beat you to death with this very bar! He needs to know what it's like to lose the one person he cares about more than anyone."

"Then do it." She glared at him. "I'm not going to beg for my life, not now or ever."

He smirked. "You're no coward. Why else would you come here alone? It was a grave mistake, I'm afraid. Simeon wants you dead, I want to hurt Lucian— it's a win-win for me."

J.D. frowned. "Why does Simeon want me dead?"

"Not just you. He wants the entire d'Aubigne line gone. He left your mom in that house to die with her unborn twins, but your father saved her. Simeon killed your father, and he's hell bent on finishing you off once more. First you, then your brother, then that freak of a cousin you have." He lifted the bar. "Don't worry, I'll make it quick."

No don't!" Dominique shouted.

When he brought the bar down, it struck J.D.'s head so hard that she only felt pain for a short second before she blacked out. While she lay there in sleep-like state, she thought of Lucian. She wished she could have seen him one more time— that she could have walked down the aisle with him and had his children. But what let her finally slip away was the thought that the short time she'd had with him had been enough and that she would be okay with dying with his name in her heart.

44

Nicola pushed her way past the crowd in Dickson's Beer and Burgers and grabbed one of the menus from the stand. She had spent her entire day with Ryan getting ready for the ceremony that would be taking place in two and a half days' time. Tonight had probably been the hardest and she felt bad for ditching J.D. It was the only way to keep Ryan from being suspicious of her loyalty.

She chose the beer battered chicken and fries. It was busy for the time of night and everyone's gazes were fixed on the TV. Nicola had no interest in the news, so she pretended to be interested in the Farmer's Almanac from two thousand twenty-two. Her distracted thoughts kept her from being able to focus on the words and she kept anxiously tapping her foot.

Her attention switched from the almanac to the waitress as she approached the counter.

"Hey, you! Back again I see," the waitress said.

"How have you been, Betty?"

Betty smiled and patted her swollen belly. "About ready to pop. Gordon and I have everything ready. Now all we need is a baby to put in the crib."

Nicola loved talking with Betty. Of course, she could never discuss the dark things going on in her life, but she often spoke to her of Lucas. This was the one place besides the warehouse where she had people who she could talk to. Betty was one of them. Betty knew all about Nicola's love for Lucas and for her son. She sometimes asked for advice and Betty knew quite a bit about relationships. Being a happily married person with her first child on the way, she would always know what to say to give Nicola hope.

"I would love to have another baby," Nicola said. "If only that weren't impossible."

"Oh, sugar, everything will be all right! You'll see. When that man of yours finds out your secret, he'll adopt all the babies you want."

Nicola laughed. She couldn't imagine Lucas and her settling down with a bunch of babies in tow. He was too much of a hero for that. He wouldn't be able to resist saving someone's life or righting a wrong. And she loved him for that. However, she wouldn't mind adding another to their little family. He was so good with Colton. She had a feeling he would be a great father regardless if the children were his. That discussion would have to be brought up in a few years.

Betty's husband, Gordon, came over with the food packaged and tied in a sack. Nicola thanked him then took out her wallet to pay for it. She was handing her money to Betty when she noticed her attention was elsewhere.

"Oh my," Betty said.

"What is it?"

"Not too long ago, a young lady asked me to deliver a message to a gorgeous man with red hair, and I think he's just arrived. Gorgeous doesn't even seem to describe him."

Nicola immediately turned around and saw Lucian just as he'd come into the door. He was looking around and then finally they locked eyes. What was he doing here? And what young lady was meeting him here. Could it have been J.D.? Nicola handed Betty the money then hurried over to Lucian.

"What are you doing here?" they said in unison.

"J.D. called from the payphone," he explained. "I was to pick her up here. Is she with you?"

"No, I haven't seen her since we had breakfast earlier today. Why was she here?"

"Looking for you. She said she accidently took your phone. I don't see how, considering she has a black case with pink trim and a diamond J on the back. Yours is blue. How could she mix them up?"

"Excuse me, sir?" Betty said. She pushed the swinging door with her hip and walked over to them with a piece of paper in her hand. "This was left for you by a young woman with black hair and eyes the color of the Hawaiian waters. She said you were her fiancé."

Lucian took the paper from her and read it. He then groaned and handed the paper to Nicola. She read it too and recognized the address. It was the warehouse where Dominique was being kept.

"We need to leave," she said.

"Agreed. Thank you, miss for passing the message."

Lucian put a hand on Nicola's back as they hurried through the crowd and she got into the passenger side of the Scion. He informed her of everything that was going on with the police and the family. Apparently, the San Antonio immortal task force put out an APB for Gallard, Melody, Cherish, and Kevin. They were the only ones that were mentioned in the reports having to do with Lela's case. As far as he knew, all but Lela were safely hidden.

He had to speak quickly because the warehouse wasn't too far away. He parked in front and they both hurried out. She wasn't too worried about J.D. discovering Dominique, but she was concerned that Ryan might be lurking around. He'd forbidden her from visiting, but unlike his other demands, she'd refused to abandon her sister.

Lucian opened the door and when she water running, her heart lurched. She had been concerned about the pipes during her last visit, but Dominique assured her that the pipes had been making noises for weeks. They must have finally burst.

"Dominique! J.D.!" she screamed. She rushed inside and down the stairs with Lucian behind her. The water had reached the fourth step, leaving barely any breathing room. The gap between the surface and the ceiling was about ten inches at the most. She plunged into the dark water then came back up feeling her way down the hall.

"Are you sure the room is this way?" Lucian asked.

"Positive!"

While she swam, she bumped into something and her heart skipped a beat. It was a body. She quickly turned it over and gasped in shock when she saw the person's face. Ryan's face. There was a stab wound on his neck and he was pale from loss of blood. Someone had murdered him, but why?

She pulled his coven necklace from his neck then pushed him out of the way. Swimming further, she found the door then took a deep breath before going under. Her night vision kicked in and she saw that there was a chair shoved underneath the doorknob. Ryan must have found J.D. there and locked her and Dominique inside.

A rage she'd never known coursed through her as she jerked the chair away and Lucian kicked the door in. Together, they swam inside, and she saw the two women. Nicola broke through the surface and took a gulp of air as she moved towards them.

"Nicola!" Dominique called.

"Thank God you're alive!" Nicola said. "I thought I was too late!"

She and Lucian sped over to them, Lucian taking J.D. in his, arms and Nicola latched onto her sister. There was now only a head's length of space left and she needed to make the most of it so she could get her sister to the stairs before she ran out of air. As she swam, she looked over to J.D. and froze in panic when she saw the cut on her head.

They swam as quickly as they could down the hallway and once they got to the stairs, Nicola eased her grip on her sister and they walked the rest of the way up and out the door. Dominique fell to the ground, breathing hard and erratic. It must have been hard for her to tread water with the chain attached to her leg and Nicola admired her endurance. Once the relief of having rescued the women had set in, she glanced over at Lucian who was frantically trying to give J.D. CPR.

"Come on, darling! Wake up!"

"What happened down there?" Nicola asked her sister, trying to focus on something other than J.D.'s pale complexion. "How did you get free?"

"She was trying to help me and Ryan showed up. He locked us in," Dominique said. "He hit her in the head with one of the bed posts. Three times."

"He must have come here to see if I was still visiting you. But how did you get free?"

"There was another man. I couldn't see his face, but he broke through the window. When he saw that I was chained, he broke it and then pulled J.D. up to the surface. He left literally thirty seconds before you came."

This man must have been the same one who had killed Ryan. He'd known Dominique was down there? And if he'd left shortly after their arrival, he could still be close by. She was curious to know who this mysterious hero was.

Nicola moved closer as Lucian breathed into J.D. and continued giving her compressions. In her heart, she knew that this was all pointless. If Ryan had hit her head, she was probably already dead from the blow. Either that or she'd drowned after losing consciousness. J.D. was too still and the cut on her head was terrible.

"Jordin Anastasia, you wake up right this moment!" Lucian demanded. "You're a d'Aubigne. You're supposed to be able to cheat death."

Dominique began to cry, and Nicola hugged her sister close to her. This was all her fault. If she hadn't been too afraid to tell someone what was going on, J.D. wouldn't have done her usual thing and tried to search for her own answers. Now she may never laugh, fight with, or share the company of her good friend again.

"I told her to leave," Dominique said. "I told her we both wouldn't make it out, but she wouldn't leave me. She wouldn't leave."

Nicola tightened her embrace and tried to comfort her. How could she give comfort when all she wanted was for someone to comfort her too? But someone needed to be there for J.D.'s family — for Gallard and —

"Lucas," she said. "We need to call Lucas! He can help her."

Lucian remained motionless. He'd stopped trying to revive her and was holding her in his arms, his eyes void of emotion. Nicola released Dominique and hurried over to him, shaking his shoulder.

"Lucian! Come on! We need to get her to Lucas!"

He slowly brought his gaze to her and then nodded, standing up. She knew he was in no position to drive, so she took the liberty of getting into the front seat. She drove about fifteen over the speed limit and the diner went by in a blur. Thankfully, Lucian had left his phone in the car so it wasn't damaged by the water. She dialed Lucas' number and waited.

"Did you find them?" Lucas asked.

"Luke, it's Nicola."

"Thank God! You have no idea how happy I am to hear your voice."

"There's been an accident. I don't have time to explain, but I need you."

"Just tell me who's hurt and what I need to do."

Love swelled inside of her. He was so trusting and willing to help.

"It's J.D. Please don't mention this to anyone, but she suffered a head injury and we've been unable to revive her."

Lucas grew silent and she could feel his anguish through the phone. Tears stung her eyes as she looked in the backseat at Lucian who was still holding J.D. and rocking her lifeless body. She was dead. Nicola knew that, or else J.D. would have shown signs of life by now. Lucas was their only hope.

"Bring her to my parents' old house. It's in Arlington. 2643 Evergreen. It's in a cul-de-sac."

"I'll be there. Lucas—"

"I know. Everything will be okay, I promise."

She hung up the phone and continued to drive while struggling not to fall apart. Ryan had mentioned wanting Lucian to pay for murdering his mother, but she never thought he would go as far as killing J.D. He had no reason to hurt Dominique so that had to be the reason he locked them in there. Her hate for him intensified and she was glad someone had killed him before he could hurt anyone else.

The street sign appeared up ahead, and she started to turn onto it when she saw the spikes in the road. She hit the brakes, but she had been going too fast and she drove right over them, tearing up all four of the tires. The car screeched as it skidded across the road then came to a halt. Her heart was pounding, and she checked everyone to make sure they were all right. Dominique was fine but shaken up and Lucian had finally snapped out of his grief-stricken state.

"What happened?" he asked.

"I think we're in trouble."

Not long after she spoke, a dark figure appeared in front of her. By the style of the cloak, she recognized the man as a coven member. She started to get out when four more cloaked figures appeared, and she realized what was going on. This was a trap, no doubt. A glare formed on her face and she opened the door, getting out and slamming it behind her.

"Get out of my way," she threatened.

"Or what?" one of the men said. "You are outnumbered. You've been causing problems for too long and we're here to put a stop to it."

She clenched her fist, preparing for any fighting she would have to do. Someone came up behind her and she quickly went into action, elbowing him in the face. Another approached her and she quickly did as Lucian taught her and rotated her hip more before executing a kick, knocking the man onto his back.

Someone caught her off guard and started choking her from behind. The frame felt small and she discerned it was a woman. But this woman had no idea that she was a vampire with strength twice that of a night-walker. She flung the woman over her shoulder, slamming her to the pavement.

The other men had started to come at her, but she could see the hesitance in their eyes. A smile formed on her lips. They were afraid of her. This was the best feeling in the world — to be the one inflicting fear instead of the one being fearful.

"Let us by or I'll do the same to the rest of you," she threatened.

"We apologize," one of the men said.

He removed his hood and knelt to the ground. Soon, the rest of those who were present one by one did the same thing and then every single one of them were bowing to her.

"We have been waiting for you," the man said. "Ask anything of us and we shall do it."

That's when she recognized the man.

"Zeke?"

He looked up, and though it was dark, she could see his golden eyes.

"Yes, it's me. I've been looking for you, Nicola."

"Get up you fools!" someone shouted.

Nicola turned around to see another man emerge from the darkness. He was tall, about six-one and had dark hair and blue eyes. He was as young as the man in her mother's picture album. All these years and she was finally face to face with her father.

"Simeon," the Ezekiel said. "What are you doing here?"

"I came to find you. I was told you were not at your assigned location."

The car door closed, and she saw that Dominique and Lucian had gotten out. She wished her sister would stay in the car where it was safe. Spencer had been the one who locked her in the warehouse because she'd defied him and had an affair with a man outside of the coven. That man was now dead, and she was forced into temporary exile.

"Hello, Spencer," Nicola said. "Or Simeon. Whatever your name is."

He slapped her across the face before she even saw him raise his hand. This wasn't exactly the way she'd imagined her first physical contact with her birth father would be. A handshake, maybe, but not a slap. She should have known, since he was a Christophe after all.

"You disgrace me," he said. "Killing members of your own coven. Gallivanting around with *him*."

Lucian stepped forward. "I don't care that you're my grandson. If you strike her again, I will make you wish your mother had never laid eyes on your father."

Simeon threw his head back and laughed, startling everyone present. It gave Nicola chills and not in a good way.

"Sometimes I wish the same thing. But then, you wouldn't have this," he put an arm around Nicola, "lovely woman as a descendant."

Lucian's eyes flashed with astonish. "What are you saying?"

"Lucian Christophe, meet your great granddaughter Nicola Atherton."

"What!" Lucian looked at Nicola. "This whole time. She's so much like my daughter and I thought it coincidence."

"I do regret having children of my own, but maybe if they were raised in a different time, they would not be so rebellious."

"You said they. What do you mean *they*?"

Simeon's gaze wandered over to Dominique and Lucian's followed. He looked at Nicola and then back at her sister, the realization clear in his eyes. Nicola longed to go to him and explain everything, but Simeon's hold on her was too firm and the bones in her shoulders ached.

"What is your business here?" Lucian asked.

"My daughters have disobeyed my orders. Dominique is exiled and Nicola is well on her way down that path as well. She was to be bonded with Ryan Aspen, thus making her a member of the coven but now that he is dead, she upsets my plans for her. It doesn't matter. I still intend to start a war against the mortals."

Lucian smirked. "A war you say? It appears we have the same idea. Only ours does not involve violence, unfortunately."

Simeon raised an eyebrow. "Similar ideas? Do explain."

"I assume you know Lucas. He currently has people out gathering troops for our cause."

"Is that so? Since when does the infamous Lucian Christophe answer to the likes of a fledgling like him?"

"Well, he is your grandson's father after all. If I were you, I would meet the man and join forces. No one else need be harmed because of conflicting interests."

Nicola held her breath as she waited for Simeon's reply. This would be too good to be true— for both sides to join for a similar cause. There wouldn't be any more plotting or fighting. She could finally be honest with her family and maybe she wouldn't be forced into binding herself to a member of the coven. The whole point of it was to ensure she would be on their side during the war. But if both sides became one side, plans could change.

"Get me a meeting with Lucas," Simeon said. "And I will consider your request."

"If I arrange the meeting, you have to let me take Nicola and her sister into my care. None of that degrading ceremony and blood mate rubbish. Nicola is to be released from her engagement and Dominique pardoned for whatever she was exiled for."

Nicola was suddenly jealous of Melody and Cherish to have such a great father.

"We have a deal. Tell him to come to the football stadium in Bradford. He has three days to comply or I will alert the police of you and your family's whereabouts." He released his grip on Nicola's shoulders. "Goodbye, my daughter. You must be relieved to not have to go through with the ceremony. It doesn't matter to me. I've never met a greater disappointment in my life."

A black limousine drove up and he gave her a malicious smile before getting in and the rest of the coven members followed. Immediately after, Dominique shuffled over to her, dragging the clumsy chain behind her and hugged Nicola. She knew exactly what her sister was feeling— free. They were no longer bound to the coven and its demands.

Lucian reached into the back seat of the car and lifted J.D.'s body out. She could see he was struggling to hold himself together. Nicola clasped Dominique's hand and together, the three of them walked the rest of the way to the safe house.

45

I couldn't handle being there when Lucian brought J.D. into the house. I left the room and went to the backyard, struggling to not have a catatonic episode. Memories of Mona flooded my thoughts and I nearly buckled to the ground. Nicola hadn't explained what had happened over the phone because she was pressed for time, but I didn't want to know. J.D. was dead and now all the pressure was on me to ensure she would come back.

While I stood on the lawn, I felt the ground begin to shake. It was subtle, but I took a few deep breaths to try and calm myself down. My mom was in jail and J.D. was dead. How much worse could this day have gone? At least the rest of my family was safe.

Seeing Lucian in such anguish was like witnessing Micah grieve Mona's death all over again. The overwhelmed part of me didn't want to fix this, but to run away from these issues. The part of me that still hadn't given up was determined to turn this situation around.

I sank until I was crouching on the ground and wept. I wept for J.D. I wept for Mona. I wept for the danger my family was in. And I wept for Micah, who was still waiting for me to come back to Florida and rescue him. There was so much at stake and all of it seemed to be weighing on me. I tried to hold the family together while Gallard was away and even when he'd returned. I'd failed.

Someone put a hand on my shoulder, and I was too emotional to turn around and see who. Whoever had come out to comfort me, I appreciated it. I had stopped weeping as heavily as before, but my chest still ached from the sorrow. I almost wished that I was more like Gallard and didn't have a heartbeat. Maybe my heart wouldn't ache if I didn't have one. It even hurt to breathe.

Looking up to the sky, I did something I had never done before. The Wrights were not religious, aside from Scott's mother and the Taylors were Catholic, though not practicing. I didn't think I believed in God, but lately too many miraculous events had occurred. My entire life, I'd heard of the Sharmentino Curse, and yet I was blessed with abilities anyone could only dream of.

"God," I said. "I probably should have spoken with you sooner, but . . . I wasn't sure how. My family's in danger, and I don't know what to do. All I want is to right all the wrongs. I don't know why I have these gifts, or why my uncle thought I was the best person to wield them, but I could use some guidance."

+"Even the Lord Jesus himself wept when Lazarus died," my comforter said. "He knew he would be able to resurrect him and yet he still grieved the loss of his friend."

I recognized the voice and stood up. "Solomon? When did you get here?"

"Gallard called me immediately after he learned of Lela's imprisonment. I flew straight here, and David is coming with Arnaud."

I embraced him, feeling as if a million pounds had been lifted from my shoulders. He had no idea how much his return had given me hope. We needed him terribly and here he was just when everything was starting to look hopeless. With him and Gallard both leading us, we were bound to come up with a plan.

"Is she still . . ."

Solomon nodded. "I examined her when I arrived. It appears that she is currently in transition. Her body is cold, yet she is not showing signs of decay or rigor mortis. It is almost as if she were asleep. Her eyes are also changing colors. It is a very intriguing thing to see, but also so devastating."

"I will do everything in my power to help her. I only needed a minute."

"Take your time, Lucas. She is not going anywhere."

I closed my eyes. "Her body might still be here." I then opened them again. "We can't say the same thing about her soul."

We went back inside and, I inquired about J.D.'s whereabouts. Melody and Cherish had taken her upstairs to clean her up and get her into some dry clothes.

While I waited, I went searching for Nicola. She'd disappeared somewhere in the house with the other woman and I was curious to know who she was. I went upstairs, listening for voices. I heard two coming from the bedroom at the end of the hall and I knocked on the door.

"Come in," I heard Nicola say.

I slowly pushed the door open and was greeted by her smile. She and the woman were sitting on the bare mattress, bundled in blankets and they looked so cozy.

"Lucas, I would like you to meet my sister, Dominique. Dom, this is Lucas. Colton's father."

"I'm glad I can finally meet you," Dominique said. "You can't tell by looking at us, but we do share a father."

I studied this woman who was apparently also a Taylor. She looked nothing like Nic. Dominique was taller than her, curvier, and had dark brown hair that hung barely to her shoulders. She also had fuller lips she'd inherited from Cherish.

"It's a pleasure to meet you," I said. "I hear that you tried to help J.D."

"Only after the mysterious man saved me first. If he hadn't broken my chain, we both would have died."

"Mysterious man?"

Dominique filled me in on the events of that night. I wasn't one hundred percent sure, but I had an idea who this person might be. I would think about that later.

"Do you think you can help her?" Dominique asked.

I wanted to say that it was inevitable, but I didn't want to be over-confident. I could heal people more easily now, but Robin was the only person I'd ever brought back to life and that had been unintentional. I was afraid to promise anyone anything in case it didn't work. I had to believe it would, though. Everyone was counting on me. Lucian was counting on me.

Someone knocked quietly on the door and the two women stood up as Gallard entered.

"She's ready for when you are," he said in a somber tone. "We're putting her on the couch. Is that okay?"

"The couch is perfect. I'll be down in a moment. I just need some time to prepare."

I looked back at Nicola and Dominique must have sensed that I wanted to speak with her alone because she followed Gallard out of the room, closing the door behind her. It was difficult not throwing myself at her and sinking into the comfort of her embrace. I had to control myself and speak with her first.

"Your sister seems nice," I said as an icebreaker.

"She's great. It's like we've known each other our whole lives."

We both grew quiet and I tried to think of what I would say. I didn't have to lie and pretend I didn't know the truth about her and Ryan. I needed her and couldn't wait a second longer for her to be in my arms again.

"Do we have good news?"

"Yes." She smiled. "Simeon made a deal with Lucian. I'm no longer tied to the coven."

I did what I desired most and wrapped her in my embrace. My arms had felt so empty without her there and now that everything was out in the open, I never wanted to let her go. I loved her for making such a hard sacrifice and nearly binding herself to another man all for the sake of our son. He had one hell of a mother and I had one hell of a girlfriend.

"I have to help J.D.," I said once we'd shared a comfortable silence. "But I can't do it without you. My gifts always seem to work better when you're with me."

"I'll be at your side. Now, tomorrow, and every day after that. I love you, Lucas. Thank you for waiting for me."

I leaned in to kiss her then stopped. "Next time we fake break up, don't kiss my dad. It's gross, no matter how young he looks."

"Lucas, I never—forget it. I'm done arguing. Just kiss me."

I pressed my lips to hers, kissing her as if this were the first time I was doing it. I wanted to stay this way for hours, never letting her go but J.D. was counting on me. I didn't know what to do about my mother yet, but I had faith that with my dad and Solomon's help we would figure everything out.

Hand in hand, Nicola and I went down the stairs and found everyone in the living room. Solomon and Cherish were holding hands. Gallard seemed a little lost without my mother there and was leaning against the wall with his arms folded and his head down. Melody had an arm around Dominique, and I assumed she'd learned from Lucian that they were related.

Lucian was kneeling by the couch, staring at J.D. as if he were waiting for her to miraculously wake up. Occasionally, he would reach over and stroke her hair and then he took her hand in his and pressed his lips to her knuckles. I hated seeing her so lifeless— so still and quiet. She had never been as long as I'd known her. Gallard said she'd been talking since she came out of the womb and I believed it.

With my free hand, I touched Lucian's shoulder, and he looked up at me before reluctantly letting go of J.D.'s hand then moved so that he was sitting on the coffee table. All the furniture had come with the house since it was a rental. I couldn't believe this was the very couch where Lela often spent her time reading or talking with Gallard. There was so much history in this house.

I took a deep breath and Nicola kissed my cheek before taking a seat next to Lucian. I then held the hand that Lucian had been holding and struggled to keep from falling apart. Her touch was as cold as death, much like Gallard's. I also noticed she was wearing a ring on her left forefinger. She never mentioned that Lucian proposed. This made her resurrection more urgent. I needed to do for Lucian what I had been unable to do for Micah.

"Hey, Jordin," I said. "You can't stay out of trouble, can you?"

Everyone in the room chuckled, but it was a sad chuckle. I would have given anything to have to rescue her from another scrape than to have to worry about whether or not she would wake up. I would trade anything for her not to be in this situation.

"You may not be stealthy or strong or fast, but that doesn't mean we aren't lost without you. You're brave and smart and hella funny with your conspiracy theories. This family wouldn't be the same without you, which is why I need you to fight." I took her face in my hands and pressed my forehead to hers. "Please wake up, Jordin."

I waited for the same hum that I felt the night Robin had come back, but it never seemed to come. My body remained the same and it became so quiet that all I could hear was my own heart pounding in my chest. This was not a time for my gifts to have a glitch. Every other time, I was able to perform them on command, other than the levitation thing.

Nicola hugged me from behind, resting her head on my back, and I listened as she began to sob. Her touch was comforting and heartbreaking at the same time. But somehow, it acted like a jumpstart and I felt tingling in my fingers. It spread to my arms and then I could feel it throughout my entire body. Someone moved closer to me and by their scent, I knew it was Gallard. I kept my eyes closed as the electricity grew stronger and stronger and I heard the familiar humming noise.

Then something changed. J.D.'s cold skin began to heat and soon she was at a healthy body temperature. Everyone grew silent as we waited for whatever would happen. I opened my eyes and stared at her, looking for any sign of change. Her appearance was the same, only with more color. I was going to try and listen for her heartbeat, but then she squeezed my hand tightly. Everyone gasped and slowly moved closer. Her eyes fluttered a little and then finally they opened. They were blue green, which meant I had successfully stopped her from transitioning.

"J.D?" I whispered. Her eyes turned to mine, and she didn't say a word. She looked around at everyone who was gathered around her and she started to withdraw and shrink closer to the couch. She jerked her hand away and slowly sat up.

"Who the hell are you?"

I blinked, not sure if I should be more surprised that she was alive or that she was confused. Lela never mentioned disorientation when she'd awoken and neither had Cherish or Melody. Everything about J.D.'s resurrection was odd.

"J.D., do you know why you're here?" I asked.

She stared at me, scrutinizing my face and then did the same to everyone else. Each moment that went by without an answer made my anxiety triple. Why wasn't she talking like she used to? I expected her to say some sort of joke or something extremely British. Instead, she continued to remain quiet and search everyone's expression.

"No, I don't," she said.

My heart clenched. Even her accent was gone. What was going on?

"Darling," Lucian said. "Are you all right?"

She shook her head. "I'm really sorry, but . . . I don't know who any of you are."

Disappointment filled the room. J.D. had lost her memory as a result of her head injury. I didn't know how it happened or why. I felt for Lucian the most. If she didn't remember him that meant she didn't remember how she felt about him — that she was in love with him or that he was in love with her.

"What about your name?" Gallard asked. "Do you remember that?"

She shook her head once more. "No, I don't know who I am."

Lucian stood up and walked out of the room. I wanted to do the same because inside I was screaming. Was this any better? Was having her alive and not remembering us better than her being dead and taking the memories with her? I wasn't so sure.

I couldn't stand to watch her stare at everyone anymore. She reminded me of a child lost in a crowd. No one dared mention the V word to her in case she would freak out like any normal person would. We decided it would be best to ease her into the know slowly but surely. She seemed to be most comfortable with Melody, so J.D. stayed close to her.

While nobody was watching, I slipped upstairs and closed myself up in the room at the end of the hall. I was tired and hadn't slept much the night before. I hadn't been sleeping well because of the case and the worrying. That mixed with my erratic feeding made me tired and overly emotional. At least I wasn't grouchy.

I opened my eyes when I heard the door open and shut. Someone padded over to the bed and then I felt a blanket around me along with the warmth of Nicola's touch. I knew her arms and her scent better than anyone's other than Colton. I turned around and was soon curled with her in the same position we'd slept the night after the frat party.

"Everything will be okay," she said. "Don't stress too much."

I chuckled. "How did you know I was stressed?"

"Because I love you, and I know you very well. You spent two months taking power naps when we broke up the first time. Napping is your go-to stress reliever."

"Just like painting is yours." I found her lips in the dark with mine. "What am I going to do? My mom's in jail, the police are after half of us, and now J.D. doesn't even remember her own name. I don't know where to start."

"Start with resting and save all that worrying for tomorrow."

She started kissing my neck and I sighed, thankful to feel that again. I hadn't kissed her in twenty days, nine hours and twenty minutes. I'd counted even the seconds up until I'd kissed her earlier that night.

"Are you trying to seduce me?" I asked.

"Maybe. Is it working?"

"Yes. But I don't think it's a good idea. Too many people around here."

I tugged her closer to me until I had my arms around her. We didn't speak for the rest of the night, but the situation spoke for itself. We were back together and we weren't going to let anything tear us apart. Eventually, she fell asleep and I drifted off as I stroked her back.

What woke me up was the sound of the door opening once more. I opened one eye to see that it was morning and the sun shone through the window. Someone jumped onto the bed and I came face to face with Colton.

"Are you still sleeping?" he asked.

Nicola opened her eyes as well and she moved the blanket so Colton could crawl in with us. We hadn't done this since Arnaud attacked me a few months before — have all three of us sleeping together as a family. It had felt right for reasons I didn't understand back then and now I knew why. They had been my family all along.

"Morning, bud," I said.

"Grandpa told me to see if you were still alive."

"Oh, really? Well, you can tell him mom and I are fine, and we were just making up for lost time."

Nicola cuddled Colton close to her and I smiled at my little family. I never would have pictured myself with an amazing girlfriend and a wonderful son at twenty-two, but I was very fortunate. I wouldn't give them up for anything and I was going to protect them with my life. I thought back to what Nicola and I had discussed a few weeks earlier and I realized that I'd made a mistake. Adding another child to our nest would make me the happiest man alive. But there was one thing that might just make me happier.

"Colton, what do you think about mom and I getting married?" I asked.

Nicola looked up at me in shock.

"Married?" Colton asked. "You mean like grandma and grandpa?"

"Exactly like grandma and grandpa." I smiled at his mother. "Nicola Rose Hendrickson, would you do me the honor of being my real wife and not just my fake wife?"

She burst out laughing and Colton laughed too. I'd already proposed twice, once to ask her to a dance and another to beg for forgiveness. I had wanted to give her a serious proposal but serious wasn't my style.

"Hey, Cole, could you give your dad and me a moment alone?" she asked.

"Okay, mamma."

She kissed his forehead then he hopped off the bed and hurried out the door, closing it behind him. When we were alone, she sat up.

"Lucas, why are you asking me now?"

"Because I'm in love with you, and I want to make you mine. I started to ask you that night we went to the festival, but as you know things didn't turn out so well. I don't want anyone to ever try and take you away and they can't if we're married. I also want to have more children with you like you said, and I want the whole picket fence life with the dog and the house and the trampoline in the back yard."

Her silence was deafening and my good mood was quickly disappearing. I thought this would be something she wanted. I had given it a lot of thought and my conclusion was that I wanted her to be my wife. Why didn't she want to marry me?

"I'm . . . confused," I said. "You love me, right?"

"To death. But we aren't in any position to get married right now. You were right about us having a child being bad timing." She took my face in her hands. "Hey. This doesn't mean I don't want to marry you. I only think we should wait." She gave me a quick kiss then hopped off the bed. "Now let's get up and go talk to your family."

I wasn't entirely pleased with how this conversation had gone, but I was willing to agree . . . for now. As we walked down the stairs, I mulled over what I could possibly do to change her mind. I didn't want to wait. I didn't want to hope for a better time because that may never happen. I wanted her now and I was sure that I could convince her to reconsider.

46

Robin shifted and accidently bumped into something. She was confused at first but then remembered Abe slept next her the entire night. The fire had long died, and the cabin was slightly chilly from the morning. She slowly turned around and smiled when she saw he was still asleep.

She lightly kissed his cheek and took this as her chance to get up and eat something. To her disdain, there was no food in the fridge so she managed to sneak into town in the truck and purchase breakfast items. She also picked up a few things for herself.

When she got back, she saw Abe had gotten up and moved to the couch. He was probably tired from worrying about the family and being up most of the night driving as well as from their passionate rendezvous.

She wanted to have breakfast ready for when he woke up, so she tried to be as quiet as possible while she cooked. Carefully, she took the pan of eggs off the stove and put it on one of the unused burners.

Robin heard footsteps behind her and turned around to see Abe entering the kitchen. He was wearing the same jeans from the day before and no shirt. She'd worn it to the store. She loved that it smelled like him, and she understood why J.D. wore Lucian's shirts all the time. He hugged her to his side as he studied the stove.

"Where did you get all this food?"

"I found it on the porch! Someone must have known we were in need."

He laughed. She hadn't heard him really laugh before and she loved it. It was nice being able to laugh with him, despite everything. She was also glad he'd given in to her seduction. She'd never seduced anyone before and it was empowering. He'd tried to talk her out of it and she'd convinced him otherwise.

"Gallard would throttle me if he knew I allowed you to leave this place without chaperoning you."

"I don't need a chaperone. Nobody knows we're here. Gallard said everyone was safe and that they'd got a hold of Nicola and J.D. My sister is the only one who needs help now."

Abe rubbed her arm sympathetically. Robin hated thinking about what Lela was going through. She'd known that Lela was tortured by Samil after Lydian had taken her to safety. Were they treating her terribly now? She shuddered at the thought.

"This breakfast looks amazing," Abe said. "Shall we eat?"

She smiled and nodded. She was grateful that he was getting her mind on something else. While he grabbed the plates and silverware, she uncovered the eggs and put an oven mitt on the table before setting the pan there and placed the plate of bacon next to it.

They ate mostly in silence, but it was a nice silence. She felt a little more tired than usual and attributed it to needing some blood. Despite Lela's suggestion, she hadn't been taking her pills as often as she should have. She was going to start getting sick if she kept that up.

"Since I'm tasked with staying at your side at all times, what should we do?" Abe asked.

"We could go out. You said there was a place to fish down the hill from here."

"Or we could stay in."

"That too. I'm sure this place has board games or maybe movies, right? I still haven't seen *Dirty Dancing*."

A smile crept onto his lips and he stood up, taking her hands in his and hoisted her out of her seat as well. She had an idea what he was thinking because she was thinking the same thing. Now that she'd purchased contraception, they wouldn't have to worry about anything. Staring at him, looking all sexy with his shirt off was tempting her.

"Could we watch an action movie instead? The kind with a lot of violence and no romance whatsoever?"

"Sounds like a plan."

He leaned in and kissed her, softly at first but then he started getting more intense. She returned them and soon they were back to the same place on the couch that they were the previous night. A half hour later, she lay with her back to him and they had a blanket around them.

"We're so bad," she said, chuckling to herself.

"But you're so good." He kissed the back of her neck. "I promised Gallard that it was over between us. He would kill me if he knew we'd taken it this far."

"Then let's hope he doesn't find out. I can keep a secret."

Abe sat up and so did she. His expression became grave, and she wondered what he had on his mind.

"Not for long," he said. "I don't want you to be my dirty little secret. Eventually, I want him to know about us. You're not a one-night stand, Robin Shepherd. I want you for the rest of my life."

Her heart clenched, and she had to break eye contact. She wanted so badly to say she felt the same way, but she couldn't. Not while the wound from Erik had yet to close. Abe made her pain go away, but she needed more time before she could honestly say she loved Abe.

"I'm . . ." she cleared her throat. "I should get dressed."

"Okay." He lightly kissed her lips. "I'll be down here."

Stealing the blanket from him, she went upstairs to change into clean clothes. While his shirt was comfortable, she wanted something lighter. She changed then went into the bathroom to brush her teeth and tie her hair back.

After she finished getting ready, she looked in the mirror. She remembered the night before any of this ever happened. Before she'd even gone on a date with Erik or even experienced her first real kiss. It was the night they went to the club. The woman she'd seen was timid and sad but determined to carry on. The woman she now was broken completely and self-destructing in ways she never thought she would. She didn't like this new person very much.

Tears escaped her eyes and before she knew it, she was crying. Robin undressed herself then turned the water on the hottest setting. She then got in and took the washcloth, rubbing the soap bar against it until it was extremely foamy. Using the cloth, she started scrubbing every inch of herself. She felt dirty. She wanted to wash off what Matthew had done to her, what Ash had done to her, and what she'd done to herself by using two men to mask her pain.

"Babe?" she heard over the hum of the shower. "You in here?"

"Yes. I'll uh . . . be out in a little bit."

She resumed with the scrubbing, hoping that Abe would leave, but then she heard him walk towards the shower. She didn't want him to try to come in. The water was turning red and she couldn't bare it if he saw her like this.

"I just thought of a new rule," he said.

"Oh?"

"I think from now on, no one should be allowed to bathe you but me."

More tears poured out of her eyes as she continued to scrub herself raw. Why did he have to fall in love with her? He deserved someone who wasn't broken. Who wasn't on the verge of losing her mind with the hurt over what had been done to her.

"Babe?" Abe asked again. "Are you all—"

He pushed the curtain away and she cowered in shame.

"Go away!" she shouted

"Robin, what have you done to yourself? You're bleeding!"

"I said go away!"

Abe took the bloodied towel away from her then lifted her out of the tub. Using one hand, he grabbed a body towel off the rack then wrapped in inside of it. As he rocked her, she continued sobbing heavily, struggling to breathe.

"Why?" he asked her. "We were happy just a moment ago. What happened between then and now?"

"I haven't been happy for a long time," she said between sobs. "I'm disgusting. I finally had a chance to be with my family again. Then Ash took it away. He made me this awful person who used you and Erik. I'm a slut."

"Robin . . . you're not a slut."

"Yes, I am. I hadn't even kissed Erik when I fooled around with you. And we were barely broken up for five hours when we slept together. I'm a disgusting, selfish slut."

"Oh babe," He held her tighter, smoothing his hand over her back. "It's going to be okay. I promise you. I'll do whatever it takes to make you happy again."

Once she'd calmed down, he helped her clean up. It was strange watching him handle her so gently when he'd been a fighter for most of his life. He used a cup to pour water over her legs and washed the blood away. When she was clean, he gave her some privacy so she could get dressed.

She'd just come down the stairs when someone knocked on the door. Abe, who had been waiting at the bottom, mouthed that she hide in case it was the police or an enemy and she went further into the house. Despite the awkward situation, she hoped it was a family member coming to retrieve them. She hadn't heard from Gallard since he'd said they were looking for J.D. and Nicola and was dying for an update.

"What the hell are you doing here?" she heard Abe ask.

She hurried to the door then froze. Erik was standing there with the saddest expression on his face. He wasn't in uniform, and he looked like he hadn't slept at all.

"I need to see her," he said. "Please, I only ask for ten minutes."

"How did you even find us?"

"Lucas told me where you were."

Abe grabbed Erik by the jacket and pulled him into the house. Robin wasn't going to come forward just yet. She wanted to wait and see what Abe would do and how Erik would respond. He was the last person she expected to come here and the last person she wanted to see. What could he possibly have to say that he hadn't yesterday?

Abe slammed the door then corned Erik against the wall. "Start talking."

"I know you have no reason to trust me, but you have to believe that I'm telling you the truth. My dad set me up. He bugged my apartment, my truck, my desk. He knew from the moment he met Robin that she was somehow related to Diane Fontaine. He said the resemblance was too uncanny and it was too much of a coincidence that they were both from Miami. After I was injured, he saw it as the last straw and decided to make a move and arrest Lela. I was afraid that he would go for Robin next, so I called Lucas and warned him before we arrested Lela. I had to go along with the arrest so they wouldn't know that I was the one who helped them escape."

Robin covered her mouth in shock. She couldn't believe this. Erik had been trying to help her? He'd lied about turning her sister in? If he was telling the truth, this changed everything. It would mean that Erik truly was the good man she'd believed him to be. It also meant that she'd admitted to cheating on him when he truly did care for her.

She moved away from the wall so that Erik could see her. They locked eyes and the anguish in his expression turned her stomach. That was genuine regret she saw in his face. If only she knew how much worse her actions were. Now she was more confused than ever.

"Is this true?" she asked. "Did you really lie so I would be safe?"

"I swear to you that I'm telling you the truth. I lied because they were still listening. They would arrest me too. If you don't believe me, ask Lucas. He'll explain everything."

She turned her eyes to Abe, and she could see he was feeling the same way she was. In light of everything, she had betrayed Erik with Abe.

"Um . . . okay." She shifted her eyes between both men. "Abe, could I have a moment alone with him?"

He was hesitant but then nodded and went outside. Erik moved sluggishly and sat on the couch. She had hoped they could go outside instead. It was bad enough knowing what she'd done but her stomach knotted at the thought of speaking with him on the very couch where only ten minutes before she'd been sleeping with another man.

"Is your family safe?" he asked.

"Yes. Thank you for asking. Yours?"

His face formed a pained grimace and he looked away. "My mom is a mess. When she found out that your sister was here and that she'd never made the effort to come forward, she was hurt. Your sister was her best friend in high school and she never got over her sudden disappearance." He closed his eyes. "To make matters worse, she overheard an argument between my dad and me and she found out about . . . his past relationship with J.D. She started crying and kicked my dad out of the house."

"Oh, Erik. I'm so sorry! I'd hoped that this would never touch your family. It's all my fault."

"Your fault? It's not your fault that I fell in love with you."

"I shouldn't have said anything. I should have let you think I had no idea who you were or your connection to my family. Now your family is being torn apart. You could be arrested for aiding and abetting criminals."

He smiled. "Aiding and abetting. You sound like a cop already. Too bad you never got the chance to have that secretary job. I would have loved having you at my side."

The tears fell freely from her eyes and he reached over and wiped them away. He probably thought she was crying because of his confession when really she was crying because she hated this situation.

"Robin, before I left, you said you cheated on me with Abe." He turned his eyes to hers. "Was that true? Or did you say that to hurt me?"

"Erik, there are still some things you don't know about me. Things I've been too ashamed to tell you." She sighed. "Those things have led to me making poor choices. But in the end, I chose you. I put an end to my stupidity and decided I only wanted you. Now everything is just confusing."

By the look on his face, she knew he was heartbroken. This must have been how Mark felt when he learned her mother had cheated with David. It was an awful feeling and she felt like a terrible person. She deserved to feel this way.

"I used to believe infidelity was a deal breaker," he said. "It was the one thing I felt was unforgivable. That was before I fell in love with you. I don't know what it is that you feel you can't tell me, and I'm willing to wait until you're comfortable. But you must know that I want to fight for you. Tell Abe game on because I'm not letting you get away that easily."

He leaned forward to kiss her but she turned away. Having been so wrapped up in Abe, she'd forgotten how much she'd loved Erik's kisses. They were innocent and tame and so tender. Abe's were hot, passionate, and intoxicating. She wanted so much to feel both passion and tenderness with just one man.

Two men had claimed to love her, one who treated her better than anyone and whom she adored and one whom ignited a passion inside of her she never knew existed. It wasn't supposed to be this hard. Until she decided what she wanted, she couldn't kiss either of them.

47

Someone outside started shouting and they both stood as it grew louder. The door burst open and a man came flying into the house. Abe rushed in not long after and just as the man bounced back up, Abe hit him with a punch so hard that it made a sickening sound. Robin didn't recognize the man. He'd probably followed Erik here, which meant there could be others.

The attacker tried and failed to fight back. He couldn't match Abe's skill and soon Abe had him pinned to the ground with his arms behind his back. He jerked him up and Erik stepped forward, tossing some hand cuffs to him. Robin dragged a chair from the kitchen and Abe forced him to sit down.

"What are you doing here, you scum bag?" he asked through clenched teeth.

"I'm just a messenger," the man said. "My will is not my own."

Abe punched him in the jaw, causing Robin to flinch. She'd never seen this side to Abe and in a way, it was frightening. Watching old clips of his fighting matches didn't compare to seeing him in action. She knew he would never hurt her or anyone innocent but knowing he had the ability to inflict real harm was eye opening.

"Don't give me any of that riddle crap. I'll ask you again – who are you?"

"Ezekiel. I followed you here to report to my leader where your friend was. I'm sorry."

The door opened again only this time she knew the person. It was Simeon.

"Uncuff him," he said. "Now."

When nobody moved, he rushed over to Abe at a speed only seen in immortals and stabbed him with what looked like a needle. Abe attempted to fight him off, but this man was too strong. He incapacitated Abe with one nudge of the knee.

"Uncuff him or you'll regret it."

Erik moved forward, taking keys out of his pocket and obeyed. Once the mortal man was free, Simeon tossed another knife to him and Ezekiel held that one to Erik's throat. Robin snapped out of her momentary numbness when she realized the lives of two men she cared about were in danger.

"Hello, Robin," he said. "I got your message. And here I thought I would be getting a booty call."

"Yeah sure. You may be hot, but your terrible personality overshadows your looks. Plus, you're kind of a creep."

Abe winked at her as if to say *atta girl* and she tried not to smile.

The smile left Simeon's face. "I'm not here to make nice. You threatened me and I'm here to respond."

Robin didn't like where this was going. Simeon was here for a reason and she had a feeling he had malicious intent. Why else would he be threatening Abe and Erik? She wasn't anywhere near her phone and they were well outside of screaming distance. Instead, she did her best to try and not tremble to show she was afraid.

"What do you want from me?" she asked.

"What do I want?" Simeon passed the knife to his minion who then pressed it to Abe's throat again. "What I want is for a proper partner to be on my side. I was going to recruit Nicola, but I see now that isn't going to happen. Not with Lucas' strong influence over her. He has her thinking that she can do whatever she pleases without considering her loyalty to the coven or her family. And we are her family."

Robin shrugged. "No offense, but your family kind of sucks."

Ezekiel laughed until Simeon punched him in the side. Robin's sarcastic mood instantly left and she began to take this threat seriously. If Simeon would turn on his own, what would he do to them if they resisted?

"Okay, I understand."

Simeon laughed. "How could you possibly understand? Everyone in your family practically worships you. You're the one they watch over most. The one everyone loves and who bends to your every will and all you have to do is put on your best pathetic smile. You have everything handed to you."

She clenched her fist, her rage beginning to grow. He could spout off all the information he'd gathered by spying on her. He could judge her based on what he'd seen from afar, but that didn't mean he knew her. He didn't know the half of it.

"My life isn't perfect," she said. "I've had my fair share of suffering and hardships. Just because I have a smile on my face doesn't mean I'm not dying inside."

"Fair share of suffering," Simeon jabbed. "What kind of suffering have you had? Everybody treats you like a child and nobody really understands you? Sister wouldn't let you see your cop boy toy? No, I have a better one. He betrayed you and now you're here shagging another man."

"Okay, you got me there. That's what you see but it isn't who I am. You want to know who I am?"

"I would love to know who you are."

She took a deep breath before replying. She hadn't really opened up to anyone besides Lela and Abe about everything she'd experienced and she definitely didn't want to get into it with this horrible man. He obviously had zero empathy and she wasn't hoping her story would somehow magically change his heart of stone. But he was taunting her, and she wasn't taking it.

"When I was four years old, I was molested. He was a vampire and worked for a man who wanted my sister and her husband dead. He told me that if I let him touch me, he would make sure my sister was let go and unharmed. I believed him. Two days later, she was dead."

Simeon's jaw clenched but he didn't say a word. Abe looked like he was in utter shock. This was one of the few things she'd left out of her past. She was trembling now, feeling emotional from thinking about that terrible time, and because she was in a lot of pain but she kept going.

"A year later, I was tossed off a balcony. I suffered from brain damage and my siblings were informed that if I ever woke up, I would be mentally impaired and most likely a quadriplegic. My brother thought that turning me into a vampire would save me from that life, but instead he cursed me to an eternity as a child. My sister, out of the love in her heart, decided to end my life instead.

"Fast-forward twenty-two years. I was brought back to life by accident. In the course of less than twenty-four hours, I aged from five years told to twenty-eight. My family believes it was a result of my vampirism being cured. I don't tell many people, but I have to drink human blood every so often to keep from getting sick.

"But that isn't the worst part of it. I was walking home with my brother after being separated from him for all those years and we were given a ride by a couple of police officers. I soon realized that they weren't what they seemed and one of them forced himself on me while the other tried to set my brother on fire. They planned to kill me, but he overpowered the one who hurt me and killed him. The man who survived said he would have my brother burned alive if I said anything."

She had to pause because her back was starting to hurt. It was like cramps, only worse. She almost stopped with her speech, but she continued anyway.

"So, you see, I may smile. I may laugh and act as though I'm on top of the world, but I'm not. I still have nightmares. I still have dreams where I feel like I'm still in that coffin where I woke up. That I'm in the trunk of that car, drugged and unable to move. Go ahead and judge me. Threaten me, and threaten those I care about, but don't act like you know me. And don't think for one second that I won't go down without . . . without . . . a . . . Ow!"

Her back hurt so much that she fell to the ground. Her body contracted and she yelled in pain. The man who was holding Abe suddenly left his post and started towards her but the Simeon stopped him with one look.

"I could help her," Ezekiel said.

"Move another inch and I'll slit your throat."

Robin curled up into the fetal position and yelled in agony. Abe used the distraction as a chance to go to her and he got on the floor next to her.

"What's wrong?" Abe asked.

"It hurts!" she managed to say. "It hurts so much."

He lifted her up from the floor and carried her over to the couch. Ezekiel and Simeon had stopped holding Erik back as well and Erik rushed to her side. Whatever the source of the pain was, it remained centered towards her hips. Something was wrong, she could feel it. Abe grabbed the quilt off the couch and draped it over her.

Ezekiel dropped his knife then took off his jacket, walking towards her. Simeon grabbed his arm, stopping him from going any further.

"You help her, and you're finished. You hear me? You're done!"

"Then be done with me! I'm not leaving her here. She could die!"

Simeon glared at him. "Very well. You'll regret this, son. I assure you — you will regret this."

After Simeon left the room, Ezekiel went over to Robin's side. She was hesitant to let him help, but she could see the kindness in his eyes. He didn't have the soulless gaze that Simeon did. Maybe he wasn't really their enemy.

"Do either of you men know her medical history?" Ezekiel asked.

"She's pregnant," Abe said. "Seven months, I think."

"What?" Erik asked. "No, there's no way!"

"Tell me where it hurts," Zeke said quietly, ignoring Erik. Robin tensed up then placed her hand over her pelvis. He looked at Erik and Abe for a moment then back at her. "Robin . . . I'm going to need to undress you. Do you mind?"

"I mind," they said in unison.

"I assure you I have your friend's best interest at heart. I took the Hippocratic oath when I became a nurse — First, do no harm."

328

"Just do it!" she shouted, too preoccupied with the pain to care. The pain was so severe that she couldn't do it herself so he pulled off her jeans and then her underwear. Erik held her hand while Ezekiel spread her knees with his hands and looked under the blanket.

"Oh my," he said. He dropped the blanket. "Robin . . . I think you're in labor."

"What!" she and her friends said at the same time.

"You're dilated. Quite severely."

"That's impossible. How can I—ow!"

She bit her lip until she tasted blood as another wave of pain went through her. Her hips and back hurt terribly. No matter which position she was in, she was uncomfortable. Abe started yelling something to Erik about hot water, scissors, and the rest was muffled by the sound of her own painful wails.

"Robin, you're going to have to push," Ezekiel said calmly.

Push? How could she push? This wasn't happening. There was no way she could be in labor. She still had two more months to go.

She should have gotten a checkup sooner and this wouldn't be happening. This had to be a horrible nightmare. She couldn't be a mother yet. She'd barely grown up and was just now learning how to be a woman. And she wasn't even sure whose baby this was. There were two possibilities and neither was better than the other.

No matter how this was happening, one thing was certain. She was going to have to push. This baby wasn't going to disappear because she wished it. Erik had come back with the pot of hot water and all the other items Ezekiel had requested.

"Robin, if you sit up, this will be a lot easier. Your friends can hold your hands, and I'm going to guide you through it."

A tear fell down her cheek. "You've done this before?"

"Yes. I've delivered all my nieces, nephews, and all the coven's babies. I haven't lost a patient yet, or a baby."

His words were comforting and inspired her to sit up. Her friends helped her, and as he'd suggested, they each held one of her hands. She sat with her lower back against the middle couch cushion and Ezekiel was directly below her. On his command, she pushed.

"Okay, stop," Ezekiel said.

"Should she keep pushing?" Erik asked, speaking for the first time in several minutes.

"No, she's only supposed to push with each contraction. The baby's doing what it needs to. Any extra strain, and we could risk damage."

She felt like she was going to throw up she hurt so bad. If it weren't for Abe's encouraging words and Erik's comforting touch, she probably would have passed out by now. She could feel liquid pooling beneath her and she became even more concerned.

"Am I bleeding?" she asked, trying not to panic.

"No, your water just broke," Ezekiel assured her. "You're doing well, Robin."

He instructed her to push again after about forty-five seconds passed and she did. She squeezed her friends' hands so hard she feared she was hurting them. This went on for several hours and she began to get tired.

Ezekiel looked under the blanket and then smiled.

"I see the head. Keep pushing, Robin, you're almost there." When she did nothing, he lightly touched her knee. "Robin, you need to push. Just one more time and it'll be out."

She closed her eyes, taking one last moment to appreciate her life. She'd done a lot of growing up over the past few months but this would be the ultimate test. Everything was going to change and she would now be responsible for another life. She hadn't even had a chance to get used to the idea. If she'd found out about the pregnancy in the beginning, she would have been able to prepare, mentally and emotionally. There was no time for that now.

Taking a deep breath, she gave one last push, using every bit of energy she had left, but instead of feeling progress, she felt pain more intense than anything else she'd suffered and cried out in agony. She could feel something cracking.

"Get it out!" she heard Erik shout. "She's going to die!"

"Nobody's dying here!"

Robin could feel Ezekiel's hands trying to coax the baby out but she could no longer help him. Her body was about to give out and everything was getting blurry. Her ears were ringing and she could barely move.

Then she heard it. A wheezy cry echoed throughout the cabin. It was all so surreal, and her body felt light. She slowly opened her eyes, allowing for her vision to clear and she watched as Ezekiel cut the cord and then carried the tiny human over to the warm water. He'd placed several folded towels on the floor and used a washcloth to gently clean up the infant. Curiosity encouraged her to study it more intently. The baby was pink and had a shiny bald head. She couldn't see the eyes from where she was laying.

"Abe," she said, her voice weary. "How is she?"

"She's beautiful."

Ezekiel wrapped the baby in one of the free towels then handed her to Robin. She didn't hold out her arms at first. Holding the baby would make all of this too real. Was she ready for this? It didn't matter anymore. This child was hers and she would take care of it. She took the baby from him and cradled it close to her. The little girl was small, most likely because she was a few weeks early. She was still crying and wheezing, and Robin tried rocking her to sooth her.

"I'm going to call an ambulance," Abe said. "Erik, stay with her."

"Where else would I go?"

Abe left the room and Erik continued to dab her forehead with the cloth. The baby girl opened her eyes for the first time and Robin stared at her in wonder. She had grey eyes—as grey as a vampire's. She attributed it to the baby being born with the vampire gene.

"How are you feeling?" Ezekiel asked.

"Confused, tired. Mostly terrified. I had a baby. I'm a . . . I'm a mother."

"It's because of what happened to you, isn't it?" Erik said. "Robin, why didn't you tell me you were raped?"

She shrugged. "I don't like talking about it. I didn't want you to be afraid to be with me because I cared about you enough to give us a chance. I thought I could move on but . . . I can't anymore."

The baby's tiny hand curled around her finger and she held her breath. More than ever she wished that her sister was there. She couldn't do this alone and she was going to need help.

Erik continued to stroke her hair, occasionally kissing the side of her head while she gently rocked the baby. Holding a baby was a first for her. She'd been too small before and no one in her family had any babies now. Not until this little one made a surprise entrance.

"Thank you so much," Robin said to Ezekiel. "You saved me."

He nodded. "Anytime." He lightly put his hand on the baby's chest. "I think she's having trouble breathing. Try to keep her upright until the ambulance gets here."

"Ambulance is on its way," Abe said. He knelt down beside her and smiled, stroking the baby's cheek. "Are you doing okay?"

"I'm not in too much pain. Mostly tired."

Ezekiel stood up, probably to go and wash his hands and Abe followed him. She listened in on their conversation, just in case Ezekiel told him something he was afraid to tell her.

"I can't thank you enough," Abe said. "Why did you help us?"

"I would have done it for anyone."

"That woman . . ." Abe took a deep breath. "She's my life. And you just saved her. I will never forget that."

"For years I've submitted to Simeon. It ends now. I've waited my entire life to save my family from his control, and I intend to do that now. Do you think your family would be willing to help us?"

"Of course! When they hear what you did for Robin, they'll welcome you in a heartbeat."

"Then I must go. I'll get my family and bring them to yours."

The red and white lights flashed through the window and Abe opened the door so the paramedics could come in. They gave her another blanket for modesty and then lifted her onto the stretcher. One of the EMT's took the baby from her and rushed ahead to the back to give her a checkup. There was no room for the other men but she trusted they would meet her at the hospital.

"We'll be there soon, Robin," Erik promised. "Just hang in here."

She smiled at him just as the doors closed. The EMTs tried asking her questions but she was feeling exhausted emotionally and physically. All she wanted to do was sleep because if she didn't sleep, she would break. She'd lost J.D. but also gained a child. One life was lost and another began. If she could rest, then maybe when she woke up she could handle the struggles ahead.

48

I stood on the porch and watched J.D. as she sat in the middle of the yard. Watching her struggle to remember an entire lifetime worth of memories made my heart ache. I waited for her to crack one of her jokes or say something incredibly inappropriate. Instead, she remained silent and distanced herself from those who loved her.

As much as I wanted to find a solution to her problem, I had to focus on my dire needs. My mom was in jail and we were still hiding from the police. I'd spoken briefly with Erik over the phone and urged him to go and hide with Robin and Abe.

Everyone on our task force was being questioned and forced into a polygraph to see if any were in league with me and my supposed diabolical plan to infiltrate the police department with vampires from within. That was the official suspicion anyway.

I felt a small hand tug on mine and I reached down and lifted Colton into my arms. All of this was confusing to him and he only believed we were on vacation. When he asked why he couldn't go to school, I told him that he wasn't going to be in school for a while. I hated that his life was being disrupted over something he had no control over, but I needed him safe.

"Why is J.D. sitting by herself?" Colton asked.

"She isn't feeling well, bud. She got hurt last night and she's recovering."

A sympathetic expression crossed his face and he rested his head on my shoulder. He said nothing more and I was feeling the same way. What was there to say? How could I explain all of this to my four-year-old? He'd already had a glimpse of how cruel this life could be when he'd lost Mona. Even if I could bring people back, that didn't stop me from fearing for the lives of those I loved.

"Lucas?" I heard my dad say. "Dominique says she has some information on the Romani coven she thinks we should know."

I nodded then set Colton down, sending him off to play. I had been putting off having a serious discussion with the others long enough and it was time to start planning. Obviously, we couldn't leave town with Lela still here and we were all in agreement that a jailbreak was not a good idea. The question was what we should do next.

We gathered in the living room, no one showing any signs that they were as eager for this conversation as I was. Lucian looked utterly devastated. Cherish, however, had taken off to take care of something. She hadn't left us with much to guess for what she was up to but I trusted whatever it was, it was important.

"My father may have called a truce, but that doesn't mean he's forgiven past wrongs," Dominique said. "When Nicola made him think she killed Ryan, she got herself banished and basically declared war."

"Wait, *you* killed Ryan?" Melody asked.

I shot a quick glance at Nicola and Lucian. As far as we knew the four of us, including Dominique, were the only ones aware of the mystery hero who saved J.D. I figured it would be better to let them think Nicola had done it and let the question of the real savior be answered later on. I was putting a lot of problems on the back burner and I was getting stressed.

"Like I said, she made him think she did. Coven members don't kill one another," Dominique continued. "That's one of the only rules that none of them break. Other than marrying-slash-consorting with people that are not members. Anyway, he wants Lucas in exchange for my sister and me."

"That is not going to happen," Lucian said. "I made a deal, but I have no intention of keeping it. He is not coming anywhere near my godson or my granddaughters."

Melody smiled and linked arms with Nicola. I was still reeling from the news that Lucian and Nicola were related. That meant that Colton was his descendant as well, thus making all of us related in some way. Not that we weren't family before, but this revelation made it even more so.

"Okay, well I guess I'll give Gallard the floor and we can decide what to do about my mother," I said.

Gallard looked up then glanced around the room as if he'd been caught off guard. I'd figured he should be the one to come up with a plan since he was basically the leader of our group. Either him or Solomon. Though Lucian was technically the oldest, Solomon had always seemed like the patriarch type figure for us. Maybe it was because he was a religious man.

"Why don't you take the floor?" Gallard finally said. "I would love to hear your suggestions."

I raised an eyebrow. He wanted *my* suggestions? Why? I wasn't much of a leader and I'd proved in the past that my ideas weren't always so great. The whole trapping Henry thing, the breaking into the clinic stunt, not to mention the failed attempt at taking down the MITF.

"Sure. Sure, I'll come up with something." I started shifting nervously. What was there to be nervous about? This was only my family. "Okay, so she's being charged with the murder of Grey Meyers. We all know that unfortunately, she is guilty of that. I wish I could say I understand but I don't. I mean, I've never taken a life."

Lucian looked at me funny, and I almost addressed it but continued.

"Anyway, it makes me wonder about the brother, Richard Meyers. Has he really been missing all these years?"

"He has," Gallard said. "No one has seen him since the night Mark let those vampires loose in Orlando. We've all assumed he took his life."

"Or he's just hiding. You know better than anyone how to make sure no one knows where you are. Too bad we're pressed for time or I would suggest we find him. Since we can't do that, we should try to come up with a good case for her. Solomon, how would you feel about defending her?"

"Really? Well, I did study law while in the seminary, but those were Italian laws and are very outdated."

Though I'd thrown the idea, I didn't really think we should go through with it. Waiting or my mom's case to go to trial would waste time we didn't have. Each second we were in Texas, I could feel Micah slipping further and further into the clutches of MITF's influence. And we were all in hiding. We couldn't hide out in this house that long. Hiding and worrying was exhausting. If only we didn't have to hide anymore. If only...

"I have an idea," I said. "I have to forewarn you — my idea may sound ludicrous but I need you to hear me out."

"You have our full attention," Lucian said. "As long as it includes violence. Considering the night I've had, I need to hit something very badly."

Nicola took his hand and he gave her a forced smile as he covered her hand with his other one. I hadn't realized how close they'd gotten and it showed just how tight the bond was between all of us. And for some reason they were counting on me to save us all.

"Sorry, Lucian, but my plan does not involve violence."

"Only when it's necessary, am I right?"

I frowned. "I'm sorry, is there something you have to say? By all means speak up."

"Yes, I have a problem. I have a problem with everyone around here treating me like I'm a time bomb. Like I could snap and kill someone at any moment. Well you know what, I think everyone here should know what really happened that day at the Sharmentino house."

I had no idea what he was talking about. He hadn't seen what happened, I was sure of it. Nicola and I kept that between the two of us and Lucian couldn't have known what really happened. He'd insisted on taking the blame for Henry's death and I had adamantly protested that but he wouldn't listen. Was he resenting that?

"What are you talking about, Lucian?" Gallard asked.

"I didn't kill Henry Wright. I said that because I was protecting Lucas. I knew everyone would worry if they found out what he'd done, so I let everyone believe I had done it. It was easier to believe, was it not? Anyway, I'm telling you all this because I don't want anyone here to believe for one second that violence is never the answer."

Everyone grew quiet and I contemplated what I would say next. Lucian thought that I had killed Henry and because of his grief induced anger, he was saying things he probably didn't mean. Outing me as Henry's killer wasn't exactly the best thing to do right now. I was already worried about letting everyone down and now I had to deal with this.

"Is he telling the truth, Lucas?" Gallard asked, pity riddled on his face.

"I would rather not discuss that right now. We have more important things to talk about. Anyway, about my plan. Your entire lives, you've been running. Now I know the past has been forgiven, so I won't go into all of that. Frankly, running is getting exhausting. Here is what I propose. What if we all just came forward? We could all turn ourselves in to the task force and then explain our case. We'll make them see that eradicating vampires isn't going to solve the problem. Make them understand us instead of seeing all of us as monsters."

"Or, they'll just douse us in gasoline and set us all on fire," Lucian said. "What's plan B?"

"I think it's a good idea," Gallard said. "We were able to convince Richard Meyers in the end. There have to be more people we can get through to. I don't know about you guys, but I'm going to turn myself in."

"While you guys do your thing, Nicola and I will go to Simeon," Dominique said. "I think we can convince him to partner with us. He wants a war and so do you, correct?"

"How do you intend to do that?" Gallard asked. "I don't know if I feel comfortable letting you or your sister back in that man's grasp."

Dominique's expression darkened. "Trust me. I have a plan that will guarantee his cooperation."

"And then we can rip out his throat if he doesn't comply," Lucian said.

"We're not killing anyone," I said firmly. "I mean it. Not a single drop of blood will be shed on our part. You're going to stay here and keep an eye on the remaining women and my son. Please, Lucian. We can't do this unless I'm sure my family is safe."

"When do we turn ourselves in?" Gallard asked. "The sooner the better."

I checked my watch. "It's nearly noon. If we leave now, we'll be in Arlington by two o'clock. We could make a goal to be at the precinct by four."

"That plan works for me. I'll call Kevin and let him know to pass the message to the others."

49

I sat in the driver's seat of my SUV outside of the Euless police department. My dad, aunt Melody, and Kevin were all in the car with me. We'd made it back in town at the time we planned and now came the hard part— turning ourselves in.

When I'd come up with the idea, it all sounded too simple. Show up, hold out our wrists, and let everything follow. The truth was, I was terrified. What if Lucian was right and they doused us in gasoline and burned us alive? Killing us would be a lot harder than it would be to exterminate a night-walker. Or they could put us in jail and that would mean I would never free my brother.

Gallard reached over and put a hand on my shoulder. He really had no reason to trust me to lead our group. I hadn't been in the game as long as he had. He had been leading people since he was barely eighteen years old. Now he was three hundred and oddly felt the need to hand over the reins to me.

"Are you sure you're up for this?" I asked him.

"All the way. You're right—we have been running for too long. It's time that we come forward. Terrance Fox can finally die and I can go by my real name."

"I doubt I will get hard time," Melody said from the back seat. "I only helped someone escape prison and knocked out one security guard."

"That's basically what I'm being accused of, Mel," Gallard said. "Oh, and kidnapping both Lela and Robin. And helping Lela kill her parents. Wow. I'm in deep *merde* aren't I?"

"I still don't know why *I'm* here," Kevin said. "I never did anything. Technically, I'm a victim."

"You're a Sharmentino so that means you're automatically guilty." I said. "Would you rather stay at the house and wait? I'm sure that would be fun. Hours and hours and hours of chess games with Terrence. Unless he's too busy hooking up with Celeste. Then you can hang with Ramses and talk about Egyptian history."

Kevin raised an eyebrow. "Yeah, I think I'll go with the jail time."

"Thought so." I opened the door and got out. "Okay, here it goes. Kev, you riding back seat?"

"If you mean Gallard's pocket, then no. I think I prefer Melody's purse."

I started to get out when I noticed about six cars had showed up. They weren't police vehicles, so this got me curious. They parked side by side and then about thirty women flooded the parking lot. I recognized one of them as Lela's boss. Gallard got out first and I followed him.

"Marcelle?" he said. "What are you doing here?"

"Hey there, pumpkin." Marcelle hugged Gallard. "Why else? We're here to protest your wife's arrest. I brought back-up too."

"Yes," another woman said. "Every single of one of us has been touched by her in some way. She's saved our hair, our relationships. She made us all feel like part of a family. We're not letting this happen to our sister."

Gallard smiled. "We appreciate your support. I'm sure Lela would say the same thing. But, Marcy, this might get dangerous. I wouldn't want any of you ladies to get hurt."

Some of them giggled and I nudged him. Gallard was basically a cougar magnet.

"Well, we should go inside," I said. "All of you, we would love to have you on our side. But like Gallard said, stay safe. We don't know what could happen today."

Kevin transformed and then Melody created a cozy space for him next to her wallet and pepper spray. The three of us formed a line and held our heads high as we walked towards the door. Almost all of the police cars were gone, probably because they were out looking for me and my family. I opened the door and let them in before I followed behind.

The first person I saw was James. He was on the phone by his desk and when he saw me, his jaw dropped. He muttered something into the phone then hung up. He approached me rather quickly and took out his gun, holding it to my chest.

"Before you say anything, I want you to answer one thing. Where is Erik?"

"He's safe. He made sure Robin got away and then he joined her."

"Oh, yeah? You didn't kill him to shut him up?"

"I think it's a little late for that. If that were my plan, I would have killed him the moment I found out he knew my uncle was a vampire. Believe it or not, James, but I was as devoted to this task force as you are. That's why I'm here. We're not the real threat to this town." More officers entered the room and I saw Tyler. He looked like hell and he moved like a zombie. He made eye contact with me and then he looked at Gallard. For a few long seconds, they just stared at each other. I hadn't anticipated the awkward reunion, but at least no one was throwing us to the ground and pulling guns on us, other than James.

"Hello, Gallard," Tyler said. "I'm sorry your daughter is past curfew."

I turned to Gallard for explanation, but he didn't say a word. It must have been an inside joke between them.

"Where is she, Tyler?"

"Hopefully still alive. I left her with Grey Meyers' children. They're the heads of SAITF. I have a feeling they aren't going to play nice."

A sick feeling formed in my stomach. I'd stayed away from frightening thoughts concerning my mom for hours in fear that it would send me over the edge. J.D.'s amnesia, our exposure, and Lela's arrest were all I could handle. Then I heard what I was trying to find and what I had been dreading. Lela's yells accompanied by the sound of harsh blows.

I started to move towards the sounds when James held up his gun again.

"Take one more step and I swear to God I'll shoot."

"Put the gun down, James," I said, my rage growing. Lela's yells were growing louder and they were all I could focus on.

"Give me a reason to."

"You have no idea what I'm capable of. Put it down or you will regret it."

I heard James cock the gun and that set me off. I punched him in the stomach and grabbed the gun from him. Three officers rushed towards me and all it took was for me to hold up my hand and they flew back against the wall. Milliseconds later, I picked up the gun and shot James in the leg. He cried out in agony, clutching at the injury.

"Lucas what are you doing?" Gallard asked. "You said no violence!"

"Wait!"

Nobody moved so I knelt down next to James. He was bleeding pretty badly and I guessed that I'd hit an artery in his thigh. He flinched when I pulled out the bullet but it was necessary. I gently touched James' leg and closed my eyes. My erratic emotions were helping me harness my powers better and the buzz I would always feel when I used them had begun to resonate through my body at a constant.

I removed my hand from James after a few seconds and he gazed in wonder at his healed leg. All the other officers were stunned speechless as well. Tyler was backed up against the wall, whiter than ever.

"Wha . . . how?" James asked.

"The same way Erik miraculously recovered from a broken spine. Like I said— I'm not here to hurt anyone. I'm here to help."

The initial shock of what had just happened wore off and I ran down the hall. I knew exactly where they were keeping Lela and I found the door in no time.

"I'm going to ask you again," a man said. "Where is Richard Meyers?"

"I don't know! I haven't seen him in over twenty years."

I rammed it with my shoulder a couple of times before I knocked it down and I met the gazes of three stunned people. Two men and a woman. One of the men was crouched down next to Lela and had his fist in the air as if he were preparing to strike her.

"Get away from her," I ordered. "Now."

"Who are you?" the man asked. "The boyfriend?"

At that point, I was done playing nice. I looked down at my mom, who was on the floor bloody and bruised. She was perfectly capable of fighting them off and yet she hadn't because she knew it was wrong. She had an unfair advantage and because of that, she wasn't willing to abuse her power.

"Which one of you is in charge of this case?" I asked.

"I am," the woman said. "My name is Jennifer Meyers. I'm the head of Immortal Investigations. I'm basically in charge of every task force in the country, second only to the Vice President." She turned to Lela. "And I've been waiting years to get my hands on this one."

"I understand what it's like to want revenge. But this isn't the way. The fact that she isn't fighting back should show that she is willing to accept the punishment for her crime."

"Prison time isn't enough. She needs to suffer for what she did to the two most important men in my life. She took away my father and my uncle. My family was never the same after that."

Two officers came in behind me and attempted to hold me back. I shrugged them off easily then shoved them out the door, slamming it behind me. This wasn't going as planned. The point of turning ourselves in was to prove a point but now that I saw how they were going to treat us, plans were changing. I had hoped that revealing my true power to the mortal race would not have to happen until much later on. I had a feeling that time was nearer than I would like.

"You think we're monsters," I said. "You think we deserve to die because of what we are. You really need to take a look in the mirror. I think you'll find the true monster there."

The taller man rushed towards me and punched me in the stomach. I didn't fight back this time. His blow had barely hurt because I was freshly nourished. I wanted to be up to my full potential. It must have made him mad that I hadn't responded to his attempt at inflicting pain because he kneed me in the stomach then knocked me to the ground by striking my back with his elbow.

"Enough Brian!" Jennifer shouted.

"He's a sympathizer." He kicked me in the ribs. "He disgusts me more than any parasite."

"Brian stop!

"Why?"

"His brother is my son!"

I looked up at her and the officer who had been beating me stepped away. I couldn't believe what I was hearing. Lela sat up as well and I knew by her expression that she hadn't known this either.

"You're Micah's mother?" I asked.

The anger on her face quickly turned to anguish and then she backed up until she was leaning against the table. This whole time, I thought that Micah's mother was just some poor woman who was forced into it or bribed with a lot of money when in reality she was someone who was very influential when it came to immortal eradication.

"Brian, Daniel, take the Sharmentino woman to her cell," she said. "I need to talk to Lucas."

50

Nicola slowly sipped her mug of blood as she watched Lucian from the window. He'd been on the porch watching J.D. for at least twenty minutes and she was starting to get worried. It had been tough seeing how devastated he was when he'd pulled J.D. out of the warehouse. Ever since that moment, he'd been getting progressively more hostile. A thing she tended to do whenever she felt hopeless.

She finished the blood then filled a clean cup before going outside, unable to take it anymore. She wanted to talk to him so he could vent and get out his pent-up rage. There was still time before Cherish and Solomon were scheduled to come back. Until then, the six of them were ordered to stay put unless told otherwise.

To break the ice, she held out the cup to him. He looked at it, appearing to be confused then took it with an appreciative smile on his face. He took one sip then only held the cup as he continued to watch J.D. as if he were afraid she would suddenly get her memory back and he didn't want to miss it.

"You're tense, Red Coat," she said. "Are you going to chill and stop verbally attacking everyone or am I going to have to try another kick on you?"

He chuckled. "You are the only one who is brave enough to try." He took another sip. "You were very impressive when you fought those men last night. If I were your father, I couldn't be more proud."

She playfully nudged him in thanks. After meeting Simeon for the first time, she hadn't felt as disappointed as she'd predicted. She'd known

343

for a long time that he was a waste of space of a human being. Even when she was young, she knew better than to hope for father-daughter activities like dances and tea parties. He was definitely not a candidate for whom she would want to walk her down the aisle on her wedding day.

"I wish I could say the same about you," she said. "Telling everyone Lucas killed his brother — not cool, man."

His shoulders sank. "I know. I did not mean it. But I do think everyone should know, for his sake. Once you take a life, it's hard to stop. It is like an alcoholic having to struggle with his addiction while living in a wine cellar."

She contemplated if she should tell him the truth. She'd shared almost everything with him and he had been the one to convince Simeon to release her from any ties to the coven. He deserved to know what had really happened because it was very possible the same thing had happened with Ryan.

"Lucian, Lucas didn't kill Henry."

He turned his gaze to her. "What do you mean? But, he was dead. You were injured and there was no one else there."

"Actually, there was. After Henry shot me, someone showed up at the house. He saw what was going on and he went after Henry. Neither of us recognized him."

"Did he tell you his name?"

"No. Lucas doesn't know who he was either. He came out of nowhere and said he was making up for not protecting him in the past or something like that."

They both stopped speaking when J.D. stood up from the grass. She wiped the excess blades off her pants then turned around and walked towards them. Nicola gave her a friendly smile. There were few things that remained the same with her friend. One of them was the way she walked. J.D. always had a confident walk. Another was how she had one hand in her back pocket while the other hung at her side. Everything else was foreign, especially the not so starry-eyed way she was looking at Lucian.

"Hey," she said, still lacking in her accent. "I'm sorry I've been acting like a loner. Actually, I'm not even sure if I usually am that way. Was I?"

Nicola didn't respond right away because she was still surprised that J.D. was even speaking. After she'd woken up, the only person she didn't avoid was Gallard which was understandable.

"No," Lucian said. "In fact, you were quite the opposite. Your brother used to compare you to a puppy."

J.D. laughed. "A puppy you say? Wait, I have a brother? Was he here?"

"Oh no, Abe!" Nicola said. "Has anyone talked to him?"

"Not that I know of," Lucian said. "Last we checked he was still with Robin in Bedford. He confirmed that Erik had taken refuge with them."

344

J.D. gave them a confused eyebrow raise and Nicola realized that she probably had no idea what they were talking about. There was a difference between not knowing you had a twin and forgetting that you had one. Nicola dreaded having to see the look on Abe's face when he would learn that his own sister had no memory of him.

"Okay, well, I'm officially lost," J.D. said. "Why don't we start with proper introductions?" She held out her hand to Nicola. "I am Jade. Or was it Jane? J something or other. And you are?"

The moment their hands touched, something flashed in J.D.'s eyes. If Nicola wasn't mistaken, it almost looked like fear. Why would J.D. be afraid of her?

"I'm Nicola, your . . . well, I'd like to say we're best friends but we're sort of like family. I'm dating your cousin."

"I see." J.D. quickly took her hand back. "Wait." A sneaky smile crossed her face. "Am *I* dating anyone? Do I have someone to keep me warm at night? I noticed I'm wearing a ring and it looks very expensive."

Nicola glanced at Lucian and waited for what he would say. She couldn't imagine how she would cope if Lucas forgot her—if he forgot every moment they'd shared, every kiss and every touch. Every thoughtful word and every longing gaze. J.D. had been so in love with Lucian and he felt the same way. Now they might have to start all over again.

"Not at the moment, no," Lucian said. Nicola could see how much his words pained him. "That ring was a gift for your birthday."

"Well, that's a relief," J.D. said. "I would feel bad for the poor guy I might have forgotten. So, who are *you*?"

"Lucian Christophe. Family friend."

Nicola heard footsteps behind her and turned to see her sister coming out of the house with Colton in tow. He smiled at Nicola and she picked him up, kissing his cheek. Dominique had borrowed some of Melody's clothes and they showed off her figure better than the tattered shirt and sweats. She was definitely curvier than Nicola and at a healthier weight. Nicola's diet had declined when the whole Ryan thing started and she'd lost some of her progress. She was determined to get back on track with Melody's help.

"We were just doing introductions," Nicola said. "J.D., this is my sister Dominique and this little guy is Colton, my son."

The two women shook hands and Nicola nearly passed out. If she wasn't mistaken, J.D. had unabashedly checked out Dominique. Her gaze had lingered longer than necessary. Dominique didn't seem to notice but when Nicola glanced at Lucian, she knew that he'd seen it too. What was going on? What had happened when Ryan hit her with that post?

"Aren't I lucky to have a bunch of good-looking people as my friends and family?" J.D. said.

A door opened and shut inside the house and Lucian ushered the group inside so we could regroup. Cherish greeted everyone then went over and hugged Lucian. Nicola was so relieved when it was cleared up that Cherish never hurt her. Now everyone was reunited and there were no more secrets or misunderstandings.

"I'm sorry to drop this on you, but we have to leave," Cherish said.

"What for?" Lucian asked.

"Simeon is headed for Euless. He's afraid that if we combine forces against the mortals, we won't do things his way. He wants to challenge the leader of our group to establish himself as the dominant immortal for this cause."

"He really thinks he stands a chance against Lucas?" Nicola asked. "He has to be an idiot."

"That's not all, I'm afraid. He's not only planning to fight Lucas, but he wants to make an example out of Texas. There's no real significance, but he wants to kill as many people as possible as a way of saying he can't be stopped."

"He plans to do this tonight?" Dominique asked.

"Tomorrow night. And he's not bluffing, he's done it before. He killed fifteen people in Kansas nearly fifteen years ago. They were written off as ritualistic murders but it marked the beginning of his war against the mortals. It was around the time when nearly three hundred immortals were slaughtered by the task forces across America. He wanted to prove a point: kill us and we'll kill you."

"We have to tell the others," Lucian said.

"I've already tried Lucas and Gallard, they won't answer their phones. The police are all distracted with the big walk-in visit from them and Simeon sees this as an opportunity. No one is watching the streets."

"But we will," Nicola said. "There may be eighty of them and only seven of us but that doesn't mean we can't try."

"Seven?" Cherish smiled. "Oh, hon, we have way more than that. Follow me."

The group went through the kitchen and into the garage. It was dark so she turned on the light and that was when Nicola saw that there were two black windowless vans parked there. They hadn't been there the night before. The passenger side opened, and David got out. He greeted everyone then he shook Lucian's hand.

"Shepherd," Lucian said, extending his hand. "I hear that you married my daughter behind my back. I suppose that makes us in-laws."

"Never thought that would happen, did you?" David asked. "Speaking of, where is my wife?"

"She turned herself in along with Gallard and Lucas. Solomon is talking with his personal handler to prepare in case he needs to represent them in court."

"As long as I know she's with Gallard, I won't panic just yet. Are we ready to go?"

"Let's show everyone our army first," Cherish said. She pulled open the door to the first van and Nicola's jaw dropped. There had to be at least fifty bats inside, all hanging upside down from bars that had been screwed into the ceiling. All the seats had been taken out and there were even some on the floor. They peered at their audience with their little grey eyes, chirping at random.

"There are twice as many in Arnaud's van," David said.

The doors to the other van opened and a man with spiky hair and an outfit straight from Bikers R Us walked around to join the group. Apparently, they had picked up Ramses, Terrence and Celeste on the way because they got out of the van as well.

"Thank God we have more day-walkers around here," Arnaud said. "Do you know how hard it is to drive with covered windows? Nearly rolled the thing a dozen times on the way here from Canada."

"So, this is Lucas' army?" Nicola asked. "And here I thought you spent this whole time tanning on some beach."

"We've been very busy," David said. "Which is why I am handing these keys over and shutting my eyes for this trip." He looked around at the group and frowned. "Where's my daughter?"

"If you mean Robin, she's with Abe in Bedford."

"Well, we should bring them here. I would feel more at ease knowing that she's near."

"I can go get her," Nicola said. "It only takes twenty minutes to get there and then ten to get to Euless. I'll take Colton and my sister with me."

51

Everyone prepared to leave and Nicola quickly packed Colton's things. He was still confused about what was going on and played obliviously with his toy train. She stuffed everything into his bag then tied his shoes to make sure they were snug. She was glad he would be with her or else she would just be worrying about him the entire time.

"You ready to go, baby?" she asked.

"Yes, mamma. Are we gonna see dad?"

She smoothed his hair. "Not yet. We will soon, though. Your dad is doing something very important and we have to help him with something while he does that. Right now, we're going to see aunt Robin and uncle Abe."

Someone stepped in the doorway and she helped Colton stand before approaching Cherish.

"I don't feel comfortable leaving you alone," Cherish said.

"We'll be fine. With Lucian's tutelage, I've developed a mean drop kick. No one will mess with me anymore."

She sighed. "But . . . you're so young. All those years ago, I failed to save my son from the same coven that is threatening us now. You're my granddaughter and I don't want to fail you or Dominque. This is my chance to get it right."

To make her feel better, Nicola gave her a hug. Cherish had every right to worry because she wasn't even sure if she trusted herself to succeed either. But she was going to have to work on her confidence as a vampire sometime.

"Okay, Colton. Say goodbye to your great grandmother."

His eyes widened. "Aunt Cherish is my great grandma? Does that mean she's Gallard's mom?"

Cherish and she both laughed. "No, baby. Cherish is *my* grandmother. I know it's confusing."

Cherish tenderly stroked Colton's hair. "Don't worry about your father, sweetheart. I won't let Simeon harm him."

"Take care of yourself too," Nicola said. "And if you see Simeon, kick him in the balls for me."

Dominique insisted on driving and Nicola had no objections. All three parties left at the same time, following each other until the van Lucian drove took a different exit. Nicola was now officially forced to put her trust in the woman behind the wheel.

The drive wasn't long, but she read Colton a story anyway to keep him occupied and they had the radio playing soft music. Nicola was trying her best not to worry about Lucas and the others.

Turning themselves in had sounded like a good idea on paper but there was no telling how horribly they would be treated. She'd seen the videos Lucian had of the experiments that were done on vampires and how they were treated in prison. Lucas wouldn't let them treat him that way, would he?

"Don't worry about your man, love," Dominique said. "He can take care of himself."

"I know. Doesn't mean I'm not concerned. He's too good for his own good. He won't hurt anyone even if they hurt him."

"It might not even come to a fight. Not if my plan works."

Nicola set the book down since she'd finished reading. She handed Colton another that he could read to himself.

"What is your plan, exactly?"

Dominique didn't answer right away. Though Nicola had spent several hours with her over the past several weeks, there was still a lot she didn-'t know about her sister.   Dominique had said that the reason she was in exile was because she fell in love with someone who wasn't in the coven. Nicola could understand why that would piss off Simeon but there was still a lot about Dominique's life in the coven that Nicola wanted to know.

"Do you trust me?" she asked.

"In theory. Why?"

"There are some things you don't know about me that I would be happy to talk with you about. But for now, I just need you to keep an open mind."

"Dom, you're scaring me. Open mind about what?"

Instead of answering, Dominique pulled over to the side of the road. If she couldn't say it while driving, it had to be serious. She even killed the engine and Nicola held her breath.

"I'm Simeon's blood mate."

Nicola felt like she'd been punched in the gut. This woman that she'd trusted with so many secrets and whom she'd confided in for the past several days had lied to her. She should have known better than to trust anything Ryan told her.

"You were spying on me?" she asked.

"It started out that way. Simeon wanted me to scare you into joining the coven. He would have me lock myself up down there and hide the key until you would leave. We had someone watching the place so I would know when you were coming. But after I met you and saw what a kind and thoughtful person you were, I couldn't do it anymore. I told him I was done and that's when he took my key and flushed it down the toilet. For the past four days, I've been locked down there for real."

Nicola bit her lip. "You lied to me. How am I supposed to know you're not lying now?"

"Because my lie was only half a lie. Nicola, I am your sister."

"How is that possible? You just told me you were Simeon's blood mate."

Dominique gave her a pointed look and Nicola let that information sink in. She was his blood mate and she was his daughter. She could have thrown up.

"I didn't know he was my father until our son was born. He had several birth defects and the doctors told me privately that they were consistent with inbreeding. When I confronted him about it, he admitted to being my father and forced me to remain his blood-mate. I hated every moment of it. I felt awful being with him like that when I knew who he was."

Nicola covered her face with her hands, trying to let all this sink in. It was a lot to process and she understood why Dominique pulled over. She didn't say anything for a while, and they got back onto the road. Colton never said a word because he probably didn't understand anything they were talking about. How could she explain to her four-year-old that his own grandfather had tried to kill him and that his aunt was in on it? She didn't have it in her.

"Are you mad?" Dominique asked after a while. "I understand if you are." She paused. "You know I was a twin as well. Simeon split us up when we were five years old. One day, I plan to find out where he is. It's the reason why I wanted to escape. It's taken me years to finally break free from the coven, and I couldn't have done it without you. I am forever in your debt."

"I am mad, but not at you. I'm mad at Simeon. God, I could punch him in his stupid face over and over. I'm sick of him! I can't believe I ever wanted to meet him in the past. I wish I'd never even heard his name."

"You and me both. I had to remain his blood mate for three years after I found out about who he really was. By then, I was in love with him." She turned tear filled eyes to Nicola. "Am I sick?"

Nicola reached over and took her sister's hand. She knew better than most that life was too short to be angry at your siblings. She'd lost Mona and that had ripped her heart out. She was going to do everything she could to make sure the same thing didn't happen with Dominique.

"I'm going to take care of you now," she said. "Lucas' family is awesome and they'll welcome you in a heartbeat."

Dominique smiled. "Yeah, they are pretty great. I'll never forget what your friend J.D. did for me. I love our great aunt Melody. Cherish is wonderful too. I must say that you are one lucky woman to score a man as delicious as Lucas."

Nicola often thought the same thing. She'd loved him since childhood and never dreamed that they would get together. She couldn't imagine having a better man at her side.

"I am lucky, aren't I?"

"Damn straight."

Colton gasped from the back seat. "You said a bad word!"

Both women laughed. Nicola knew that Colton had to hear a lot of bad language because he was around J.D. and Cherish, both of whom had colorful vocabulary. Melody often scolded Cherish for dropping the F bomb too much. So far, he hadn't picked up on any of it.

"Colton, you're not allowed to swear until you're eighteen okay?" Nicola said.

"Why eighteen?"

"Because then you're a legal adult and you can do whatever the hell you want."

He scrunched his brow in confusion then smiled. "Okay!"

Everyone laughed again. She was glad they were able to switch to a less serious conversation. Nicola had a feeling they wouldn't get many chances to laugh in the next couple of days and she wanted to make the most of the time they had before everything would get ugly. Simeon wanted blood and there was a chance he might get that.

A black car raced up behind them and slammed into the bumper, causing Nicola to grab onto the door support. Dominique looked back then tried to speed up, but then the car approached from the side and rammed into them again. After it hit a second time, Dominique pulled over. If she didn't, they would probably end up rolling and that was more dangerous than stopping.

The black car slowed down then parked behind them and Nicola unbuckled her seatbelt.

"Stay in the car," she said. She got out, slamming the door behind her and stalked towards the vehicle. The driver didn't get out, but she could see it was a Simeon.

"Get out!" she yelled. "Get out or I'll drag you out myself!"

Five seconds ticked by then the door opened. As the driver got out, Nicola glared at the man who had given her half his DNA. That was basically all he'd contributed. She thought she was done with him.

"Why are you here?" Nicola asked. "You said we were free from the coven!"

He gave her a menacing smile. "And I am true to my word. However, I failed to inform you of certain rules." His eyes slid over to the car. "As my blood-mate, she has to answer to me."

Against Nicola's wishes, Dominique got out of the car. Nicola couldn't believe this was happening. When did he ever quit? Why couldn't he just leave them be?

"What do you want, Simeon?" she asked.

"I believe we have unfinished business, my love." He swiftly moved over to her before Nicola could stop him. "You know the rules."

Dominique's eyes widened in fear and she began to tremble.

"What are you talking about?" Nicola asked. "What rules?"

"Your sister is my blood-mate. That means there is only one condition for her to be released from our union." He stroked Dominique's cheek. "So, what's it going to be, Dom? You going to come back to me? Or suffer the consequences."

The fear in her sister's eyes turned to defiance as she looked up at his face. "I will never go back to you, you sick bastard."

Nicola sucked in an angry breath through her nostrils then sped towards Simeon, knocking the knife out of his hand then grabbed him by the throat. If she were to ever revive the Redheaded Fury, this was the best time to do it.

"I don't want to listen to you anymore." She squeezed harder. "You have done more damage than Dominique ever did. You tried to have my son killed. You spread lies about Cherish that nearly turned her family against her. Let's not mention you tried to frame me for murder. At least Dominique had motive. You're just a sick son-of-a-bitch who likes to screw with people for fun."

Simeon smirked. "Just you watch, honey. You think framing you for murder was bad? I could do so much more. I will make you wish that your mother had given you to me instead of —"

Nicola frowned. "Instead of who?"

He chuckled. "Still haven't figured it out yet?" He leaned close to her ear. "Check the coffin."

He shoved Nicola away from him and she hit the ground with a hard thud. He got into the car, staring it, and she got back up with the intent of stopping him. As he smirked at her through the windshield, she did what Cherish would have done and flipped him off.

Instead of starting a fight she would probably lose, she urged Dominque to get into the car and they drove away. She needed to get to Robin and Abe before any more coven members tried to stop her.

"You doing okay back there, baby?" she asked Colton.

"Yes, mamma." His voice was quavering. "Why did that mean man want to hurt Dominique?"

Her sister forced a smile and looked at him in the rearview mirror. "Because he's a bad person, Colton. But you don't have to be afraid of him. We'll protect you."

52

Robin heard the door to her hospital room open and she smiled when she saw Abe. She'd hated being away from him while she underwent an examination and hadn't expected them to give her a sedative. Apparently, she'd broken her tailbone during the delivery, which wasn't that uncommon.

She'd slept through the afternoon and woke to hear her report. The doctors said she was fine and very lucky. She never would have gotten through it without Ezekiel and she would forever owe him.

Abe leaned over and lightly kissed her forehead. Her five seconds of bliss ended at that moment and she felt guilt once more. She'd never thought that she would be torn between two men. But it felt like an unimportant thing to worry about now. She had new priorities, and one of them was lying in a glass basinet next to her bed.

The surprise infant had been born weighing six pounds and four ounces. She was sixteen inches long and was suffering from respiratory problems. A side effect from Robin smoking while pregnant. If she'd known, she never would have picked up a single cigarette.

She hadn't held the little girl since the EMT's took her away in the ambulance and she was afraid to now. She went from getting her driver's license to having her first kiss to experiencing her first time, and now she was a mother. She had wanted to grow up but not this fast.

"Where's Erik?" she asked.

"He's in the hallway. He's still a little freaked, but he does want to see you. How are you feeling?"

"Like I just had a baby." She glanced at the basinet. "What the hell am I going to do with her?"

He chuckled. "Did you just say hell in front of your newborn?"

Abe reached his hand into the basinet and let the baby grip his finger. It was odd to see him so good with the baby. Robin never pictured him as a father, and yet he acted like he was already attached to the tiny human. He was more attached than she was. It still hadn't quite sunk in yet.

"We should name her something unique," Robin said. "Something sophisticated that can also have options for a nickname. When I was in school, all the girls were Katelyn or Ashley."

"Yeah. That's an idea." He took his hand back and shoved it into his pocket. "When I found you in the shower earlier, you'd gone to a dark place. What happened?"

"I didn't like who I was becoming. I was smoking, drinking, cheating on my boyfriend, sleeping with you even though you claimed to be in love with me and I wasn't sure of my feelings. I hated myself."

He lay on the bed next to her and held her in his arms.

"You know I'll love you no matter what, right?"

"Yeah, I know. I just don't want to hurt you, Abe. What if I can't love you the way you love me?"

"Then I'll settle for being your best friend. I'll be there to help you with your baby or to teach you basic life lessons or give you a boost if you can't reach something on the top shelf."

They both laughed. It was true that she was significantly shorter than him, but she was still very tall for a woman. She had David's side of the family to thank for that. Poor Kevin got stuck with the short genes.

"Hey, could you watch her for me?" she asked. "I'm going to talk to Erik."

"My pleasure. Take as long as you need."

She slipped out of his arms and got up. She was tired of lying down and her legs were stiff. She gave the baby's head a gentle farewell pat then gripped her IV rack and left the room. She still needed to speak with Erik, and she didn't want to leave him hanging. The nurse informed her of where the waiting room was, and she headed in that direction.

It was a little busy since it was around two in the afternoon, but she spotted Erik right away. He was sitting in a chair fast asleep. He'd probably been up longer than he had, and she almost turned around so she could let him sleep. Instead, she shuffled towards him then took the seat to his right. He still didn't wake up, so she leaned over and kissed his cheek. That caused his eyes to open. He stretched then turned his attention to her.

"What are you doing here, beautiful? You should be resting."

"I did rest. I slept like a baby—no pun intended."

His expression became grave. "You scared me today. I thought I was going to lose you."

"I fought for my life. I couldn't have done it without Abe or you at my side. I'm sorry I scared you."

His jaw clenched and he looked at his hands that were clasped in front of him. She wanted to reach over and hug him, telling him over and over that she wished things could have turned out different. His confessing that he had lied about betraying her had allowed her to forgive him. That didn't mean she didn't feel something for Abe.

"Do you love him?"

"In a way, I do. He's my best friend. But now that I'm a mother, I have to make her my priority. I want her to have a good father figure in her life because every girl needs a father. Since we have only been together for a month, I can't ask you to take on the role of dad. You're young, successful, and you have so much ahead of you."

He looked away again. "I suppose you're right. Since we're being honest, I have to say that I'm not ready to be a father just yet. Someday, but not now. This whole situation is weird and confusing. So, where does that leave us?"

Taking his hand, she said, "I really do care for you, Erik. You are a wonderful, wonderful man."

"You're just not in love with me." He gave her a half smile.

"To be honest, I don't know what I feel. I care for you, but I also care for Abe. But the bottom line is that I just can't be in a relationship right now. Not while I'm trying to adjust to being a new mom. She has to be more important than my love life for a while." She leaned back in her seat. "I also need time to focus on myself. To figure out who I am outside of a relationship. What I did — cheating on you was very wrong. That doesn't mean that our night together didn't mean anything to me. It truly was wonderful. It was the first time I was with someone when it was my choice, and I will always remember that."

He took her hand and brought it to his lips. "I'm glad. That night was amazing, and I wouldn't give it up for anything. I'm not going anywhere, Robin. I will wait until you know for sure that I'm not the one you want to be with."

"I can't ask you to wait."

"Then don't. Let me make that choice."

Robin leaned over and rested her head on his shoulder. She was glad they were able to have this conversation without yelling or crying. He was a good guy that way and she was grateful that she'd stumbled into his life. Whether she chose him or not, she hoped he would be happy.

"I'm actually starving," Erik said. "You want anything?"

"Got any spaghetti with buffalo sauce?"

He laughed. "That I cannot do. You okay with McDonalds?"

"Do you even have to ask?"

He kissed her cheek then got up and stepped into the elevator. While she walked back down the hall, she heard the sound of a baby crying.

356

There were several other mothers in the ward with babies, yet somehow she knew it was hers. She looked at the basinet and then the bed. Abe was gone. She stood there stunned for a moment but then remembered the baby and picked her up. She rocked the baby and spoke in soothing tones. Despite being tiny, the baby was a little heavy for her weak arms.

"It's okay, baby," she said. "Don't cry."

"I think she's hungry," someone said. A nurse must have heard the crying too and came into the room.

"Oh. Uh . . . is there a bottle I could use?"

"Why don't you try breast feeding her?"

"I guess I could. I wouldn't know where to start. I'm so unprepared."

"That's quite all right. I have a few more patients I need to check on, but as soon as I get back, I'll help you get started, all right?"

The nurse left the room and Robin lay the child back in the basinet. This was really happening. Her head was still reeling from the events of that morning. How was she going to do this? She could barely take care of herself, let alone an infant. She'd never babysat Colton alone. Being responsible for a newborn twenty-four-seven would be even more difficult than watching a four-year-old.

Recognition lit up the infant's grey eyes and Robin picked her up. The entire night, she'd tried to come up with a name and nothing seemed adequate. The baby would have to live with it for the rest of her life. She'd wanted something classy and that's when J.D.'s middle name came to mind.

"Anastasia," she said out loud. "Anastasia Shepherd. Anya for short."

The door opened again, and she turned, expecting to see Abe. She turned around and then froze when she saw the strange man in black. She was getting tired of strangers sneaking up on her and this was the last straw. Instead of cowering in fear, she glared at him, backing towards the wall.

"Whatever it is you want you can't have it. I know some karate, and I won't go down without a fight. Now go on your way or you'll be sorry."

The man laughed and closed the door behind him. What surprised her was that he didn't lock it. If he meant ill will, he would have locked it to make sure no one else came, wouldn't he?

"He didn't warn me you would be feisty," he said. He took another step towards her and she grabbed a syringe from the table. She had no idea what it was filled with and she didn't care.

"I will stab you if you come any closer!"

"Even if I'm here to help you?"

"Help me how? You work for Simeon, don't you?"

He laughed again then took a step back, folding his arms then leaned against the wall. His demeanor was strange. His dark clothing and black hair made him appear foreboding, but his smile seemed genuine. He also had a Texan accent. None of the coven members were Texans that she knew of.

"Ma'am, I truly am here to help. I don't work for Simeon, but he is on his way here as we speak. He plans to take you, but we're one step ahead of him."

She lowered the syringe. "He wants me? Why?"

"I have some ideas." He unhooked a bag from his shoulder and handed it to her. "I bought some clothes. As soon as you're dressed, we need to find your friend and go."

"What do you mean *we*?"

"That I cannot say just yet."

While she was speaking to him, she hadn't even noticed he'd moved closer until he was directly in front of her. He looked down at the baby in her arms and she held her tighter. Her baby had already been threatened by one man and she couldn't endure it if another one did as well.

"He didn't mention you had a baby either. She's precious."

"Anya. Her name is Anya. Short for Anastasia."

"The name fits. She's as beautiful as the grand duchess herself." He stepped away from her once more. "I will return in ten minutes As for your other friend, leave him a note to find Lucas at the station in Euless. I will tell Abraham the plan."

He swiftly left the room before she had a chance to ask questions. What was his name? How did he know her? Why was he so bent on saving her?

53

I sat on the floor in our holding cell, counting the cracks in the ceiling. It had been fifteen hours since Jennifer Meyers confessed to being Micah's mother and she explained how it was possible.

For some reason, she needed time before she would come back and formerly charge us. My patience was lessening but at least I wasn't worried about Lela anymore. In exchange for my cooperation, she agreed to not let my mom suffer from police brutality.

Gallard, Kevin, Lela, and Melody were all in my cell with me. When I told them everything I learned, they were as shocked as I was, more so Gallard than the rest. This was all very strange for him. It was different learning that Nicola had a child by me because we were in a relationship and cared about each other. Gallard didn't know this woman and being the good guy that he was, he felt guilty even though he hadn't known what was going on.

According to Jennifer, she got involved with the whole immortal task force corporation when she was only seventeen. She'd been having problems at home, doing poorly in school, and getting caught with drugs. When she learned that Lela and Terrence Fox were in MITF custody, she bought a ticket and flew down to Miami.

Scott was impressed with her dedication to the cause and helped her emancipate herself so she wouldn't need her mother's permission to subject herself to tests. Scott informed her that the government was secretly trying to build an army made of super soldiers who had all the characteristics of immortals without the need for blood. She said she would do anything to make that happen.

They told her that she was going to be impregnated by a vampire, but she wasn't given the man's name. She was somewhat skeptical but decided she was all in. A month later, tests showed that it had taken, and she was five weeks pregnant. She was then kept in the lab, but had her own room and access to cable, internet, and room service. She remained there for eight months and then she gave birth to a boy, Micah. To prevent any attachment issues, they didn't allow her to see the child or to hold him. The only privilege she was allowed was to name him.

Because of her volunteer work, Scott gave her a great recommendation letter and she was then transferred to D.C. where she became an intern for the new branch in the White House. Over the past twenty years, she worked her way to the top until she got where she was today. That was what Henry wanted to do, both him and Ash. Their goal was to come up with a way for worldwide extinction.

Gallard had given Lela his blood so she was able to heal her wounds. She looked as good as new after having a few hours to recuperate. But the tears and bloodstains on her prison garb still made me angry. Jennifer's brothers had beaten her terribly because of what happened to their two family members. The only reason she'd spared Gallard from the same beatings was because he was the father of her son.

"Dad, can I see something?" I asked.

"Nobody is getting nude in here," Melody said.

Gallard chuckled. "No worries. I wouldn't want my mother-in-law to see me anyway."

I walked over to Gallard and he gave me a puzzled look. I hadn't used my memory prying ability on him yet and I wanted to see if I could see back when everything happened with Jennifer. He said he never remembered seeing her but the perks of my ability was that I could see memories whether he remembered them or not.

I took his head in my hands and closed my eyes. I had to concentrate and try to relax or else I would end up seeing sporadic pieces of the past. Lucian was able to do this when he was inside of Lela's head but he couldn't do it outside of the body like I could. I fished through everything over the past couple of months. Some memories were heartbreaking, like the moment he told Lela that I had taken my life. He was crying but she wasn't and she'd sat in a chair and stared off into space while he held her. I had been the same way for days after Mona died.

Finally, I found the memory I was looking for. Gallard was strapped to a table and wearing scrubs, minus the shirt. A doctor, whom I recognized as Andrew Barrington, injected him with a syringe filled with a red liquid. Luckily for me, I could skip ahead in the memory and I watched as Gallard's hair slowly turned from black to blonde and his skin had more color. After he was successfully turned mortal, they knocked him out with some gas and started doing all sorts of tests on him, taking samples as well.

I was going to release him but then I saw something interesting.

Gallard was walking down a hall, limping because they'd taken bone marrow, and there was a young woman there as well. I recognized her as Jennifer, though she was twenty years younger than she was now. He had on his eye patch and accidently bumped into her.

"I'm sorry," he said. "I should wear a sign: Caution: one eyed man."

She laughed. "Don't worry, I'm not even bruised."

He smiled and then gestured to her stomach, which I had just noticed was round with child. "When are you due?"

"May. I'm four months along, and I'm already tired of being pregnant."

"That will change once it's born. My wife and I couldn't wait for our son to arrive."

"Really? I'm having a boy too. I'm trying to decide if I want to name him Micah or Grayson."

"Do those names have any significance to you?"

She shrugged. "Not really. Grayson is a variation of my dad's name, but Micah is something I came up with."

A guard entered the hallway and roughly shoved Gallard against the wall. They said something crude about interspecies mating and that he needed to keep his eyes off of the young woman. She tried to assure them that he wasn't doing anything wrong but they ordered her to go to her chambers then hauled him away.

That was when I let go of him.

"You met her," I said. "In the lab. You ran into her and she was telling you what she wanted to name her baby."

"That's incredible. I don't remember that at all. She probably didn't know who I really was, or she wouldn't have been nice. I am the reason her father is dead after all. I wish there was something I could do."

"You did," Kevin said. "She let her brothers beat Lela to a pulp and you didn't retaliate. You did a great favor. If it were Lucian, he would have snapped her neck right then and there."

"*I* was going to start snapping necks when they started beating Lucas," Lela said. She pulled her feet onto the cell bench and hugged her knees to her chest. "Not really. I'm so tired of violence. I'm tired of being forced to hurt people to save myself or others and I'm tired of people hurting those I love."

Gallard nodded in agreement then turned to me. "Lucas, was Lucian being honest when he said that you killed Henry?"

I relaxed against the wall and shut my eyes. I'd replayed that day over and over in my head, but it never got easier to think about. Ever since I'd nearly killed Mona in a feeding frenzy, I swore to myself I would do everything in my power to not take a life. Now I was in control of my thirst and my only struggle was not taking vengeance into my own hands. I wasn't sorry that Ryan had died but I don't think I could have killed him had I been blessed with opportunity.

"No, I didn't. I was too preoccupied with keeping Nicola alive to pay attention to Henry. Someone else showed up and killed him."

"Someone like who? Lucian wouldn't lie about it. He actually likes to take credit for those sort of things. Well, he used to."

"It was someone I don't know. But I think he knows you. He said '*I will be watching. Both of us will.*'"

"What does that even mean?" Gallard asked. "He's working with someone?"

"I think so. I have no idea what he's doing but he has a partner. Do you have any idea who they could be?"

The door opened before he could answer, and I was almost relieved to see it was Tyler. He was the only one who seemed sorry that we were in custody and he hadn't inflicted any harm on any of us. He didn't look sad now but frantic. I stood up from the floor.

"What is it, Sherriff?"

"I'm here on my own accord. The others don't know I'm speaking with you and I could lose my job over this."

"Go on."

He looked around then shut the door behind him. He seemed scared out of his mind about being alone in a room full of vampires, but he had to have a good reason if he was being this brave. Either that or he trusted I wouldn't hurt him.

"I just received a call from a David Shepherd. I know him as Mikey, but you already know that. Anyway, he said that the man who hurt my son is a leader of some vampire coven and he plans to kill a lot of people. He begged me to release all of you. He also said that he knows you are good people and that you would willingly return to our custody after you help us elude this threat."

"Did he happen to say why this man is doing this?"

"No, he didn't. He only explained how urgent this situation was. Lucas, we're not equipped to handle a threat this massive. I wouldn't ask if I weren't desperate. I love this town and I intend to protect it in any way that I can. Including investing the help of vampires."

There was no question about whether we would help. If people were in danger, we would help them. Simeon had caused enough damage already to my family and now to Erik's. Nicola had mentioned to me the previous night that there were eighty coven members and there was no telling how many of them were immortal.

"What would you have us do?"

He unlocked the door then looked around before waving me over. "All of you, follow me."

"You go," Lela said to us. "I'm staying."

"No, you're not," Gallard said. "You're coming with us."

She shook her head. "I'm done trying to escape my past. It's time for me to own up for what I did." She smiled. "I'll be fine, old man. Ty won't let them hurt me anymore."

I hugged her and then Gallard gave her a kiss. We immediately filed out the door behind Tyler. There was no one else in the hall and like he had the first time I went there, he led us through the back way out. He checked the break room and once he was sure no one was there, he went in. We'd probably been caught on camera, but considering how preoccupied everyone was, I doubted they were paying attention.

We exited the building and I shielded my eyes from the bright sun. Kevin had transformed again, and Melody hid him under her jacket since they'd taken her purse. We continued to follow Tyler until we reached the back where the station parked all the squad cars.

"Take the green van. No one uses it and they won't even notice it's missing," he said.

"Thank you, Sheriff." I opened the door then stopped. "Tyler, I truly am sorry for not being honest with you."

Tyler gave a weak smile then shook my hand. "Just keep my son safe. I don't know if he'll forgive me for what I've done, but he's chosen his path. All I can do is try and support him."

"Hey!" someone shouted. The group turned around and my heart lightened at the sight of Nicola and Dominique running towards me. I reached out so that I could take her hands. She was supposed to be hiding, not chasing after me.

"Why are you here?" I asked.

"Lucas, Robin is gone!"

"What?

She had a hesitant look on her face, and I had a feeling she wanted to tell me something but was choosing not to. She started explaining how David came into town and how she and Dominique were going to pick up Robin and Abe from the cabin in Bedford. She said she ran into Erik and he said Robin and Abe disappeared from the hospital and left a note saying they were safe but that he needed to come back to Euless.

"What was she doing in the hospital? Was she hurt?"

"I'll explain that later, but Lucas, we need to find her! I think Simeon took her to make her his new bloodmate."

I let out a frustrated groan and leaned against the van. This was perfect. Simeon was not only threatening to commit mass murder, but he was creating a distraction for us. We would be too busy worrying about Robin to put our full effort into a fight with some of us would be trying to find her.

"Okay, here's what we're going to do. You and Erik are leaving with Gallard and Melody and you're going to meet up with David and prepare for when the coven will strike. I'm going to find her."

"I think I'll be of better use helping you instead."

"Nic." I took her face in my hands. "You don't need me. You're stronger, emotionally and physically."

"Lucas —"

"You *are* stronger. I believe it, now all you have to do is believe that for yourself. With Lucian and Cherish's training, you could be unstoppable." I leaned in and kissed her, but reluctantly pulled back. "Take care of our son and our family. I'm going to find Robin. Go with Gallard and I'll take care of her."

She smiled at me before taking my place in the passenger seat of the van and Gallard assured me that he would look out for her. I nodded and shut the door and he left the parking lot to go meet up with David. I was glad he didn't ask me about my plan because I had no idea what I was going to do or where to start looking. I was afraid that I might have to resort to violence and I hated violence.

"Is there anything I can do to help?" Tyler asked.

"Yes." I started heading for Nicola's car. "Don't let them kill my mom."

54

Gallard drove the van over to where Erik was parked and Nicola got out. They had ridden together back into Euless and Erik explained everything what had happened on the way. She didn't have it in her to tell Lucas about the baby. It would only worry him and he would be distracted. She knew how easy it was for him to feel overwhelmed.

Erik was playing some hand game with Colton. Nicola smiled at the sight of them. She was a sucker for men who were good with kids. She waved, reluctant to interrupt their game. The smile left Erik's face and his expression became serious as he took Colton's hand and walked closer to her.

"What's going on?" Erik asked.

"I'll tell you in the van, but we have to go."

He followed without another question and even strapped Colton in. Once her son was successfully transferred to the van, the two of them got in and Gallard left the station. David had texted her again and he said they were trying to think of a place to meet that was far from the busier part of town. The less witnesses to a vampire fight, the better.

"I don't think Lucas should go after Robin alone," Gallard said. "They could eat him alive."

"Oh, come on Gallard," Melody said. "He's not a two-year-old anymore. Lucas did manage to survive both of Henry's attempts on his life. He was thrown from a car and tumbled down a cliff and that was while he was only on blood pills. He can handle himself."

Nicola was half on Gallard's side and half on Melody's. The thought of someone hurting him made her sick, but she had confidence that he would safely get the job done. The ceremonies were always held late at night and the final part known as the blood bonding ritual would take place at midnight. Before that was the consummation ritual and Nicola hoped to God that Lucas would find Robin long before that.

"What I want to know is why Simeon took Abe too," Gallard said. "Why not leave him behind?"

"The note said Robin was safe," Erik said. "That whoever they left with wouldn't say who they were but promised their protection. Abe wouldn't have gone along with it if he even suspected it was Simeon, but . . . I don't know."

Gallard swore and hit the steering wheel with his hand. Nicola was worried as well because Abe wasn't immortal. He was strong and a great fighter, but mortal nonetheless. Simeon would see him as the one thing standing in his way of getting to Robin so he'd probably made sure to eliminate that threat. She prayed that wherever they were, they were together and safe.

Gallard suddenly slammed on the break and Nicola felt the seatbelt squeeze her. Everyone else in the car had to brace themselves as well. She was going to ask why the sudden stop when she looked up ahead and saw that there were four people in the road. By their garb, she knew they were coven members.

"To run them over or not to run them over," Gallard said.

"No, don't!" Dom said. "They're not dangerous."

"But they're coven members, are they not?"

"No," Dom said.

She got out of the car and Nicola chased after her. Though she recognized Ezekiel, she wasn't sure if she could fully trust him. He worked for Simeon, kind or not.

When Dom reached them, she threw her arms around him.

"Thank God you're safe!" Zeke said.

"I have good people looking out for me. I was worried you wouldn't get out in time."

"Wait, what's going on?" Nicola asked. "You're friends?"

"She told us that your family was kind and that they would help us escape," the woman said.

"You were planning to escape the coven too?"

She nodded. "We had it all figured out. You were going to find a way to free Dom and then we were going to follow you."

"Why me? I was as much under the control of the coven as she was. Why did she think I could help her?"

When the woman didn't answer, Nicola studied them further and noticed for the first time that these people looked a lot alike. They shared many facial characteristics and two of them had the same color of dark brown hair while the woman had copper hair. Zeke was shorter in stature than the other men and his hair was lighter. He had a black eye that looked like it recently happened. Their ages appeared to range from late twenties to early thirties.

"Because you are the only child of Simeon that made it to the immortal phase," Dom said. "He keeps us human because he wants us weak. As long as he's the only immortal in the family, he can't be challenged by one of us to be his successor."

"One of us what do you mean?"

The tallest man, one of the two with the darker hair, sighed in annoyance. "We're your family, Nicola. Simeon is our father."

She glanced back at the van to see if the others had heard this and the door opened. Melody got out and so did Gallard but he stayed behind. This was important news to her because Simeon was her nephew, making her every bit as much of their family as Nicola was.

"Does he know you're here?"

"No," the shorter brunette said. "We overpowered our guardian and went to that house in Arlington. When we saw no one was there, we came back here. We heard of our father's plan to challenge Lucas for dominance and tried our best to find you."

"All right, well, get in the van. I'll explain everything to everyone and we'll keep you safe."

They followed her and Gallard opened the back for them. There were hardly any seats left so they were forced to sit on the floor. I explained to Erik and Kevin what was going on and they agreed that we could trust them.

"Welcome to the group," Gallard said. "What are your names?"

"I'm Klara," the woman said. "I'm the oldest, and these are my brothers Ezekiel, Jean, and Casper."

Nicola's phone vibrated and she looked at David's text. He was asking where they were going to meet and what they planned to do once everyone was all gathered in one place. There weren't many places in Euless that were discreet because of how small of a town it was. The group discussed different options while they drove with no real destination in mind.

"You could go to the fairgrounds," Erik suggested. "They're abandoned because there aren't any schedules events until spring."

"That's actually a great idea," Gallard said. "The area is big enough in case this turns into a full-on battle and it's far enough from town that will keep civilians from being caught up in it."

Nicola texted David the news. They may have had over one hundred vampires on their side but having more day-walkers was always comforting. She hoped Lucas would join them soon. Simeon was the only one on his side. They had their army taken care of and now the next order of business was hoping Lucas would find Robin and Abe and bring them back in time for the battle.

55

I stopped at my destination and stared up at the magnificent building. The Catholic Church was probably the nicest building in all of Euless and I wondered why I hadn't taken the time to stop by before. Solomon had texted me to say he would be waiting there until we gave him further instruction and I was eager to speak with him.

I spent about four hours searching the town for the coven's hiding places and I had come up with no results. Nic told me they changed locations often to stay hidden.

The warehouse had long been demolished after the flooding was discovered and the gallery was locked and riddled with alarms. It wouldn't be open anytime soon since Ryan was dead. I was a little ashamed to admit that his death wasn't all that devastating to me. He'd crushed J.D.'s skull and ruined her memory. I was done with this coven and if Robin was touched, they would have to deal with me.

The bell rang to signify that it was noon and I went inside. I hadn't been to church since I was two and I almost felt like an intruder. One way or another, an immortal would feel uncomfortable in a holy place. Lucian said his ears would bleed and Lela said when she went, the sounds would amplify until her head hurt. I had yet to learn what the church would do to me.

I dipped my fingers in the water and did the sign of the cross on my forehead before entering the sanctuary. There were a few people praying in the pews here and there and I spotted Solomon in the fifth row from the front. Before I approached him, I admired the stain glass windows. They were beautiful, but not comparable to the church in Miami, from what Lela told me.

I sat in the pew in the very back and observed what the other people were doing. They were all praying silently and none of them were crying out or murmuring. I decided to do some more praying as well. I definitely had much to pray about. For my mother's safety. For Robin while she was in the coven's captivity. For my group as a whole, who could possibly suffer casualties during this war. And for Micah, who was waiting for me to come back for him.

Unsure of where to start, I pulled down the bench and got down on my knees. For the first time in years, I prayed. I prayed for all of my fears and worries, and I asked for guidance. Not just for the next few hours but in the years to come. This was only the beginning and I knew that I couldn't live comfortably in a nice neighborhood and have a day job anymore. My real purpose was much bigger than that.

Lucas, a voice said. I nearly looked up, but the voice couldn't have come from someone in the church. There was so much command behind it— power and purity. My entire being told me to respond.

I'm listening.

You were right about your purpose surpassing the boundaries of this small town. You were once a humble servant of mine, and I've chosen you to complete a task. You have the power to change the way things are. The immortals have been separated from me for too long. It is time that you bring them back to me.

I thought back to what Gallard had said almost a month ago. He said that God told him the only way to restore the immortals with their souls was for me to die. Did he really mean that there were no other options? Was it too big of a mission to just fight for their rights?

You want me to die?

I want you to speak. Curing immortals will change nothing. It doesn't teach the rest of the world anything. They have to want to accept them despite their species. It is what I have been teaching for generations. Love your neighbor as you love yourself.

How can I get them to think that way? They believe us to be monsters.

Do you trust me?

I didn't know how to answer that. How could I say no? That would be offensive. But if I said yes, how could I look past all the doubt in my heart. This cause was so much bigger than me and I would need as much help as I could get.

Yes. I am choosing to trust you.

Good. You will not be alone, Lucas. I have given you someone whom you cannot do this without. He is the key to your finally harnessing all of your gifts.

He? You mean—

In time, you will know. He suffered greatly but will soon learn his purpose. Together, you can accomplish great things. Tonight, you will be tested. Do my work, and I will reward you.

He never spoke again after that. I opened my eyes, standing up from the bench and I noticed that several people were staring at me. I hadn't been talking out loud, so that couldn't be it. I wasn't wearing anything particularly odd. Even the priests were staring. I finally found Solomon in the crowd and he shared the same look as the rest of them.

"What is it?" I asked.

"You're . . . kind of glowing."

My eyes widened and I took out my phone to see my reflection. I wasn't glowing like a light bulb per say but my hair had turned white again and it was bright. After Gallard had given me my gift back, Lela had to dye my hair blonde but that had all been undone in one prayer session. Solomon finally came over to us.

"Get me out of here," I said. He nodded and we hurried out the door before people would start asking questions. I heard one little boy ask his mom if I was an angel and the priest she was speaking to said he was wondering the same thing.

When we got outside, I was hit with this overwhelming tug. My heart lurched in my chest and I nearly fell over. I felt it to the core and it was like I was being pulled in all sorts of directions. After a few moments, it lessened, and the pull became subtle. It was as if unspoken words were being whispered to me and something inside kept telling me that I needed to go west.

"Uncle Sol," I said. "Where are the others?"

"Lucian texted me not five minutes ago. He said they are all gathering at the fairgrounds to prepare for Simeon's attack."

So, my instinct was right. I was being pulled to that location and if my family was there, it meant Nicola was there too. I remembered what Lela wrote in the journal about feeling a pull before she'd died and how it linked her to Gallard, David, and her friend Lydian. It had to be what I was experiencing, and the pull was drawing me to Nicola.

Go, the voice said again.

But I can't. Robin and Abe are still in danger.

They are safer than you know. Someone has already gone to their aid. Your place is with your family right now.

I shrugged inwardly. If the voice was saying that they were taken care of, I was going to trust it as I'd promised. Robin and Abe were in his hands now and I was to go and help my family.

"Shall we fly or take the taxi?" I asked.

Solomon chuckled. "Personally, I would love to see you fly. In human form, that is. Have you attempted it at all since you first did it?"

"I haven't. But wouldn't the satellites pick up on me and my glowing hair?"

"I have a feeling that the world is going to know about you soon enough. Why not start now?"

I nodded in agreement. It was only a matter of time before I would become a public figure. My mom was already notorious and nearly every task force in the nation knew about the infamous Lela Sharmentino. Would I be known as a good guy or a sympathizer? The more I thought about it, the less I cared. It didn't matter what people thought of me but how they would respond to what I had to say.

"Let's get out of here, shall we?" I said. I put an arm around Solomon's waist and launched myself into the air. Unlike the time I'd tried and failed to transform back in Miami, I had more confidence. I soared higher into the sky and never did I falter.

As I flew, I took in the view of the city from above. It was beautiful. The trees looked so different from that angle and the people below were so tiny. Then I noticed that a lot of the traffic was stopping, and people were getting out of their cars and looking up at me. Normally, I would have been embarrassed by the attention, but instead I laughed and waved back. Some were taking pictures, and some were staring in amazement.

The fairgrounds came into view and I saw the vans that were parked in the middle of the field. I spotted Lucian first because of his red hair and then the rest of my family. I slowed down a little but not quite enough because when I landed, the three of us crashed and rolled. All my confidence instantly vanished. Solomon thought it was funny though and laughed while he stood up. I'd cushioned his fall, thank goodness.

"What are you doing here?" Gallard asked. "I thought you were going after Robin."

"I was. But someone informed me that she was safe."

"Someone like . . .?"

"You know." I smiled and then he nodded once he understood. "Well, now that I'm here, I guess we should prepare for tonight, huh?"

"We are one step ahead of you," Lucian said. "Cherish and Nicola are giving our new friends some lessons in fighting."

I looked towards the other side of the field and saw there were three unfamiliar people gathered around Cherish. No one had mentioned recruiting more help. J.D. was there as well and practicing alongside them with Erik and Nicola. The pull surged through me and at the same moment, Nicola looked at me and smiled.

"I think I'll join them," I said. "Just because I can throw people across the field with my mind doesn't mean I shouldn't know how to defend myself in combat.

I walked with Dominique over to the group and Cherish gave them a break so everyone could be introduced. The four strangers, including Nicola, all enveloped Dominique in a hug. Nicola briefly explained her relation to the four people and why they were on our side now. I had no problem with that. Her family was my family now. I was willing to welcome anyone who wanted to be a part of us.

"So," Klara said. "You're the one Simeon is so scared of?"

I laughed. "I don't look that intimidating, do I? It's the hair, isn't it?"

She smirked. "Not just the hair. Your face, your . . . happy attitude. You're just a kid. How old are you anyway, twenty?"

"Twenty-two. I'll be twenty-three next month."

She shrugged. "I still have eighteen years on you, kid. But if my sister has faith in you, then I suppose I could give you a chance."

"And Lucas isn't happy all the time." Nicola circled her arms around my waist. "You haven't seen how grouchy he can be. He may look harmless, but you don't want to be around when he wakes up on the wrong side of the bed."

"I won't wake up on the wrong side if said side is already occupied," I said. I leaned in and kissed her, causing Klara to groan and her brothers let out taunting *oohs*. I pulled back then draped my arm over Nicola's shoulder. "Okay, aunt Cherish. Let's get this class going again. We have until midnight to be somewhat decent."

56

J.D. practiced with the group, finding this whole fighting thing rather easy. Though they wouldn't let her fight, she needed to do something to distract herself for a while. Trying to remember a group of people she'd known her entire life was mentally exhausting, and she feared she would crack if she strained her mind any longer.

At least the voice had stopped. Occasionally, she would hear it speak and it was frightening. It was bad enough that she couldn't remember anything and now she had to deal with voices in her head. She wouldn't dare tell anyone about it. They would think she was crazy and probably put her in a hospital.

She was afraid to sleep too. Her dreams were disturbing and most likely not something she should share with the others. They had told her countless times that she could always talk to them about her feelings and what she was going through. She appreciated it and it made her feel close to them, despite their being strangers, but how could she tell them she was dreaming of a woman? Or that she felt so out of place? It wasn't just that she had no memories. It went beyond that. She felt incomplete or wrong.

"J.D.?" someone said, snapping her out of her daydream. It was Cherish— the lovely woman with the red hair. Or at least one of them. All the women in this family were beautiful. The only exception was Klara.

She could have been pretty if she didn't have such a huge scowl on her face all the time.

"Yes, Mrs. Sharmentino?" J.D. finally replied.

"Wow, so formal. Why don't you rest? You've had a rough couple of nights and all this exercise isn't really necessary."

She wanted to protest and say that sitting still was worse than unnecessary exercise, but instead she held her tongue and went back to the van. The back doors were open and the redheaded man, whom she learned was Cherish's father, was sitting there. He'd gone into town to pick up food for those who ate and was observing the fighting lesson from there.

"Are you hungry?" he asked.

"Not really. I am thirsty, though."

He reached into the pack and slid a pack of bottled water closer then pulled one out for her. She thanked him then took a sip. The cool water felt wonderful going down her throat. She'd worked up quite a sweat trying to imitate Cherish's moves and the water reenergized her.

"How are you feeling?" Lucian asked.

"Like I've been sucked into a horror movie and the director forgot to tell me who I'm supposed to play. And what's with that man who came out of the sky? He was the first person I saw when I woke up."

"He is your cousin. He's very gifted and you wouldn't be here today if it weren't for him."

Dominique came sauntering over to the van and pulled off her shirt as she went. She had on a green camisole and wore it well. She took J.D.'s water out of her hand and poured it onto her head. When she was finished, she flipped her hair around then took a full bottle and gave it to J.D. to replace the one she'd taken. J.D. was surprised at her actions and slightly intrigued.

"Hey," Dominique said. "It seems we've both been resurrected by the blonde angel."

"Yeah, it appears so." J.D. smiled. "I don't remember it but Nicola told me that I tried to help you when I was killed. I'm glad you got away all right."

"Thanks. I'm glad you're alive as well."

They shared an awkward silence for a bit and J.D. was glad that Dominique ended it.

"Are you going to continue the fighting lessons?"

"No. I mean, I don't know. I'm kind of tired actually. I was going to take a nap."

Dominique smiled. "I actually had the same idea. Would you mind if I joined you?"

J.D. shook her head then they both went around to the front of the car. She climbed onto the hood then held her hand out to help Dominique. The moment their hands clasped a small trill of electricity went through her.

She ignored it and finished helping her then they relaxed against the windshield as J.D. ate. She'd only slept two hours the night before and now she was barely able to stay awake.

Dominique drifted off first. J.D. decided she would shut her eyes only for a few minutes. Long enough to get some rest but not too long to start dreaming. She finished the burger then crossed her arms and closed her eyes.

Despite her attempts to keep her nap short, she fell into a deep sleep.

The dreams came with the sleep and she was once again thrown into another world of confusion. She saw the woman again, and this time she was close enough to touch her. The room she was in was exotic and decorated with foreign paintings and the walls were painted a very shocking purple. She soon realized that she was on a bed and the woman was next to her.

"Well, we did it," the woman said. She had a Texan accent, which threw J.D. off. This had to be a recent memory, being that they were currently in Texas.

"Yeah we did." Her own seductive tone was astonishing. Why was she addressing this woman in such a way? She didn't even know her. It was as if she couldn't control what she was doing. She hugged the woman close to her and then started kissing her neck.

"I didn't mean that! I meant that we finally got them together. I told you it would happen eventually."

"Wait . . . did you know that she was coming? Did you call her here?"

The woman gave J.D. a sneaky smile. "No. She came on her own. But I told her long ago to make a move and she finally did. I'm a genius."

"A beautiful genius." She kissed the woman again. "But we still have a lot ahead of us. We may have a plan but I'm afraid it won't be as easy as we believe."

"I know. However this turns out, at least I'll have you with me." The woman sat up and stared deep into J.D.'s eyes. "No matter what happens, promise me you'll always love me. Because I love you and I need you at my side."

"I could never stop loving you. Je veux passer toute ma vie avec vous."

She then kissed the woman even more passionately than before and wrapped her arms around her. For a moment, everything was okay and she hung onto her bliss for as long as she could until the dream faded away and she woke up.

J.D. was still curled up against the windshield and she sat up. It didn't matter that she had no idea who that woman was or what they were talking about. All she knew was that she loved her and the dream had not been enough.

"Hey," Dominique said. She put a hand on J.D.'s shoulder. "You okay?"

"I don't know. Just had a weird dream is all."

She slid off the hood and Dominique did the same then they headed back towards the group. J.D. was able to vent all of her frustrations while doing jabs and kicks and didn't have to worry about not knowing anyone because the majority of those in the group were new as well.

Before she joined them again, she picked up a couple of water bottles. She knew she would need them even though the sun was starting to go down. It had to be at least five o'clock but it was Texas and the weather was still pretty warm.

"Shall we try for more sparing?" Dominique asked.

"I guess so. What else are we going to do?"

Dominique turned so that she was standing next to her and side by side, they observed the others. The woman with the copper hair, Klara, was getting frustrated by one of her brother's inability to execute a move and was bossing him around.

"Can I ask you a personal question?" she asked Dominique.

"Sure."

She hesitated before speaking again. She barely knew this woman, let alone anyone else around her and here she was asking for her advice. Somehow, J.D. could feel she wasn't as close to her as the others. Dominique was newer in her life and thus easier to talk to. J.D. wouldn't have to worry about upsetting her with her disturbing thoughts and fears.

"Have you ever felt as if everything around you was wrong? Like that one experiment where smoke leaks under the door and everyone but one guy ignores it?"

"I don't think I understand."

"Let me word it differently. I feel like something isn't right. People keep telling me facts about my life and stories from back when but none of it feels familiar. And then . . . never mind, I don't want to make you uncomfortable."

"I don't mind. I reached uncomfortable long ago when I learned my husband is really my father. Now I'm helping my grandmother's family fight against my own coven who wants to make a meal out of this town and my disgusting aforementioned husband-slash-father took my sister's boyfriend's aunt because he wants to marry her."

Dominique was spot on about everything. She hadn't exactly had much time to adjust to the whole vampire thing and now she was preparing for a vampire war. Of all the things that were concerning to her, that should have been at the top of the list. Not her weird dreams or the voices in her head.

"Okay, this might be a little personal, but I have to tell someone. I keep dreaming about a woman. Not just dreams but very intimate dreams, if you know what I mean."

"Oh . . . Oh! Wow that's—"

"I've made you uncomfortable, haven't I?"

"No, just confused. Aren't you engaged to a guy?"

This was news to her. She had been told that she didn't have a significant other in her life. They had lied to her! If they lied about that, what else were they keeping from her? What if they didn't approve of the woman she was with and that was why they never said anything? What if this so-called fiancé was a cover for her real relationship? It had to be the answer because if she was in love with a man, wouldn't she be dreaming about *him* instead?

"Who is this supposed fiancé?" she asked, her anger growing.

"Lucian. Nicola told me he proposed with that ring you're wearing."

Her gaze found Lucian among the crowd and she furrowed her brow. He'd straight up lied to her face. She didn't care that he was trying to protect her. She wanted to know the truth. Knowing things might lead to remembering and he wasn't helping her at all.

Without warning Dominique, she stalked across the field and straight towards him. He saw her coming and smiled but when he saw the expression on her face, the smile instantly disappeared. He must have figured out that she knew the truth.

"Hello, J.D.," he said. "You have a nice rest?"

"We need to talk."

He said a few words to Gallard then followed her back towards the vans. She couldn't even look at him. Not only was she angry but she was confused. If she had feelings for him then why wasn't she feeling them now? It would make sense if she felt a slight attraction to him if she had in the past, but she felt nothing. Nothing but annoyance and anger and frustration.

She pulled him around to the other side so no one could witness their conversation. This was going to be slightly awkward for them, more so her. Before speaking, she took a few moments to calm down. She wasn't sure if she was the type to start yelling or to maintain a calm and collect demeanor. Getting hostile wasn't going to make this problem go away, though.

"Why didn't you tell me that we were involved?" she asked.

"So you know. I guess it was bound to come up at some point." He leaned against the van and kept his eyes away from her. "I did not think it would change anything. You do not remember me or what we meant to each other."

Her anger softened and she felt her annoyance disappearing. She never thought about how much harder it would be for him. How close had they been? Were they as close as she was with the woman in her dream?

"Did I love you?" she asked.

He sucked in a breath and turned even further away from her. That was her answer. She felt like crap now.

"I proposed and you said yes. I was searching for you that night, and when I finally got to have you in my arms again, you were dead. I've never felt emptier than in those several hours you were gone and when you came back and I learned you couldn't remember me it was almost like you'd died all over again."

Unsure of what else to do, she reached over and put a hand on his shoulder. In a way, she understood. Her dreams were a perfect example of what it was like to love someone and not be able to fully be with them — to touch them, or to hold them. That was all a fantasy, though. Her dream could mean a number of things but Lucian was right here and in the physical world. He actually lost something real.

"I'm sorry," she said, no other phrase coming to mind. "I wish I could remember."

He touched her hand then slowly turned around. His gaze was intense and she wasn't sure how to take it. He continued to hold her hand in his then brought it to his lips.

"I would rather show you than try to coax the memories." He leaned in and softly kissed her lips then pulled back "I am going to kiss you seven times. A kiss for every year since I started falling for you up until I proposed. By the seventh kiss, I am determined to make you remember me."

Lucian walked back to the group, leaving her there feeling more confused than ever. Because when he'd kissed her, he hadn't sparked memories of love or passion or even friendship. What she saw was quite the opposite. She saw visions of him trying to kill her.

57

Robin groaned in frustration as she tried and failed to nurse Anya. The nurse never came back to show her how, so she was left trying to guess. Ever since Abe and she left with the mysterious savior, she'd been full of questions and received no answers.

After leaving the hospital, they'd gone to one of Simeon's abandoned safehouse where they remained for several hours. Abe did his best to keep her distracted but after a while she noticed he looked tired. He slept for a bit then woke when their savior returned with food. The man hadn't given his name, but he was kind and so far hadn't done anything to hurt him.

Anya started crying, and tears filled her eyes as she attempted to soothe the infant. She sat on an old couch with a blanket around her legs and patted the baby's bottom.

"I know, baby. I know. Mamma wants to feed you but I don't know how."

Her baby continued wailing, and her breathing was very raspy. Robin hated that sound, and she was angry with herself. Her baby's lungs might never be normal all because she'd smoked while pregnant. Maybe Lucas could heal her so it wouldn't hurt to breathe so much.

Abe, who had been in the bathroom for quite some time, flushed the toilet then came out. When he wasn't asleep, he was in the bathroom. She thought he may have eaten something bad but remembered he hadn't had anything since breakfast. She'd ended up eating his portion of the dinner too.

"Hey," she said when he sat next to her. "Are you feeling okay?"

He took a deep breath then forced a smile. "I think my body is just getting used to my change in diet. I went from strict Keto to eating whatever I wanted."

Robin didn't buy it, but she didn't bug him about it. She lay her head on his shoulder, and he stroked her arm. Anya had stopped wailing and was smacking her lips with her eyes closed. If only she could get some formula, but they'd been told not to leave the house alone. Their savior promised to return later that night and he would take them to their family.

The door opened, and they sat up as the man himself came in. He wasn't dressed in all black as before but more normally with jeans and a hooded sweatshirt.

"Alright, everything is in order. Are you ready to go?"

"Just about," Robin said. "I just need to use the restroom and put my shoes on."

"Why don't you do that?" Abe said. "I'll put the baby in the car."

She kissed his cheek in thanks then went to the bathroom. She didn't really have to go, but she wanted a moment to herself. She had been so overwhelmed with the sudden birth and the responsibility of being a mother while running from the enemy was taking its toll. If she didn't have Abe, she might have lost her mind.

Turning on the sink, she splashed some water on her face then fixed her poor excuse of a French braid before going back out. She expected to see their savior, but there was someone else in the room. Someone wearing a hooded cloak. He stood hunched over, like his back had been injured in some way.

"Hello, Robin," he said. "Are you all right?"

"Yes, thanks to this man and . . . who are you, exactly?"

The savior smiled. "Richard Meyers. I'm sorry for all the secrecy. Simeon has eyes everywhere, and we needed to ensure you were truly safe."

This was a bombshell. She'd been told all the stories about him and what he'd done to her family. She also knew that in the end, he'd switched sides and became a great help.

"Why are you here?" she asked. "After all this time?"

"I kind of owe your father. He saved me from making a terrible mistake years ago and I am helping him with his cause."

"My father?"

The hunchbacked man slowly removed his cloak, revealing his face, and she was speechless. He had wavy grey hair and wrinkles around his hazel eyes, but she could still recognize him anywhere. He was her father, or at least the one who had raised her for the first five years of her life.

She'd grieved his death and later struggled to come to terms with what had really happened and learning to forgive him.

"Mark?" she said in disbelief.

"It's hard to believe the little girl I used to get McDonalds for is a woman now."

She couldn't think of anything to do besides hugging him. Despite the past, he had been a great father to her. He never let the divorce effect their relationship and there was always the fact that he'd loved her even though she wasn't his. His hugs were the same as she remembered only he was feebler.

"What happened to you?" she asked.

"After the vampires were let loose in Orlando, I climbed onto the roof to reflect. Richard joined me and by then the sun was rising. He was going to let himself burn but at the last minute I stopped him. In the process, we both fell through the already unstable roof and I broke my back and shattered the bones in my left leg. I never healed right."

"All these years, you've been with Richard Meyers?"

"Well, not the entire time," Richard clarified. "I helped him with his physical therapy and in return, he used his funds to keep me hidden from the rest of the world. I wanted my family to think I was dead so they wouldn't come looking for me. We've only just recently reconnected when we heard of what was going on with Lucas and the MITF."

"We should move this conversation to the car," Mark said. "I promise to explain everything. For now, let's get you to your family."

Robin quickly put her shoes on then they followed Richard through all the secret passageways until they were outside. The entire building was practically vacant. Robin nearly laughed when she saw the car that was waiting for them outside. It was Mark's Toyota 4Runner. After all these years, he still hadn't gotten a new car.

She climbed into the back seat with Abe and smiled when she saw Anya was safely strapped into her car seat. She kissed the baby's little nose then let Anya hold her finger as they began to drive. Abe held her other hand and everything felt so right.

"I never told you I loved Anya for baby Shepherd," Abe said. "I love it. J.D. will be honored."

He grimaced a little and she turned her attention away from the baby. This wasn't the doings of too many carbs. Something was definitely wrong.

"Abe, no more lying. What's really wrong?"

Richard glanced back at them but quickly looked ahead. They were hiding something from her and she didn't like it. Abe was the person who always told her everything and this wasn't the time to start keeping secrets.

"Robin . . . something happened when Simeon attacked me at the house," Abe began. "He didn't just stab me. He injected me with something"

"You mean he poisoned you?"

He nodded then gave her a forced smile. "It's working pretty slow, but I can handle it. You've helped distract me from the pain."

"Oh, no! Abe, no!" She hugged him and tried not to cry. This couldn't be happening. "Lucas can heal you though. Right?"

He never answered her, so Mark spoke in his stead.

"I did research on the poison while I was biding my time. The average person can survive up to four hours. Abe's size and metabolism has helped him survive longer. It's already been eight."

"Technically, I could have made it to Lucas, but I chose to stay. I couldn't leave you, not even to get help."

"Abe!" she was sobbing harder than ever. "Why did you do that? Why didn't you save yourself?"

He leaned in and kissed her tears away. "Because my whole life, I've never been there. Not for my family, not for my sister, and not for you. I made a promise not to leave your side and I'm not breaking that promise, even if I am dying."

Dying. That very word made her feel as though she were poisoned too. Her heart ached and she couldn't breathe. She hated losing people and she hated the tragedies that this life brought. She could only be so strong and endure for so long.

"It's not forever, babe. Just like Lela, Cherish, and Melody I'll come back. I don't know how long that will take." He gave a half smile. "Look, I know you're still sorting out your feelings. Maybe by the time I come back, you will have decided. But you will always be my girl. Got it?"

She pressed a soft kiss to his lips then rested her head on his chest and remained quiet for the rest of the ride. There was no telling how much longer he would last and she wanted to make the most of it. Lela had been dead for a year before she came back and Melody and Cherish were asleep for over six months. It felt like such a long time and she hoped he would find the will to awaken a lot sooner than that.

Richard finally pulled onto the highway. She'd forgotten to ask where they were going and assumed they were taking her to the rest of the family. While they'd left the building, they explained what had been going on with Lucas and the police as well as Simeon's plan to kill people. With her being human and Abe being sick, she wasn't sure what part they would play.

"Where are we going?" she asked.

"The fairgrounds," Richard said. "Your family and friends are meeting there."

It was a relief they were going to her family. She'd been afraid she would never see them again and she wanted to warn them about Simeon's plan. Simeon may have been temporarily stopped, but now he was probably very angry. He wouldn't be so kind when he retaliated and the more prepared they were for him to strike, the better.

58

Nicola held her breath as she guzzled down the water bottle full of blood. Strength coursed through her and she felt powerful. Like no one could harm her. This was exactly how she needed to be for the battle. Night had fallen and they were forty-five minutes away from Simeon's appointed time. The night-walkers had all come out of the van in their human forms and were meeting with Lucas about that night's strategy.

Even after sparring with the group for several hours, she wasn't tired. She could see that Lucas was looking a little worn out, though. Colton had long passed out in Gallard's arms and the mortals in the group had pitched tents to get in quick naps to reenergize.

Everyone had moved to the rodeo arena and Lucas was standing on the bleachers so the group could hear him. He requested that she stand next to him and she gladly complied. There was no place she'd rather be.

"We're not here to shed blood," Lucas said. "David and Solomon probably already told you this when they asked you to be here, but I have to make sure that it's clear with everyone. Our purpose for tonight is to protect the mortals. To show them that we still have our humanity. All we've ever wanted is to not have to hide what we are and that won't happen when they're afraid of us.

"Simeon has another agenda. He wants the mortals to fear him and he wants to establish dominance. Only pain and tragedy will come from that and we must make sure that doesn't happen. If any lives are lost, it will only be immortals. It would be unrealistic of me to ask that you don't take lives during this battle because we may have to. I want you to do everything in your power to ensure the safety of the people in this town."

The night-walkers let out a victory cheer and Nicola smiled at this man she loved. He had always been so quiet in school and hardly ever spoke in class, though he was very smart and a complete goofball around her and Mona. Now he was leading an army. He had come so far from the timid sick boy she remembered. This Lucas was confident, strong, and determined. She loved him before and she was growing to love him even more now.

The large group separated and began talking amongst themselves. Lucas' family as well as hers came forward for a little debriefing and she could see the pride in Gallard's eyes. She understood because she was proud too.

"That went very well," Solomon said. "I believe we have a good chance of standing up to Simeon."

"Let's just hope that we can keep anyone from dying tonight," Lucas said. "At least we know that Robin was successfully rescued. She and Abe are on their way as we speak."

"Abe rescued her all by himself?" Gallard asked.

"Not exactly. It appears they were never in any danger. She said their saviors were keeping them safe from Simeon."

"I guess we'll have to wait and see. Until then, you two should get some rest. We have a long night ahead of us. There are some more free tents in the van."

Nicola gave Lucas a sneaky smile. "I'm not sure staying in a tent is the best idea. Lucas might push me again."

He laughed. "That won't happen. I'm not in a hurry to push you away anymore."

Gallard raised an eyebrow and Nicola sensed that he was leery of their true intentions for going off together. She would never suggest they get intimate with Lucas' entire family only a few feet away. She did want some time alone with him though. They may have had a lot of people on their side but that didn't mean she wasn't nervous about this fight.

"Don't worry, Gallard," she said. She kissed the sleeping Colton's cheek. "I won't compromise your son. I'll take care of your baby if you take care of mine."

He chuckled. "Sounds like a good deal to me." He adjusted the sleeping boy in his arms. "I have to know. Did Simeon tell you to kiss me?"

Lucas groaned and Nicola squeezed his hand to reassure him.

"Gallard, I did a lot of things I'm not proud of while under their clutches. I lied to everyone I care about, and it nearly cost Cherish her life. But I—"

"It's okay. I completely understand. Let's just forget about it, shall we? I know you're completely devoted to my son." He winked at Lucas. "Now go rest. We have a long night ahead of us."

While she was glad they were dropping the subject, she did wish there was some sort of explanation for Gallard's claim. The coven had her do many wild things but kissing Gallard wasn't one of them. She would have remembered doing something that drastic. What could he have been talking about?

Lucas took her hand and they went to the van to get a tent. Together, they were able to set it up quickly and they climbed into the sleeping bag. She curled up against him so that he was behind her and he started stroking her arm like she always loved. She would be asleep in no time.

"Are you awake?" he asked.

She laughed and turned around. She should have known he wasn't going to let her sleep.

"No," she said, only it was a playful no.

He stopped stroking her arm and rested his hand on her hip. Slowly, he slipped his hand under her shirt and rhythmically massaged her lower back. She liked that even better and she lay on her stomach so he could reach the entire span of her back.

"If you marry me," he said, "I will give you back rubs every morning for the rest of our lives."

"Wow. That's really tempting. But sorry, no. I'm sticking with my answer."

"Why?"

Nicola smiled then spoke in a deep voice. "Because, Luke, I'm in love with your fatha!"

He stopped touching her and rolled over onto his back. Usually jokes like that made him laugh. She could feel his demeanor changing so she sat up to look at him.

"What's the real reason Nic?" he asked. "Is it because of what happened with Henry? Did he turn you off to marriage?"

She should have known he could see right through her. There were several reasons she was afraid to say *I Do* and the secret she'd been keeping him was one of them. Her fear for their future was another. She was scared that something would happen that would tear them apart for good. Something worse than a stupid fight or an enemy forcing them to break up. They had a history of events pushing them apart and though she kept fighting, there was always a fear in the back of her mind that they hadn't experienced the worst of it.

"I feel like getting married right now would jinx us," she said. "Whenever we get to a place where we're incredibly happy, something happens. The first time, I was assaulted and forced to leave town to hide my pregnancy. The second time, Henry started hurting those close to you to keep you quiet about your findings. The third time, my own father threatened to kill our son if I didn't break things off with you. What's next? Either you or I could get killed tonight."

He hugged her close to him once more and she clung to him as if he would disappear. He stroked her back again, but this time it was to comfort her. Being close to him was somewhat soothing her anxious thoughts but it would only last for so long. In less than half an hour, they would be fighting for their lives and the lives of the residence of Euless.

"I have faith that we're going to get through this night," he said. "God told me he has a purpose for me and that it goes beyond helping the people in this town. If that's so, then he wouldn't let me or you die in this battle." He lifted her chin then leaned down and kissed her. "I'm not going anywhere, and neither are you. Not tonight anyway. And if I have something to look forward to, I will be even more motivated to succeed. Marry me, Nicola Hendrickson. If not now, then in the future as you've suggested. I want everything you talked about— my brother back with Mona, peace between the races. Everything."

He reached into his pocket and then held a beautiful ring in front of her. It was rose gold and had a round diamond with tiny ones surrounding it. It was vintage but vintage was exactly her style. She stared at it, speechless and utterly happy at the same time.

"Lucas, where did you get this?"

"I stole it off one of the vamps around here." She smacked his arm and he laughed. "It was David's mother's wedding ring. He was going to give it to Melody when he proposed, but they married on a whim and he chose to buy her a new one instead. He gave it to me before he left and said I might need it in the future."

She felt tears sting her eyes and she quickly wiped them away. She wasn't usually a sap, but this was a wonderful gesture. She never considered herself a material person or in need of a flashy ring to show off that she was taken, but this— she couldn't turn him down now.

"Yes," she said. "I will marry you."

He smiled and threw his arms around her, knocking her down and they were sent into a fit of laughter. So much for no one getting pushed tonight. Once they'd composed themselves, he got up and slipped the ring onto her forefinger. She doubted that they were going to be able to rest now.

But there was something still bothering her. She hadn't told Lucas about what she'd learned earlier that day and she didn't want any secrets between them.

"Lucas, I have a couple of things that I need to tell you."

"Uh oh. Are you airing your dirty laundry?"

"No. But they aren't good things. Would you like me to go from the least bad to the worst or vice versa?"

He sat up and supported himself with his hands. "I think I prefer to gradually get to the worst part."

"Okay, here it goes. Those bruises you saw on me — they weren't from being hurt. They were from fertility injections. They were supposed to help, but I can't have any more children. I'm sorry that we won't have the future of our children running around our yard. It seems Colton will be our only one."

"Oh, Nic!" He hugged her again and she could tell he was as upset about this as she was. She'd hoped for a big family and she'd desperately wanted the children to be his. For a while, neither of them spoke, and they held each other.

"What's the worst thing you were going to tell me?" he finally asked.

This news was by far going to send him over the edge, and there was no way so tell him delicately. She tried to come up with different ways to say the same thing but every possible version of *Robin had a baby and it might be yours* sounded more insensitive than the last.

Before she had a chance to break the news, the tent door unzipped, and Lucian stepped inside. He didn't even bother to announce himself first.

"Oh good, you're decent," he said.

"Would you have come in even if we weren't?" Lucas asked.

"Yes. I'm afraid I have a bad report. Jennifer Meyers just showed up with a lot of back up. They found out about the vampire threat and they believe we are the ones behind it."

The two of them scrambled to get out of the tent and instantly, she saw the sea of red and blue lights flashing on the opposite side of the field. Along with the squad cars, there were three tanks, a SWAT van, and a helicopter was swooping overhead, lights beaming down. She grabbed Lucas' hands and they both ran towards the night-walkers who had formed a stance side by side, making about ten rows. Gallard informed her that Colton was with Erik, Dominique and J.D. in the van then she and Lucas took their place in front of everyone.

If Nicola wasn't mistaken, Lucas' hair was whiter than ever, almost creating a light by itself. His hand was warm and she started to feel a tingling in her own, as if his power were starting to transfer to her. He was radiating with it.

He continued to stand tall even as the officers got out of the cars and approached him with guns. Knowing that Jennifer Meyers was Micah's mother made Nicola sympathize with the woman. They'd both had their children taken from them after they were born, and both had suffered the loss of a loved one.

Jennifer and her two brothers stopped about ten feet away from Lucas and held their guns towards the sky. Nicola had an idea of what was in those guns. She'd been drugged by V.S. before and it wasn't a great thing to experience. It paralyzed the body and with enough, knocked the person unconscious. If these officers freaked and started shooting at everyone, they were in danger of losing half their army. They couldn't afford for any of them to be unconscious.

"You didn't really try that hard to hide," Jennifer said. "The fairgrounds, really? There are cameras all over this arena."

"Who says we were hiding?" Lucas said. "If we were, we would have chosen a better location, let alone left Euless."

"What are you doing, Lucas? I told you that I wanted to make a deal. Your mom in exchange for the freedom of your father and aunt."

"I can't make that deal. I've already traded Micah's freedom for Colton's and I'm not doing that again. But I will fight for the people of this town. We're not the real threat here."

Nicola looked to the sky and saw that three more helicopters had arrived. If Lucas couldn't convince them that they were in fact the good guys, this situation could get hostile very quickly.

"You expect me to believe that there's another hoard of vampires in this town and we haven't seen them yet?" Jennifer asked.

"That is correct. They've been right under your noses for the past month. I tried to use the task force to seek them out but I never realized how massive they were. That's why I've brought some backup."

Jennifer narrowed her eyes as if she were trying to see if Lucas was lying. Nicola could feel the night-walkers getting anxious but as they were instructed, they weren't launching an attack. Lucas had been very adamant about no mortal blood being spilt and she hoped everyone would hold to that agreement.

"Let's say we believe you. How can we be sure you're telling us the truth?"

Nicola and she turned to see Klara had come to her side. One of the officers aimed his gun at her and Nicola quickly blocked her. She'd grown attached to her four siblings rather quickly and after losing Mona and nearly losing Dominique, she wasn't about to let another family member die a senseless death.

"Lower your gun," Lucas said. "She's mortal."

"And I have crucial information." Klara stepped around Nicola. "My father is the leader of the opposing vampire group. They consider themselves a coven. They used to be peaceful people and kept to themselves. It wasn't until after my father learned of his heritage that he became their leader. There are currently eighty members, all who are elders whom he's turned over the past five hundred years. They follow him because he's unique. He's immortal yet he doesn't drink blood but he can still turn another into a vampire. Every decade or so, they commit mass murder to make a statement."

"Eighty you say?" Jennifer asked. "How many do you have?"

"One hundred and fifty," Lucas said. "Not including my son. If you and the other SAITF officers work with us, we'll have even more. What do you say?"

"I will never fight next to a parasite," the other officer said.

He then spat on the ground, and the tensioned kicked up a notch. Never in her life had Nicola imagined herself being of the very species that many despised. She'd suffered a lot from Ash and Henry, but this was pure hatred she saw in these three peoples' eyes. If anyone could convince them that not all immortals were monsters, Lucas could.

"I don't know," Jennifer said. Her gun was lower than before but her face still held a hostile expression. "I don't know you— any of you. Trusting you based on your word is not something I can ask my men to do."

There was some loud commotion on the other side of the field. The officers were trying to stop a vehicle from entering the premises and were seemingly failing. The car was driving rather quickly and dodged all of the squad cars. Jennifer and her partners held up their guns again and aimed at the oncoming vehicle. The taller man shot at the windshield and Nicola grabbed Lucas' hand. The car finally came to a stop and she counted the seconds before the surprise visitor would open the door.

59

I watched as the doors to the Toyota 4Runner finally opened. When I saw Robin get out I let go of Nicola's hand and sprinted towards her. Brian and Daniel tried to stop me but I dodged them easily and once Robin was in my arms, everything felt a little more right. All that was missing now was my mom.

I had been so worried when they told me someone I didn't know had whisked her to safety. I put my faith in a claim from God and it paid off. I looked up to the sky and mouthed *thank you*. When I pulled back, I studied her. I'd imagined her being treated terribly and possibly going through what she had in Miami, but she seemed fine.

"How's my favorite aunt?" I asked.

"I'm perfect." She looked inside the car. "I brought a few extra people, is that okay?"

"It's so like you to pick up strays."

The other doors opened, and I smiled when I saw Abe. I had been worried about him as well. However, he looked a little sickly. Somewhat how I looked up until I started drinking blood. He went over to the person sitting in the passenger seat and helped the man out. But when the driver got out, I immediately recognized him.

"You!" I said. "You're the man who intervened when my brother shot my girlfriend."

"Yes, that was me. I told you we would be watching." He held out his hand. "Richard Meyers."

I heard a loud thud and turned to see Brian and Daniel had dropped their guns. Tonight was a night of reunion for many. I could see the emotion in Richard's eyes as he smiled at his niece and nephews. They were speechless and Jennifer looked like she was going to cry. I was going to say something but then I got a look at the man whom Abe was supporting. Granted he was twenty years older and had grey hair, I knew who he was. Mark Sharmentino.

"Dad?" I heard Kevin say.

He broke from the group as well and hurried towards Mark. The old man reached for him and I smiled as I watched them embrace. It was like witnessing my reunion with Gallard. The Meyers siblings hadn't moved yet though.

"Anyone else you're hiding in that car?" I asked Robin.

"Actually, I am."

She released me from the hug and went to the other side of the car. I was going to ask her who it was when I heard a familiar cooing sound. She shut the door then came back over to me and I was stunned. She was holding a baby girl— a very cute baby at that. Judging by her size, she had to be born recently.

"Robin, whose baby is this?"

"This is Anastasia. My daughter."

I could have thrown up. I had to lean against the car so I wouldn't fall, and yet I couldn't take my eyes off of the child. How had she given birth? The doctors said they'd given her a morning after pill to prevent this. She'd been as flat as a board for months and now she had a baby? Was this baby mine?

"Lucas, I know this is a lot to take in, but we came to warn you," she said. "We overpowered Simeon for the time being but he told me something while we were dancing. He doesn't want to just fight you — he plans to kill you."

Gunfire rang out and I heard screaming. Another shot sounded and I told Robin to get into the car and I ran towards the group. Richard Meyers was lying on the ground clutching a wound on his side and Jennifer was holding him.

I wasn't worried about him since he was immortal but Jennifer looked completely distraught. Daniel was yelling at Brian and they were fighting over the gun. The first shot was accounted for but I wanted to know who had been hit by the others. That's when I saw Nicola and Klara leaning over someone and I realized Jean who was hit. He was bleeding from a wound in his chest. Upon further inspection I saw David had been hit as well and was clutching his shoulder.

"What happened?" I asked.

"One of them shot Richard," Nicola said. "The other tried to grab the gun from him and he accidently shot into the crowd."

I heard a hard thud and turned to see Brian had overpowered Daniel and hit him in the head. This was going to get out of control if something wasn't done.

"I'm not listening to this anymore!" He shouted. He took out his radio. "All officers position yourselves for incarceration. Ready the nets!"

"What the hell are you doing?" I asked. "You need to calm down!"

He pointed a smaller gun at me and shot, hitting me in the shoulder. It hurt like hell but didn't knock me down. That's when I noticed that the helicopters had swooped closer and there were men with guns hanging from ropes and the tanks were coming closer. When the gunfire began, the night-walkers scattered. Lucian had lifted Jean into his arms and Nicola, Melody, and Cherish acted as shields while Gallard carried David.

"Robin, I need you, Abe, Mark, and the baby to get in that van over there. Erik and J.D. will get you out of here."

I opened the van and J.D. stared at us. I never told Abe about the amnesia thing, but he would learn soon enough. Once they were safely inside, Erik got into the driver's seat.

"Take them to the hospital. Make sure all of them are in once piece, all right?"

I looked at my injured people. I would have healed them, but I was needed elsewhere. I promised myself that if any of them died, I would bring them back. No one was going to die tonight if I had anything to do with it.

Erik started the car and I moved back as he drove away. Now that they were taken care of, I could try and save the nightwalkers. I looked up to the sky and saw that those in the helicopters had successfully hit several of the night-walkers with V.S. bullets and were now preparing to land so they could round them up. The sight of them broke my heart and those who hadn't been hit were doing everything they could to drag the unconscious ones away.

The power began to radiate through my body, and I somehow knew what to do. I held my hands up towards the helicopter and it stopped flying midair. The men yelled in panic, and I could feel they were trying to resist me by turning to the left. I was stronger. My anger intensified, and I sent the helicopter spinning then dropped my hands. I wanted to let it crash to the ground. I wanted them to know that we weren't going to be pushed around anymore.

But that wasn't me. I would never kill a helpless human being, no matter how angry I was. Just as it was about to hit the ground, I held my hands up again and it stopped about five feet above the grass. The abrupt stop caused the men to tumble out, but it wasn't that far of a fall. I then slowly lowered it down, careful not to accidently set it on some. The men crawled away and at the last minute, I decided not to approach them.

"Lucas!" Gallard called. He ran over to me and Lucian was with him. So far, my family members were accounted for and Nicola's half siblings were all in the other van with Kevin as the driver.

"Where are the others?" I asked.

"Solomon, Melody, and Cherish are trying to get the rest of the night-walkers to safety. Do you have a plan?"

"Not at the moment. We just need to get everyone out of here. I have to find Simeon. If I don't show up, he might go through with the massacre plan and we're not equipped for that with all the police around here."

More shots rang out in our direction and I saw a bullet go through Lucian's chest. He fell over and Gallard and I knelt down next to him. I knew that a bullet couldn't kill him but that didn't keep me from worrying. Lucian's death would prove catastrophic for all of our kind. Gallard managed to pull it out then I took Lucian's hand and hoisted him back up.

"Bloody hell. Why does everyone want to kill me?"

"Well count your blessings, Lucy Goosey," Gallard said. "Twenty-two years ago, I wanted to kill you and now I don't. They're a lot less foreboding than me."

A cry of anguish from captured my attention and I scanned the crowd. No matter what was going on around me, I could always recognize the pain of loss in a person's voice. I didn't even say goodbye to the two men but ran towards the sound. It was a man's voice I was hearing and I quickly found the location. My gaze locked on him. It was Daniel and Jennifer was lying on the ground. Richard was next to her as well.

"What happened?" I asked.

"She was caught in the crossfire," Richard said. He stroked her hair. "Oh Jenny. I wanted her to be safe. I stayed away so she wouldn't get caught up in this."

I went to check her pulse, but Daniel swatted my hand away.

"Don't touch her, parasite!"

"Daniel!" Richard shouted. "She's dead and your prejudice is what got her here. Lucas is the only one who can help her."

I reached again and felt a faint but present heartbeat. She was bleeding quite a bit and wouldn't last for much longer. There were so many different worries weighing on my mind. I couldn't worry about my family, fight off the police, and challenge Simeon all at once. But if I could do one thing, I would make sure another Meyers wouldn't fall pretty to a death brought on by association with vampires.

I placed my hand over the wound and closed my eyes. Daniel tried to come at me again, but Richard held him back. I could feel the power working faster this time. The electricity started instantly and once I released her she'd woken up. Richard let go of Daniel and he held her close to him, weeping with relief.

"Jenny? Are you okay?"

"I thought I was dead," she said.

"I've given you a second chance," I said. "And I am asking that with that chance, you choose to help us."

Daniel helped her stand then Richard and I did as well. I let her have a few moments to get her bearings before I would start getting impatient. I needed her answer so I could leave, knowing that she was going to call off the round-up. Several of the unconscious immortals had already been netted and thrown into the Hum V's.

"I won't side with immortals," Jennifer said. "Not after my father was killed in cold blood."

"Jenny —" Richard said.

"Wait, I'm not finished." She stepped away from her brother. "I see the good you are capable of. And because you're my son's brother, I can't bring myself to hurt you. I won't stand up for the vampire race, but I am willing to convince the government to hear you out."

"That's more than I can ask for," I said. "Thank you."

She nodded. "I'll call off the round-up. But if one drop of blood is spilled by one of yours, I won't hesitate to burn all of you."

We shook hands to seal the deal and I could tell Daniel was not pleased. As they walked away, I heard her speak over the radio to command all units to hold their fire and to release the prisoners. I turned to Gallard who smiled and nodded. We were safe, for now. And I had most of my army to help in case Simeon's attack went through.

60

J.D. hated waiting for a report from the doctors, but she didn't have any choice but to sit in the waiting room. Seeing her twin brother for the first time was more than she could handle, and it had brought on emotions she hadn't felt for anyone else in the group. She hadn't even introduced herself to him but she had felt a connection. Somehow, she knew in her heart that she loved him.

David and Jean were both in the ICU, but Jean was in worse condition. David had maintained consciousness the entire ride and he was out of the red zone. Abe, however, was quickly deteriorating.

When Robin told her that he'd been poisoned, she hadn't expected to feel so heartbroken. She wanted to see him so badly, but the doctors were still trying to find ways to stop it from spreading. She hated being kept from him and hated that no one was telling her about his progress.

Almost everyone in the waiting room was glued to the television. Reporters had arrived at the fairgrounds sometime before they'd left and were showing live feeding of the chaos. Every now and then, J.D. would see glimpses of people she knew. Lucian had been shot but recovered and Lucas' confrontation with Jennifer Meyers and her brother was caught on camera, though they weren't able to get close enough to hear what they were saying.

"After a very frightening incident with some injured and a near freak accident with one of the choppers, the Immortal Task Force Director has officially called off the arrest," the newscaster said. *"Not all the details have been released to the press, but it is still believed that there is another hoard of immortals that prove to be the real threat to the town of Euless. Police have advised all residents to remain in their homes and all streets are being heavily patrolled by SAITF officers. Until the threat is stopped, no one is allowed outside until sunrise."*

"J.D.," someone said. She turned around to see Robin standing behind her. Robin's eyes teared up and she hugged her. J.D. hugged her back because she felt that she needed it.

"They said we can see him now," Robin continued.

"How is he?"

Robin started crying again. "There's nothing they can do. The poison has hit all his internal organs. He'll be gone within the hour."

J.D. clenched her teeth to keep from losing it. She hadn't even had time to get to know her brother again and now she was hearing that her chance was slipping away. If only she could magically get her memories back. If only she hadn't wandered into that warehouse as she'd been told and stayed in the diner where it was safe.

Robin took her baby from Cherish then J.D. followed her to Abe's room. She couldn't get there fast enough and ended up walking ahead of her. The door was open, and she froze in the entryway. Closing her eyes, she tried for yet another time to will herself to remember. She fished through her mind for something, anything that was related to her and her brother but all she hit was a wall.

Tell him you love him, the voice said. J.D.'s eyes flew open.

Don't talk to me. I told you to go away.

Please. Just tell him. And forgive him too.

She didn't know how she did it, but she ignored the voice and soon enough it quieted again. She then went into the room and stopped in front of the bed. Robin had gone in ahead of her and Abe was holding her baby. He rocked the infant for a bit then looked up at J.D. and smiled.

"She sure makes cute babies, doesn't she?" he said.

Robin lightly shoved him, and he laughed. J.D. forced a smile and moved closer to him.

"Is she yours?" she asked him.

"You would assume that, wouldn't you? Sadly, I am not the father of this precious munchkin."

"But you will be," Robin said. "I want you to be on the birth certificate. If you're willing."

"I'm willing if you give me a kiss. I know you're deciding, but it would be nice to say I died with your kiss on my lips. So romantic, isn't it?"

397

Robin pressed her lips to his then pulled back after a short second. He smiled lovingly at her and in a way, J.D. envied them. He was looking at Robin the same way the woman in her dream had looked at her. That was when something came to mind. A tattoo. Instinctively, she reached up and touched her side. She turned around for a moment and lifted her shirt so she could look at her ribs. When she saw her skin was clear, her heart sank. Maybe she really was crazy.

"*À jamais dans mon cœur*," she whispered.

"J.D.?" Abe said. "You okay?"

"Yeah." She pulled her shirt down and cleared her throat. "How are you?"

Robin took her baby back then said she would give them some time alone. She shut the door behind her, and J.D. took a seat in a chair next to the bed. Abe reached over and held her hand in his, which she hadn't anticipated but the action seemed so natural. She returned the gesture by covering his hand with her other one.

"I'm so glad you're here, J.D. They told me what happened in that warehouse. Just couldn't stay away, could you?"

As far as she knew, no one had told Abe about her amnesia, so he was under the impression that she was the same sister he'd grown up with. Here he was, dying with the relief that she had survived and the thought of breaking his heart with the news of her memory loss felt cruel.

She decided to pretend. She would have to do a hell of a good job and that would include faking an accent. She would do it for him. For this man whom she undeniably loved in some way, though she had no memory of him.

"I couldn't leave you behind," she finally said. She even used an accent. "We came into this world together and as far as I'm concerned, we're leaving it the same way."

He chuckled. "As awesome as that sounds, I would rather you not follow after me this time."

Remembering what Lucian had mentioned before, she said. "Like a puppy, right?"

"I haven't called you that in years. I remember mom was pissed when she found out I had convinced you that you were a dog and made you drink water out of a dish."

"You could get me to do anything."

The smile left his face and he squeezed her hand harder. "I'm sorry that changed. I don't know exactly when we drifted apart, but I regret that every single day. I love you, *mon soeur jumelle*. I hope you can forgive me."

His grip on her hand lightened and she could feel in her heart that he didn't have much time left. He closed his eyes and his breathing became shallow. She stood up and lay on the bed next to him. She felt like she couldn't be close enough with him and this was the only way she could think of.

She studied his face, trying to find familiarity. It was obvious that he had her nose or rather they shared the same one. His jaw was a lot like Gallard's. But there was something there that she couldn't quite grasp. He looked like someone but she couldn't quite figure out who. Their father maybe? She'd seen a picture of their mother on Cherish's phone, but no one had a picture of their father.

The voice had asked that she forgive him and she had no idea what that meant. But she felt the need to say the words so he could have peace of mind.

"I forgive you," she whispered.

He opened his eyes. "Thank you. That means more . . . than you know."

J.D. felt him stop breathing moments before he flat lined. Tears escaped her eyes and she sat up and stroked his hair. As she did this, she began to cry harder to the point where she was nearly inconsolable. She didn't even protest as someone lifted her off the bed and carried her out of the room. That same person set her down and kept their arms around her as she continued to sob.

The person tipped her chin up and she found herself staring into Gallard's eyes. He was crying too and he leaned in and kissed her forehead. She hugged him once more and the longer he held her, the more comforted she felt. She felt the same familiarity that she had with Abe. She started rambling on and pouring her heart out to him about all the things she'd been holding in since the moment she woke up.

"Why do we always lose people?" she asked.

"What do you mean? Are you remembering something?"

"No. I don't remember anything. I just have a feeling. I can't even remember my own brother and now he's gone. All I can remember is this feeling of loss. I lost something . . . someone. The tattoo is gone and the woman . . . she keeps haunting my dreams."

"Wait, tattoo? Woman? What woman?"

"The dark-haired woman. I dream of her and she told me she loved me."

Gallard's jaw dropped and but then he closed it. She couldn't believe she was telling him this. Her brother just died, and she was crying about her own personal problems. But this might have been a personal loss if she could remember. She cared for him, yes, but only because of a gut feeling.

"J.D, I think you're a little overwhelmed. You've been through a lot and this probably sent you over the edge."

"I've been over the edge since I started hearing voices," she continued. "Well, one voice, singular. I figure out how to make it stop but occasionally I hear it again. It keeps going and going sometimes it won't shut up!"

"Jordin—"

"There's something else." J.D. looked around to make sure they were alone. "I get this feeling whenever I'm around Nicola. She scares me. I don't know how to explain it, but I think she hurt me."

"Okay!" Gallard said. "Breathe, sweetheart. You're making me hyperventilate and I don't even breathe." He walked her over to the chairs and helped her sit down. "Now what was this about Nicola?"

"I don't know. Maybe I'm just stressed out like you said. I could be completely wrong. She said we were close, and she seems like a nice person. Forget I said anything."

Gallard sat back in his seat, crossing his arms. "My entire life, I've had to trust my intuition when it comes to others. So far, I think I've been very good at judging whether someone is a friend or foe." He looked at her. "If you have this feeling towards Nicola, maybe you should talk to her about it."

"I don't know, maybe." She leaned her head against his shoulder. "I think I just need some time."

She tried to do as he suggested and calm down. It was enough that she was grieving a brother she never knew she had and trying to make sense of the other confusing things in her life wasn't helping. She would keep her thoughts to herself for the time being. Maybe everything would become clearer after she had time to breathe.

Robin held Anya and rocked her as she watched her family grieve Abe's passing. She couldn't bring herself to cry about it anymore. Crying would imply that he was gone forever, and he wasn't. He was going to come back and she would be there when he opened his eyes for the first time. For now, his family was going to keep him comfortable.

Erik came over to her and he had Colton in tow. How he'd gotten tasked with looking out for Lucas' son, she didn't know. He'd said he wasn't ready to be a father and yet he was great with Colton. She was more surprised that he'd stuck around.

"What are you still doing here?" she asked him.

He told Colton to go see Melody and he did. Robin then handed her baby to Dominique so she could talk with Erik alone.

"I told you. I'll be here for you no matter what," he said. "I'm also here because I'm fighting for what I think is right."

"You should go to your family. Your dad is probably in jail because he broke my family out."

"I'm not going anywhere. Besides, he could use some time to reflect. I still haven't forgiven him for using me to get to your sister." His anger softened. "But he's my dad. I'll talk to him eventually."

Smiling, she squeezed his hand affectionately. The breakup had been hard for her, even if he didn't think so. Their relationship meant something to her and out of respect for that, she'd been determined to keep things civil between them. Erik had been her first for a lot of things — the first man outside of her circle that she trusted, her first boyfriend, the first man she'd ever really been with, besides the assault. This was going to be a tough choice. At least she didn't have to make one now.

"Is there any way I can convince you to run to safety?"

"Not a chance, beautiful. To hell with what people think. I'm already supporting vampires. Might as well break all the rules."

The elevator door opened, and Lucas stepped into the hall with Richarrd, Nicola, and Lucian. She smiled at Lucas, and he gave her one of his hugs that she loved. Melody then handed the baby back to Robin so she could get an update from Lucian.

Anya's eyes opened slightly, and she reached a hand towards Lucas and he kissed her little fingers. Robin wasn't sure what to make of that gesture. Could her newborn know who her real father was? Besides Abe, Anya tended to cry if anyone else held her. Robin had hoped deep down that Ash was the father just so it wouldn't make the whole situation so awkward but part of her almost wished Anya was Lucas' because he was the better man. Either way, Abe said he would claim Anya as his daughter and she would stick with that decision.

Lucas picked up his son and for a while he hugged him tightly. She could see in his eyes that he was tired, emotionally and physically. It couldn't be easy having so many people depending on him to lead the army of immortals. Robin then hugged Nicola and the three of them went over to talk to the rest of the group and get an update.

"David's awake," Melody said. "His wounds are healing nicely. Jean, however . . . the bullet passed through an artery. He has internal bleeding."

"And Abe?" Lucas asked.

"He's gone," Robin said. "He was too sick. But he asked that you don't interfere. He wants to transition."

"Are you serious? Why? I thought —"

"He wants to be able to help. He hated that he could easily be overpowered, and he felt inadequate to protect the family in his mortal state."

Gallard stepped out of a room down the hall and J.D. came with him. Both looked very upset and Robin hated seeing them that way. But she was glad that J.D. was alive and that Abe had gotten to see her before he died. She had faith that they would be reunited again. They had to be.

Soon, everyone was gathered in the waiting room and the group filled up the entire space. Lucas informed everyone that the night-walkers had all recovered from the attack and were waiting patiently in the vans for the next move. Kevin had been tasked with keeping up on local news to make sure Simeon wasn't trying to pull a fast one when they weren't looking.

"Robin, do you have Simeon's phone number?" Lucas asked her

"I do," she said. She took out her phone and texted it to for him. "Why are you calling him?"

"I need to end this. He's either going to work with us or he's going to have to get out of my way. Judging by his previous actions, I'm going to make a guess and say that he's not the most rational guy. He slept with his own daughter for crying out loud. He had my son nearly run over, he hurt Erik to send a message, he impulsively kidnapped Robin, and he poisoned my cousin. I don't know how everything will turn out, but I will stop him somehow.

"Wise decision," Gallard said. "What will you have the rest of us do?"

Luca

s looked around at everyone. "I think that you, Solomon, Kevin, and the rest of the night-walkers should watch out for the coven. Simeon enjoys shedding blood and I want to make sure the town is protected."

"And what will you do?" Lucian asked.

"I'm going to challenge Simeon like he asked. And I want you and the rest of your family to be there. Maybe if you're there — "

"You think we can convince him to change his ways?" Ezekiel asked. He chuckled. "Please. I've been trying to do that for thirty-five years. He's been a psychopath from birth. You can't rationalize with him. You have to kill him."

"No," Cherish said.

That conviction seemed to hit everyone in the room. Robin always knew that there was a possibility that someone would get killed. They always vanquished the bad guy if there was ever a threat to their family, save for Lucian and Mark. Gallard killed Samil and Lucian killed Matthew, both of whom took part in the murder of her mother. But Robin also knew Lucas felt very strongly about taking lives. Even the life of a person as disgusting as Simeon

"I don't want to kill him," Lucas said, putting a reassuring hand on Cherish.

"Why not?" Lucian asked. "Every single person in your family has taken a life with justification. They're good people. They're not evil." He put his hands on Lucas' shoulders. " *You* will not become evil if you kill Simeon while fighting for your life. Because if you don't kill him, he will kill you."

"I'm not killing him. No one is beyond saving. You of all people should know that, Lucian."

"Lucas—"

"It's settled. I will fight Simeon Atherton and I will incapacitate him if necessary, but I won't kill him."

No one said anything else about it. Robin could understand where he was coming from. She didn't feel comfortable taking a life either. She may have knocked one guy around with a broom in a fit of rage, but she wouldn't have killed the man.

"Robin," he said. She looked up, removed from her daydream.

"Yes?"

"I need someone to look out for Cole while the rest of us are busy. You up for it?"

"Of course. Where should I go?"

He looked around the group as if scrutinizing who he trusted most to be her bodyguard now that Abe was currently on leave.

"Take Erik, Mark, and Richard with you. Go the police station and see if you can try to get them to release Lela and Tyler."

She pretended to groan. "Great, I get to be babysat by the Dukes of Hazzard?"

Everyone in the room laughed except for Erik, who seemed to be confused. She didn't blame him. That was a pretty old show and even she wasn't born yet when it came out. But now everything was settled. The only one staying behind was Melody, who wanted to be with David and keep an eye on Jean who was still in surgery.

While the rest of the group filed out, Robin strapped Anya into her car seat. The only perk to her captivity with the coven was that they'd provided her with much needed baby supplies like diapers, wipes, several onesies, and even a fold up stroller. Thanks to Richard's smuggling skills, he'd packed all of it into the 4Runner.

"Is the pretty lady ready to go?" Richard asked.

She let out an exasperated sigh. "I'm flattered, but I must decline your flirting. I've already had a brush with promiscuity, and I've decided that I'm not sleeping with anyone until I know for sure that I want to be with them for the rest of my life."

He laughed. "I was actually talking about the baby."

Her cheeks flushed. "Oh. Sorry."

"Don't be. I would flirt with you, but your dad made it clear that you're off limits."

She smiled. Of course Mark was looking out for her. It was what everyone did. After being kidnapped by Simeon, she decided she would never take their over protectiveness for granted ever again. She'd accepted that because she was mortal, she was an easy target.

"To answer your question, I've got her all strapped up. Whenever you want to leave, we're ready."

Erik came over to them and both men reached for Anya's carrier. Robin laughed to herself, thinking of how her little girl was already having men fight over her. For her sake, she hoped that this would die down by the time she was old enough to date.

"I'll take her," Robin insisted. She picked up her baby and slung the diaper bag over her shoulder. "After you, gentlemen."

61

I put the van in park and sat in the seat for a while. I'd called Simeon at the hospital and he asked that we meet in Pennington Field in Bedford. Apparently, he wanted our fight to be in an environment that resembled an arena. I agreed with his terms to avoid any altercations. The guy was unpredictable enough without my being uncooperative.

"How much time do we have?" Nicola asked, breaking the silence.

"He said he would be here at sunrise. That gives us a half hour at the most."

I turned my face to hers and saw that she had a mischievous smile on her face. I knew exactly what she was thinking, and it was a temping idea. In less than thirty minutes, I would enter the arena and fight for the leadership position.

There was a chance, and I wasn't exactly sure of how big it was, that I could die. It would be a good thing for the vampires, but I wasn't quite ready to leave Nicola and Colton behind. There was so much more I wanted to experience with them. I wanted to marry her and watch Colton grow up and support him at *his* wedding. I wanted to see my brother again and give him the woman he loved. Most importantly, I wanted my family to not have to run anymore.

"Are we alone?" I asked.

"Yes. Lucian is talking with Cherish and Ezekiel outside."

"Good."

We both climbed into the back of the van and before I even had a chance to get comfortable, she tackled me and began kissing me. I chuckled then kissed her back and for a few moments, all my problems were miniscule. I wanted to make the most of the time I had before someone was bound to show up and interrupt.

She slid her hands down my chest and nonchalantly unbuttoned my jeans. I laughed to myself, thinking about how I had been the one who had to try not to cross any lines with her and now she was initiating all the fooling around. I could sense things were getting very heated, but I was in no hurry to stop.

"*I want to be with you,*" I whispered in French.

"*I want you desperately.*"

I stopped kissing her for a moment. "Where did you learn that?

"J.D. She's a great teacher. You know what else she taught me?" She leaned close to my ear. "*I want to get you naked.*"

My heart rate picked up as her hand moved lower and my body responded to her touch. She found the sensitive spot on my neck and began kissing me there. I didn't even notice she'd removed her pants until she straddled me and started rocking against me. I sat up and held onto her as she continued. I wanted more. I wanted her so badly and all my promises seemed to disappear along with my inhibition.

When she took off her shirt, I suddenly came to my senses. It was hard and one of the hardest decisions I'd made in my life, but I managed to think clearly for the first time in ten minutes. I'd promised myself weeks ago that I wouldn't let this happen between us in primitive conditions and I intended to keep that promise.

"Nic," I whispered.

"What's wrong?"

I sighed then buttoned my pants to avoid any temptation. "I can't do this. Not here."

She looked away then picked up her own pants and covered herself. She didn't seem mad but disappointed. I understood how she felt. I wanted this to happen between us just as much as she did.

"Is it because we're in a van?" she asked. I nodded and she laughed. "Lucas, you're such an honorable man. We've been together for eight months. We're engaged and we agreed to be together upon making that commitment." Her expression became serious. "You could die tonight. I don't care if we're on a couch or in a van. I know it will be wonderful and special because I'm with you."

"I know." I softly kissed her. "But I see you as more worthy than any treasure in the world. I love and respect you too much to do this here. You deserve more than this. Not on a couch or in a van." I lay on top of her and started kissing her neck. "Not on the floor or on an afghan."

She started laughing. "Stop!"

I thought of more. "Not in a tree or in a tent. Not on Easter or during Lent."

I couldn't think of anything else and by then she was laughing so hard that she was crying. She was so beautiful when she laughed. There was a moment back when she lay bleeding on the floor that I thought I would never hear her laugh again. I wanted to hear her laugh for the rest of my life. If I was going to die that night, I would die with the memory of her laugh still ringing in my ears.

"You're such a goober, Lucas Taylor." She tugged her clothes back on then smiled at me. "But you're *my* goober. I love you to the moon and back."

"Same here."

I kissed her again then we lay with her in my arms. I quickly checked my watch and saw that we had ten minutes to spare. Every second of those ten minutes would be spent there in her embrace.

Or at least I hoped so. Someone knocked on the side of the car and we both groaned. We should have known our alone time would be interrupted at some point.

"Come in," I said, not even bothering to sit up. The door slid open and Lucian stared at us with mock disappointment.

"You better not be defiling my granddaughter in here," he said.

"Quite the contrary. She was compromising *me*. My reputation is ruined and now no respectable woman will marry me. Not even with my decent dowry."

He laughed. "Sounds like a true Christophe to me." He winked at Nicola then his expression became serious. "I hate to interrupt but Simeon just arrived."

"Sun's up already?" Nicola asked.

"Afraid so."

The two of us got out of the van and I gave Nicola one last hug. I didn't dare say goodbye because I had faith that I would make it through the night. God wouldn't have told me to speak on the immortal's behalf if he planned for me to die. Either way, I didn't want to be overconfident either. Simeon let me throw him down once but tonight he would fight back.

Nicola linked arms with Lucian then blew me a kiss as we parted ways. I walked through the entrance and through the gate into the field. I'd been there one time to see a football game back in September and it was a descent size. The lights were off, but I could see the early rays of sun from behind the stadium. Besides, my night vision was good enough to not need the light.

I was halfway to the center of the field when I saw someone approach me. It was a man in a dark cloak and he had about ten men with him. I looked over to my left and smiled when Cherish waved at me. Lucian, Dominique, Klara, Ezekiel, Casper, Nicola and she were all sitting on the bleachers. We may have only been related through Colton, but I felt just as close to Lucian's family as my own. They were there to cheer me on and I felt even more confident with them in the stands.

Simeon motioned for all but one of his followers to go onto the bleachers as well and they sat one section over. He probably brought them there in case he needed back up. We'd had the same idea. There was no way I would have met him alone. I didn't trust him as far as I could throw him, and I could throw pretty far.

We came to a stop in the center and stood about thirty feet away from each other. He removed his cloak and then gave it to the man who accompanied him and the man then joined the others on the bleachers. Simeon was dressed in black pants and shoes but no shirt. He had several tattoos on his arms, all related to his coven. He looked sinister, and I could see why Klara was so skeptical that I was his opponent.

"Greetings, Lucas," he said. "How is that cousin of yours? Abe, was it?"

I flipped him off and he laughed.

"I apologize for my attire," he continued, "but it is customary for coven members to be bare-chested during a match. I hope you don't mind."

I shrugged. "I don't mind at all. It makes it easier for me to draw blood."

My group began slamming their feet on the bleachers in a rhythmic drumming and then let out a short battle cry. I smiled. In a way, it was a fancier way of saying *ba dum tsh.*

"Then why don't we make it fair?" Simeon asked. "Remove your shirt."

"Wow. You could at least ask me to dinner first."

I did as he asked then tossed it to the side. I'd showered while I was in jail, but I was wearing the same jeans from when we first turned ourselves in. It would be hard to maneuver in them but I could make due.

"Before we begin, we should state the terms," he said. "Since I am the one challenging you, you get the privilege of going first. Have you any specific preferences?"

"Yes. If I win, then your coven will abide by my terms for this cause, no questions asked."

He nodded. "Fair enough. Let's not dilly dally any longer, then."

"I'm not finished. You will abide by my terms *and* Lucian takes your place as the coven leader."

Gasps erupted from both groups and Simeon's jaw tightened. He hadn't expected that one. I hadn't really given that part of the deal much thought, and I had only come up with it at that moment. I wanted to ensure that no one would be victim to his tyranny ever again and the only way to do that was to strip him of his leadership.

"You are bold, young man." He crossed his arms over his muscled chest. "Now I will state mine. If I win, your family, including my children, will be free to do as they please. They can continue with their cause with or without me and I will not interfere any further."

I raised my eyebrows. That didn't sound like terms to me. It sounded like a bargain that was too good to be true. I expected worse from him.

"Okay, lets—"

"I'm not finished," he said in a mocking tone. "I get the privilege of wiping out the d'Aubigne bloodline. That includes Lucian's lover, your father. Hell, I'll even hunt down that brother of yours. Micah, is it?" He gave me a menacing smile then turned to look at my group. "And I'll save Colton for last."

"No!" Nicola shouted from the bleachers. Cherish put an arm around her and tried to soothe her. "Hell will freeze over before you touch him!"

"If you do not abide by the terms, I will slaughter anyone in my way. Starting with Robin's baby."

As much as I hated these terms, I had no choice but to agree to them. It only gave me more motivation to win this duel. I couldn't let what happened to him happened to my family, especially Colton.

"I will abide by the terms," I said.

Simeon then took a knife out of his boot and sliced his hand as he stepped closer to me. He handed the knife to me afterwards and I did the same. We joined hands to seal the agreement then he returned the knife to his boot. My hand healed quickly and I could feel the power within me start to activate. I wanted to use it so badly, but it gave me an unfair advantage. I would fight this fight with my physical strength and nothing more.

"Are there any rules?" I asked.

"Only one. No weapons that are not attached to your body. Oh, and no mouth shots. We may be immortal, but we can't regenerate more teeth."

"Sounds good to me. Your looks are probably all you have going for you anyway."

Simeon's face wrinkled into a snarl and he shoved me backwards with full force. I tumbled head over heels, and I was about to collide with the bleachers when I used my power to steady myself and I stopped, suspended in mid-air then lowered myself to the ground.

"What are you?" Simeon asked, disbelief riddled on his face.

"Someone you don't want to piss off."

I flew at him and knocked him off his feet and onto the ground. We had more than enough space to compensate for our strong throws and kicks and we made the most of it. His blows were painful, but I quickly learned to block out the pain and fight back.

I got him into head lock, and he struggled for a while. I thought I was gaining the upper hand when he punched me in the side, breaking my ribs. I let go of him and fell to the ground, gasping for air. It was painful but tolerable. Not as bad as when I went through the windshield and tumbled down the cliff. It was kind of gross feeling the bones knit back together but at least I was healing fast.

Simeon kicked me again and basically re-broke the ribs. This time, I didn't stifle the yell that was building in my throat. I could hear my group booing in the stands. It took a very low person to kick someone while they were down, but there were no rules against it. For him, this was a fight to the death, and he intended to kill me.

"Get up!" he shouted. He kicked me again and I grew dizzy. "Come on! You're a day-walker. You should be more resilient than this!"

"*Brûle en l'enfer*," I whispered.

He wrapped his fingers around my throat and lifted me into the air so that I was facing him.

"Say that in English, you little fledgling bastard!"

"I said, 'Burn in Hell.'"

I head-butted him and he yelled as he let go. I hadn't meant to aim for his nose but I was sure by the sound that I had broken it. I remembered my mom told me she'd used the same move when fighting several times and I was grateful that it came to mind at that moment. My head was cut in the process and blood dripped into my eyes. I had to wipe it away as best as I could. The maneuver gave my ribs more time to heal and once I was recovered, I went for him again.

I punched him in the jaw after he stood up then kicked him in the chest. He fell back and took his time standing. I hadn't kicked him *that* hard, but he was acting like he was running out of energy. I soon realized I'd underestimated him. He feigned nonchalance but then came at me swing so hard and fast that I could barely block any of the blows. I felt my spleen rupture as his fist met my side and I responded by grabbing his arm and flipping him over my shoulder.

Once he was on the ground, I jerked it to the left, dislocating it. He cried out then kicked me in the shin, fracturing the bone. My knees buckled — a big mistake on my part and he kicked me in the head, causing me to do a one-eighty turn and I landed on my stomach.

"You fight like an amateur," he said. He kicked me in the side, breaking my ribs yet again. I was starting to get the feeling that this was his favorite move. "I expected more from you!"

"What . . . for?" It was hard to speak through the pain. Blood filled my lungs and I was pretty sure the blow to my head had fractured my skull.

"You're their leader! They're expecting you to lead them into war and you can't even execute a decent punch. Sure, you can heal and resurrect the dead but in battle, you are useless."

Since he wasn't hurting me, I forced myself to sit up. He had a good point. I had decided to become the voice for immortals all over the country and yet I wasn't this big strong warrior. I'd spent most of my life in a hospital and at times I could be clumsy. I wasn't a violent person and the thought of causing someone pain bothered me. The only reason I'd agreed to fight Simeon was because I wanted to somehow stop him from hurting those close to me. I went into that arena knowing full well I would probably lose. That didn't keep me from walking away — my love for my family did.

"You're right," I said. I stood, wincing as I tried to favor my broken calf bone. "I can't fight. I suck at it. The only fight I've ever been in was when I was nine and I hit a guy for beating up my little brother. And it wasn't even a real fight because after I overexerted myself, I passed out."

I could feel my body had restored itself, so I stood up straighter. "I never pretended to be something I'm not. Yeah, I can't fight, I get very depressed, and, well, I'm a virgin. That goes to show that I don't have much life experience. I'm only twenty-two, for crying out loud, and you're over five hundred. But none of these facts matter because I care. I care about our race and I want to use what gifts that I do have to help them."

Simeon's lips curled into an amused smile. "You talk far too much. Perhaps your tongue will inspire our kind to follow you. Unfortunately, I don't care much for talking."

He took a step forward and I backed up.

"Let's just end this now, Simeon. We can work together and compromise. Either way, I'm not going to kill you."

"Pity, because I want to kill *you*."

Somehow, his words gave me an idea. He started moving close to me and I knew I had to act fast. As soon as he was close enough, I used my abilities to keep him from being able to move any further and I took his head in my hands. Instantly, images began forming and I saw everything.

I witnessed the heartbreaking reality of his childhood. A young boy who tormented his older sisters endlessly — who did cruel things to them, only to laugh when they cried. He was equally as cruel to his stepmother and she often beat him, only to get no response. She would scold him for disobeying her rules and he would stare at her with no remorse whatsoever.

I saw his early adulthood. He would enchant women of all ages and seduce them, only to admit he did it for fun. He even convinced a married Duchess to leave her husband and children for him and after they'd crossed the ocean to America, he murdered her in her sleep and left the body in his house to rot. He'd taken Florence Christophe with him and they spent several centuries together.

Skipping forward in time, I searched until it was the nineties. He was attending college in Florida and he was intrigued by a blonde woman who was laughing with Florence. I recognized her as Sheila Sharmentino, my grandmother. They were at a party and he tried to make a move on her. He started getting inappropriate and then Mark showed up and put him in his place. It was odd seeing him so young while he was so old and feeble now.

The final memory I saw was from about three years before. He'd gone to a hospital and went into one of the rooms. Dominique was lying on the bed and crying. She told him that their son had been born with severe birth defects, including being without a set of lungs. He'd died minutes after he was delivered.

"They say these defects are only common in children born from two people with similar DNA," she said. *She looked up at him, tears streaming down her face. "Are you my father?"*

"Don't be ridiculous, Dom."

"Are. You. My. Father?"

He clenched his jaw then a sheepish grin spread across his face. "All right, yes. I am your father. So what?""So what? So. What?" She slapped him across the face so hard that even I flinched, though I wasn't there. "You're sick! You disgusting, vulgar, perverted bastard! I loved you! I was in love with my own father! How could you deceive me like this?" She began sobbing. "I hate myself. I want to die. Please just kill me like you killed the others."

In one swift move he reached out and clutched her throat as he had mine. She struggled for a bit but then she stared up at him with gratitude and it broke my heart. He must have seen it because he let go.

"I won't make it that easy for you. You'll forgive me in time. But if you die, it will be on my terms and mine alone."

I let go of him, unable to watch anymore. I had hoped his memories would show me why he was the way he was. Why he felt the need to kill and destroy those around him. Instead, I saw a lifetime of pure insanity. He didn't even have hate inside of him. It was something else. And I realized that I couldn't save him.

"What did you do to me?" he asked.

"I broke the rules. I see now that talking really is pointless. Nothing I say will change your mind about killing me."

I saw movement in the corner of my eye and turned as Lucian stood up. He was pointing at something and shouting but I couldn't hear him. I strained my hearing until his voice registered by then, his warning was too late. Simeon pulled his dagger from his pocket and drove it into my chest. He only pushed it about an inch, but it brought me to my knees nonetheless.

I could hear my group yelling and screaming but it was warbled. They were running towards us and at the same time, his followers left their place and attempting to block the way. My heart continued to beat but each pound sent blood spurting from the wound. It was working overtime to keep me alive and I could feel it losing the battle.

"You broke the rules," Simeon said. "Now it's my turn."

He shoved the knife all the way until the hilt touched my skin and I could feel as it severed something crucial. An artery maybe or my aorta. The pain lasted only for a few moments and then my body became light. My gaze found Nicola and I smiled at her before there was a brilliant flash of light and I felt my body flying backwards and everything went dark.

62

Gallard watched the horizon as the first signs of daylight began to appear. There were no signs of the coven and soon it would be too late for them to fight. It would be nice if they didn't show up. He would rather get to his son and make sure Simeon didn't wipe the floor with him. Lucas wasn't a violent guy and he doubted Lucas had an ounce of bloodlust in him. He wouldn't kill Simeon unless it were necessary. Or maybe he wouldn't. He hadn't even killed Henry after Nicola was shot.

Terrence groaned out of boredom and kicked a rock off the roof they were watching from. Solomon, Ramses, and Kevin had all taken positions lower down while Gallard, Terrence, and Arnaud were the eyes from above. Having a stakeout with these men reminded Gallard of the old times, back when they were young and naïve boys and itching to shoot anything that moved.

"This is *merde cheval*," Arnaud said. "I come here for a war and the only action we get is a couple of trigger-happy yanks."

"If I recall, those trigger-happy yanks knocked ye out with a V.S. bullet," Terrence taunted. "Shows how useless you are."

"Do not talk to me of uselessness. I did not spend the past three hundred years as a bar bouncer."

"No, you spent the past three hundred years sitting on your arse and waiting for someone else to start a war for ye."

Arnaud started to lunge at Terrence when Gallard put a hand to his chest to stop him. Just like old times, the two men weren't getting along. Terrence's hate was not misplaced since it was Arnaud's fault that he had to turn. Gallard never asked for them to like each other but he wanted them to be civil to maintain unity among their army.

"The wars were so much more fun back in our day," Arnaud said once he'd calmed down. "We were legendary. I will never forget the look on their faces when Gallard returned from avenging Dyani."

Terrence laughed through his nose. "I remember. When Gallard returned he brought their bodies with him on a cart. When he got to the Shawnee camp, he dumped them in front of Lalawethika's tent and the whole family watched them burn."

That had been one of Gallard's darkest days. When Bodoway's cousin had shown up at Gallard's father's house and told him the news of Dyani, he'd lost it. He made the mistake of seeing her body and it sent him spiraling into a rage.

"I remember they called me White Death," Gallard said. "For years you two and Bodoway were the only ones who called me by my name."

Terrence's smile left. "I miss B. I was his bouncer for thirty years. We had many a good talks during those years. Mostly we would bet whether or not you and Lela would end up together."

Gallard laughed. He remembered too well the excitement on Bodoway's face when he'd told him that they were married. *You married the shark wrestler?* He'd said. It amazed Gallard that long before he and Lela were even romantically interested in each other that he'd seen Lucas in Lela's future. First he thought it was Tyler and then himself. The end result was better than he could have imagined.

"Since we may die tonight, there's something you should know," Gallard said to Terrence.

"I thought we knew all your dark secrets," Arnaud said.

"Not all." He sighed. "I never slept with Celeste."

Terrence's eyes grew wide. "But I saw ye! You were with 'er in yer house!"

"I only made you think you'd caught us. I'd arrived merely minutes before you did. I found her with Gaspard."

Arnaud's jaw dropped. "You're kidding me! Your baby brother?"

"Yes. He'd been in love with her for a while. They spent a lot of time together while Terrence and I were at war. I guess they had an affair when he was sixteen and it lasted until we returned. She claimed that she felt alone, and she feared you would never marry her. While I didn't approve of the deception, I owed him for when I had been with Dyani after they married, so I took the fall."

"That little bastard," Arnaud said. "Then again, Gaspard had always been the best of us, hadn't he?"

Gallard smiled. "Yeah, he was."

Terrence put a hand on his shoulder. "Thank you for telling me."

"Up ahead!" Gallard heard Solomon shout.

The three men moved closer to the edge and scanned the area. The streets were dead because everyone was on lockdown in their homes. He saw the figures moving down the street and by their cloaks he knew they were the ones everyone had been waiting for.

They jumped down to the ground just as their section of the army gathered on the streets below. Solomon rounded the corner with his group, and they met in the middle of the road just as the coven stopped ahead of them. Gallard stepped forward to be the spokesperson.

"Okay, let's be rational here," he said. "We have one hundred and fifty and you have eighty. We don't want to hurt anyone."

"Actually, we do," Arnaud said. "We want to crush your skulls in our fists."

Gallard elbowed him in the ribs. "We do not want to hurt anyone. So what's it going to be? Are you going to fight and lose or are you going to compromise and come to an agreement?"

"Your cause is futile. You saw what that task force did to our people tonight. They will not listen. Which is why Simeon is going to make them listen. We will tear humanity to pieces until they have no choice but to surrender."

"Right, because genocide has always answered our problems in the past. Starting back in Egypt. The Pharaoh felt like the Israelites were growing too numerous and feared for their lives. So they killed the firstborn sons. Hitler wanted a pure race, so he targeted those who disabilities, those of different sexual orientation, and let's not forget the Jews. Now they're doing the same thing to us. Violence begets violence."

The man gave Gallard a condescending smile. "That was a lovely speech. But I didn't come here for a history lesson. I'm here to distract you."

Gallard exchanged a quick glance with Solomon. "From what?"

"Simeon. He made you believe that we were going to start an attack so that you and your army would be far away while he killed your son." He chuckled. "Brilliant, isn't it?"

"Gallard go!" Solomon said.

He pushed his way through the army and they began clearing the way for him. He should have known that this was a diversion. Knowing Lucas, he wouldn't kill Simeon, so Gallard would have to do it for him. He gladly would. But he needed to get there in time before Simeon took away one of the most precious things to him.

Gallard was halfway through the crowd when suddenly a pain in his chest stopped him. He doubled over and put a hand to his heart. Whatever it was, it went away quickly. He started to run again, but the pain came back. The man next to him groaned as well and he looked up to see that everyone else was touching their chests.

"What's going on?" he whispered. He forced himself to stand up straight then turned around, heading for Solomon. Something wasn't right and he wasn't the only one experiencing this.

Then he felt it. A rumble in his chest. Heat gathered there and gradually began to spread throughout his body. His heart was beating and he was starting to gain circulation.

"Gallard?" Solomon pushed his way towards him and Gallard saw the excitement in Solomon's eyes. "Do you feel that? Is this happening?"

Gallard reached forward and touched Solomon's neck. He too had a heartbeat. Kevin, Terrence, and Arnaud had joined them as well and even in the dim light, Gallard could see the color in their complexions. Not only that, but they were breathing. Their breath was fogging in front of them from the cold December air.

The sun was completely visible now and everyone present had forgotten they should have been hiding. The night-walkers cowered in fear but several moments passed without any of them catching on fire. They began raising their faces to the sun in wonder.

Then Gallard realized what was going on. If their bodies were coming to life and the sun no longer caused them to burn, it could only mean one thing. The initial excitement turned to terror.

"Lucas," he whispered. "No."

"What is it?" Solomon asked.

Before Gallard could answer, the ground began to shake violently. His fear began to intensify as his realization became clearer. Earthquakes only meant one thing — someone powerful had died.

"We have to go to him," Gallard said. "My son he . . . he can't be — "

Solomon cut him off by grabbing his arm and running off. They still had the ability to run quickly, which Gallard was grateful for. The rest of their army followed behind and his heart raced as he prayed and prayed that he wasn't right — that Lucas wasn't dead because if he was, he would be devastated. He may have had a heartbeat, but he wouldn't really feel alive if his son was gone.

63

A strong force shook the jail cell so hard that Lela awoke from her short nap. She was wide awake in less than five seconds so she sat up and looked around. Tyler was clinging to the bars as if to steady himself.

"Did you feel that?" he asked.

"Yes. Was that an earthquake?"

He started to answer but the shaking began again, only this time it was so powerful that she was knocked off the bed. Attempting to stand up, she tried to figure out what was going on. She knew that Texas was known to have earthquakes but not like this. The quakes were way to strong and felt familiar. The last time she experienced a tremor this massive was in Orlando when Jordan died. Or rather when . . . Lucas died.

"No," she whispered. Lucas wasn't dead. He couldn't be. She'd already had her heart ripped out twice and she should have been used to the attempts on his life. But this earthquake was worse than the first time when Aaron killed him.

Coming back to reality, she noticed the ceiling was starting to crack. Tyler was struggling to stay grounded and then a huge chunk of plaster fell from right above him. Thankfully, she was up to her potential and in a flash, she pushed him out of the way and set him down on the other side of the cell. He was a little shocked by how fast she moved but recovered quickly.

It seemed that the earth was shaking even more and soon even she couldn't stand. Hanging onto Tyler, she fell to the ground and cradled him a little to keep his head safe from any falling debris. After all these years, she still felt protective of him.

"Shouldn't I be shielding *you*?" he asked.

"If you want to, be my guest. But I'm the one with the bones of steel here."

"I forgot how nurturing you are."

She was puzzled by his comment but figured he was trying to get both of their minds off their frightening situation.

"Gallard thinks I was born with motherly tendencies. I've always wanted children but never dreamed I would miss out on twenty years of his life. I was cheated out of motherhood."

And I might be again, she thought to herself. Whatever was going on out there couldn't be good. For now, she needed to get Tyler out of there so he wouldn't get crushed. There was only so much she could do by shielding him with her body.

He stared at her with so much bitterness that she couldn't look him in the eye. After all these years, she may finally be able to explain everything to him. That had always been one of her regrets.

"I don't even know what to call you," he said. "You were Diane to me for so long."

"I haven't used my real name in twenty years."

"Is that so? Tell me, after all this time, what brought you back to Texas?"

She shrugged. "I have a lot of good memories here. But honestly, I have been here for a lot longer than you know. When I came back, I made sure to live somewhere I knew I wouldn't run into you. I've changed my appearance three times since two thousand sixteen and used different aliases. I never thought we would cross paths again."

"Not until my son became involved with your sister. You've got quite the entourage here with you. My men counted sixteen people living in the three homes all next door to each other. I already know that Terrance Fox also known to me as Gallard Fontaine is one of them. Your father hasn't aged a day."

She smiled. "He's not my father, remember? He and I are the same. Over the years, we fell in love and now we're married."

He didn't reply right away. She understood it was a lot to take in. Tyler always addressed Gallard as Mr. Fontaine, abided by Gallard's rules for dating me, and always told her how much he'd liked her dad. To hear his ex-girlfriend ended up with her fake dad was quite a blow.

"I see. And what about Lucas? Who is he?"

She hesitated. Revealing that Lucas' identity would change everything. She'd told him long ago that she couldn't have children and at the time, she couldn't. She hadn't had the ability until she was twenty years old but he probably wouldn't believe her. She'd already told too many lies. It was time for her to be honest.

"He's my son."

"Really? You said that wasn't possible. Who is he really?"

"Ty, I'm not lying to you. After all this time, what reason would I have to lie?"

His mouth twitched and her harsh tone died down. He hadn't been around while she was being harassed and she doubted he condoned it. The Tyler she knew wouldn't have intentionally inflicted harm on another person, let alone allow it. She could handle the pain, but that didn't mean there wasn't a second she longed for Gallard's comforting embrace. She hated not knowing if he was okay.

"Lucas was born less than a year after Gallard and me were married. Gallard has another son that was born via a surrogate. He's in the custody of the MITF because of his supernatural abilities. He traded himself so that we could be let go."

"So, they pardoned your crimes all for one child?"

"He's not a child, he's nineteen years old."

She was starting to fall apart thinking about Micah. It had taken her five minutes to get attached to him, though he wasn't her biological son. If she thought about what he was going through too much, she would drive herself crazy.

"Tyler, you have to believe me when I say that all this is bigger than you know. The task forces aren't who they say they are."

"Wow. I always knew you were a sucker for a good mystery, but I never took you for a conspiracy theorist."

"I'm not a conspiracy theorist. I have files and videos— proof that they're doing unethical practices. Lucas figured it out because he was living with the captain of the Miami precinct for twenty years. They took him away from me and adopted him. They did experiments on him!"

"Okay, stop. Dia . . . Lela, you are sounding like a crazy person."

She forced herself to look into his eyes. "Did you really think I would hurt you? After I told you what I was?"

He didn't respond for the longest time but then he shrugged. "I didn't know what to believe. I felt like those three years were a lie. Then I realized that I made a terrible mistake. By that time, you were long gone. For a while, I was able to move on. I married Mandy and had three beautiful children with her. But I still was haunted by what could have been. That lead to me cheating on her and I regret that. When I learned you were back in town, I expected all my old feelings to come rushing back."

Her throat tightened and she swallowed. "Did they?"

"No. I feel like seeing you again gave me closure. I wouldn't give up Mandy and the kids for anything."

That brought a smile to her lips. "And I wouldn't give up my husband and two sons either. We're right where we're supposed to be."

He nodded. "Just the same, I shouldn't have walked away when they interrogated you. What they did was wrong. Torturing you like that. I'm sorry you were hurt."

"Thanks, Ty. That means a lot to me."

The room shook again, and more plaster fell from the ceiling. It was apparent that staying there was no longer safe for Tyler. She got up and started pulling on the bars. At eighteen, she had torn the doors off a maximum prison. If she could do that she could bend a couple of cell bars. The steel bent a little and she pulled harder. The space was large now but not big enough for a grown man to fit through. If only the other officers would show up and let them out. This was an emergency, after all.

"There, I think that's good enough." She squeezed through the opening she made and managed to get through. "Think you can fit?"

"Yeah, maybe fifteen years ago. I'm not the short beanpole I used to be."

He was right, it was too small for him. She began looking around for something else she could use, and her eyes found one of the emergency hatchets. She broke the glass with her elbow then pulled it out. Thankfully the lock on the cell was old fashioned and not the electronic type that were seen in most jails. She struck it about five times and then the door sprang open.

"Come on!"

Tyler hurried out with her and they dodged the debris along the way. The rest of the precinct was a mess and it looked like everyone had cleared out. She pulled him towards the door. No one was there and the place was dead silent. Even the parking lot was empty

"Go home to your wife," she said.

"No, I'm coming with you. I need to see my son."

"You can't, Ty. You're going to get yourself killed."

A car pulled into the lot and Lela recognized it. She hadn't seen the 4Runner in years. Not since it was stolen twenty-three years ago.

The car stopped at least three inches away from her knees and she nearly jumped out of the way. The door opened and when Robin got out, Lela didn't even scold her for the reckless driving. She pulled her sister into her arms.

"I'm so glad you're safe," she said, trying not to cry. When she pulled back, she noticed Robin was already in tears. "Honey, what's wrong?"

"It's Lucas. Lela, something happened."

"Tell me in the car. We need to go to him."

Tyler got in first and she followed. The Toyota had seven seats, but they were already spoken for, including the driver's seat. Erik took over as driver, so Robin sat in her lap.

A cooing in the back seat startled her and she looked to see there was a car seat. "What the hell? Whose baby is that?"

Robin looked down for a moment. "Mine.

"Yours! Yours and whose?"

"Care to explain, son?" Tyler said.

"Think about it, dad. Do you really think if it was mine that she would have given birth in a month?"

"I don't think we should discuss this now," Robin said to Lela. "But I promise you we will when tonight is over. But just so you know, dad is here. Our other dad, that is."

She looked around that's when she realized who exactly was present.

"It's good to see you, Lela," the man in the passenger seat said.

"Wait, Mark? How? When?"

"I came with Richard."

Lela looked over to Richard and he waved. Twenty years and here these two men were. She'd always wondered what happened to them. Richard filled her in on everything she'd missed, and it was a lot to take in. Now her priority was getting to the fairgrounds.

64

"Lucas! Lucas, wake up!" Lucian shouted.

After Simeon stabbed him, Nicola had gotten to Lucas first. He was still bleeding when she went to his side and she'd hoped it would stop after she pulled out the knife. She was covered in his blood now.

"He's not breathing," she said through sobs. "Why isn't he healing?"

"Don't waste your tears," Simeon said. The remaining members who hadn't been killed while trying to stop Lucian and Cherish from stepping onto the field had joined him and put his shirt back on. "Lucian, it would be wise to inform me of the whereabouts of Gallard and that woman of yours. Oh, and Colton too, please."

Lucian's nostrils flared and he stood up. In the past, Nicola would have encouraged him to keep his calm, but not now. Not when Simeon had killed Lucas. He had crossed the line long ago, but this was unforgivable. Not just because she loved Lucas, but because he'd killed a man who had bravely refused to shed blood. A man whom Simeon could never live up to.

"You're dead," Lucian said. "I don't care that you're my grandson. Lucas was more dear to me than any son could ever be. You think you're this fierce leader whom everyone fears. You're nothing compared to what I could be."

"And what is that, dearest grandfather? What are you? The infamous Lucian Christophe? The man whom everyone feared and whom the coven felt the need to put down because of what? A crime you didn't even commit? You're not terrifying."

Simeon stepped closer. "You're nothing but an idea. I am perfection. I am everything you could have been but decided not to be because you're soft. You had a chance to be notorious and you gave all of that up for a woman. Where is that woman, Lucian? Oh, I remember."

He began circling Lucian like a vulture. "That woman is currently married to another man. And it was her son that I killed tonight. So, it was all for naught—your path to redemption, your whole honorable man mentality. Where did it get you? You're still alone. Your family and friends still see you as a potential killer. Even your own fiancée doesn't remember you. Who would want to remember a coward any—?"

Lucian grabbed onto Simeon's throat and Nicola continued to press on Lucas' wound while she watched. Lucian's hair began to darken until it was black, and nobody moved. This was it—he was finally going to snap. His rage had been building and building ever since J.D. died then came back with fractured memories.

"You forget one thing, Simeon," he said. "Lucas isn't the only one who is gifted."

Lucian let go of his throat, but Simeon remained floating in midair. Nicola was terrified and intrigued at the same time. Lucian hadn't displayed any abilities before. It must have had to do with the power Gallard had spoken of. The power he'd obtained from Maximus.

"You have caused many so much suffering. But nothing compares to two thousand years' worth of pain."

As Lucas had, Lucian placed his hands on Simeon's head and he started yelling in agony. Whatever Lucian was showing him must have been terrible. She'd never seen Simeon so terrified. Nicola watched as blood began flowing from Simeon's mouth, nose, ears, and even his eyes. This was more gruesome than anything she'd ever witnessed. And it wasn't self-defense.

She didn't want to leave Lucas' side, but she had a feeling this situation was urgent. She waved Dominique over to take her place then she and Cherish approached Lucian from behind.

"Father stop!" Cherish said. "Please, he's my son!"

"Your *son* killed J.D. Or at least let it happen. Your *son* poisoned Abraham. Your *son* wanted you dead and has now killed Lucas! How can you still feel any love for him?"

A tear slid down Cherish's cheek. "The same reason I felt love for you after everything you did to me. After you ignored me for months after I thought I lost my child. After you killed a man in front of me when I was only five. Because you're family. And he's our family too."

Lucian turned back to Simeon who was now paler than before and motionless.

"Your pity is useless," Simeon said in a raspy voice. "You were never my mother. Never needed you to be, nor do I wish it."

Ezekiel put a hand on Cherish's shoulder. "Grandmother, we must agree. If we don't kill him, he will cause the death of more than just Lucas. He's too dangerous." He stepped away from her and approached Lucian. "Let Casper and me be the one to do it."

Lucian didn't move at first but then released Simeon, who fell to the ground. Ezekiel picked up the knife and he and his brother approached their father. Cherish went to stop them but Lucian held her back. Nicola watched as Casper held Simeon down then Ezekiel basically did to Simeon what had been done to Lucas, only he cut out his heart. Simeon twitched once but then his body went limp and Nicola knew he was dead.

Cherish cried out in anguish and Lucian held her, attempting to comfort her. Nicola began crying as well, not for Simeon but for Cherish. She had been in the exact state of emotion when the nurse informed her that Colton died in his sleep.

"Twas long overdue," Lucian said. "He would have taken Colton, probably killed us, then killed thousands of people."

She pulled away from his grasp. "I know. That doesn't change the fact that he was my flesh and blood and I loved him despite his cruelty. It may have been the right thing to do, but I still need time."

Ezekiel and Casper were able to successfully transfer Lucas from the field to the van. Ezekiel was confident that he could help Lucas. Nicola was shaking, and Dominique was attempting to keep her calm. How could she be calm when the man she loved was dead? He didn't have a heartbeat and he'd stopped breathing. She felt like she had as well.

Everyone had insisted that Nicola stay out of the van while he and Cherish tried to revive him and she'd reluctantly agreed. All she wanted was to hold his hand and kiss him. He had to wake up. He needed to wake up. For those who were counting on him. For his family and friends. For Colton. And for her.

"I don't understand," Ezekiel said. "The knife is out. He should be healing."

"We need to get his heart beating again," Cherish said.

She then bit into her wrist and started feeding her blood to Lucas. Nicola's legs gave out but her two sisters kept her from falling over. She thought she was over her aversion to blood. At least to the point of passing out anyway. But having Lucas' blood on her and seeing Cherish's was forcing her into old habits.

"Hey!" Dominique said. "He'll be fine!"

"How can you be so sure? He's not breathing, he's cold, and all I want is for him to open his eyes! Why won't he open his eyes? I love him. I can't lose him. And Colton . . . I don't want him to lose his daddy."

"No one is losing anyone!" Ezekiel shouted from inside the van. "Where's the knife?"

"Why?" Klara asked.

"I need to massage his heart."

Cherish nodded then pulled her own pocketknife from her back pocket. When she flipped it open, Nicola lost it and threw up on the side of the van. She had nothing in her stomach but blood and water and this made it even worse. Dominique held her hair back until she was finished. It was so strange being the in the role of younger sister. She'd always been the one who looked out for Mona and now she had two big sisters at her side. Klara was forty-one and Dominique was twenty-eight. Their comfort felt nice and somewhat soothed her anxiety. But nothing would make her feel completely at ease until Lucas woke up.

"Zeke, wait!" Cherish shouted. "Look, his artery is healing!"

Those words were music to Nicola's ears. Klara gave her a bottle of water and poured it onto a handkerchief so she could clean herself up. Once she was finished, she climbed into the back of the van to see if Cherish was telling the truth. It was hard staring at the gaping wound in his chest, but it was clear. She could see the cut healing and in a way, it was fascinating.

The arteries reconnected and that's when Ezekiel stuck his hand inside of Lucas' chest and began squeezing his heart. That part wasn't so fascinating, and Nicola nearly vomited again. He did it in even movements, somewhat like a heartbeat. Squeeze and release. Squeeze and release. Cherish moved a little so Nicola could be at his side when he woke up and she stroked his hair. Even in death, he was beautiful. His hair was perfect and his face was so serene. He'd even smiled at her before collapsing.

Lub dub.

Once the wound completely closed, everyone grew completely silent. Nicola knew that they'd heard what she heard and now came the aggravating waiting period. She took his hand and pressed her lips to his fingers and held them against her cheek. He always said that his gifts worked better when she was with him so she did this in hopes that it would somehow speed up his healing process.

"Guys," Klara said. "Look!"

They turned their attention outside. The football arena was filled with people. Nicola recognized some of them and it was clear that they were the ones David and Solomon had recruited. But what was strange was that they were outside even though the sun had risen at least an hour before. They were night-walkers. How were they able to be in the sun?

Someone came running towards them and she saw it was Gallard.

"Oh no," he said when he saw Lucas. "Please tell me he isn't —"

"He's improving," Ezekiel assured him.

Lub dub . . . Lub dub.

That was two heartbeats this time. Nicola nearly cried she was so happy. But she wanted to know what was going on as well.

"Gallard, what are they doing here?" Lucian asked.

"That's what I came to tell you all. Something happened just before sunrise. The coven showed up and we were going to fight when everyone nearly fell over. I felt something that I usually don't feel unless Lela gives me her blood. A heartbeat. I thought it was just me but then Solomon, Terrence, and Arnaud were complaining of chest pain and we noticed the coven acting strange as well."

Cherish got out of the van and placed her hand on his chest. Her eyes widened and she looked at the rest of the group. "It's true. His heart is beating."

"And the night-walkers aren't sensitive to the sun."

"But we're still vampires," Solomon said. "We have strength and speed, just like we used to."

Another group of people showed up at that moment. It was Lela and Robin along with Richard, Mark, Erik, and even his dad. Robin was holding her baby and Lela had Colton.

"Mamma?" he said when he saw Lucas. His lip started quivering. "Is dad okay?"

"Yes, baby. He's going to be okay."

Lub dub . . . lub dub . . . lub dub.

His heartbeat was becoming more consistent now. The only abnormal thing about it was that there was still a scar. It was similar to the one her grandfather had after he'd had open heart surgery. Nicola didn't mind it, though. He always told her that her scars were beautiful because they reminded him of Colton and how it was a miracle that he was theirs.

Nicola gasped in shock when his hand tightened around hers. She was so excited that her first reaction was to lean down and kiss him. He was still covered in dry blood but that didn't stop her from putting her head to his chest and listening to his heartbeat. Then his chest rose and fell as he took his first breath. It was almost as magical as when she first heard Colton cry.

Then he opened his eyes. Their color wasn't blue as the used to be but a color she had never seen before. Almost like opal.

"Lucas?" she whispered.

He didn't even say a word but sat up and got out of the van. She followed after him and observed his movements. He seemed stiffer than before. The way he walked and looked around was robotic. When he finally did speak, it wasn't in English. It didn't even sound French. He kept saying the same thing over and over.

"What's going on?" Lela asked.

"It's Aramaic," Lucian said.

"How do you know?" Gallard asked.

"When Maximus gave me his power, he imbued me with the understanding of the ancient language. He's saying, *The time is near. Do not think I have come to abolish the law or the Prophets — I have not come to abolish them, but to fulfill them.*"

"Matthew five-seventeen," Solomon said.

Lucas said a few more lines before Lucian translated again.

"*Blessed are the merciful, for they will be shown mercy. Blessed are the peacemakers, for they shall be called children of God. Blessed are those who are persecuted because of righteousness for theirs is the kingdom of God. The times may be hard now and they may seem to get worse but do not falter. Do not give up.*" He let him finish then continued. "*Rejoice and be glad because great is your reward in heaven, for in the same way they persecuted the prophets who were before you.*"

Lucas stopped speaking and nearly fell when Gallard caught him. Nicola crawled out of the van and supported him from behind. He lifted his head a bit and she found herself staring into his eyes. They were still that odd color, but he seemed to snap out of whatever trance he was in. He smiled and reached up to touch her face.

"Did we win?"

65

I apologize for the weirdness. I was told that I would be given the words to say. I see that you are noticing something's different. How you liking the sunshine out here?"

The group cheered then I climbed on top of the van so I could get a better view of the crowd. I reached down to take Nicola's hand and she grasped it seconds before I hoisted her up with me.

"This is only the beginning," I continued. "Immortals all over the world are feeling a little more human. You have an advantage and what you do with that advantage is crucial. You can either become hostile and go against those who persecuted us. Or you can prove a point. Prove that just because you can feed during the day that you choose not to be violent. I made a pledge back when I first learned of my heritage. I want to finish this cause without taking a life. For many of you, taking a life equals survival. You need blood to function and I understand that. I want to change that for us. I want to find a way to help nourish our kind without the need to hurt people. But first we must get the rest of this country on board. I don't know how we're going to do that, but I'm sure as hell not giving up until every unjustly incarcerated immortal is set free."

The cheers came once more then I did a sort of follow up. The hoard would be separated into groups of five, putting thirty in each. Two from the family would be assigned to them and the remaining members would be given a different task. The agenda for these groups was to raise awareness in the most influential cities of America.

Once the commotion died down, I used one of the water bottles to wash off the blood then put my shirt back on. The first person to hug me was Lela who was joined by Gallard and I hugged both my parents at the same time. Terrence and Arnaud both ruffled my hair then Kevin hugged me as well. The last person I acknowledged was Lucian. He looked different, but I wasn't worried yet. I took him aside so I could speak with him.

"Where's Simeon?" I asked.

"Taken care of. After you were injured, Ezekiel and Casper dealt with him."

"I see. And you helped?"

He nodded. "I had to. They wouldn't have been able to kill him had I not aided them. He needed to be stopped. However, I may have lost Cherish in the process."

I put a hand on his shoulder. "She'll forgive you. You're her father."

"Maybe. Unless this time I have done something truly unforgivable. Only time will tell."

The last person I approached was Ezekiel. I held out my hand and he shook it.

"Thank you. I know what you did for Robin, and your kindness for Nicola. And lastly for saving my life. I owe you."

"No, I owe you. Without you, we never would have been free of our father."

Catching Nicola's gaze, I thanked him one last time before going over to her. I wanted to take some time to be alone with our little family, so I took Colton from Erik then clasped her hand in my free one. We walked over to the side of the stadium and I hugged her to my side and for five solid minutes, we stood in silence and just enjoyed each other's company.

I then leaned down and pressed my lips to hers.

"Ew," Colton said in a tired voice. I laughed and pulled back.

"Trust me, bud. When you grow up and meet a girl as amazing as your mom, you won't think it's gross."

Nicola smiled up at me. "I thought I lost you, you know."

I planted a kiss on her forehead and then on her cheek. "I know. I'm sorry you're not off the hook for marrying me."

She punched my arm. "I don't want to be off the hook. I'd marry you right now if we had a license. But you have a job to do, and I am willing to wait until that job is finished."

"It's why I love you. Speaking of jobs, I wanted to talk to you about our part of this mission."

"Name it and I will do it. I'm at your side forever and always, Lucas Taylor. Now what's my mission?"

I gave her a sly smile. "I want you to help me rescue Micah."

She laughed. "What? Lucas, you're crazy. How am I going to do that?"

"I don't know. That's for you to figure out. I can't be seen Miami or Scott will kill him. But he never said anything about banishing *you*. I know you, Nicola. You were known as the Redheaded Fury in high school for how brutal you were on the volleyball team. People feared you and you can make them fear you again. I have faith in you."

EPILOGUE
MIAMI CHRISTMAS

The smell of baked ham wafted through the house, contrasting well with the scent of pine from the Christmas tree. Everything was decorated for the holidays, and each ornament was perfectly in place. Green and red lights spiraled up the stair railing and there was a garland of holly draped along the fireplace. The hooks were in place for the stockings. Six—one for each member of the family.

Of course, Regina knew it was silly to put them all up. Only one son was left in the family and she had a feeling he wouldn't be up for sentimental traditions. Not when he spent his time locked inside a high security facility. Scott told her that Micah was away at the police academy in Tampa, but she knew better. He hadn't visited at all in five months because he wasn't allowed to.

The strong ham smell alerted her that it was ready to be taken out of the oven. She finished applying her makeup then gave herself one last look over before heading downstairs. Her parents were going to arrive soon, and she'd spent the entire afternoon entertaining her in-laws. Scott's sister Cecelia had come into town with her three children and so had his unmarried brother. Usually, they would invite Gabriella and Edison, but Scott claimed he was done with the Taylors and the Edisons.

"Reggie, you look gorgeous," Cecelia gushed. "I swear you look as young as you did when you married Scottie."

Regina forced a smile. She knew Cecelia was being kind. Her hair had gotten greyer in the past several months and her wrinkles were more prominent. Losing a child really wore on a person. She'd lost three. Lucas and Colton weren't technically gone like Henry was, but they might has well have been. The rest of the world believed that Lucas was killed at Henry's hand and that Colton was taken by his biological family. It was hard keeping the truth to herself.

"When is that boy of yours getting here?" Steven asked. Scott's brother worked in a different branch of Immortal Order Control. He usually collaborated with his brother but after speaking with him, it was clear to Regina that he had no idea what Scott was really up to or what he was doing with Micah.

The FBI had raided the precinct as planned, but they never found anything. It was believed that Henry and Ash alone who had conspired with the hospital. Their immortal accomplice was dealt with as most immortals were and the case was closed. They had no idea that there was still corruption going on under the surface.

"He should be in town soon. Cec, why don't I take the nog from you and I'll put in the kitchen."

"Thanks, Reggie. You're an angel."

The front door opened, and Scott came into the house. She'd sent him to the store to get some macaroni salad since his mother had forgotten to bring some. Again. Every holiday she would promise her signature salad and every holiday she would forget. Usually it didn't bother Regina, but this year she was feeling less sympathetic. She was already in charge of the ham and the bread and the apple pie. Not to mention she was hosting. In light of everything, she was feeling a tad overwhelmed.

"We were in luck. There was only one left," Scott said. He leaned over and lightly brushed her lips with a kiss. "The ham about done?"

"Yes. I was just about to take it out."

She walked into the kitchen in a robotic manor and opened the oven. The ham looked heavenly and smelled even better up close. Slipping on her oven mitts on, she took it out and set it on the red cloth on the counter. Loud conversation erupted form the living room and she assumed his parents had arrived. Instead of going out to greet them, she continued to slice up the meat and place the sections onto the plate that she used every year.

Footsteps came up behind her and she turned to see Scott. He had his phone in his hand and she was worried that he was being called into work. That was happening a lot these days and it was hard to be alone in the house all the time.

"Just got off the phone with Micah," he said. "He's not coming to dinner."

She stopped mid slice and started to tremble. This was a lie. One big, stupid lie. Did he think she was oblivious? Did he really think she believed Micah was in New Hampshire working as the Concord Immortal Task Force Lieutenant? He'd just lost the woman he was going to marry. Micah wouldn't go off to start a career. She knew him better than that. He would be too distraught to even think about his future.

"How could you?" she found herself saying. "This is the only time I might get to see him. How could you—" she realized what she was accusing him of. She couldn't allow him to know that she knew his secrets— the experiments, the immoral medical practices. All of it. "You didn't try hard enough to change his mind."

"Regina, you're going to have to accept that Micah doesn't want to be part of this family. He resents us for lying about his adoption and he sees us as a reminder of what Henry did to Mona and Lucas."

Hate coursed through her and she nearly gave herself away. Because of his crazy agenda, her children were gone. Her home that had once been filled with children's laughter and the brotherly banter of her boys was now dead silent with the ghosts of what used to be. This wasn't supposed to be her life. Scott wasn't the same man that she married. All he cared about now was killing vampires and he didn't care what he had to do in order to achieve that. Including having their son murdered and holding another captive. Well, she was done with it.

"You're right." She wiped away her tears. "He'll come home when he's ready." She smiled at him. "Why don't you go spend time with the family and I'll bring everyone a glass of egg nog?"

He pulled her into a hug, and she relaxed into him. When he released her, she finished slicing the last bits of ham then got out enough cups for everyone. Cecelia's egg nog was a hit every Christmas and they could finish an entire jug in one day. She began pouring it into the white Christmas cups with the gold trim and holly painted on it. The set had been in her family for generations and it was tradition to drink the nog from them.

Once the cups were filled, she set one aside then slipped upstairs into the bathroom. Opening the cupboard, she began looking for something in particular. She held used her finger to trail through the labels until she found what she was looking for—Ambien. She grabbed the bottle, stuffing it in her pocket, then went back downstairs. Nobody even noticed her as she walked past the living room. Everyone was in deep conversation, just the way she needed them to be.

When she entered the kitchen, she quickly opened the bottle and dumped the pills into her herb bowl then began to grind them. There had to be at least ten of them. More than enough. She smashed and smashed until they were nothing but powder then she dumped it into the set aside glass and stirred it in. Her hands trembled while she put them on her Christmas tray.

432

With a smile on her face, she went into the living room and set the tray on the coffee table.

"Who's ready for Cece's nog?" she asked. Everyone cheered excitedly and she handed each person a cup. Once everyone was served, she took a seat next to Scott. "Before we drink, I would like to propose a toast." She raised her cup. "Scott and I have been through so much this year. It has been a difficult time and I don't think we could have gotten this far without you guys. You're our family and your support means the world to us."

"Yes, I agree," Scott said, taking her hand.

"Anyway, I'm glad you are all here. We love you guys and I have faith that we will get past this. We will heal in time." She raised her glass. "To family."

"To family," the company said in unison.

Regina watched as everyone took a long sip of the nog then drank hers last. The conversation continued, but she was mostly quiet. Nobody questioned her about her lack of contribution, and she was glad for that. She couldn't speak while she was waiting. Waiting for the pills to kick in. Preparing for how everyone would react. They wouldn't have a clue what was going on. She'd hidden the bottle inside of her bag of flour where it would never be found. The deed was done. And now she would wait.

Made in the USA
Monee, IL
06 March 2020